P9-AGU-058

PRAISE FOR

THIS IS THE NIGHT

"Part parable, part thriller, and part love story, *This Is the Night* will keep you turning its pages until you reach its remarkable ending. Could our contemporary lives look and feel like this? Yes: they could and they do. Just start reading, and believe it." —Charles Baxter, author of *There's Something I Want You to Do* and *Feast of Love*

"A beautifully written, flashlight-under-the-bed page-turner, reminiscent of *The Handmaid's Tale* and *Never Let Me Go* . . . a chilling novel that will stay with you." —Michael David Lukas, author of *The Oracle of Stamboul*

"Sirott knows what William Gibson meant when he said, 'The future is already here—it's just not evenly distributed.' Put another way: *This Is the Night* is so right it's a little scary. I couldn't put the damn thing down." —Justin Taylor, author of *Flings*

THIS IS THE NIGHT

THIS IS THE NIGHT

A NOVEL

JONAH C. SIROTT

Little
a

This is a work of fiction. Names, characters, organizations, places, events, and incidents are either products of the author's imagination or are used fictitiously.

Text copyright © 2015 Jonah C. Sirott

All rights reserved.

No part of this book may be reproduced, or stored in a retrieval system, or transmitted in any form or by any means, electronic, mechanical, photocopying, recording, or otherwise, without express written permission of the publisher.

Published by Little A, New York

www.apub.com

Amazon, the Amazon logo, and Little A are trademarks of Amazon.com Inc., or its affiliates.

ISBN-13 (hardcover): 9781503947641
ISBN-10 (hardcover): 1503947645
ISBN-13 (paperback): 9781503947658
ISBN-10 (paperback): 1503947653

Cover design by Cyanotype Book Architects

Printed in the United States of America

For Leah

YEAR 22

I.

Three police officers stood beneath a harsh, generator-powered street-light. Their shiny badges seemed to momentarily blind Lorrie as she let up on the gas and rolled the car into the checkpoint. Next to her, Lance stiffened. Already one of the officers was approaching the car. Terry, who sat in the back, remained quiet. The highest-ranking officer gestured for Lorrie to roll down the window while the other two walked around to the passenger side and stood with their arms folded, eyes on Lance.

"Another round of attacks," the officer explained. One by one, she applied her gaze to the three passengers, daring them to break contact.

"By whom?" Terry asked.

"I think it's *who*," said Lorrie.

"Who do you think?" the officer said. "Foreigns. Ideology Fivers. Maybe Fareon freaks. We got lucky, though. Whoever those mother-rapers are, they can't even build a bomb right. The thing didn't blow."

"This just happened?" Terry asked the officer. "Right now?"

"What's a Fareon freak?" said Lorrie.

The officer ignored their questions.

Lance slunk low in his seat. He knew better than to talk to a person with a gun more than was necessary. He knew what was coming next. But Terry spoke first.

"So can we go?" she asked.

"Can you go?" The officer seemed amused. "You think we're just out here looking for terrorists? Let's see your papers, young man."

Lance handed them over, and she walked in front of the car so her colleagues could inspect his documents. She leaned in toward them and made some sort of joke, and the three women burst out laughing. She strode over to the passenger side window, the seed of a smile appearing on her face. "My goodness," the officer said, glancing down at Lance. "I see your time is coming soon." She was looking, he knew, at his birth date.

As the officers waved them on, Lorrie misjudged the width of a gaping pothole, jolting her passengers as the car plunged in and causing a loud bang that echoed in the night. They were silent for a long while. Finally Lorrie spoke. "Don't worry about it," she said. "We'll figure something out."

We. Lance glanced at the clock on the car's dashboard. Twelve hours since they'd first met.

❖ ❖ ❖

That morning, the third day of his third week as head technician and sole employee of the small, poorly equipped photo studio, Lance's future had suddenly come into focus. The studio was nestled in the back room of the town's only bookstore. Just weeks into his new job, Lance's life was yet again engorged with sameness. Though Lance had long had the hazy notion that he was destined for a life of vast joy and fulfillment, little in his world suggested a trajectory that would end up any different from his brothers. Until finally the day came when life proved him right. He went to work, the sun was shining, and there, in his store, was Lorrie.

She and a friend were lost, she explained, having strayed far from the expressway. And while they had chosen the loose gravel of the back-roads on purpose, they had gotten lost in Lance's town unintentionally. Their car had a flat, and while they were waiting on the mechanic, they had decided to walk around in search of adventure.

"What's with all the tinsel?" Lorrie asked, placing one palm on the counter. "Something special happening around town?" She had an overflow of hair and stood with her other hand fixed against her hip, a posture that wrung Lance's heart clean. He was not sure if she was making fun of him.

"Oh c'mon," he said. "You know what today is. The entire Homeland is celebrating." At first Lance thought it was her unruly spritz of hair that made his heart throb—or maybe her small breasts softly swaying beneath her dress, or those round, round eyes, perhaps it was the eyes—but a moment later he realized that such a woman could not be broken down into distinct parts. One focal point did not do justice to her beauty.

"It's the prime minister's birthday, isn't it?" she said.

"His ninety-sixth, I believe."

A flash of distaste crossed her face, and he watched as she did her best to quickly transition her expression back to neutral. Though he could not make out her reason for disliking the man who had ruled the Homeland for as long as he could remember, the thought came to him that if he could keep her talking, he just might find the sort of endless depth—or maybe it was a looseness—that he immediately realized was completely absent from his own life.

"It's just," she began, her voice lowering, "twenty-two years is a long time to be at war, you know?"

Lance did not know. The Homeland had always been at war. Though his family had suffered, he knew his story was just one dark cloud in a stormy sky that was full of them, one of thousands. War was what was happening, what had always been happening. In two weeks he would be eighteen, and the same thing that had happened to his brothers would happen to him. Until this moment, he had never thought to invent a different ending.

"That's why me and Terry there"—she gestured to a woman smoking a cigarette on the sidewalk—"we needed to get out of the city and clear our heads."

Their eyes met. Lance could see that she was a woman who would not let him in without effort, which was, of course, the entire point. Anyone who offered up his or her heart too soon surely deserved to get it stomped on.

After a moment, Lorrie explained that not only did they not know where they were on the map, but even after having the tire repaired, the car was still jerking to the right when they drove.

"Almost like it led you here, like fate?" he joked. The small curl to Lorrie's lip followed a skewed wrinkling of her forehead. Either she didn't get Lance's sense of humor or she didn't like it.

The woman named Terry poked her head through the door and gave a cool, practiced look around the shop. Immediately Lance spotted a vague suggestion of non–Majority Group features in her relaxed face that was rare in these parts of the Homeland.

"So here's the deal," Terry said. "I just picked the car up from the mechanic, but it's still pulling to the right."

None of this was surprising; with no money to repave the roads, sunken indentations in the blacktop were the norm. Lance told the single customer browsing in the mystery section that he would be right back and went outside to look at their car, an old hay-colored Brand 8 pocked with rust spots over the rear wheels. All the tires were worn down evenly but still had plenty of tread. He checked the springs and saw that they jounced strong and even.

"It's Terry's car," said Lorrie. "See that rust there? Do you think that has anything to do with anything?"

"Well," Lance said. He bent down to take a closer look, sneaking a sideways glance at Lorrie's unpainted face. From every angle, she was stunning. He felt Terry's disapproving eyes on him and returned his focus to the Brand 8 and its rusted quarter panels. Lance had taken only one course of shop and had spent most of it making intricate line drawings of air hoses and locking nozzles in his sketchbook. When it came to component parts of combustion engines, he understood their form but had no idea of their function.

"She had bad oil leaks last winter," Terry was saying. "But I got that taken care of. Of course when the first snow hit, exhaust came right through her vents along with the heat. Just driving was enough to get a girl tipsy."

"Hmmm," Lance said. The Brand 8 didn't look like a she. He gave a light kick to the passenger front tire that he thought looked authoritative. The idea came to him to check the tire pressure.

"I don't like this much," Terry said.

"The car?" Lance asked.

"No, asking you to fix it," Terry said. "It doesn't go with what we're trying to do."

"You asked Dan Cummins for help," Lance pointed out.

"Who's Dan Cummins?" said Terry.

"I think that's the name of the mechanic," Lorrie offered.

"It is," Lance said, happy to agree with Lorrie about anything, no matter how insignificant.

"And I think Dan Cummins, the one-legged mechanic, screwed us," Terry said, her voice rising. "I don't remember her veering like this before he fixed the flat."

"That's crazy," Lance said. "That man saved his whole battalion, held off a band of Foreigns for twenty-seven hours until a rescue team came in." Dan-the-Mechanic had served with Lance's oldest brother, and the mention of their ordeal made his brother's narrow forehead leap into his memory, the rest of his face following quickly. With a silent apology, Lance pushed him out. Like so many others in town, he was well acquainted with the problems with dead people: they still insisted on making themselves felt, even as the world moved on without them.

"Fighting Foreigns doesn't make him a good mechanic," Terry said. "Everyone who gets shipped off fights Foreigns. If anything, it probably rattled his brain like the rest of them."

"You think Dan damaged your frame?" Lance said. "He just patched your tire."

"Then maybe it was you," Terry said to him.

"All I did was check the springs!"

"You kicked her, too."

"If it's the frame, a kick won't make a difference."

"Says who?"

"Terry." Lorrie crossed her eyes. She turned to Lance. "We appreciate your help," she told him, "but we're not about to depend on men. Now, where can we get some good coffee around here? Terry and I need to figure out our next move."

"I'll come along," Lance said. They didn't object, but they didn't agree, either. "Wait here," he said. It was unclear if they would.

"Hey, get lost," he hissed at the browsing customer. "We're closing early." The man, an old drinking buddy of Lance's father, had already lost two boys to the Foreigns and hadn't heard from the third in months. Plus there'd been a younger brother, Lance remembered. His words tugged the man's face downward, but he shuffled off without complaint. No big deal. He wasn't going to buy a book anyway; no one ever did. With a sharp push, Lance slammed the cash register shut and headed out to the street. He willed the two women to still be there. They had to be.

"Took long enough," Terry said once he returned to the sidewalk.

Lance pointed the way to the one diner in town and hoped they weren't in the midst of a blackout. On the walk over he smiled as he heard them agree that it was probably the frame that was bent after all, and that it had been that way for quite some time. The busted tire was probably just a coincidence. On every block, the preternaturally triumphant grin of the prime minister gazed down from bannered lampposts, his face standing out brightly in the warm sun. Lance felt around his pockets, caressing the Currencies he knew were already there. Going out to lunch would not be a problem.

As a boy, Lance's pockets had overflowed with small-denomination bills. Other students always followed him around school; chances were a few crumpled Currencies would jump from his pants onto the ground, and anyone alert enough to notice would be able to grab at least enough for an extra dessert or after-school snack, maybe even a whole meal.

The means by which Lance collected his classmates' allowances and filled his pockets to overflowing were transparent: each day at recess he set himself up with pad and paper in a corner of the playground, interruptible only for new orders of the pencil-and-ink portraits his fellow students commissioned of themselves. Lance's clients were charged with providing the pebbly, textured paper that was his preferred medium, and boys and girls—though they were mostly girls—would line up, sheets in hand. Lance's process was straightforward and direct: step one, collect their Currencies; step two, take the textured paper from the excited girl or bashful boy's optimistic hand; step three, internalize the face that stood in front of him. Before the final bell of the following day, Lance would return the piece of paper to the correct classmate/customer, portrait now included, a large profit realized.

How many of these he sold he couldn't say, only that by ninth grade, business was so good that he raised his prices and lowered the quality of his work. Nothing anyone noticed, of course, just small steps to save time: a skip of some shading, the failure to vary his line weight. At first he thought doing a crap job might make him feel bad about his art, but he found that as long as he told himself he wasn't trying, he felt fine. Though his strokes were sloppy, his customers were always satisfied when the end product appeared to at least represent their particulars. In addition to his living customers, Lance was often commissioned to draw a portrait of those killed in action, usually the older brothers of his classmates.

For these pieces, he charged double and always drew from memory. He always had enough Currencies for the movies, plus a date, even when he didn't want one.

Mostly, people said, there was something about Lance's eyes. Others claimed his face was far wiser and more erotic than was reasonable for a boy his age, particularly one in such a far-off and isolated part of the Homeland. Traveled eyes, the people around town liked to say. Only Lance had never traveled anywhere, and on most days, he had little desire to. After all, everyone in his family who left had simply failed to come back.

For one family to have given so many boys to the war wasn't right, people mumbled to one another in the aisles of the grocery store, whispered over pews at church, shouted above the splashes of children at the community pool. At the local veterans' shrine, where pictures of forgotten boys from Lance's town stared down at the few visitors, wall space was now at a premium. Quite a few of those pictures were of people related to Lance, and though the effort was unspoken, folks wanted to protect the next up in this long-suffering clan. Now that next boy was Lance—almost of age—possessor of those soothing eyes and that smooth, uncut skin. Their town was a small, Young Savior–fearing place, people reminded each other, and they were not those cold, unruffled heretics who lived their lives stacked vertically in metropoles like Western City North. In Lance's town, deep in the Homeland's interior, townsfolk celebrated the prime minister's birthday every year with gusto, neighbor helped neighbor, and family watched out for family, especially when that family's suffering was of such endless magnitude.

Those people could have been us, husbands and wives whispered across mattresses. And so it came to be that people around town, particularly those without daughters, tended to go out of their way in order to help Lance out.

Among the people who wanted to help was Mrs. Miller, his art teacher. During his final year of high school, Lance had spent every evening in the art room, painting and drawing until the night custodian jiggled his keys and told him to run on home for dinner. He was the sixth of seven children, each more unwanted than the one before, that early history now buried with the rough news of every brother shipped home cold. Although as a boy, space in Lance's home had been hard to come by, his world had shifted, and now there was far too much of it.

Mrs. Miller—one of the few who approached Lance with a genuine curiosity unformed by his tragic losses—had pushed him into the world of oils and color, but really, he would have jumped into whatever dimension she asked him to. Mrs. Miller and her husband had arrived in town as refugees, relocated from the Eastern Cities after First Aggression. Though treated by old-timers as if they had only just arrived, the Millers had lived in town for decades. Then again, few could believe that the war was in its twenty-second year, either.

Even so, not a day went by without the Millers being pelted with questions about life in the Eastern Cities before First Aggression, that fateful series of coordinated attacks in which the Foreigns had cast the first stone so long ago. No one was under any illusions that the shuddering emptiness of such a small, out-of-the-way rural location could ever compete with the former cultural capital of the Homeland. But still, the townspeople had questions. Mr. Miller, who thanks to his service was missing an ear and several toes on his left foot, had told Lance that people were far more interested in the screaming gearshifts and unending high-rises of the old Eastern Cities than any of the balled-up gobs of horror he had witnessed fighting Foreigns in the jungle. Lance was convinced that the Millers were from some raw-edged place that he couldn't yet understand but that might one day become the course of his life, if only he paid attention. As long as the path opened into a clearing different from that of his brothers. He did whatever Mrs. Miller told him.

"Construct the difference," Mrs. Miller said. She stood over Lance's shoulder, ignoring the other students as she whispered advice into his ear. "Each stroke must address the logic of the entire production."

Lance nodded. He found it nearly impossible to understand her pronouncements, but a hush welled up inside him whenever he actually got down to work. All the questions about what Mrs. Miller meant fell away, and an idle grace washed over him that softened his body and allowed his hand to take charge.

Around this time, Lance's father headed west with a woman who was not his wife. No one knew who the woman was, only that the two of them had met either at the old train station on the north end of town or over on the east side, with its cluster of overgrown cattails and rickety houses built for First Aggression refugees. Most said the train depot. It made sense; ever since the takeover of the trains, the warped and empty building had offered darkness and privacy while double-stacked boxcars rushed by with the raw materials of war.

Wherever it had happened, the story was the same: Lance's father, a sporadically employed lineman, was assisting with the effort of electrification, finally bringing long-overdue power to the farthest homes at the edge of the Sector. The project was already unpopular—why give more people electricity when the rolling blackouts still afflicted those who had it? But the assignment was clear, the funds earmarked, and providing access to electricity that the Homeland didn't have was what Lance's father had been doing when a woman in a domestic Brand 22 automobile, or maybe it was a bubble-roofed Brand 12—the stories differed—pulled onto the shoulder and asked for directions.

Lance knew his father had never been spontaneous and thought the whole story strange. One conversation with a woman in an unknown car and his father had tossed his family aside for a new life? But as unlikely as it seemed to Lance, it was also real and true. To some, it made sense: undamaged men were a catch these days, the woman had been young, and Lance's father, though fierce, was a handsome man. And with all the boys being sent away, why should the remaining older fellows not trade in for a newer, younger model? Wasn't this sort of thing happening daily in bigger cities throughout the Homeland?

With his home life a murkier blend of sadness and bewilderment than ever before, Lance threw himself even further into his work and Mrs. Miller. She allowed him to pursue special projects and during class left him to labor away in the corner of the room on whatever he wanted while his less gifted classmates practiced fundamentals of perspective and proportion. If she knew about his brothers, she never asked, never offered up those pale and wiry smiles of sorrow and sympathy. For this act alone, Lance loved her.

Alongside the twelve daily newspapers his mother subscribed to, a cascade of brochures for art school poured into Lance's home, each glossy page soaked with complicated directions regarding the proper way to submit a portfolio, block letters demanding obscure widths of slides bathed in tungsten lighting and ordered in an ambiguous numbering system. In even smaller print, a rigid warning that prospective students who ignored these rules were wasting the school's time as well as their own. No photo studio within two hundred distance-units could conjure up the equipment to meet these stiff requirements. Well, said Mrs. Miller, you'll just have to send them originals.

"You've got to bring each package inside," the mailwoman at the post office told him.

"I can't just drop them in the box?" Lance asked.

"Not since the latest round of attacks. Damn Ideology Fivers."

Soon another deluge of mail began to arrive. Rejections all, though some included critiques that both chastised him for not following the directions and used phrases to describe his art like "amateurishly macabre."

College, Lance had been told, had become increasingly competitive with everyone applying to avoid the Registry, though there were rumors that this exception, too, was changing. Art schools, he was convinced, were bogged down in applications from scared men with mediocre skills trying to get out of the war. Not that it would have mattered. Tuition, it seemed, had risen nearly 200 percent since the year before. After the twelfth thin envelope, Lance decided he couldn't stand one more rejection and dropped out of school. Though he knew his failures were not her fault, an iron dislike for Mrs. Miller and her ripe praise overtook him.

"I never want to see you again," he told her on his last day.

With Currencies on loan from Lance's second-oldest brother's widow and her one-armed new husband, he plunked down a small deposit on a dark efficiency in the sleepy center of town. There was no resistance from anyone in his family; Lance's mother was too busy trying to figure out what had happened several years ago with a young woman on the edge of town. The emptiness of her home and the deaths of her sons had become nothing more than strange distractions as she slipped far into her unanswerable questions of why and how.

Lance's mother visited only when she didn't see him in church. He didn't have a phone. All of his clothes and possessions fit easily into three paper grocery bags. A small and poorly equipped photo studio in the back of the town's only bookstore hired him to work shifts in both. The job was easy; his life became simple, prefabricated. And then, he wanted to say to the woman in front of him at the brightly lit diner, I met you.

❖ ❖ ❖

Lorrie and Terry were as strange to Lance as a pair of left-handed scissors. In the diner, Lance learned that Lorrie was from one of the few inhabitable cities in the Eastern Sector of the Homeland. Her father had just moved to Interior City for work. She had met Terry at University 282—a very elite institution, they explained, as the three-digit schools were the most discriminating—and the two of them had read some book in a literature course and realized they both wanted to drive across the Homeland and get rough-and-tumble when and if the situation called for it. Together they had skipped most of their classes and spent their time, they said, bumming around "the city." Exactly which city they were referring to, he wasn't sure. Like so many others, Lance had almost no geographical knowledge when it came to the intricate, Swiss-cheese disorder of the Eastern Sector of the Homeland after First Aggression. Even all these years later, keeping track of which of those distant cities had been fenced off and abandoned was a difficult task.

Lorrie continued to overload him with information about her life. A father who served in the early, tame years of the conflict, cousins and uncles lost to the Foreigns, but no brothers. Lance kept silent about his own losses; the compassion of strangers had never moved him, no matter the extent of their beauty. As Lorrie went on, Lance found himself driven by visions of the dark hair of his arms against the skin of her slightly rounded stomach. He decided he had a perfect idea of what her belly button looked like and made a note to himself to transfer the vision to paper.

"You know they're going to admit men soon," said Terry. "Everybody says it's just a matter of time."

Lance hadn't known University 282 was for women only, though he did understand that most schools were now de facto single-sex institutions anyway.

"Not that there's any to admit," Lorrie said.

Terry rolled her eyes at this statement of the obvious. As Terry and Lorrie debated the impact of a male presence on campus—a presence they both agreed would consist primarily of very rich men's sons—Lance took large gulps of coffee and lifted his eyes from the lip of his cup to steal long glances at Lorrie.

"I don't even know where exactly you girls are going," he said.

They exchanged a quick look he noticed but could not interpret and told him they planned to start new lives in Western City North or Western City South. They couldn't decide which.

The waitress—whose tangled and desperate love for Lance he had neutrally noted and promptly ignored since the days when the two of them had struggled to master the alphabet around a kidney-shaped table in a small classroom—came over and refilled Lance's coffee.

"Anything else, Lance?" she asked.

"I'd like a soda," said Terry.

The waitress frowned.

Lorrie and Terry both seemed amused. "Have you ever seen the ocean?" they asked him.

"Which one?" He hadn't seen any.

"How about this menu?" said Terry. "You would think they still had fruits and vegetables outside the cities."

Lance had not realized that produce was still affordable anywhere in the Homeland. At least in his sector, the authorities had been very opposed when it came to allowing females to be farmers. Too many women doing traditionally male work, they said, only made the lack of men more glaring. Better to carry on as usual, though "usual" meant rampant shortages and rationing. Perhaps it was different elsewhere. Still, Lance knew better than to display his ignorance and instead nodded wearily, hoping the expression on his face mirrored that of the two Eastern Sector sophisticates across from him. "The pies are pretty good," he said, gesturing at the laminated menu. "Banana cream is their specialty."

"Bananas?"

The light in their faces saddened him. Had he not made himself clear? The "bananas" were nothing more than silken tofu pulped with marshmallows and a spray of liquid flavoring.

Lorrie accepted the artificial banana news with a sigh and began to share a vague future plan of taking night classes with the eventual goal of being the person who took patients' blood pressure and stabbed them with needles but wasn't a nurse. Mostly, she said, the job would be to fund her political work.

"What kind of work?" Lance asked.

"Political," she said, slower this time. "Do you know about the Coyotes?"

"Coyotes?" Lance asked.

Two men in the booth across from them turned and stared.

"Not so loud!" Lorrie said. "We'll talk about that later."

"So why Western City South?" he asked.

"Or North," Terry said.

Terry and Lorrie explained to him the differences between the two far-off cities and how they wanted to put distance between themselves and their former classmates, most of whom were focused only on the race to marriage, the need to find a healthy vet or a suitable older man. The blood of Lance's brain carried the information that left Lorrie's lips through the proper nerve fibers and pushed it into the appropriate cerebral sections, but even so, Lance found he couldn't really concentrate. To calm down he looked across the table at Terry. She uttered a few comments that made it clear she would prefer Western City South. Not as many blackouts there, she said.

"Do you like living in such a small town?" Lorrie asked him. "Does everyone know each other? Do they all get along?"

Just looking at Lorrie from across the table showed him a thousand new possibilities. He considered her questions and answered them as thoughtfully as he could. Lorrie and Lance began to talk like Terry wasn't there, and after a while she got the picture and took a walk around town. As the conversation shifted into new and different concerns, Lorrie quoted a Foreign author Lance had never heard of in a way that she said was a perfect description of the current muck the Homeland was caught in.

"Oh?" Lance said, and raised his eyebrows.

She loved to read the Foreigns, she told him. Again, more glances from nearby tables. Homeland authors were too provincial, she went on, too sensitive to trends in their own mass culture. "The Foreigns have an awful lot of answers," she said.

"Isn't that Ideology Five?" Lance whispered.

"Absolutely not," Lorrie snapped back. "Haven't you noticed that the prime minister calls everything he dislikes Ideology Five? When you do the research, the actual ideas behind it—"

"Here's your soda," the waitress said, plunking the glass down just a bit too hard. Lance wasn't certain if the look of disgust on her face was because she had overheard their conversation—both of her brothers, he knew, had been lost in the jungle—or simply because he had always ignored her advances and was now sitting across from a beautiful stranger. Once the waitress walked away, Lance tried to move the conversation toward an area in which he had more to contribute, but Lorrie wouldn't let him.

"It's scary, almost," she said. "Dangerous how much those Foreign books have in them. Sometimes I don't want to see that deep into people, you know?"

Again, Lance didn't know. He found himself wondering how flat words on dead paper could ever be dangerous or help anyone see into somebody who was real and alive. Lorrie raised her eyebrows, waiting for him to speak. "Of course," Lance said. "For sure." Lance had no idea what he meant, but he knew that she had sucked him into a current of desire against which he didn't even bother to struggle. When had he last read a book? And one by a Foreign at that? Whatever. For this fantastical goddess in front of him, he realized he would drain his eyeballs dry. *Just point me to a library.*

Lance pulled a pen from his pocket, and while Lorrie went on about her favorite Foreign book, he captured the fine lines of her fingers in sticky blue ink on the napkin in front of him.

"Hey," she said, glancing down at the drawing. "You really know what you're doing."

But Lance didn't hear. He was light and airy and indestructible. He was working.

As Lance and Lorrie were leaving the diner, the lights flickered out. The other patrons groaned and gripped their coffee cups as though they were the very source of life themselves. The day's first blackout.

Good timing. Lance and Lorrie smiled at each other. *Good timing.*

Wherever they were going, Lance knew it would be better than where he was. "Take me with you," he said.

When they met back up with Terry, Lorrie pulled her aside and explained Lance's promise to pay a third of the cost to realign the frame and more than his share of food money. From his vantage point, Lance could see a distinct lack of enthusiasm on Terry's part, but after a few minutes of Lorrie gesturing, he finally saw Terry shrug and nod. When the two of them looked his way, he could feel a wide smile making its way across his face.

❖ ❖ ❖

Walking down the block to the bank, Lance withdrew his entire savings. Once that piece of business was taken care of, he headed home and grabbed his three paper bags of clothes. On top of his unmade bed he left a note for his landlord and dropped two postcards in the mail: one to the widow of his second-oldest brother and the other to his mother's on-again, off-again best friend. By the time the recipients got around to telling his mother, Lance figured he would already be in Western

City South or North. The bricked-up buildings and flat-faced residents of his small interior town would be left behind. With only two weeks until his eighteenth birthday, he would sweep himself into someplace entirely different.

In a moment of excitement, Lance told Lorrie they could talk the whole two thousand distance-units to the coast.

She gave him a funny look. "What are you, crazy? We're driving a Brand Eight. No matter how good a shape we get that car in, it's going to moan and sputter so loud all the way, you won't be able to hear a thing. Everybody knows you can't have a conversation in a Brand Eight."

"I've never been in one," he said.

"Don't you read books?"

"Books say that Eights are loud?"

"Some do."

She was right. The three of them cranked down the car's sticky windows and shouted to one another over the rattles and clanks as they passed through strange cities and towns. Around them spiky plants popped out of the dry dirt, the perfect light tracing the edges of their hard, dark leaves against the nothingness of everywhere else. Twelve hours after they began their journey, they were pulled over at their first checkpoint.

The next morning, there were three more. Dark and hungry potholes threatened to swallow the entire vehicle, the wide, axle-scraping muddy pits yawning widely in the roads. Often they were forced to drive at what seemed to Lance like no more than a fast trot.

Headed due west, the three of them argued Western City North versus South. The simple fact that Terry had a slight preference for the southern end of the Sector made Lance push for the north even harder. None of them had ever visited either city, though Lorrie had read a good deal about both. Unable to decide, they agreed to split the difference and aim for somewhere in between.

On the last day, they didn't stop to sleep. All through the night, they kept themselves awake by debating the Homeland's efforts to control the makeup of the workforce. Sure, there were women cops, women janitors, pretty much women everything. So why wouldn't the Homeland let them farm?

"Do we even know that's what's happening?" Lorrie said. "I read that these crazy jungle bugs are eating all the crops. They hitch rides in the eyebrows of returning soldiers."

"I hadn't heard that," Terry said. "And I read all the papers. There aren't any bugs. They just won't let us farm."

"It's a morale thing," said Lance. "If we let women do everything, it's like we're going extinct or something. But damn, what I wouldn't do for an apple."

As Lorrie cleared her throat and readied her rebuttal, Lance saw the road sign he had been waiting for.

"Take that route!" he shouted.

"But it's totally out of the way," said Terry.

Lance pressed his case for taking the coastal corridor toward the edge of everything, the brim of the Homeland. Once there, Lance knew his mind would be calmed by the fact that he couldn't go any farther. In the end, the two women agreed, if only to quiet him.

After a few distance-units, the mountains parted, and for the first time, Lance saw the ocean. They parked the car and headed down the craggy path to the beach, where Lance realized that not only had he never seen the ocean, he had never seen people like this. The beach was packed. His eyes fell on an enormously fat woman in a ridiculously small suit rubbing cream into her dog's fur. So even the dogs out here had sunscreen. Next to her lay an oiled-up old man in a stained bathing suit slurping watered-down fruit juice through a straw, the red liquid spilling from his lips and sliding down his cambered chest. Lance watched the two of them adjust their ripstop nylon chairs to maximize their sunlight. He noticed that Lorrie was watching the heaving chest of the man drinking the fruit juice. At first Lance thought that she might have a thing for old guys, but after a moment, he realized she was looking at his drink.

"Let's grab a spot," he said. Nearly every speck of sand was taken.

Patterns emerged, the ways of the beach. The young women rotated themselves on schedules, the middle-aged men beside them daring Lance to look. Most of the women seemed unable to help themselves and threw long, possessing glances in Lance's direction. A few of the more lecherous ones yelled their plans and fantasies at him, but Lance kept on walking. The rotating women were everywhere. None of these beachgoers were casual tanners, poseurs pretending at a lifestyle. Lorrie had described it beforehand: anthropologically, she had said, these people were the beach. She had read several books on Western Sector beach culture, simply, as best Lance could determine, for fun. The white sand and the blue breakers, she explained, this was their natural habitat, like those specialized parasites that can only survive in the ear of a cow. Take it away, and they wouldn't just be lost or confused. Without the beach, these people would be drained and sapless, close to dead.

Lorrie went around a corner and changed into shorts and a bathing suit top patterned with small birds, and the two of them left Terry to explore, taking off down the shoreline. Lorrie's shoulders, Lance saw, arched in perfect coexistence, beautifully sloped and delightfully muscular.

They walked on the beach together for a long time. Lance decided that, if anything, he had underestimated the moving production of her beauty.

"I want to ask you so many things," Lorrie said. "But I don't want to overwhelm you."

"Ask away."

Lorrie looked toward the ocean for a moment before turning back to him. "Are you scared to go to war? Do you think you might have a way out? If you did have a way out, would you feel guilty about it?"

He had never even considered the fact that his own freedom might come at the cost of someone else's. Though her carefully considered inquiries about his life touched him, he did not dwell on her actual questions, and he didn't want to think about his impending induction. For it was not what she asked, Lance realized, but how she asked it. There was such an overflow of passion that the intensity of her emotions spilled into him.

Once their legs tired, they sat next to each other on the warm sand and looked out at the shallow sandbar before them, the joyous blasts of hot wind so welcome after long hours glued to the sticky seats of the car. Lance did his best not to gaze for the ten millionth time at the bright fabric birds flying across her breasts. Above Lance and Lorrie, shrieking gulls, dazzling red cliffs, and everywhere beautiful women, though none of them, Lance knew, beamed brighter than the woman next to him. They sat upright, staring out at the sea, doing their best to ignore the jealous glares and wordless grunts of the envious women surrounding them. Why, the women seemed to be asking, should *she* get a healthy one?

A few minutes passed. His stomach making short leaps, his breath shallow, Lance reached over and placed his hand on the smooth spot just above her knee.

"This," said Lorrie, still looking outward, "is amazing."

Lance felt her weight shifting, and soon he brought his hand higher up, sliding from knee to thigh. Together they lay flat in the sand, rolling waves in their ears, runs of foam at their feet. Right here, Lance thought, ear to the earth, the world was perfect. The wind turned and began to blow over them, a warm unraveling rushing over their bodies. First her soft, loose lobe, then her neck, then finally his lips touched hers. On his skin, he felt the narrow beams of warmth shining down from above, and he moved his hand onto her breast, his palm smothering the bright birds of her swimsuit. Through his fingers, he could feel the radiant energy of her low breaths, the soft push of her hard nipple.

Eyes closed, bodies joined, he could not see anyone, could not hear a single soul, could no longer feel the collective ache of the missing men his age. There was nothing but Lorrie.

But it was all too idyllic, the sheer beauty of it all, Terry complained. Somehow she had found them, despite Lance's best efforts to lose her. "The heat must shrivel their brains," Terry added, gesturing at the beachgoers surrounding them. "Up in Western City North, it's colder, more intellectual."

Lance and Lorrie shrugged their shoulders and slapped the sand from their feet with their socks. Right then it was decided: the three of them would head up to Western City North.

On their way out, they drove past another beach, this one slightly hidden in a small cove and bordered by ramshackle homes. "Stop the car," Lorrie said. "I've read about this place, too." Lance pulled over at a graveled lookout point with an expansive view of the sea. The hike down the cliff was steep, but even from their perch on high, the three of them could see that the beach below was different. White sand, blue water, sure, but there were no rotating women, no umbrellas, no nylon chairs. No women at all, just young men, rubbing and blinking, scratching at their bandages, turning their good ears to hear each other, reattaching the cuff straps of their plastic legs around the residual limbs that remained.

No one spoke. Finally, after a dismal pause, Lorrie cleared her throat and told them what they already knew. Veterans Beach, she said, was where men recently returned from the jungle went to sunbathe, partly so no one would have to see them, but mostly so they didn't have to be seen.

"Let's get back on the road," said Terry. "We have plenty of driving left."

Lance quickly agreed with her, one of the few times he had done so after several days in the car. They drove away quickly, speeding over potholes rather than swerving.

By nightfall, they had arrived in Western City North.

Terry surprised everyone by deciding on her second day that the city was not for her. She sold the old Brand 8 to a man with half a nose who asked her why she didn't want it anymore. "I'm going rural," she explained. "Once I get where I'm going, I'll get a new one. Besides, you can't really see this country from a car." Lance and Lorrie saw her off at a bus station. Lance watched a small stripe of tear run down Lorrie's face as they waved good-bye. He wiped it away for her, but he wasn't sad to see Terry go.

Lance and Lorrie had no possessions, but the city was well stocked with furnished apartments. "Registry-runners," the disgusted landlord told them at the first place they saw. "The last boys just up and left. Two more upstairs I'm keeping an eye on. You can't always spot the weak ones."

Lance and Lorrie nodded.

"Overall, it's a good building," the landlord continued. "Six units total. Some immigrants from Neutral Country P right across the hall. Bad smells, but great cooking. In that other unit, a friendly asthmatic gal. Her husband was a hero. We've got good people here."

"We'll take it," Lance said.

"A good omen, taking the place today."

"What's today?"

"Don't you two read the papers? Today's a day for celebrating."

From the side of his vision, Lance watched as Lorrie made a rapid attempt to rebuild her face, quickly working to disinherit the scowl that had appeared the moment the words left the man's mouth.

The landlord seemed to take the masked looks in front of him as close emotional bonds and continued to speak. "That's right. Just last night our boys took back a nice little chunk of the jungle. Sure, we lost a few, but those cold-blooded Ideology Five fanatics, may the Young Savior curse their name, lost even more."

"Seven hundred casualties," Lorrie mumbled, "is not 'a few.'"

Lance elbowed her, and the two of them shook hands with the landlord. He had no idea whether the number of dead referred to citizens of the Homeland, Foreign, or both. A feeling of relief passed over him that he didn't read the newspapers.

Inside the apartment were pots and pans and even a pair of jeans that Lance found fit him quite well. The two of them slipped right into those other people's lives. Lorrie put up a new pair of curtains and slowly began to toss out the old occupants' things and replace them with their own. Lance wanted her with him at all times.

2.

Outside, the air was warm; the deep-red sun burned hot and luminous. Joe and Benny were both broke, but their empty pockets were the least of their problems. They could hear the landlord on the stairs, showing the empty apartment below. Both knew that come Monday, they would have nothing to offer to the wiry old man with the harsh teeth and pale scalp when he tapped on their door to collect. Their imaginations had been stunted, and Joe and Benny had censored their thoughts away from what they were sure was unthinkable. Now they had nowhere to live and much bigger worries. The Registry had found them.

"The girl sounds hot," Benny whispered.

The two of them sat on their old couch, doing their best to limit all sounds of life.

"Be quiet," said Joe. "I think he's showing the place to two girls."

"Yeah, and one of them sounds hot."

"You know that 'sounds hot' is a stupid concept, right?"

Benny shrugged. Insofar as Joe was concerned, a Benny shrug was a concession to the rightness of his own point. They waited for the landlord's footsteps outside their door, for the terrible knock, but when they heard him mention heading out for lunch, the two of them began stuffing clothes into bags. They would take only what they could carry.

"So we'll meet on Friday, right?" Joe said.

"Right," said Benny. "At the Blue Unicorn."

Joe felt a serious terror when they parted because he knew their carefree times were gone. Not that their time together had always been so great; the fear came because Joe had no idea what kind of life might replace it.

Benny headed out first, his cracked leather bag slung across his shoulder.

First, the familiar sounds of Benny's hard footsteps, clunking down the stairs. But then a pause, the chiming voice of what could only be one of the neighbors. Joe had seen the guy and his girlfriend around for a few days now, and had even run into them a few times in a coffee shop, but with each encounter, he had made sure to be as bland and quick as possible. *Destroy all references,* the saying went. Leave no images behind. He overheard that the couple had moved to Western City North from elsewhere, that the guy was some sort of artist, and that the girl was interested in hosting political meetings for some cause or another, but that was it.

Pressing his ear against the glazed glass of the doorway, he heard Benny and the male neighbor exchange greetings. Benny was careless like that. Had Joe encountered someone on the stairs, he would have lowered his eyes and mumbled a soft greeting without breaking his stride. But Benny wasn't the type who might stop and think that for anyone with an exacting eye, a living, breathing young man with a well-stocked bag around his shoulder was unlikely to return to wherever he was departing from.

Through the door, Joe heard the guy introduce himself to Benny. *Lance.* Just another name, just another roadblock. He squeezed his eyes shut and willed Benny the smarts to give a fake name back. He did, and Joe let out a long breath he did not realize he had been holding.

Why make it any easier for the Point Line than he had to? Whoever this Lance was, Joe wished he would head back indoors. He too had a bag to carry out, a life to leave behind.

❖ ❖ ❖

Joe caught a ride across the bridge to a student co-op in a small college town. The next two nights he spent in a wall closet, a pile of clothes stuffed into a pillowcase under his head. That night, he dreamed of a soundless Benny, gesturing to him wildly, unable to speak, further details slipping away the moment he woke. On Friday, as planned, Joe went back to the Blue Unicorn and waited for Benny to show.

As Joe sat in the café, an emptiness skidded across his stomach, and he sneaked small bites of forgotten food when no one was looking: stale bread, hard cheese, salted beef. A full day of waiting, and still no Benny. Normally, Joe liked to be alone, needed it even. Most people drained him or filled him with a profound sadness that human interaction was, by definition, such a chore. But not Benny. Around Benny, his gloom was swept away. Benny recharged him.

After hours of waiting, Joe hitchhiked back across the bridge to the co-op. It was an old building with an apexed roof that dropped shingles onto the front yard at menacing speeds. Inside, the hallways were lined with paint streaks and posters offering discredited or fanciful explanations of official versions of events. Every door was closed, but from behind each one escaped loud, thudding music, the scratches and wobbles of banged instruments shifting at an ever-changing tempo. These days in the Homeland, there were only two types of music: clanging songs of war or the sad, slow tones of women who wept alone.

There were so many people in and out of the co-op that no one gave Joe any trouble. Women and vets, for the most part, a few of them Substance dealers, none of them with any idea of who was lost and wandering and who actually belonged. A few of the dealers had approached him, but Joe turned them down. He knew Benny messed around with Substance Q occasionally, but it was clear that these folks were slinging new derivatives that were much more extreme.

That evening, Joe called his parents collect. He knew they would want to hear from him, and besides, maybe they had some information he could use. His mother yelped when she heard him on the end of the line.

"Calm down, Ma," Joe said.

"Where are you?" His mother always began conversations like this.

He told her he was at a co-op for college kids, and she began to cry. "Are you going to church?" his mother sniffed. "Tell me you go. I do hope you're going, Joe. I really do."

A bone-thin man without a shirt walked by and blinked his eyes in Joe's direction a few too many times. Joe let his eyes pass over the man's thin limbs and sunken chest, noting his missing ear and scarred torso. "Look, Ma, this is collect. Don't you want to call me back?"

A debate broke out between his mother and father over which was more expensive: a collect call or a long distance one. After a few moments of letting them argue, he shouted the co-op's number over their voices and hung up. The shirtless man walked past again. A small gust of desire drifted into Joe's chest, but he stamped it out quickly. There were no friendly faces in this strange place. Besides, the man in front of him had some sort of problem.

"What?" Joe asked the man.

With a slim finger, the man pointed to the phone.

"I'm waiting for a call," Joe said.

The man's face got tight, but he kept quiet. He took a cross-legged seat on the floor, folded up at Joe's feet. Eyes closed and breaths slow and troubled, the man seemed to be shutting out all external stimuli. Finally the phone rang again, Joe's parents already midargument the moment he picked up. His father's hearing had begun to fade; each word was initiated with an excess of volume. He heard his father grunt something to his mother about *telling him now*. Not yet, the pitted voice of his mother said. Whatever his father thought he should know was put on hold; she had more to ask him: Where are you, how are you doing, and what is it that you think you are doing wherever you are?

Well, Joe thought about telling them, there's a one-eared cross-legged man with piped veins and heavy breaths folded at my feet. "It's my turn now," he heard his father say. An involuntary clutch pressed into Joe's back and thrust his spine straight. Even though it had been two years since Joe had been under his roof, the voice of his father still whipped his skin; each sound he spoke birthed tiny welts in the center of Joe's chest.

"They came in person, Joe. The Registry. Showed up at our door at dinnertime."

Joe said nothing. The cross-legged man lifted his head and looked up at him. As their eyes met, the man unfurled his palm to reveal a fiery flash of red. It was a crumpled peony; Joe recognized the flower from his mother's garden. What he meant by it, Joe had no idea.

"'Three notices,' they said. Three notices you ignored. Scared the heck out of your mother."

"Tell her I'm sorry about that." Below him, the bright red petals of the peony lay flat on the cross-legged man's upturned palm. Maybe he was one of those vets Joe had heard about: stable on the surface, but saddled with an inner world of deluded landscapes and bristling misconceptions. Unless the flower was some sort of signal. But Joe's father was still talking: notices ignored, official documents, last chances.

"You can't ignore the Registry, Joe."

For once, his father was right. So many years into the war, the Homeland was getting desperate and the Registry more vicious.

Joe's eyes needed to rest themselves on something that wasn't unfolding into madness. Tacked on the wall in front of him was a piece of newsprint with the headline *Secret Reggies*, followed by small photographs of half a dozen men. Joe squinted at the tacked-up newsprint to try and make out what and who they were.

"It's not a game, Joe," his father was saying. "Twenty-two years now, these guys know what they're doing, how to get you."

Below the bolded *Secret Reggies* was a small, italicized explanation: *A Gallery of Wolves in Sheep's Clothing.* Undercover Registry agents, the article explained, posing as wildhairs, as normal citizens, as drug dealers and criminals. The agents, the article said, were everywhere. The largest photograph was of a man said to be operating locally. He had sloped shoulders and curly hair and wore a fringed vest.

Joe stared at the pictures.

None of those men, he thought, *look any different from me.*

"You know what they told me?" his father was saying. "They said, 'tell your boy that even if he's too chickenshit, that's not how you go about it. Tell him you don't ignore.'"

"Got it." You used to be able to ignore, Joe thought. But no, the Homeland had been fighting for long enough that no one was slipping through.

"You go, you cough, you let them grab your balls, and then you see what happens."

"Is that them saying that or you?"

"Does it matter?"

The cross-legged man rose to his feet. *We're the same height; our eyes are completely level,* Joe thought. The two of them pushed their stares toward one another, and Joe could tell from the shrunken pupils across from him that this man had a raw edge that was ten worlds away from him. Were they done playing make-believe? Just as Joe was about to point to a spare closet he had seen with a lock on the door, the man leaned forward.

"History is a nightmare," he whispered in Joe's ear.

"What's that? Speak up, Joe, I can't hear you," yelled his father into the phone. "I can't make out a word you're saying."

All the signs had been wrong. Perhaps Joe was still too new at playing the game; he had let his eyes linger too long on the man's childish
limbs, his corduroyed thighs. Too much enthusiasm drizzling and oozing out of him like a lost puppy. The man let out a high-pitched sneeze
and dragged the outer bone of his wrist across his nose before strangling
Joe with his eyes one last time. After that, he was gone, down the hall to
some other part of the dilapidated co-op. Even so, Joe allowed himself
a smile. One day, he promised himself, he would get it right.

"So get this down, Joe," his father was saying. "You're up on First
Tuesday, six p.m. Today is Friday, so that means you have four days to
get yourself together. The induction center is at Fourteenth and a street
called Clay. You got that?" his father said.

"Got it."

"You have to go to this one, Joe. You really do."

"Ask him about church again," he heard his mother say.

"Your mother wants me to ask you about church," said his father.
A few hard-to-parse mutters and his mother's voice came on the line.
"You have to soak yourself, Joe, or it will all fall apart. Get drenched in
the Young Savior now, understand?"

She had, Joe knew, no idea what she was talking about. How could
she? His mother wasn't in Western City North. Up here, Joe had seen
people who were soaked, drowning, really. Get soaked. A good chunk
of the people in Western City North were so soaked in the Young Savior
that their lungs were plugged and their hearts were suffocating. Every
day in Western City North someone heard the Young Savior's voice and
put a bullet in their own heads or someone else's. Whole quadrants of
the city constantly wished to be elsewhere. But Western City North was
the edge of the Homeland. This was the farthest they could go.

"You do understand what I mean when I say 'soaked,' don't
you, Joe?"

What did she know about being soaked? She meant the white-
haired minister at their church who raised his voice ever so slightly

when a passage struck him as illuminating a fundamental truth. She meant the brief tingle on her neck when the vocal lines of the congregants congealed in harmony on "Oh, the Burden Faced Down by My Bleeding Young Savior." But she certainly did not understand what it was to be soaked in Western City North. His mother lived in Prison Complex J, an empty prairie of convicts and the people who kept them in.

"Yes, Mother," Joe said.

"Soaked!" she repeated triumphantly.

He could not help but roll his eyes into the phone. Immediately the Young Savior's voice entered his head to chastise him: *Do not remove thyself from the earthly wisdom of thy family.* Quotes from the Young Savior had a knack for burrowing into his mind at the most annoying times. Too much damn religious school.

"And one other thing." His father had wrested control of the receiver once again. "Benny Dorton called. Long distance. I am not an answering service. You tell Benny that, you hear?"

Sudden circuits of joy burst forth from the balls of Joe's feet, pausing for a moment before racing up his body and rolling deliriously around his temples. "What'd he say, Dad?"

"You'll tell him that, won't you? I can't be called at all times of night."

The levels of joy began their imperceptible ebb. "Did he leave a message?"

"He said you could find him at the millhouse. Does that mean he finally has a job? Benny Dorton with honest employment? Mr. Dorton will be glad to know, if that is the case."

Joe said nothing.

"Joe? You're still there, aren't you?"

"Yes."

"If you do happen by Benny, be sure and ask him to call home. I ran into Mr. Dorton, and he asked me to tell you that, in case you saw him."

"I'll tell him."

"It's an important matter about his brother, I believe. And one more thing—"

"Nope, gotta go." He had everything he needed. More, really.

Joe hung up the phone and stepped out to the street. For the first time in a long while, he didn't feel exhausted after a conversation with his parents. He asked the first wildhair he saw for the cross streets of the Millhouse, and headed that way.

❖ ❖ ❖

The place was easy to find, but the neighborhood wasn't pretty. Even the vets looked more mangled, more in need of repair. As Joe walked, the hungry, gleaming stares of women followed him across the pavement. Most were subtle: a slyly cocked head, an eager smile, but a few of the older ones—women who sparked the moment their shining eyes spotted a male gait—called after him.

"What's your name? Where you headed to?"

Joe kept his head down. None of it was personal. They were calling after ghosts, mostly: husbands or boyfriends who were gone, their bodies decaying in the soil of the jungle.

Finally Joe spotted the Millhouse. On the side of an old motel next to the coffee shop was a large billboard: "Point Them Out" the letters demanded. No one knew what actually happened when you called the Point Line on someone, only that if that someone was on shaky status with the Registry, once the Point Line had the person's name, that was it. Poof! Top of the pile, and then you were gone. Pointed.

"Spare Currencies?"

An unpleasant voice hoisted up from the sidewalk below. Joe paused to look at its owner, a man sitting there with his shaved head exposing a lacerated scalp. *Newly returned from the jungle, probably just a year or two older than Benny or me,* Joe thought. A red cleft adorned the right side of his head, an injury that looked pretty bad until Joe's eyes spotted the man's feet. One leg had been poorly amputated, and the skin of the nub was badly infected.

Joe shook his head. "Sorry."

"I don't need your sorrow," the vet said. "I need some Currencies."

Joe took a breath and pushed his way into the coffee shop.

There at the counter was Benny, asking for a free refill. All the blood in Joe's body crowded into his face. To Benny, he could have said a million things.

Benny spoke first. "Oh, wow." His voice was a chilly reminder of the distance between them.

But there were other problems, too, Joe saw, much more obvious ones than Benny's stormy inner weather. To begin with, Benny's face didn't look good. Scabs marked its surface, and he needed a splash of water. Joe absorbed the expression of his oldest friend and felt a sad shudder within. No, Benny was not excited to see him. Never in the same way. *Young Savior help me,* he thought. But that phrase was automatic, and Joe pushed it out of his mind, too. The Young Savior had never helped him with anything.

"What do you mean, 'oh, wow'?" he asked Benny. "I waited for you. At the Unicorn. We were supposed to meet this morning. Where were you?"

"Long story." Benny shook his head. "Just got some free coffee, though." A wide smile appeared on his face, and in a flash the scabby version perished and the old Benny came into sight, the one that gave Joe a route, a course. Here was the Benny he had been missing.

They angled themselves toward an empty table. Neither had any money for food, but judging from the scattered plates abandoned on almost every surface, their poor finances were probably for the best. Even the panhandling vet outside would have rejected this stuff: spotted eggs boiled for so long their yolks were covered with a sick green film, bowls of damp figs with a rotten mold smell, old bread, sour yogurts.

"Yeah, sorry I didn't show," Benny said, taking a seat. An unseen force pushed his eyelids down and hooded his pinhole pupils. He looked around more than Joe thought necessary.

"Why are you over here? We never come here."

Benny shrugged his shoulders. He was dressed in the exact same clothes he had been wearing when they had said good-bye last week, only now they hung off his frame as though the dirt had stretched the fabric loose.

"So according to our greetings," Benny said, "we've got four days." Reaching in his pocket, he came out with a crumpled letter.

"Our greetings?" Joe looked at the paper. There was no runaround like on some of the forms. In bold letters at the top of the paper, this one said exactly what it meant: *Order to Report for Induction.* Right below was the prime minister's seal and the sad black type that said it wanted to take him.

"Everybody calls them *greetings* now," Benny said.

"Oh." Joe paused. "I read somewhere that the first Tuesday of every month is the biggest induction day."

"Right," Benny said. "First Tuesdays are the worst." His fingers tapped the uneven table, and a pearl of coffee rolled down the side of his cup.

"Did you even go to the Unicorn?" Joe asked.

"Yeah." Benny sniffed.

"This morning? I was there for hours."

"Yeah?" Benny's eyes dug holes in his coffee.

"No one had seen you around."

"Laying low, you know?"

"I thought maybe you got caught up in that thing over in Quadrant Three."

"What thing?"

"You didn't hear about that? Some car was stuffed with bombs, almost blew up a warehouse?"

"Why a warehouse?"

Joe shrugged.

"Fuckin' Foreigns."

"Well, get this: people are saying it wasn't Foreigns. The car, the prints on the bombs. They were Homeland citizens."

Benny took a deep breath. "Whoa. Sympathizers. That's new."

"No one really knows. Some say angry Homeland Indigenous or something."

"In Western City North? Those guys aren't around here."

Joe nodded, but he needed more. He waited without hope to hear what Benny had to say. He didn't need hope; Benny always had something.

Leaning toward him, Benny drummed his fingers against the table-top. "Look, Joe, I heard about this book. It's hard to track down, but it can help us. It tells you how to beat this thing. It's for us, exactly for us, is my understanding. All that killing to stop the Foreigns from spreading Ideology Five crap? Not for us. Not anymore. I've got this. *We've* got this."

"A book?"

"A special book. Twenty-two years of hidden information."

"That's all you've got?"

"Fuck you."

They both smiled, but Joe was devastated. A book? He wanted a plan. *I'm not going to let these guys take us,* he thought. *The Registry can't do this to us. Take those other guys, those strangers on the street. But not me and Benny.* He took a deep breath and rubbed his eyes. "It's got real info?"

"Yeah. They say it does."

All that sleeping in a closet had made Joe stiff and stale, but he could see it had done something else to Benny. Wherever Benny had slept, it hadn't killed his fire, and just like always, Joe could sense that he still believed in an out, even when all evidence pointed to the fact that his fierce desire to believe was just that. *What's the name of the book?* Joe could have said. *How come no one else has figured it out? How come we're the only ones who can get it?* And finally: *You think the words in some book are special enough to get us out of this?*

"Don't look so mad, Joe. We've got a plan. We're not going to let these guys get us."

But he was mad. What the two of them had was special. And once the Registry pried it apart, Joe could not see how they would get it back again. Even the Young Savior had said it: *What you truly love, you do not let go.*

Above, the lights flickered off, the voltage around them slipping down to nothing. Another rolling blackout.

Benny got up to go to the bathroom. Joe forced himself not to watch that familiar dragging stride, drew his eyes away from the brush of Benny's thighs. A man in a fringed vest stood up and followed Benny into the bathroom. Onward yet.

With Benny in the bathroom, Joe's mind began its automatic reversion to a more joyful time. The two of them had grown up in the same complex, just a few blocks away from each other. Both their fathers worked in the prison, but Joe's father wasn't a guard and neither was Benny's. At the time, the two boys were sure this made them special. In the mornings before school they would steal the newspapers off their neighbors' porches and read the comics out loud on the walk over. On the way, they would dodge gangs of refugee boys, angry kids whose worlds had been broken apart after First Aggression and now loved nothing more than to throw a fist at the natives. As soon as class let out, Benny and Joe waited for each other outside the chain-link fence.

Sometimes other boys wanted to play with them; Joe always said no, but Benny could usually convince him otherwise.

After what seemed like a long time, Benny returned from the bathroom. With an electric groan, the freezers, stoves, and lamps came back to life.

"I mean, here we are, you and me, sitting in a coffee shop," Joe said, "and all the while the Registry has got its fingers at our throats."

"Yeah, yeah," said Benny, waving his hands. "Let's talk about something else."

"Fine. Have you been reading the papers?"

"Not really."

But what papers were the ones that needed reading? Years ago, as one of his first moves in office, the prime minister had showered grants and tax breaks on anyone looking to start up news channels, newspapers, even radio stations. For the public good, for an informed citizenry, he said. Currencies were bestowed upon anyone who correctly filled out the forms. What's the plan for today? the joke went. Oh, nothing much, just starting up a national newspaper.

Only now, years later, there was far too much information, and Joe had little idea if any of it could be trusted. As a result, he paid attention to almost nothing. Except, of course, to what was right in front of him. And in front of him now, he saw, was a wolf in the guise of a sheep.

"That guy in the fringed vest," Joe said, indicating the man with his chin. "He's been watching us the whole time. He got up and followed you when you went to the bathroom."

"C'mon, Joe. You're always so worried about people. Don't worry about him. He's whatever." Benny leaned in closer. "But how about that other guy?" He pointed to a man with short-clipped hair and black-rimmed glasses on the other side of the café, cracking peanuts out of the shell one by one.

"You think he's Registry?" said Joe. "I mean a Reggie?"

Benny's laugh was spare and gravelly. "Not everybody's an under-cover. He looks like that kid we used to have chemistry with." The man with black-rimmed glasses pushed another peanut shell with his thumbs. A little part of the peanut flew an unexpected path into the lens of his glasses.

"Are you serious?"

"Yeah, you know who I mean. What's his name, who was always taking notes and wouldn't share them. Not that I remember much from chemistry. Well, maybe something about particles being matter, or matter being particles, but that even these rules are just, like, experimental facts, not—"

"We shouldn't be talking about this, Benny. These are the wrong things to talk about."

A drip of sweat slid down Benny's forehead, stopped briefly at his temple, and picked up speed as it cleared a path through his stubble and fell to the floor. Strange, because it wasn't hot in the Millhouse.

"For real," Joe continued. "The Registry has called us in. And we've got no plan, nothing at all."

"Yeah, besides, whatever we did or didn't learn in chemistry is probably useless by now."

"Are you even listening to me?"

Benny tilted his chin. "I already told you. We do have a plan. The book."

Again the lights flickered out. This time they stayed off. The second rolling blackout in less than an hour.

A silence hovered between them. Friends for their entire lives, they were unable to talk about the only topic they should be talking about.

"It is weird, though, right?" Benny had always had a habit of beginning his thoughts in the middle of a conversation. "When you really think about it."

Usually Joe was able to follow the swirling gusts of Benny's rapid shifts in thinking. But even a few days apart from Benny could make him hard to interpret. "What's weird?"

"That this old man can make us do whatever he wants."

"I think it's a little more complicated than that."

"I mean, what is he, ninety? Ninety-five? If some random old guy came up to us right now and was, like, 'pour your coffee on the floor,' you'd just say no. But because it's *this* old guy in particular . . ."

Joe shrugged. The only way to believe that the prime minister's age was an issue was to read the underground papers, and neither of them had bothered to do it. "Do you think it's our fault?" he asked Benny. "Do you think we should have known more? Read more papers or something?"

"Are you serious? First off, even if you could do it all over again, you still wouldn't watch the news or read the papers. There's so many of them, it's impossible to choose what information to pay attention to. And when you do listen, it's completely demoralizing. Second"—Benny was smiling now—"the fact that there's way too much news does nothing to change the other fact that every paper, every program just says the same thing over and over again. It's a simple equation. Big paper equals: the war is going well—"

"But watch out for terrorists at home," added Joe.

"Right. And for the smaller papers, it's even simpler: the war is wrong."

"Plus a sympathetic little box in the corner for the latest round of domestic crap."

"Totally. 'Small Bomb Dents Registry Truck.'"

"'Foreign Sleeper Cell or Domestic Sympathizers?'"

Benny sighed. "Same question. Every damn time."

And yet this world Benny was describing was already becoming simple, unfamiliar. Lately, Joe had heard, a new strain of the underground press had emerged, radio stations and newspapers that let facts whip about wildly like an ocean storm. Not only were they fixated on the prime minister's health at age ninety-six, these new papers also made an issue of his closest associates, many of them in their eighth and ninth decades as well. A result, these papers claimed, of Fareon. How they explained that it was the Foreigns who controlled and maintained the world's only deposits differed. But beneath the surface, all the claims were similar: Fareon was helping old men feel young. And the only ones who had access to it happened to be the architects of the war.

Of course, a handful of new radio stations and papers had recently popped up solely to refute these claims. The only thing Joe knew for sure was that the war was absorbing men at astonishing new rates. And here he and Benny were, up next.

Just a handful of days to figure out his entire everything. The Registry had squirmed its way into Joe's life, and it seemed that the more he thought about his options, the narrower they became.

"I'll track that book down, and we can meet up tonight at my uncle's cabin," Benny was saying. "There's a bus in a few hours for you and one for me a little after." He sniffed in again. "We'll lay low for a while, get out of the city. The cabin is completely isolated. It'll give us some time to think before Tuesday."

"Why don't I just come with you?"

Benny waved his hand. "I just have to handle a few things first. I'd let you tag along, but you don't want anything to do with these guys."

Joe wondered what kind of guys had books but were dangerous, too. And why split up? Why not just stick together? Benny hacked a syrupy cough into his napkin. "So we go to this cabin—"

"And we'll be in this amazing forest, and we can sit and think and maybe forget about all this Registry crap for a minute. Maybe for a hundred minutes."

"That's like an hour and a half."

Benny laughed. The laugh was his real one, Joe knew, rare and deep, and to Joe, the sound was as joyful as the jump of a small child into a warm pool.

In some ways, the plan seemed perfect. Solitude, a completely new setting, just the two of them, a calmness that might lead to the ability to make a real decision. But why split up beforehand? Joe was just about to press again for Benny to invite him along to whatever he was doing when his eyes linked up with the man in the fringed vest who had followed Benny to the bathroom. No matter what Benny said, it was clear that the man was just dirty enough, Joe thought, to be too dirty, the kind of grime that had been carefully applied in front of the mirror in some Registry agent locker room.

"This coffee tastes like shit," said Benny. "I want an apple."

"Don't talk about apples."

Benny began to talk about apples. He missed them all, the sweet mush of the golden yellow kind used for baking, the tart fire of the miniatures that had been the last to go. But Joe's thoughts were elsewhere—into the territory of the jungle, into the idea that either of them fighting a war seemed like a case of mistaken identity. They were being pushed into the wrong era. It was not an era either understood or belonged to, but now they were flooded with letters from the impossibly old prime minister, letters demanding physicals, letters claiming they did belong, after all. They were the right shape, of acceptable heights, the right sex, but these letters were made of words, and those words demanded things: packs of muscles, rows of teeth, a thick skull, and internal organs that pumped and drained and performed the proper tasks at the required times. *We are,* Joe thought, *human clumps with the right tools to go and do something we don't know how to do in a place we have never thought about.*

Benny scribbled out the directions to the cabin on a napkin he grabbed from the small metal box on the table. Joe pretended to study the directions carefully, but it didn't matter. Right then he knew: he wouldn't let Benny slip away again.

3.

No details had been provided to Alan about the Southwest Sector School for Homeland Indigenous other than the fact that he would be departing for its distant campus in two weeks. He had been twelve years old when they'd told him, almost thirteen. No one referred to the place by its full name. *The School*, they said. Somehow, in the shortening of the proper name of the institution to a generic one, Alan had felt even more frightened at the prospect of leaving his family for this unknown place of learning. Though he could not have known it at the time, his fear was more than reasonable. Within days of his arrival, the truth—as it so often does—made itself plain. The School was a brutish, nasty place.

Now, four years later, Alan sits on the floor of a bright, concrete room. Above him, two bars of light buzz and flicker. Thirty-six hours have passed since he has last seen darkness. The constant neon shine is part of his punishment. Until today, he had never thought of darkness as a privilege. The idea of an outside world, of red sunsets, of passing grey clouds, all of it had faded in the first nine hours of confinement. And just his luck, there had been no blackouts. The room has no windows, only a hard mattress, a metal toilet, and three cups of warm water meant to last him the entirety of his stay.

For his first three years at the School, Alan had dutifully followed the arbitrary rules of the nuns and fathers. He completed his homework on time and performed his work duties beneath the hot sun. But as he entered his final year, he had begun to think more about how he had arrived in the first place. And right now, he has plenty of time to think.

❖ ❖ ❖

It's not a choice to go, it's an order. Alan can see the pain on his parents' faces, the way their mouths breathe sick, slow breaths and their eyes turn sliced and narrow. They must have held this information all night; they probably hadn't slept a second.

"Why don't you have a seat?" his father says gently.

As Alan sits down, he takes in the living room: parents across from him on their new couch, wood with whitewashed finish. The new couch came with cushions that are puffed out and swollen, and lately, the three of them have to sit more often than they'd like so as to deflate the sofa to normalcy. Alan places himself in the low chair across from his parents. The small table separating Alan and his mother and father is packed with objects. The cast of knickknacks rotates frequently, but right now the table is glutted with two wax apples in a cherry wood bowl; an empty wine bottle filled with a mixture of topaz and garnet that an unemployed cousin gave Alan's mother for her birthday; a white rectangular serving platter with scalloped details; two rams, a large deer or a small elk, three sea captains, and a wire-haired fox terrier, all glazed ceramic; and four folded newspapers, still unread. For a moment he considers flinging a ceramic fox against the nearest wall. Anything to break the awful mood of the house. His parents continue to explain themselves.

"There's no more room at your school," says his father.

Do they really think he is this stupid? School is twelve minutes away—three turns, one stop sign, and no traffic lights. In every classroom, there are empty desks. No, they must have some other agenda they are trying to cover up. He waits, nodding slowly, playing dumb.

"No room," repeats his mother softly. Her head sways from left to right, and her bare foot rises to the coffee table, her bean-shaped toes curling around the edge. The scalloped platter and the bowl of ornamental apples clink together musically with the trembling of her foot.

Today cannot be a normal day. On a normal day, no one would put bare feet on the coffee table.

"We had a visit," says his father.

Alan's mother jumps up, grabs him from behind, and squeezes. The fact that she's hugging him already, Alan thinks, shows that the situation is much worse than he understands. A semisolid picture forms, telling him that whatever this conspiracy is against him, his mother is not behind it. From outside, he hears the wearied bark of one of the stray dogs that use their yard for shade.

"You'll have to go away," says his father.

"Because school is too crowded?"

"And because the new school is better."

A pressure on his shoulders, around his neck. His mother still has her heavy arms wrapped around him, is still bent over him and squeezing hard. Alan feels a wet drop on his chest, and then another, a third, a fourth, a fifth. Her tears drop tiny polka dots onto his shirt.

"Let him go," says his father. "Let him go for just a minute."

His mother releases him and returns to the couch. An orange light shines through the window and falls across their knees and ankles. Alan stares at his father, watching his spinning eyes. Is he the driver behind this plan or just another easily manipulated man?

"He's so young," his mother wails to no one in particular. "Too young!"

His father places a hand on his mother's shoulder but locks his gaze with Alan's. "Come outside," he says.

Of course he wants to separate us, Alan thinks. He must know something that she does not.

Outside is better anyway; the zone is scheduled for a power outage, but for some reason the lights and air conditioning are still on. The two of them stand up and leave his heaving mother on the couch. On the way out, his father grabs a small canvas bag and hooks it over his shoulder. Even as he presses the heavy oak door shut, Alan can hear the sobs of his mother.

The view from the front steps is the same as always: dry and even earth dotted with saguaro cacti and sage, the long-eared jackrabbits shooting from one bush to the next, the flat tops of the buttes jutting up in the distance. This landscape is alive. On their driveway, a keeled snake, twisted into itself and soaking up the idle warmth of the concrete.

"Like I said, we had some visitors," his father says.

Alan squints up at him.

Father and son walk down the unpaved path. The heat is strong and full, and their bodies wade through it. Though their destination is unannounced, both know they are headed to the library. The library is in a poorly ventilated trailer dotted with tiny star-shaped spores of fungus and mold, and Alan has read most of the books there. Still, he knows that if he says that, his father will tell him to read them again. This fire within, the desire to know as much as possible, Alan decides, is the one useful thing his father has given him.

"The men came," his father starts again, "to tell us to send you to a new school."

"But I like my school."

His father's eyes, always sharp and small, seem all of a sudden deeply sad and inky.

"Why do we have to do what the Homeland says? They can't tell us what to do."

"I think this new school will be good for your future," his father says. His face doesn't match his words; his tone is out of sync with his drooped eyelids and risen brows. Alan doesn't believe a word he says.

"Where is the new school?"

"Far," his father says. "Too far." This last part is only a whisper.

"A school like Gran went to?"

His father stops walking. "We aren't the kind of people you can fool like that." He bends down to place both hands on Alan's shoulders. "Nothing like that will happen at this school. I promise."

True, his family is not like the other families that surround them. Yes, they live in a specially zoned Homeland Indigenous District, but Alan's parents have two nice cars, one of them a flashy new Brand 19 with a bright chrome fender that looks like a sneering upper lip. But the car is secondary to the fact that the house is bolted to the ground and can't be towed away, that inside the house the floors are shiny vinyl, the water from the tap is cold and sweet, and that both his mother and father have salaried, air-conditioned means of earning their Currencies. They are sharp, his parents, having risen from humble roots, and they don't believe everything a sweaty Majority Group man in a suit who pulls up their driveway in a government-issued Brand 23 tells them. Or so Alan had thought.

"Did you ask them whether we had a choice?"

Rocks crunch beneath their feet as the two of them start to walk again.

"Of course."

"You asked the government man? Directly?"

Alan's father shakes his head. "I don't expect you to understand the difference between a request and an order. But this man—"

So his father had crumbled. Alan has always suspected that the man who raised him is weak. Now he knows for sure.

"I tried," his father said. "I really did."

But you didn't try enough, Alan thinks. He switches to a new tactic. "People say those schools starve kids. They work fifteen-hour days."

"Not true. You'll see. The library is ten times the size of this one."

"What does that matter?"

"That means they're serious. A big library means a place is dedicated to giving you a worthwhile education." His father stops, lowers to one knee. His face is pinched, but his hands find Alan's shoulders, pressing him even deeper into the dirt. "The knowledge they're going to give you at this school is going to last you forever. You need this. *We* need this. What do we always say our people have to do?"

"Be twice as good—"

"And they might give you half," his father finishes.

But Alan has saved his final justification for last, the one that just might break through. "But kids from that school are the first ones to go to war."

"The prime minister." His father stops and looks around, making sure the two of them are alone. "What is he, ninety-one? Besides, wars don't go longer than twenty years. Just the idea, it's obscene! People simply wouldn't stand for that long a conflict! They would . . ." He pauses, then starts again. "By the time you graduate, this war will be over. Guaranteed."

Alan stays silent. His father's voice is tender, he thinks, but his answers are empty. How can they be anything but? His father has not fought to keep him.

"I want to give you something," says his father, slipping the canvas bag off his shoulder.

A rush of wind brushes Alan's ears with dust. Though his father is still talking, Alan lets his voice dissolve into the wind. He makes a promise to himself: *I will be stronger than the man before me.*

"Take it," his father is saying. In his hand is a bright orange pouch with a zipper running along the edge. The sky is broad and open above them, the sun hot and unrelenting. Opening the pouch, Alan finds a whistle, a nickel-plated compass, and a box of waterproof matches on which is printed: "Burns intensely hot in the strongest winds." A survival kit, Alan realizes. A small group of objects placed together in a zippered pouch to help him survive.

"Don't lose this," his father says. "You're going to be in a new kind of place now."

Four years later, and Alan still has that pouch. He keeps it in a locked chest at the foot of his bed. Suddenly the lights in his cell flicker off. Finally, true darkness. Twelve more hours until his solitary confinement ends. Not that what he has to return to is much better. Even so, anything he suffers with the other boys is better than too much time alone.

4.

Western City North was a town of firsts for Lance and Lorrie. In their new apartment the two of them ate new foods and tried new positions for their new lives: oysters; draped over the bathtub—the cool porcelain an awful shock against warm skin; a rare and fresh kiwi that a radiant older woman had handed to Lance on his way to work; Lance standing while Lorrie remained seated on the tiled kitchen counter, legs on his shoulders; fresh cherries and bright blueberries, together almost half a month's rent, followed by some twisted maneuver that neither of them enjoyed called the pinwheel. Soon, with fresh fruit and quality produce scarce even in the fertile soil surrounding Western City North, their bodies were all they had left. Gone were the stone fruits, berries, and salad greens. Remaining was each other, clenched legs, crossed ankles, and all. Even when all that was affordable were sweetgrass stews and tough meats, they were still a couple possessed, marvelously fucking each night until the first hints of sunlight crept through the blinds.

❖ ❖ ❖

On his eighteenth birthday, Lance mailed his card to the Registry. It was mandated—every man had to—but as a small act of defiance he gave his address back home instead of his smoky Western City North apartment next door to the family of Neutral Country Ps. As expected, Lance heard nothing back. And while the Registry was silent, everything else around him began to crumble.

❖ ❖ ❖

First, one of them itched. The next day both of them did. They went to a free clinic, waiting for half the day while men with facial wounds and rare fungal diseases received their care. Finally a nurse practitioner hustled them into an exam room, smiled at what were surely her first patients of the day whose damage did not come from combat, and handed them a topical cream.

Once home, Lance and Lorrie followed the tiny directions on the little tube, even made a game out of it as they applied the cold cream to their ragged skin.

Two days later, Lorrie still itched.

"Don't worry," Lance said. "Give it a few more days."

A few days were followed by a few more, and Lorrie's itching did not subside.

She rubbed the cream into her skin. She still itched. She rubbed more cream, mangling the tube into spilling its final few drops.

"There isn't anything," Lance said. "I can't see a thing."

"Please." The knurled tendons in her neck rose into a ridged surface that pressed against the skin. "Just check one more time."

And for her, Lance would move around skin, squint his eyes, and look for the lice that almost certainly weren't there.

Lorrie became increasingly distressed and spoke only of contamination, infestation. The lice were on the move, migrating, she claimed, and had now voyaged out from her pubic hair and onto the rest of her body. When Lance protested they were called pubic lice for a reason, warm tears slid from the corners of Lorrie's eyes onto the sheets below. Her nose, which was long and pointed, was almost always clogged from constant wailing. They didn't discuss where the lice had come from; that wasn't a conversation either of them wanted. Lorrie recognized, of course, the aspects of Lance—the slashing eyes? The bone-crushing stare? The glaring absence of men in the city that caused women to gulp and place a soft hand on their rabbit-hearted chests?—but her focus was not on some imagined desertion on Lance's part, but rather the muffled annoyance that the bugs that had been rubbed out with one topical cream for Lance seemed to have converted in Lorrie to something else entirely.

"I know they're there," she sobbed. "Just look again. Just find something."

And so Lorrie continued to scratch. She thumbed through the phone book for laundromats. When she reached them, she would demand to the befuddled voice on the other end of the line that they recite the highest temperatures—no rounding digits, please—that their washing machines could reach. Once, then twice a week, she stuffed their bedding into large cotton bags, pulled them tight with a string, and dragged them over her shoulder and onto the bus in search of a scalding heat that would destroy the invisible colonies she was convinced had taken up residence on her clothes and body.

Each day she scratched harder. Her fingernails upended her skin, tore apart cyte and cell, transfiguring them into open sores that pocked the surface of her face.

In some ways, it was ridiculous. *You're doing this to yourself,* Lance wanted to tell her. *This is a problem of the mind, not the body.* His thoughts took violent turns, and in his dreams he lashed out at her, his nighttime self grabbing Lorrie's arms and shaking her as he spoke, each word slower than the last: *Just. Stop. Scratching.*

❖ ❖ ❖

Lance knew he only had a few hours to act while Lorrie was out. She was an active member of a group that helped organize free breakfasts for crippled veterans. However, the leadership of the small group had fractured as the vice president and her undersecretary had drafted a mission statement calling for an investigation into the flaked and fabled Foreign substance known as Fareon. *With a foundational shift in the age and makeup of our government,* they wrote, *our nonagenarian prime minister in particular, we hereby advocate for a full investigation into our leaders and their association with this material.* Or, as Lorrie put it to Lance: Why the hell were just a handful of the Homeland's leadership growing so old but staying so healthy?

Proof? There was none, raged the counterargument, not a dab, a splash, nor a splatter, nothing besides the ages of the prime minister and his closest allies, no serious evidence that some obscure mineral deep in the Foreign jungles could make anyone live longer, and even less proof that a small, shadowy cabal of handpicked legislators had this wonder potion at their disposal. Skeptics shook their heads sadly. How can we make these Fareon people see? they asked. There's no documentation, no evidence. None at all.

Exactly, came the response. They're that crafty.

Last week, the president of the organization to which Lorrie had devoted so much time had called an emergency meeting on the Fareon question. Outside, Registry agents intercepted groups of attendees and questioned them about two recent attacks, one where a bomb exploded, the other where it did not. Men were pulled aside, their papers checked.

An agent with cloudy cataracts and a limp—afflictions of war Lorrie was well acquainted with—stopped Lorrie on her way in and ran down a list of queries from his clipboard. From the wild cartwheeling of his questions, it was clear the authorities had no leads on anything.

"You guys think Homeland Indigenous are tossing bombs around?" Lorrie asked a Reggie. "That's a new one." She shook her head and headed inside.

The meeting did not go well. With the Registry having snapped up almost all the male membership, the remaining men made it clear they felt outnumbered and voiceless, though their feelings of estrangement were by no means exclusive. Divisions in the group fell less along the lines of sex and far more across the monstered lake of thoughts and feelings. Shouts and scuffles broke out repeatedly. Believers in the explanatory logic of Fareon as the clear answer to the prime minister's advanced age were baffled by the accusations of insufficient evidence, each speaker more frustrated than the next that their comrades could not see the hidden forces operating just beneath the surface. On the opposing side, the anti-Fareon contingent sat with arms folded, incredulous that an inability to end the war had now transmogrified into fanciful tales of all-powerful forces operating under shadowy rules that subverted the laws of nature and reason. There's so much more to actually fight against, things that are real, they argued.

What could be more real than a substance that won't let you die? came the retort.

In a shaky voice, the vice president of the organization read from a speech that one of the few female legislators, a Coyote, had given on the parliament floor. This particular legislator had spent years raging against the war. Members of Lorrie's group rolled their eyes. None of these people needed a civics lesson; all of them had witnessed the unfolding of what was now their hellish present. Upon completion of his second six-year term, the prime minister had run again, this time as deputy prime minister, second in command. The years that followed saw the timid man supposedly in charge push that fateful word "consecutive" into the Constitution, and soon, the prime minister was eligible to run yet again. Which he did. Repeatedly. As the prime minister's political structure hardened, antiwar legislators became increasingly rare. Now, after twenty-two years of banging on podiums, the name had stuck. Coyotes they were called. Because they may as well have been howling at the moon.

Over the jeers and hoots of the audience, the vice president of the organization continued to read the legislator's speech. Though the group couldn't even manage to get along well enough to keep serving breakfast to a few hungry vets, Lorrie still hoped to unify the factions.

"Check me one more time," Lorrie had said before the meeting. "Just once more."

Even though he knew there would be nothing to find, Lance still recognized that this nothing was feasting on the last scraps of the woman he loved. He looked some more.

Nothing. Lorrie and her scabs left for the meeting. The moment she closed the door, Lance called the exterminators.

❖ ❖ ❖

"This really isn't standard operating procedure," the first exterminator said. The men in front of him were dressed in dark work overalls and leather utility belts stocked with tools Lance didn't recognize. Both men were too old for the Registry, had probably served during the much tamer early years of the current conflict. One of the men had his coveralls zipped all the way to his neck, while the other had allowed his zipper to fall to the middle of his chest, revealing the coffee stains of his white undershirt. Behind them stood a much younger woman, also in dark coveralls, a notepad and pen in her hand.

"Our intern," said Unzipped, cricking his neck in her direction. "Not enough fellas like yourself to do the job these days."

"But back to this one," said Zipped-Up. "We don't do fakes. We're real. We kill termites. We run your carpet beetles out of the house. We zap your pests, and for a much more reasonable price than our competitors." The intern wrinkled her forehead and made a few quick scribbles on her notepad.

"Regular lice, there's a shampoo for that," said Unzipped. "You can get it at the drugstore."

"I told you guys, there *are* no lice. You're not going to really *do* anything."

The intern increased her note taking to a furious pace.

"Say again?" said Zipped-Up.

"So there's no infestation at all?" asked Unzipped.

Lance sighed. "You're just going to come in here, poke around with your equipment, and make like you're getting rid of something. It's a psychological extermination."

"Pyscho-logical," repeated Zipped-Up. "Make sure you get that down," he told the intern.

Though Zipped-Up was slow and dull, the casual way he pursed his lips reminded Lance of his second-oldest brother. He let the silence hang, hoping Zipped-Up might repeat the small movement and bring the slowly fading memory of his brother back to life.

"I can't have this kind of thing get out, the idea that we do fake exterminations," said Unzipped. "If our clients associate us with a fake extermination, it might affect their decision-making process regarding whether they would hire us to do a real one."

"And we are certainly not trained in anything psycho-logical," added Zipped-Up.

"There's barely anyone in the building," Lance told them. "Most of these apartments are empty. Registry-runners, you know?" This wasn't quite true, but he could sense that the two guys upstairs were making moves. Why not give these exterminators the opportunity to purge a bit of the contempt lying half-rotten in their bellies?

"It's just sick," said Zipped-Up.

"Disgusting," added Unzipped. "You should point them."

Lance looked to the intern, a woman his age, to see if she agreed. For a brief moment he caught her eye before she looked away.

"Look," Lance said, "I'll give you double just to not do anything." He had begged, borrowed, and saved, but whatever he might owe didn't matter.

The exterminators agreed, but demanded a verbal contract of non-disclosure. The four of them shook hands, the exterminators shrugged their shoulders and huddled with their intern, and though Lance had told them not to, they sprayed as though they were performing an actual fumigation. Lance pushed the crisp Currencies at their confused faces.

That night in bed, Lance explained to Lorrie that he had killed the lice forever. The smell of insect death hovered in the dense air, drowning out even the odors of Neutral Country P immigrant cooking that slipped beneath their door each evening and lingered till morning. Lorrie seemed to believe him, and for the first time in weeks, they began to undress each other. His fingernails were too long, the short, brittle hairs of his beard were too rough, but they squeezed and arced and twisted and followed each other around the bed. His weight pressed her deep into the mattress. He moved down between her thighs, but she pulled on his ears and brought him back up to her eye level. Nothing was normal anymore. Lance was disgusted by the lice, and with each thrust, he saw himself driving back the enemy. Only it wasn't working. There was no escape from the scratches and marks on her body, rising off her skin with bright disdain. No, this wasn't enough. He needed to hurt them, to hurt her. The flat nose and puffy lips of the intern flashed before him, but he pushed her image out. He needed to see Lorrie as she was. The next thing either of them knew, Lance turned her over and muscled his way into her. She let out a scream that was swallowed by the pillow; neither of them had ever done this before. Once it was over, the two of them lay on the bed, caught between the smells of themselves and the poison.

❖ ❖ ❖

Even after he had the house smoked, had bombed the whole place with chemicals, Lorrie still felt the lice. Lance stopped sleeping and began to rage against each tiny bug that wasn't there. After he'd scrounged up enough money and called his Substance Q dealer—a greedy, well-connected vet who also dabbled in fruit—Lance bought what he was sure was the last cantaloupe in Western City North. Lorrie refused to even try a bite, claiming she wasn't hungry. By the time Lance finally bit into it, the melon was creased and sour. Fruit having failed him, Lance tried to win Lorrie back in places where he had won her the first time.

"We must go to the beach," Lance said.

"The beach? Must?"

"And not just any beach. We're going to the good beach. Our beach." The cool air and scratchy sand, the hot wind uncoiled over twelve shades of blue: surely one of them could stop her free fall.

The two of them headed south, through the mountains and to the beach they had come to on their very first day on the coast. Lance had tossed some of her books into his duffel bag, the old kind she used to read, all the Foreigns. They drove farther, and the mountains turned dry, their shriveled tops like wrinkled blackheads. On the radio, the prime minister was giving his weekly address, condemning the latest domestic terrorism and offering up yet another warning on the dangers of Ideology Five. Lorrie switched the station, but his speech was on all of them. Since they had last been this way, the roads had slid into further disrepair. Lance took each turn slowly, ready for the rips and gashes in the concrete. From behind the wheel, he looked up and saw what he thought was a migrating bald eagle. Lorrie scratched the whole ride down.

"I read that the salt air will kill those things," Lance said. "Not eagles, but lice."

"Where's an eagle?"

Lance pointed with his left hand, keeping his right on the wheel.

"Hard to say. I'm not sure an eagle would be around here."

"Some wingspan, though. Check out that wingspan."

"Where did you read that about the salt air, Lance? A magazine? The newspaper?"

"Just some research."

He hadn't read a thing.

They spread out on the sand. The sun was white and low, and the beach was crowded once again with people—mostly women, of course, the men old or damaged—everyone on blankets and lounge chairs. Lance peeled off his pants and shirt and slipped his trunks on. Lorrie stayed in her sundress and her flat, dark shoes, but Lance could still make out the fine hairs that began at the tops of her ankles, just above the scabs where she had scratched away the skin. As they sat, Lance could feel the murmurs of those around him, audible sounds of envy from young widows wishing that they too had a man who was intact and alive and would sit next to them at the beach.

He watched the breakers; he felt the scrape of each grain of sand as the wind blew them against his skin. Lance had always found paintings of landscapes to be sentimental and ugly, but as he stared at her ratted flesh, a demented gusto swept through him, and he knew that he would one day paint some version of Lorrie's scabs against the sea.

Breathing deeply, he looked at Lorrie. She had on a new pair of sunglasses, huge platters that circled above her eyebrows and ended at the bottom of her cheekbones and gave Lance the feeling that she had stepped behind a large tinted window. She pulled out one of the underground newspapers that lay piled around their house (she currently subscribed to twelve different titles) and sighed loudly. Lance glanced at his bag and contemplated offering her one of the Foreign books that rested inside. Did she ever think about any of the big ideas she used to, or had the lice and her radical group's sectarian split over Fareon pushed them all aside?

"It says here," Lorrie read, "that a lot of Homeland Indigenous join up to go fight." She undulated the newspaper with both hands until it made a bubbling sound. "They don't even wait for the Registry. They just volunteer."

"Huh."

"I wonder why they would do that."

"Maybe they just want to help out."

"I wish Terry was here. She'd know. Her mom was actually Homeland Indigenous, you know."

"Yeah," Lance mumbled. "If only Terry were here." Lance had never met what he considered a real Homeland Indigenous, and he doubted Lorrie had, either. He distinctly remembered Terry telling him it was not her mother who had been Homeland Indigenous but her grandmother. Maybe half.

"But why now?" Lorrie said. "I mean, look at these numbers." She pointed to a paragraph near the bottom of the article. "Why would they sign up now, twenty-two years in, with higher casualties than ever before? It really makes you wonder, doesn't it?"

Lance agreed with her, but all her wondering convinced him that she couldn't even put her thoughts in the right order anymore. They were, he saw, truly breaking apart. She had invisible bugs—he had seen her sneak three furtive scratches in the last four minutes—and with the afternoon character of the water blue and calm, all she wanted to talk about were Homeland Indigenous. In front of them, the tide pushed lower, leaving a pale white film on the sand. This, Lance knew, was a brush with the worst kind of trouble: Lorrie could wonder at the problems of people she had never met, but she could not look down at the scabs on her arms and the mutilated skin on her ankles to wonder why the marks were there, and then think further and recognize that they shouldn't be there at all.

All the Foreign books stayed in Lance's bag.

Lorrie checked her watch.

"What is it?" Lance asked.

"The laundromat, the hot one, last wash is at eight. I thought maybe we could get a load in."

"After coming all this way, you want to leave so we can get a last load of already clean sheets in?"

Turning away, Lorrie edged to her side of the blanket.

"Are you serious?"

Lorrie shrugged.

A low, heavy quiver spun and hissed its way through his body before exploding in an outburst of indignation. "We washed a load yesterday and the day before that! I drove us all the way out here, to our favorite place, I packed us a fucking picnic, and still you can't think about anything else but those stupid sheets."

"Forget it," Lorrie said softly.

"No, no. That's what you want?" Lance sprang to his feet. What did she know about trouble? He was in the crosshairs, he was the one who would be gathered up to die. Couldn't she see that? Of course not. She was too worried about herself, her imaginary fucking bugs.

"I said never mind," Lorrie said.

"No, no. It's me." Above them, a stack of clouds traveled through the air, blotting out the sun. "I'm sorry for trying to make you feel better. For navigating the craters in the road, for making us sandwiches, for bringing some books I thought you might want to read. Please, by all means. Let's get out of here." He grabbed their bag of blankets, books, and sandwiches and tossed it toward her, a little harder than he knew was necessary. He had thought Lorrie was facing him, but as the bag sailed through the air, he saw that she had turned away. With his mind simmering, Lance said nothing, called out no warning, instead watching as time slowed down and the abundantly beautiful face of

Lorrie spun once again toward him, the bag slamming into her cheek as she did so.

On the drive back, Lance accelerated past Veterans Beach as fast as he could—potholes be damned—and as his foot pressed down against the hanging pedal, he saw Lorrie make the smallest flick on the tip of her nose. Just the beginning. In two minutes, he knew, she would be pawing at it furiously with her fingernails. It was the first time Lance started to wonder about her parents. Who were they, and what did they need to know?

5.

The blackout is over, and the lights have come back on in Alan's cell. How many more hours until they release him? Four years ago, the first thing he noticed upon arriving at the School was how far it was from everything, so private and lonely that not even animals came around. Not that Alan cares much about animals, though he makes an exception for the sled dogs belonging to Ricky X-P, the main character in his favorite book. The one thing Alan's father was right about: the library here is better.

Mornings at the School bring a dead, hollow silence. Back home, unseen thrushes and wrens and creepers would pile their croaks and whistles on top of each other as if they each had something to say, without being bothered to listen. At the School, the skies are always empty. The silence is creepy, but Alan knows that the broad gap in sound means nothing more than that he goes to a school on such shitty land that even the lowest animals can find a better place to be. There is a hum, a lyric vibrancy to the clamoring of the outdoors where his parents live. But here in the dead desert of the School, there is no illumination of sound, only stumped, dried trees and the plentiful acceptance of everyone wishing they were elsewhere.

Rules and regulations cling to them like vines on a tree. Outgoing mail is monitored and read, fruit is canned and sugared, cheese is old and yellowed. A stream of well-adjusted Homeland Indigenous veterans visit their classrooms, a succession of different men who have all come to the same conclusion: that duty and service must be prized above all. Students at the School are allowed to speak Homeland language only, nothing else.

The moment he arrives, Alan is determined to find a way around the ban. Homeland words don't always fit. Sometimes they're flat, filthy, worthless words that drop cold and weightless from his tongue to the floor. Sometimes he just needs to speak Group F.

Sister Ava Azor stands at the front of the classroom. "Today," she says brightly, "we will discuss your uniqueness. The Indigenous way of thought—your way—is very special, very different from Majority Group. Take these facts, for example."

She reaches for a cracked leather book on the edge of her desk and begins to read. "Members of Homeland Indigenous Group P, who suffer from bad posture, are convinced they stave off scoliosis by thanking every dandelion they see." She pauses and rotates her neck slowly, letting her eyes fall upon the class. Alan takes out *Crafty Beryl*—a new book by his favorite author, the one who wrote about Ricky X-P—and starts to read under the desk. Sister Ava Azor either doesn't notice or doesn't care. In this story, Beryl is a sailor on a boat from a country that doesn't exist, although he's on an ocean that's very real. Alan has never seen the ocean.

"It is a very old superstition," Sister Ava Azor reads, "for members of Indigenous Group T to not comb their hair at night."

There are no Group Ps in the school, so no one in the class can be sure about thanking dandelions, but there are plenty of Group Ts, all of whom Alan and the rest of the class have seen comb their hair after dark. Alan shakes his head and goes back to his book.

If thoughts are thought with words, Beryl says, *then there is nothing unsayable.*

This book is not nearly as good as the author's first one. For twelve pages now, Beryl has been staring out a window, considering decisions he made in the past. *Write a sequel to your first book,* Alan would tell the author if he ever met him. *No one cares about this new stuff.*

Sister Ava Azor continues, spewing gigantic facts that range from the Group Js at the northern border and their propensity for dining on flavored buffalo shit (the roars and groans of the class are difficult to silence for at least three minutes after she reads this sentence) to small groups on isolated islands who refuse to partake in any fruit that has already ripened. She is, Alan knows, reading failed words from failed books, words bent out of shape by time and now worn, stripped, and jammed into a wrong place in which they've never belonged.

Now, locked in a cell, Alan can still remember his response to these "facts." *Four more years,* he had thought, *just four more years until I can leave this place and get some facts of my own.*

"On to the next lesson," Sister Ava Azor had said. "Can anyone state the Homeland's purpose in engaging the Foreigns?"

No one speaks.

"Now, I know none of you were born at the time," she says, her upper lip raised and tightened, "but that doesn't mean the reasons have changed. Why, class, are we at war?"

Silence again.

"Okay, let's start from the beginning. It's very important to me that all of you understand this. When Homeland Indigenous start to misinterpret their history, very bad things can happen."

A small boy raises his hand. "What kind of bad things?"

Sister Ava Azor narrows her lips. "No need to dwell on the negative. Now, we all know about First Aggression and the origins of the conflict, but who is willing to give an explanation of the potent and hateful system of government known as Ideology Five?" Sister Ava Azor clasps her hands together and lets out a humongous fart.

Every boy in the classroom bites his lips hard. They cannot laugh. All of them know that if they do, Sister Ava Azor will screech a threat of pinching noses till their mouths fall open and she can pour detergent down their throats.

"No one"—her voice now plunged in anger—"is willing to explain the tenets of Ideology Five? No one can elucidate the nature of this tyrannical system? This system that all present will be expected to fight against?"

More silence from the class, until another gassy wheeze dribbles from Sister Ava Azor's butt cheeks.

The fart opens up a space within him. Respect is worth four gallons of swallowed detergent, and Alan immediately recognizes the opportunity to increase his sphere of influence. But he must act fast, must execute properly. First, Alan looks for the right words, and of course the Homeland language can't fit around them. The right joke would be neutered and lost if he choked it out in Homeland. He needs the raw specificity that only his own tongue can provide. A deep breath in as he turns to the three Group F boys next to him—they always sit together—and he says the joke in his language. All three of them shriek and wail, collapsing into their laughs and writhing about with giggles. The other boys in the class may have not understood the words, but the shape of the joke is clear. Mission accomplished.

"Enough!" says Sister Ava Azor.

The laughter stops.

She can't impose as strong a penalty as she would like because she doesn't know what Alan has said. Making a joke at a Sister's expense is a huge punishment. Speaking your own language is a lesser one. Alan may escape the detergent yet. Even so, the salty swallow of fluid would be well worth it. The other boys look at him, the slow bloom of respect blossoming on their faces. In the front of the classroom, a half-breed swivels his head to look at Alan. They've never spoken, but Alan knows that the halfie who has turned is Gad. Gad's face is easy to read. The heavens have unrolled before him, Alan thinks. In this cruel place, a half-breed on his side is just what he needs. From this day on, Alan and Gad are always together. With Gad by his side, the sad world around him feels just the tiniest bit happier. Since that day, until Alan's punishment, the two of them have never been apart.

6.

Benny's problem was simple: he owed his dealer more money than he had, and his dealer was starting to get unhappy.

"That was bad money, Benny, and you know it." They eyed each other across the small round table.

The Millhouse was divided by an invisible barrier: on one end, clean-shaven older men in shiny medallion shoes and ironed silk ties sat alongside young women in high-buttoned dresses and tasteful neckwear, all of them gulping down large cups of coffee before work and staring disdainfully at the other side, that section of the coffee shop that consisted of prickly, exhausted young men with ruddy smells bursting from their armpits, men with baggy eyes and last night's clothes. This second group grasped their mugs for warmth and barely sipped from them, silently staring at one another—*Who are you? Why are you still here?*—no one acknowledging that they were all about to be snapped up or had to disappear, all of them sure that at least a few in the crowd, with the dirtiest being the most likely candidates, were probably Registry undercovers anyway. Whatever. Benny knew which side he was on. Sure he stank, but those clean men would be in his place any day now.

"You understand me, Benny? You understand that this is serious?" his dealer was saying. For health or fashion reasons, Benny was never sure, his dealer always wore a flowered lei around his neck. Now the wreath sagged flat on his dealer's chest, the pinks, reds, and whites sick and wilted. "I'm not happy with you," he said. "Not at all."

"I understand," Benny told him. From the side of his vision, he eyed a woman across the coffee shop with long legs and plump lips.

"This is bad, Benny. Really bad." His words weren't friendly, but Benny's dealer had a talent for staying calm when he was deeply angry. Besides, he was right: Benny had spent twenty real Currencies in order to get the fake sixty.

"Well, give me the bad Currencies back," Benny said. "And I'll get you the real money."

"I don't like that you did that. It's not a good-faith move by a customer. It doesn't inspire confidence." The dealer rocked back on the rear legs of his chair. A thin creak floated up between them, the sound, Benny knew, of his dealer's false limb interacting with the hard floor. Benny had seen his dealer's prosthetic on a humid day a few months back. The skin color of the substitute leg wasn't even close, but then again, at least the dealer had one. With the nationwide shortage, few of the amputated had a good match.

"So we're clear? We're good?" said Benny. Was the plump-lipped woman from across the room winking at him?

"No, we're not good. You paid me in crap. Sixty worthless Currencies." The dealer closed his eyes for what seemed to Benny like too long a time, and then opened them again.

"Right," Benny said. "So now that you're awake, I'm going to need those fake Currencies back so I can get you your real sixty." Benny didn't have any other connections, and his dealer's stuff truly was the best. The plump-lipped woman smiled at him yet again, but this time Benny ignored her, the realization of his dealer's anger now occupying all of his attention. With the walls of his veins throbbing, he knew he would tell his dealer anything he wanted to hear.

"Maybe you don't understand, you stupid mother-raper," his dealer said, voice rising. "I'm keeping the fake stuff. But that bullshit money doesn't settle your debt, not even close. So now"—he leaned forward, a vein about the width of the temple tip on a pair of spectacles bursting from his forehead—"you are, shall we say, obligated to get me my sixty real Currencies."

Smile, Benny thought. *Show him that whatever he wants is no problem.* A quick thought crossed Benny's mind that he should Point Line his dealer, but he knew that all a pointing would do was save a few Currencies and leave him in the same spot: without his dealer's stuff. Then he remembered that you can't point a veteran. New tactic. Give the guy something to identify with. "I'm having problems with the Registry," he told his dealer. "I'm up on First Tuesday."

A smile followed a sneeze, the fringe on his dealer's vest flying up and then back down again along with his high-pitched spasm. "You read *A Thousand and One*?"

Benny didn't know if the conversation was turning in a way that was good for him or not. He shrugged.

"C'mon, Benny. *A Thousand and One Ways to Beat the Registry.* You want to end up with one of these?" He knocked on the knee of his plastic leg. "And that's the least of my problems. The things I saw. So many—"

"So what's this 'thousand and one'?"

"It's a book, Benny. And damn the Young Savior if you aren't going to need it more than anyone."

"How do I get it?"

"Well, that's just it. You can't just get it. Unlike almost every piece of information in this country, what with our ten thousand radio stations and two million newspapers or whatever, the stuff in this book is actually hard to find."

"Okay," Benny said.

"But luckily for you," his dealer continued, "even though you are by far my shittiest customer, you are still a customer. You're going to be in the hands of the Homeland anyway. I see that. So I'm cutting your bill in half, a debt to a future serviceman."

"You don't know that," Benny said. "I could still run."

The dealer brought the lei over his head and placed it on the table. It clumped in front of them like some bright piece of roadkill. "I feel like slapping you," his dealer said. "You don't just run. Whole underground organizations are out there, and they've given this a lot more thought than you have. Maybe someone might have been able to just up and run in year twelve, even year fifteen, but now? There's a whole industry for runners out there, if you can find them. Of course, that's the whole point. They don't want you to find them. But if you can, you've got your baldheads; they have this game where they scream at each other—I'm not quite sure how that gets people out of service, but they say it does; you've got the Homeland Indigenous Movement, not that they would help you out. The point is, you've got to plan to run, to join up with people. Running isn't just running. Running is planning." He paused and grinned to himself. "Running." He laughed. "They'll run you right down."

"Allied Country N is just a two-day bus ride."

"Right. You got a lot of places to crash in N? Do you even have a real winter coat? You think that flimsy jacket you got on will work up there?"

"I'm a friendly guy." Benny rubbed the fabric of his coat between his thumb and forefinger. "I could get those things." His dealer was right, though. It was a thin coat.

"How about you read the paper for once, listen to the news or something? Did you know that up by the border, no one is fixing the roads? That half the cars are wrecked from minicraters, that buses can barely pass? Or how about the rule changes? That you've got to show employment before they let you in now? Did you know that, Benny?"

"Sure, I know a lot of things."

"I highly doubt that. You can't even fake sixty Currencies right."

"I could get it right if you'd give them back to me."

"Shut up, Benny." The dealer sniffed loudly and closed his eyes again. Maybe the guy was allergic to his own lei. "I'm going to do you a favor," the dealer said. "Bring the Currencies—real ones—to this address. Just half, that's the first part of the favor."

"What's the other part?"

"Damn the Young Savior, you're a greedy bastard. These guys you're bringing half the money you owe me to, they have a copy of *A Thousand and One*. Tell them you know me and that your induction is just a few days from now."

Through the window, Benny spotted Joe and did a funny jump to his feet that twisted his back. "Don't talk to me for a minute," he told his dealer. "I've got to handle some stuff." Benny walked to the counter and leaned forward, squinting at the sour baked goods he did not have enough Currencies to buy. Anything to make it seem as though he had come alone.

"Get that money to that address and we won't ever talk again," said the dealer to his back.

"Why would you say that?" Benny asked, turning around to face him. His dealer really did have the best stuff.

"You're an idiot, Benny. Either you're going to be blasting little Foreign babies' heads off, fighting the good fight against Ideology Five, or you're going to be moving around every three days and looking over your shoulder. You're not going to be here, hanging out. Do you understand that? Look around." His hands slashed the air, palms up. "This is done. Over."

"Pretend you don't know me," Benny said. "I've got to take care of something."

He turned around and saw Joe standing right behind him. Wow. What the hell was he doing here? The murky memory of a call to Joe's tight-balled father, the mention that the Millhouse was his hangout now; after two nights of Substance smashing, his own motivations for calling had completely slid away from him. Right now, Joe was the last person he wanted to see.

"Where were you?" Joe said to him softly. "I waited for you."

7.

Lance sneaked the phone numbers from Lorrie's address book. He had looked in it plenty of times before; it wasn't a diary, he told himself, but now his hands felt thick and ugly. Each page stuck together, and he had to lick the tips of his fingers to separate them. With every flick of tongue against skin, he felt more and more like an animal.

He wasn't worried Lorrie might catch him in the act; she was all the way across town at a meeting of Women in the Workforce. *For sister resistors who want to organize and activate like-minded sisters to resist our exclusion from industries essential to the Homeland, please come to a meeting of fellow sister resistors,* stated the flyer on their coffee table. Lance understood their arguments. Why not encourage more women farmers, produce sorters, fish catchers, whatever the hell it was the Homeland needed? But though he would never say so to Lorrie, he also understood the Homeland's desire to keep the appearance that traditionally male jobs were still held by men. After all, nothing reminded you that all the men were dying more than looking around and seeing women doing everything.

Disenchanted by the squabbling of her free-breakfast-for-veterans group—the pro-Fareon faction had taken to accusing disbelievers of

being undercover agents sent to spread doubt and misinformation—
Lorrie had decided to use her time differently and had now been to
three Women in the Workforce meetings in two weeks. Even so, Lance
had no idea what she actually did there.

Lance picked up the cracked leather booklet with the alphabet running down the right side and turned to *M*. Nothing under *Mom* or
Mother. *D* for *Dad* and *F* for *Father* came up blank as well. A brief and
passing rage that Lorrie should have any sort of family at all hooked in
his gut. In this very moment, Lance's own mother was probably sitting
behind blackout curtains, mourning the loss of her husband and most
of her sons. And here was Lorrie, ignoring the perfectly intact family
that she had.

There was a rattle at the door, and Lance dropped the tiny book on
the floor. A split of nausea tore a path from his stomach to his chest.
Could she already be home? But wait. Women in the Workforce meetings usually went on for hours. Through the peephole he saw a tiny man
with loose, twisted curls carrying a book with a bright blue cover tucked
under his arm. An undercover Reggie, come to get him? Turning back
toward the kitchen, he did a mental marking of his best escape route.

"What do you want?" he called through the door. In the blurred
edges of the peephole he saw that the man had feminine lashes, long
and straight and the color of coal.

"Can you hear it?" the man asked.

"Hear what?"

"You don't hear anything?"

"What do you want?" Lance called again.

"I asked you what you heard. Whether you could hear that right
now?"

Would a Reggie play with him like this, chanting nonsense in order
to get him to open the door?

"You can't hear because you're not listening," the man went on. "I can help you tune in. The voice of the Young Savior is always sounding, friend. But you've got to be on the right frequency."

Quicker than he thought possible, Lance swept the door open. Reaching out, he grabbed for the man's wrist. "That's what you banged on my door to tell me?" As his insides burned, he felt his own hand cover that of the long-lashed man's. "You knock on my door and scare the crap out of me to tell me that the Young Savior is talking but I can't hear him?" He pressed the man's thumb into the backs of his fingers and bent his own palm back toward him. The one useful thing he had learned in pre-army elective.

"Ow!" the man yelped.

Lance held the twist, fixing his eyes on the quickly spoiling veins of the man's arm, the little raised lines pulsating euphorically. *Harder*, the veins whispered to Lance. *Tighter.* Obedient, Lance pressed into the hold.

"Hey, you're hurting me!"

The man's frightened tone woke Lance up. Releasing him, he slammed the door quickly.

"I'm trying to save your soul!" he heard the man shout.

Western City North was soaked with these maniacs. There was no time for proselytizers, he told himself; he was trying to save something much more real than his soul and, he was sure, much more important.

Lance gave his head a quick shake to get back on task. Her last name. Of course that was where her parents would be listed. He ran to the book and flipped through the pages. There, in Lorrie's tight script, were both her parents' names, listed as neutrally as the numbers for her dentist and the sergeant at arms for her radical theater group. People were on the other end of these numbers, real people who could help, who could solve the mystery of these invisible bugs, these painful scabs.

Five rings. Ten. At twelve rings, Lance hung up. Hours remained until Lorrie was due back from her meeting, still time to try again. In the extra bedroom that had her desk and his easel, Lance took out one of Lorrie's albums at random, this one featuring an orange picture of a machine gun on the sleeve. It was time to draw.

Even through the shrimpy little portable, the music sounded awful. Aggressive horn blasts came from nowhere. A dyskinetic drummer banged jerkily on whatever objects must have been in front of him: chairs, pots, pipes. Hard, sharp blows by the saxophone player sacrificed rhythm and melody for atonal whumpings. Who could draw to this shit? He decided to smoke some Substance Q instead. Soon the soft grey smoke curled all around him.

The second time he called, Lorrie's mother picked up on the first ring. After a brief introduction, Lance explained the situation as best he could.

Yes, we live together.

Yes, she thinks they are under her skin.

If you could not mention to Lorrie that I've called . . .

Of course, dear, the mother said. Thank you so much for informing me of this . . . circumstance. I'll talk to Lorrie's father.

It's very serious, Lance told her.

I'm sure it is, dear.

Could you reach him at work?

I never call my husband at work. He detests being interrupted.

Could she make an exception?

She could not.

Three Q cigarettes later and the once-sharp horn blasts now played soft and chirpy from the speakers. The jerky drums had turned wet and drippy. Lance heard the door rattle. He stayed folded on the couch.

"Well, it's all over," Lorrie said, standing above him. "They've sneaked their way in."

Again with the fucking bugs? An involuntary burst of cool smoke swirled from Lance's nostrils.

"The infighting, all the disagreement, you know?" She licked her dry lips.

Lance coughed, an attempt to twist the high out of his mind. What the hell was she talking about? Colonies of critters weren't having civil wars; swarms of pests didn't sit around and hash out their differences. She went on, but the confusing curves of her conversation led nowhere, so Lance nodded silently and hoped that more words plus a few facial expressions might alleviate his total failure to understand her.

"All these new members," she continued, "and every one of them divisive. They've infiltrated us for sure."

Of course. Lance exhaled. *Women in the Workforce.*

"I just thought that this was a fight that—" She paused and wet her lips with her tongue.

A feeling he quickly identified as relief ripened within him. At least she wasn't upset about the fucking bugs. He smiled up at her. "Sounds good," he said.

Lorrie walked in the bathroom and shut the door behind her.

Lance breathed out the sweet foresty smell of Substance Q smoke. It wasn't all over after all.

❖ ❖ ❖

In their small apartment, Lance entertained. Lorrie sat and smiled, but it was clear she would rather be elsewhere.

"Have a drink, Lorrie," said Rick. Rick had one leg that was significantly shorter than the other.

"Yeah," said Mike softly. "Have a drink." Mike said everything softly. He had been raised in Worship Sect Q, but was still having trouble getting his status to reflect his genuine religious dedication to pacifism. Not that it mattered. Rumor was the pacifist exception would be gone by the next time First Tuesday rolled around.

"I've got some good Substance Q," said Wilson. The rest of the group laughed, as Wilson always had good Substance Q. Only Tim and Rebecca, the downstairs neighbors, took him up on the offer. Lance contemplated the divine shape of Rebecca's lips as she wrapped them around the rolled papers.

"Did you guys hear that speech that one of the Coyotes made on the floor of parliament today?" asked Lorrie.

No one had heard it, though if they still wanted to, there would be plenty of opportunities. In that very moment, it was probably being replayed on ten channels and analyzed on ten more.

"That was a big speech," she berated them. "An important one."

Her guests nodded, but Lance could see that they were weary. Every speech was advertised as important. As a result, all of them were meaningless.

Lance tried to catch Lorrie's eye, an attempt to toss her a *calm down* look that would better capture the tone of the room. Instead, he saw her swallow, followed by the brief tremble of her lower lip. *Of course,* Lance thought. She was just getting started. Lorrie's zeal didn't recognize the need for a cold beer, a sloppy wet Substance Q cigarette while some good tunes played, not with talk of Substance-smashing soldiers chopping off Foreign fingers while smoothly aging lawmakers cheered them on from the parliament floor.

"I bet she's going to ask us about Fareon next," said Norman. A few of the others giggled, but Norman did not. Norman was Lance's most perceptive friend, though also his most obscure and maddening. How Norman wasn't snapped up, Lance had no idea, but the futile task of getting a clear answer from him demanded a level of commitment that Lance did not possess.

"I want to hear her question," said Tim. Tim always wanted to hear Lorrie's next question.

"What do you think I'm going to ask?" Lorrie's first smile of the night.

"About Fareon?" Norman said. "You'll probably set us up with some wording designed to lead us to the idea that the whispers of extended life are state-perpetuated rumors designed to distract us. Disinformation to keep us in thrall at the power of the state and all that."

"Sounds right to me," said Tim.

"Then," said the ever-perceptive Norman, "you'll circle back to the Coyotes. Should we embrace their timid, centrist plan to slowly scale down the war?"

Lorrie nodded, impressed. "Go on."

"How about another beer?" said Rick.

"Me too," said Mike, though no one heard him.

"And after we all agree how weak the Coyotes are," Norman continued, "you'll go into questions about tactics. What do we do about the recent surge of attacks inside the Homeland? Were they carried out by Foreign sleeper cells? People like us who've had it up to here? We all know those attacks make it hard on the Coyotes. But maybe it's because they're so timid. So you'll bring up whether we should be fighting to replace the Coyotes, who probably have less than ten members anyway, or give them more political support so the rumored hordes of cowardly legislators who secretly support them can feel all emboldened and shit."

"Not bad," said Lorrie.

"And if we really got into it," Norman said, "you could point to fifty op-eds for your side, and I could point to twice that against."

"About those beers—" said Rick.

Lance nodded and headed toward the kitchen.

"And finally," Norman continued, "you'll somehow combine these mysterious domestic attacks on the Homeland, the tepid protests of the Coyotes, and the insane mysteries of Fareon to that new women's group of yours. 'Don't you miss strawberries?' you'll ask us. 'Wouldn't it be nice to pop an orange wedge into your mouth?' But how it's all connected, well, I've got nothing."

"But it is!" Lorrie said. "You see—"

"Where's that other six-pack?" yelled Lance from the kitchen. With all the blackouts, keeping beer in the fridge was meaningless. Lorrie called out a few guesses over her shoulder, but by the time she returned her attention to the group, the conversation had moved on.

Wilson squinted and breathed in a long, ragged pull of Substance Q. "You guys hear about the latest attack over in Quadrant Four?"

A few people shook their heads.

"What was it?" said Lorrie. "Another homemade bomb?"

"See, this is the weird thing," said Wilson. "It wasn't a bomb, wasn't an explosion. It was charcoal."

"Charcoal?"

"Whoever it was, they broke into some Registry parking lot and filled the insides of all the vehicles with charcoal. Top to bottom."

"And?"

"And that's it. Just a bunch of armored trucks filled with charcoal."

"What the hell does that mean?"

"Maybe the Foreigns just ran out of stuff to make bombs with," said Wilson.

"Or maybe," said Lorrie, "it wasn't the Foreigns."

"Of course it was the Foreigns," said Lance. "No matter how much you hate the war, you're not going to attack your own country."

"Can we talk in the kitchen?" Lorrie turned to him.

What the hell was it now? The two of them headed to the kitchen.

"Kick these people out soon," she whispered. "WIT has an important meeting in the morning."

Lance smiled and reminded himself not to bring up yet again what a terrible acronym WIT was, as it left off the second *W* of the workforce entirely. He almost told her to relax, but he quickly caught himself. *Relax?* she would say. He knew that she would tell him that this was not a year for relaxation and that next year wouldn't be, either.

Once the letters started coming, they didn't stop. Back home, Lance's Registry board wanted him to drop in for a physical and was now sending sour ultimatums to his mother demanding he show his face. Ridiculous. Even if Lance had wanted to, he didn't have the Currencies to make his way back to his hometown. He made a note to himself to write the Registry and explain that he had moved on, that he was in Western Sector now, and that they should update their records. *Also,* he might write, *please stop sending letters to my mother's house. She is still in grief at the unique disappointments provided by the deaths of her favorite sons and the unending questions regarding her absent husband. Leave her alone. We barely talk anymore. Best, Lance Sheets, new resident, Western City North.*

Instead, Lance never got around to asking them to update their records, and his mother, he imagined, must have allowed the increasingly frantic missives to pile up on the inbuilt ledge of her hallway. Lance had no idea whether she understood what they were and where he was. Probably, she thought he had just missed church for a chunk of time. Every few weeks one of his brothers' widows would come around and see an official-looking letter with his name on it, shake the dust off, and send it his way. By the time they made it out to Western City North, the Registry had already sent a newer, angrier version.

❖ ❖ ❖

One night, after Lorrie insisted on sending yet another handful of Currencies to the hot wash, Lance struck her. He was not hitting Lorrie, he told himself, but forcing the lice to come pouring out of her in order to return her to him. Lorrie no longer seemed to like her body, and Lance thought he could hate it, too.

Once Lance had crossed the sick threshold of striking the first blow, a thought emerged: each whack to the side of her head would spill the bugs out of her. She was too beautiful, Lance raged, for these lice, for these community meetings where pastors and cops yelled and shouted, too beautiful for the wars that were happening and the wars that had been. Too beautiful, his sharp blood screamed, for all the sick events unfolding in and around her.

Later, the bruises mingled with the open sores of her scratches until it was impossible to tell the difference. So concentrated was Lorrie on the infestation and Women in the Workforce that they never talked about the night of violence that had opened up between them. She had not threatened to leave. Eyeing his latest letter from the Registry, Lance thought, it suddenly seemed much more likely that it was he who would be leaving instead.

❖ ❖ ❖

Her mother and father showed up at his apartment door, curled their noses at the Neutral Country P smells that lingered in the hallway, and cultivated their worry in an approach that Lance was sure would swallow Lorrie's final threads of sanity.

"Welcome to Western City North," Lance greeted them. "The edge of the Homeland."

"Right," said her father. He ignored Lance's hand and brushed past him into the apartment.

"Hmmmph," they said. "Tsssk," their tongues went, the heavy air whistling through their scaly teeth. "Bugs!" they exclaimed to one another at random moments when Lorrie was out of earshot. "Under her skin!" Neither of them seemed to care what they said in front of Lance.

Cures and true bed rest, the parents said, could only come from Interior City lakes and the undirected friendliness of the people who made honest lives around their banks. The Western City North winters—sea-sprayed with bursts of sunshine—made the parents suspicious. The inhabitants of this city, they seemed to think, were barely citizens of the Homeland at all. "So dirty!" they said of the streets. "So dangerous!" they said of the latest attacks.

"But we never go to that part of the city," Lance tried to explain.

"Of course not," her mother said. "It's much too dangerous."

Each minor victory of the parents toppled Lance's will and sapped his strength to argue against any outcome that was not identical to theirs. The father tuned into hawkish radio stations that Lance had not known existed, the voices from the speakers demanding a surge in troops for the upcoming twenty-third anniversary of war. A day in and it was clear to Lance that they had their differences; a few more and it was plain that the parents had no interest in looking beyond them. They would not stop, he saw, until he was wiped out, erased completely from their daughter's life.

Lance smoked Substance Q and plotted. He would not let them win. He took long walks. More letters came from the Registry. *We demand, we urge,* the letters said. Each was filled with more spite than the one before. No workable plots came to him. No self-defense seemed adequate. Questions asked of him in his own house were mandates poorly disguised.

"How about you take another walk, dear?" Lorrie's mother said. "We'd like some time with our daughter." She was slicing crosswise into a fresh tomato, an item Lance had not seen in stores for months. He wondered where she had gotten it.

Another letter from the Registry had just arrived, fingers waggling and warning him of high Currency fines he knew he would never earn over a whole lifetime, along with years of imprisonment. Lance was soon to be in violation of many laws with numbers, letters, and decimal points. A walk around the block, he decided, would help him think about those numbers and about ways to get Lorrie's parents out of his apartment and back to Interior City.

❖ ❖ ❖

The departure was executed quickly and efficiently. They must have planned it for days.

At first, Lance thought Lorrie and her parents might have just headed out on some collective errand. He sat on the couch, smoked a Q cigarette, and listened to the roaring wind batter the old apartment windows. After a while he put on an album, humming along until the songs dissolved into a series of staggered snare beats. Only after several hours on the couch did Lance notice the note, a small piece of paper folded in thirds, resting on the table, his name printed on its middle section.

DON'T GO TO WAR. DON'T COME FIND ME.

Lance was driven by everything the letter didn't say. There was no doubt Lorrie had written it, but what had she actually meant? The first part, Lance recognized, was pure Lorrie. Of course she didn't want him going off to the jungle. But the second part—he looked to her block letters as partial evidence—was so emptied of emotion that it had clearly been conjured while under a parental spell.

What complete shit. From his sunken seat on the couch, he remembered where he had hidden two more Q cigarettes. He stood up, pulled them out of their hiding place, and began to smoke. She didn't mean it. She couldn't. He picked up the paper, the block letters disembodied, nothing like her familiar script. Crumpling the paper into a tiny ball, he tossed it as hard as he could. The small paper sphere bounced off the wall and onto the floor. Pulling the Q to his lips, Lance took a long, heavy drag.

He found it impossible to forget that he and Lorrie had lived in paradise, that before the bugs came they had had a near-perfect life of fresh food and steamy bedroom tricks, and now, he thought, some mortal error, some fat sin, had banished him into a sexless, smoky apartment with clean sheets, yellowing stacks of anguished political flyers cratering the floors, and a kitchen of canned beans and hard bread. And then there was the matter of money. Lance did odd jobs, enough to make his half of the rent, but he knew he couldn't pay the whole thing for any real amount of time.

Lance looked around, started paying attention, and saw that while the lice had been feeding off of Lorrie, it was he who had returned from a walk to find his entire existence had been chewed away.

A few more drags of Q, and the veil over his situation withdrew. Nothing was fucked. Lorrie was gone for now, sure. But only by struggling with the present can one control the future. He would set off to find her.

❖ ❖ ❖

One day passed, and then another. Clean sheets became dirty ones. Each morning when Lance awoke, he promised himself that today would be the day he would take to the road in search of her. And each evening, as he went to bed alone or with someone else, the sudden violence of her departure unsettled him.

She did not want to be where she was, that much he knew. Granted, he hadn't left to find her yet. But, he reminded himself, not having left didn't mean never leaving.

Without her, his work changed. Dark, hovering shapes and obscure symbols became bright and clear portrayals with clear and obvious correspondences. In the evenings, he would close his eyes and concentrate on her face, his mind graphing whatever part of her came to him. Each night, he would sketch a new feature, the folds and creases of her lips, the dark shade of the gap between her teeth. Never did he feel the need to combine them. Each page of the notebook contained a different part of her.

❖ ❖ ❖

The final letter came. Lance called his friends. Every one of them showed up but Tim, the downstairs neighbor. Though Tim lived with Rebecca one floor below, rumor had it that Rebecca was running around Southwest Sector somewhere on a back-to-the-land Homeland Indigenous kick. Lance didn't know what that meant, and he didn't ask. Lorrie could have explained it to him, but of course she wasn't around to do so.

Right now he needed food for his guests. Lance stood in front of his pantry, eyes sweeping for possibilities. Two old crackers. A half-eaten jar of pretzels. An empty plastic bag gusted from the shelf and cascaded to his feet, giving Lance the distinct feeling that he was standing at the entrance of a deep and hollow cave.

"Lorrie's gone," Lance told his small gathering. "And I'm up. Just got my greetings. First Tuesdays are the worst Tuesdays and all that." He waved the paper in the air. "I've got a date and everything."

"Man," said Mike.

"Damn," said Rick.

"I hate First Tuesdays," said Wilson.

"Actually," Norman said, reading the letter, "you haven't been called in on a First Tuesday."

"Is that a good thing?" said Mike.

"Maybe," said Rick.

"I had a friend who was inducted on a Sunday," said Wilson.

"Either way," Lance said, "I didn't ask you here to tell you that news. Because all of you are people I can trust, I also wanted to let you know that I won't be going."

"On what grounds?" asked Mike.

"I'm just not going to go."

Silence. And then:

"Lawyer up," said Mike.

"Lawyer up," said Rick.

"You better lawyer up," said Wilson.

"They're everywhere now, you know," said Rick.

"Who is?" said Lance. "Lawyers?"

"Undercovers. Reggies. Agents for the Registry."

"No grounds?" asked Mike. "Pretty sure?"

"I believe some other factors might be in play here," said Norman.

Once they saw Lance was serious, the tips and tricks started coming.

"Don't shower for a week before induction."

"Yeah! Stink like crazy."

"I don't know," said Wilson. "I hear the Registry is on to that."

Into the night, the advice continued, his friends whispering golden information into his ears of amiable Registry boards in blurry rural outposts, diploma-mill seminaries and their inviolable deferrals granted for study of the Young Savior and his teachings. Lance could see that they thought they were saving him, that they saw every new detail as a glowing springboard to leap from, each landing pool a thousand universes of possibility: strange societies of baldheads that helped out runners, where to get fake papers, and what kind of jobs took them and didn't seem to mind. Lance copied it all down in a tiny notebook with tight springs on the binding, but after a while, he just scribbled small loops while they talked.

"You guys aren't getting it."

"What do you mean?" they asked.

"Everything you're saying, these ideas, they're all a dodge. I'm not going to run. That's not what I'm talking about."

"Then what are you talking about?" said Wilson.

"Lorrie's been kidnapped."

Silence from his friends, like a clamp being tightened on their throats. Norman giggled, Wilson had a coughing fit, and Rick and Mike stared at each other's toes. Lance attributed this mélange of inappropriate responses to the Substance Q cigarette they had shared just before he had made his announcement.

"Too many crap movies, Lance," Norman said. His head was low, his chin locked into his chest. "This is real life, man. Take a listen to yourself."

"I have," Lance told them. "All my thoughts have been put into this. This is not some off-the-head idea. This is a powerful storm of outcomes. This is what I need to do."

"But, um, Lance?" Rick, eyeing the others, clearly deciding to speak for them as well. "Think clearly, man. Lorrie wasn't kidnapped. She left you."

8.

"Time's up," a voice says.

Just like that, Alan is released back to the other boys. Punishment over. Returning to his dormitory, his eyes feel sore, unused to the many shapes and colors around him. Though he has only been gone for two days, it feels as though he has been in the cell for a lifetime.

Back in the dorm, the other boys crowd around and welcome him back. Everyone is sympathetic to the experience of two nights in solitary. Even the halfies.

The School has always been intent on pitting them against each other. Halfies versus pures. Everyone understands the two groups don't mix. Some of those halfies don't look like Homeland Indigenous at all. With all the Majority Group blood illuminating their features, a few of the half-breeds might as well be illegitimate sons of the nuns and priests. The halfies, they know, get bigger portions, softer sheets, and tufted pillows that their Majority mothers send them in large, glorious care packages. Homeland Indigenous mothers send pillows too, but the priests and nuns swipe them for themselves, they're sure of it. His fellow pure boys are the ones who show Alan which Dumpsters are worth rummaging through for dented tuna cans and aged milk in the after hours before bed. Only halfies make prefect. Officer training classes—the makeup selected by aptitude and merit, the boys are told—consist only of halfies. There's not a full-blooded Homeland Indigenous among them. And no one needs to be told of the impossibility of finding an officer on the front lines.

Four years ago, almost by accident, Alan had flipped a half-breed, brought one of them over to his side. "Roll with a halfie?" his friends had asked. Finally, after some exasperated explanations, Alan had punched one of the louder complainers in the jaw. No one had complained about a halfie in the crew since.

Still, there are times when Alan resents Gad. Whenever Alan goes to bed hollow and hungry while the halfie in the bunk below burps and gurgles into a floating sleep, he thinks about the world that despises him. These types of memories don't fade with sunrise. Each morning, as the exclamations of his stomach jolt his eyes open, Alan remembers all over again: some people are just born with fewer burdens.

But there's no denying his best friend is a halfie. Though perhaps "friend" isn't the right word. Gad listens to him, beholds his presence, but Gad, Alan had found, is not your average halfie. Almost anyone would mistake him for being Majority Group. When the two of them first met, Alan didn't understand what Gad was doing there at all. Sure, Gad had told everyone, his father was Group F, but his language skills are cracked and chippy; when speaking F, he can sound alternately like a stately young lord or a trapped prisoner whose tongue has been jabbed with the sharp tines of a thick fork. The differences don't stop there. The nuns smile at him too much—even the gassy Sister Ava Azor—praising Gad for every right answer and assigning him smooth, desirable jobs while Alan gets pinned with carpentry or sweeping the colored dust that slides across the walls of the physical plant.

"Oh, but I wish I was a pure," Gad tells him.

Of course he wishes he were full-blooded. Such a thought is exactly what Alan wants him to think. And yet their roles are as firm as a photograph.

Though Gad often tells Alan he won't stand for special treatment, that it makes his heart blur around his chest and pump strange, tangled rhythms until he needs to puke, Alan knows that importance lies not in what happens to a person, but how that person reacts when a certain something occurs. Gad, of course, has always failed this test.

So for work assignments, while Gad chops onions or washes potatoes, it is Alan's eyes that burn and his stomach that rages. The large stacks of the physical plant tower burp out clotted streams of thick and grinding smoke that smells sweet but feels hot and oily. The job is to crawl up the ladder deep within the stack and scrub the steaming yellow slime that coats the walls, each boy doing his best to make that thick coat thinner. Like the other physical plant boys, Alan rubs cough medicine in the space under his nostrils, a trick that allows the medicated vapors to drown out the anguishing smell of the purple dust that forms in the little cracks of the massive concrete tower. The method works: their sparse lunches remain in their stomachs.

The mountainous difference in their status is clear. Even so, Alan has made sure to balance the scales.

"Tomorrow in class," he tells Gad, "you should make a joke on one of the Sisters."

"Me?" squeaks Gad. "But the detergent! I'll get in trouble."

"I can't do it. I just spent two days in solitary."

"I don't know."

"Do Sister Ava Azor. You think she would ever pour detergent down a halfie's throat?"

Gad shrugs.

"Of course she wouldn't," Alan tells him.

"I don't know."

"You need to do this," Alan tells him. "Don't let me down."

❖ ❖ ❖

"One thing to always remember," Sister Ava Azor tells the class the next morning, "is that all of you have a connection, a bond with nature that I am unable to even comprehend. Your ancestors were primitive, yes, but they understood the land. They understood their surroundings. Though this has its downsides, I imagine it to be quite nice."

Alan turns to look at Gad. *Now*, he wills his eyes to say. *Do it now.* Gad raises his hand.

"Yes?"

"Sister Ava Azor, I understand nature perfectly," Gad says.

Alan can hear the shake in his voice.

"Oh?"

Gad pulls his shoulders back and steadies his hands. "I think it calls to me extra loud after a big plate of beans."

Sister Ava Azor straightens.

Alan fixes a shapeless glare in Gad's direction. *Finish the job.*

The afternoon sun blares through the window. Gad looks at Alan. Alan nods. Speaking in Group F, his tongue pronouncing the words as Alan has taught him, Gad releases the predetermined fart joke into the world. Though it isn't that funny, Alan has made sure that it contains the one thing the Sister will understand. Her name.

As instructed by Alan, every boy who speaks F erupts in wolflike laughter. Some laugh so hard their eyes fill with tears. If only not to be left out, other boys in the class—boys who do not speak one word of F but want to be part of the fun—join in.

Perfect, Alan thinks. He is referring to both the distinct relish of a plan well executed and the ecstatic shiver that only can come from having a group of people do just what you tell them. He is not sure which one feels better.

Back in the front of the classroom, Sister Ava Azor, already sensitive to her own flatulence, assumes (rightly) that the words Gad has wrapped around her name—the one sound in his sentence she understands—have formed to make a joke about her gassiness. In a series of rapid movements she leaps from her perch in the front of the classroom, runs through the aisles of desks, and stops short in front of Alan.

"Detergent!" she screams. "After class."

"Why me?" Alan says. "I didn't say anything!"

"Do you think I'm stupid?" Sister Ava shrieks. "He doesn't speak F well enough to make jokes. If you don't watch out, I'll send you right back to solitary."

The braver kids snicker. Gad studies his palms. No punishment comes to him. Reality explained.

Is Gad's heart blurring around his chest at the unfairness of it all, Alan wonders. Maybe both of them will end the day vomiting. Alan might get the detergent. But, he vows, someone else will pay.

❖ ❖ ❖

A silent slide from his bed to the floor, and Alan walks softly down the corridor until he spots Gad's toes. It's two hours before Rousing, and low snores come from all angles. As Alan does his best to move soundlessly, the shy and distrustful Hazel, dorm mascot, places her forelimbs on the front of her cage, rustling the hardwood shavings that compose the boundaries of her life. Stopping for a moment, Alan peers through the small wire frame and shakes his head at her. Hazel's tiny wheekings won't wake anybody.

All the clocks are blinking; the power must have gone off some time in the night. The floor is cold against the bottoms of his feet, but Alan can't yet put on shoes. He comes to the base of Gad's bed, reaches under his sheet, and gives his big toe a soft wiggle. This is their sign.

Gad groans but gets up. A few boys in the dorm crack an eye at them, but Gad and Alan are now in their final year of school, and if their sunrise infraction even registers, these younger boys know better than to squeal. Even so, a part of Alan wishes someone would. Alan has silenced squealers before. As he moves past the sleeping underclassmen, he sees nothing but the passive slumber of defeat. These boys, too, are dreaming of the war being over by the time they graduate.

"C'mon!" He gives Gad a sharp elbow to the rib as they begin their silent departure.

Once outside, Alan and Gad slip on their shoes. The bushes glow blue in the early morning light. Quick movements are important, so they hurry toward the woods, past the burnt brick of the inner court-yard, around the storage shed piled high with the tightly sealed upright steel barrels of gasoline the janitors pour into the generator when the school goes dark, through the dry turtle pond, away from the airless school, and toward the mouth of the unruly forest.

They are always hungry, and now is no different. The real trees, the thick ones with fanned branches and heavy leaves, are a long way from the school, but there are hours until breakfast. Gad knows how to find the nests, and Alan is a better climber. Once off school grounds, they start to talk. They are still a ways from the forest; none of the shrubs come past their kneecaps.

"Walk faster," Alan tells him. All sorts of nonsense could slow Gad down: the cast of sunlight on a shiny rock, some strange colored spot on the desert floor. Sometimes Gad is like an unruly horse, but just a quick wave of the whip is all it takes to get him back on track.

"I was dreaming when you woke me," Gad says. "All I remember is that it was really messed up. A fire, everyone running, screaming, I can't remember. I don't like to have dreams like that."

Alan sighs. What could be more boring than the recounting of someone else's dreams? The trail begins to fade, and they find themselves in a yellow meadow of dry grassland. "Maybe your dream was about next year," he says.

"What about next year?" Gad asks.

"Exactly," Alan says. The idea that he could kill a man feels fine to him. The fact that he might have to does not.

One of them steps on a twig. The crack gives a hard echo that spirals up into the fizzy sky. Two lizards chase each other over the smooth surface of a rock. Gad stops under a ponderosa pine. "Right there," he points.

Looking up, Alan nods. He's hungry, and he knows that the answer to his hunger is in this tree.

"Right there, on the third branch," Gad says, gesturing with his finger.

When exactly they figured out that crow eggs tasted as good as the normal kind from a chicken, Alan can't remember. In fact, crow eggs are even better, as lately, the eggs served in the dining hall are barely thawed and light green with syrupy yolk and tiny cracks twisting and snaking along the surface of the shell. As for the crow eggs, Gad and Alan sneak out early to find them and then steal to the kitchen late at night to scramble and salt the extra sustenance.

Alan follows Gad's finger and spots the nest. From the ground, the nest is just a clump of sticks resting in a fork of branches, though Alan knows once he's up top, that same haphazard bunch of sticks will reveal itself to be a grass-lined, deliberate structure. His stomach turns. *I want those eggs, and I hate how much I want them,* he thinks.

Even though he should have outgrown them, Alan still reads the Ricky X-P books when no one is watching. Ricky X-P has a guy in his ragtag gang of friends who challenges him for the top spot—a difficult situation for sure—but at least he can always pile a small mountain of butter atop each thick slice of freshly baked bread while he considers his next move. Ricky X-P does not have to eat anything he doesn't want to. The distance of art from life is never fair.

The nest is almost at the top of the tree. Gad picks up a rock and makes a pile of several more in case the mother crow is around. Both the mother and father bird can attack, but it's best, they've found, to take the mother out first. Once the mother has been killed, the father bird lets out a few dejected caws and gives up. Some father, they joke.

When Gad began calling them mother and father birds, a formless smirk had spread through Alan's body, cackling throughout the entire trip. Such a sad-hearted attempt for his halfie friend to try and be more Group F–like.

With arms raised over his shoulders, Alan hugs the tree. Gad stands under his feet and pushes. Alan's arms can't wrap the entire trunk; if they were only a little longer, he'd be able to clasp them together. Not being able to lock his hands makes for a harder climb. Fingers wiggling and sliding, he looks for ridges in the bark to dig into for a better grip. Palms skyward, Gad pushes up hard against the thin rubber soles of Alan's canvas work shoes. Alan's shirt bunches up, and he feels the gentle scratch of the warm bark against his belly. Finally, feet now higher than Gad's palms can reach, he begins a smooth, rhythmic motion that slides him up the tree. Small shrubs below disappear. Alan's heart beats hard against the bark. Don't look down, he reminds himself, but he does anyway, his stomach making a dizzying fist. Immediately, Alan drives his hips into the tree to make sure he's balanced. Not that he's ever fallen, but even so, being that high up isn't the same as having two feet on the ground.

"Hey!" Gad calls up to him.

"Hey, yourself," Alan shouts down. The top of Gad's head is a tight pinhole on the forest floor. "Are we good on time?"

"I think so."

Typical. Gad never knows what time it is. And yet nothing could be more important. If they are late, they'll miss their breakfast of watery porridge and black bread, the replacement for Gad being a smack in the face from the fat fingers of the priest in charge of morning count, the replacement for Alan, who is already on probation, much more severe.

As Alan nears the top of the tree, he transfers one hand to the extended branch where the nest is. With his legs and arm still wrapped around the trunk, he uses his free hand to pull down on the branch, a test of its strength. The branch isn't wide enough for him to crawl on. He will have to hang, to dangle his feet over the forest floor, to shuffle his hands, one over the other, until he's under the nest. Then he'll hold himself up with one hand and reach with the other, moving it around blindly until he grasps an egg.

Once Alan has the eggs—there are usually four or five—he'll drop one at a time down to Gad. Sometimes Gad will be in the middle of throwing rocks at the mother and father crows. Before Alan drops each egg, he shouts down a warning. How he does it, Alan isn't sure, but Gad always catches them. Gad has soft hands and uses the momentum of the egg in a way that cushions each one from the long fall. There's a satisfaction in the teamwork of it all, but not that much. Hand crossed over hand, Alan inches out on the branch until he is directly below the nest. His shoulders ache, but the pathetic pangs of his stomach burn stronger. The wood of the branch gives a groan and a creak. Alan watches his feet float above the moist forest floor, his black canvas work shoes standing out against the thick tangle of ferns and ivy. A harsh caw aims at him from somewhere he can't see. The crows are near. But then, another sound, a voice.

"Hey!"

Alan looks down at Gad, who looks right back up at him. Neither has spoken. A downward bend in the wood tells Alan to move fast, that he can only hang from the branch for so long. Already there is a bite in his shoulders, a burn and a sting. There isn't much time.

"Hey!"

The immaculate tone is unmistakable. This voice belongs to a woman.

Again Alan swings his head downward so he can see Gad, who lifts his shoulders and shrugs. Dangling in one place for too long isn't a good idea; the sag of the branch is starting to seem threatening. With his weight held by one arm, Alan reaches into the nest, feeling around for an egg. His fingers close gently around a shell. There is a squawk and a rustle, and a rock whizzes by his ear followed by two or three strong, short calls.

"There's two there!" Alan yells down to Gad. "Mother and a father." He drops the egg. He knows Gad will catch it. More rocks, more screeches.

"I said hey!" yells a woman's voice again. Alan can't see a woman anywhere. The branch creaks some more. So far, they only have one egg. One isn't enough. Alan reaches for another, and this time he hears the distinctive sound: a quick squeal like a human baby followed by a grand and definitive thump below. Gad has killed one of the crows, hopefully the mother. Between the blades of Alan's shoulders, quick, hot spasms gallop ribbons of vibration through every part of his body. The other bird lets out one bitter, sharp caw before descending into a slow, mournful keen. Yes, they have definitely killed the mother.

Alan drops another egg down to Gad. Two eggs so far. Still not enough. Both arms ache, and the narrow branch keeps up its moaning, insulted that he's taking so long.

"Stop right now, you two!"

Alan looks down and sees a Majority Group woman with wild, bushy hair. The blue stones on her fingers stand out against the browns and greens around her, even from on high. Whatever she wants doesn't matter, because Alan can't hold himself up much longer. The spasms in his back march forward; he reaches for another egg.

"What are you doing?" Alan shoots his eyes downward just in time to see the Majority Group lady kick over Gad's pile of rocks. Whoever this woman is, Alan would never allow someone to kick over his pile of rocks. He wants to make his way back down, to give this lady a shove and tell her to get the hell out of here. But first, he must grab more eggs.

The branch above Alan lets out a short snap. He feels a quick, dropping sensation, but only for a moment before bouncing up again. Though the branch might be strong enough to hold him, he is not sure if he is strong enough to hold the branch. Time is up. Two eggs it is. Alan swims his way toward the base of the tree, hand over hand, as quickly as he can. Grunts below him, some from the Majority lady, some from Gad. He makes it to the trunk, heart whipping around his chest.

Below, the strange lady is spitting and sputtering in Gad's direction. Alan begins his descent, his skin scraping the bark, folding and falling against the trunk in his desperation to reach the ground as soon as possible. The tops of Gad's and the Majority Group lady's heads become larger, closer. She is shaking a finger, one hand on her hip. As Alan caterpillars down, he spots a black pile on the forest floor. It's the mother bird, dead and still, its mothlike eyes cold and eerie.

"What the hell do you guys think you're doing?" the wild-haired Majority Group lady is yelling at Gad. "This isn't the way you're supposed to do things."

Alan sets both feet on the ground. "Who the hell are you?"

"Yeah!" says Gad. "Who are you?"

Typical, Alan thinks, for a halfie to only become emboldened once the numbers are on his side.

For a long while, they stand on the forest floor: Gad, the pile of rocks, Alan, the dead crow, and the Majority Group lady. No one moves, but the Majority Group lady's eyes call out fiercely; her face is damp with fresh dirt, and her lips are in silent motion. Alan sees that the Majority Group lady is building up, that she has waited for this moment.

"Now what did you go and do that for?" she says finally, pointing to the mother bird at their feet. "Why would you do that?"

The crow lies on the forest floor, its pathetic feathers scattered in a circle around them. A mess of red organs spills from its belly.

"So we could get these." Gad holds up the two eggs Alan dropped down to him. A wide grin stretches across his face.

Ridiculous. Why is he smiling? Two is never enough. "Don't answer her questions until she answers ours," Alan says to him. "What are you doing out here in the middle of the forest?"

The Majority Group woman pinches her earlobe. "Exactly what I'm supposed to be doing. You two are Homeland Indigenous, right? You go to that school?"

They nod.

"Wait, watch this. Let me guess." She turns to Alan, a finger pointed inches from his forehead. "Indigenous Group K."

He shakes his head.

"P, then. You absolutely must be Group P. Your eyelids scream P."

A few blinks and Alan tells her no, he is not Group P.

"Q? Are you Q?"

Qs are in Eastern Sector, four thousand distance-units away. This woman is nuts.

"Either way," she says, rubbing her hands together as though a faucet is just above them. "You two go to that school."

A raw stench floats up from the bird. The shafts in the crow's wing jut out at terrible angles, and Alan watches as the appalling recognition of the stink appears on the woman's face.

"That's why I'm here," she says. "They won't let me get too close to campus, but I know all about you." She shakes her head. "You guys don't know anything." Her knuckles are huge; her eyes are sore and overly exerted. "What I'm thinking is you two don't know what's what. If you did, you wouldn't be killing crows with rocks. You don't have to do that."

"But we *do* have to," Gad says. "School food is all old and rotten."

Alan wishes Gad would stop justifying himself to this stranger. There's a disgusting bubbling sound, and a viscous purple ooze pours from the dead crow.

"Listen," the Majority Group lady says, "you're Homeland Indigenous. I can see that. But what about you?" She points at Gad.

"Group F," Gad says. "The both of us."

Ridiculous. The sad, squirming fact is that Gad seems ready to answer any questions this stranger has. Still, the rage in Alan's chest is slipping away. Sure, he wants answers from the eccentric in front of him, but he knows that with some people it's best to let them chatter on about their topic of choice until the sound of their own voice exhausts them. Clearly, the Majority Group lady in front of them is one of those people.

"Really?" the Majority Group lady says. "You're Group F?" She points to Gad, who nods and looks at his feet. "How about that? I wouldn't have suspected."

"It's true," Alan says. He notices the feathers on the crow's neck are grey, unlike the deep blackness slathered on every other part of its body. Usually Alan and Gad don't stick around and stare at the crows they've killed.

"See that bush right there?" the woman says, pointing to a rounded shrub with dark green leaves about five feet away.

"Which one?" Gad asks. "That one with the hairy flowers?"

"Yeah, that one right there with the spiked purple dome-heads. Like an alien spacecraft, come to visit us and parked in our forest."

They shrug. "What about it?"

"You guys know what that is?"

"No," Gad says. "What is it?"

Alan crosses his arms, disgusted that Gad plays her game so willingly.

"See, that's the killer!" The Majority Group lady rises to her tiptoes, her voice escalating along with her height. "They don't even let you know about those things. For all you know, that could be some amazing breakfast, some scrumptious dessert. This is your environment. And that's part of it, you know? Your parents, or grandparents, or ancestors, maybe they were snacking on those leaves left and right till the Homeland probably tried to murder them or something. But you guys don't know, you know?" She places her hands on her hips, her tone lower now. "But what I'm here to tell you is that you *do* know. That is, you know it, you just don't *know* you know it. But it's in your blood, your hearts. There's no need to go around tossing rocks at crows. You've got a whole salad right beneath your feet and a recipe book stranded in the outer reaches of your brains."

Alan considers telling the lady that the last time he saw his grandmother, she stood behind a thick door and warned him of the dangers and pain coming to the School would bring upon him and his family. Never had she said anything about eating plants or bushes. And he could go on, he thinks, to let this Majority Group lady know that when it comes to snacking, his parents prefer cold cuts and dips to spiked bushes specked with dirt. But no, he remembers. Let this lady go on about bushes and crows and recipe books. The more she talks, he decides, the more she will reveal. There has to be *something*.

"You Homeland Indigenous kids," the Majority Group lady says, "you're all so far apart. My thing is to make sure you all know about each other, help connect you guys together in the struggle. I started out in Western City North, but right now I'm coming from another school just like yours. You guys ever been to W?"

They shake their heads.

"So I was passing by a school there, and those kids, Group F kids—"

"Group F?" says Gad.

"Maybe not F. Right, you're F. Whatever. These Homeland Indigenous kids I met, those kids are in the know, let me tell you. They put out an underground newspaper, broke into their equipment room and flipped it, right? Printed their own stuff. I know what you're thinking: there's a million underground papers. Two million probably. What's one more?"

Alan is not thinking this at all, but the woman continues, her buzzing words leaving the thinnest of odor trails, guiding them to new locations.

"Real truth perversion goes down there—you guys can probably understand. So these kids, they took control and cranked out some real strong words, you know? They told the truth in that paper. Talked about the quotas, too. Does that kind of thing go on here?"

"Truth telling?" Gad says.

"Truth perversion?" Alan tries to clarify. "Quotas for what?"

"Don't you know that all Homeland Indigenous get the worst assignments? There are different rules for you guys. Resistance isn't the same for Majority Groupers. At least they have the chance to get some sort of desk job."

"I saw on the news the other day that some woman from parliament was talking about how she's going to meet with the prime minister and convince him to draw down," Gad says. "Lower troop levels, gradually end this thing."

Alan stares at him. When did Gad ever watch the news?

The woman's wide eyes flicker. "Ridiculous. That's one of those Coyotes. All words, no action. They'll probably get ten guys sent home and call it a victory. But forget that. Do you guys know how old the prime minister is?"

"Ninety-something."

"That's right. And I won't even get into Fareon, though you Homeland Indigenous should be paying attention to that, too."

Alan makes a mental note to look up "Coyotes" and "Fareon" the next time he's in the library. His body feels rigid. He wants more information from this woman, but does not want to ask for it. Never again, he promises himself, will he be the one who knows less.

"Enough about Fareon," the Majority Group lady says. "You guys hip to HIM?"

"Who?"

"HIM. Tell me you know about HIM." She fixes her stare on both of them.

Their faces give away that they don't.

"Homeland Indigenous Movement? Woody Gilbert? C'mon, those guys are talking to you! If I were Homeland Indigenous, that's the kind I'd be. HIM. And really, I am HIM, you know? Not just some wishy-washy solidarity. I'm not just into the cause, I *am* the cause. I met Woody Gilbert once, shook his hand and talked to him. Course you can't do that anymore—he's way underground now." A new energy climbs onto her face, an excitement that expands her. "But we talked, me and him. He told me he could see how special I was, that he sensed my Homeland Indigenous spirit, and that I should help spread the message to Homeland Indigenous youth: the baldheads can help you escape the Registry, and HIM can free your mind."

Neither Alan nor Gad says a word. Alan's head is whirling; he knows that within this incessant splatter of shit are tiny drops of gold.

"Look, I'm not just on my own journey," the Majority Group lady tells them. "HIM is growing, starting to do more actions. Ever since Woody was forced underground, the movement has been getting bigger." She rummages in her bag and pulls out a ragged bunch of papers knotted in a rubber band. "Take these pamphlets. They'll let you know all about HIM. This stuff is going to break your heads wide open, guys, I just know it."

"Sure," Gad says.

"Now don't show those to anybody," she says. "HIM just got put on the list."

"What list?" Alan asks.

"It's all crap. A few bombs went off at induction centers here and there, and now we're suspects. There's a bounty on Woody's head. Membership is outlawed. Hey, how old are you two anyway?"

"Our final year," Alan tells her.

"Listen, just make sure you have something planned for when you get out of here. Don't get yourself shipped off halfway across the world, you hear me? Remember what I said about the quotas: it's harder for you guys to escape induction than it is for anyone else in the Homeland. And look at you two. You boys can't even take care of yourself in a forest, so I sure as hell don't want to see you in the jungle."

Alan turns to Gad. Gad won't meet his eyes.

"You must know the Registry is coming for you," the Majority Group lady says, leaning into them. "So get in front of it, have a plan." She is almost poking Gad in the chest now. "The Registry changes. It's smart. And it's even smarter when it comes to Homeland Indigenous; it arrives faster, harder. There's other stuff in these pages, stuff that will blow your mind," the woman tells them. "For you two, the baldheads are probably your only hope of escaping the jungle."

"Who are the baldheads?" Alan asks.

"Just read the pamphlets."

Gad takes the papers from her outstretched hands. The moment she is out of sight, Alan snatches them. *The Registry isn't random*, screams the front page of one. *Your whole life, you've been lied to*, cries another. *Better I should have these pamphlets*, Alan thinks. *Why waste them on someone who isn't ready for the truth?*

9 .

On day one, Lorrie had no ideas. Day two, her mind was still blank. At first, Lorrie couldn't see at all in that place.

"Here?" she asked her parents. The three of them stood in front of the intake building, a flax-colored structure about as large and clean as a city bus.

"Here," they said.

Atop the building, a sign in hand-painted blue letters against a white background read: "Our Young Savior's Residential Facility for the Improvement of Life and Spirit."

"Quite a mouthful," noted her mother.

"Let's just call it the Facility," said her father. "Seems more efficient."

A short, quick hug from her mother, a squeeze of fingers around her palm from her father. Her parents held each other tightly as they walked away. Lorrie lifted her hand to wave good-bye, and as she did, four of the wingless bugs that had tunneled their way to the surface of her skin fell to the ground. Each of the bugs had a bulbous little belly that glowed reddish-brown in the sunlight along with tiny patches of green dotting the walls of their outer bodies. Their tessellated eyes glittered hot and red. Lorrie almost let out a scream, but reminded herself that though the bugs were real, her parents could not see them.

She had never felt further from the city.

Two men in starched uniforms took down Lorrie's information and marched her through the compound and toward the dining hall. The architecture of the Facility was defensive, with hidden observational turrets disguised as sun decks and balconies, all ringed by deep embankments full of brackish water stocked with fish and plant life and lined with moss-covered rocks. Soothing to look at, but as Lorrie spotted instantly, also designed to pacify and contain. Beyond the Facility walls was nothing but emptiness: unused farmland, disorderly forests. Had she brought enough books? Because out here, she saw, there was nothing.

In the dining hall, long brown benches were pushed in tight against the rows of tables that lined the room. The floors were tiled, but Lorrie's eyes went up to the ceiling, which she noticed was painted sky blue, an effect that less replicated the sky and more created the feeling of eating a meal on the bottom of an emptied swimming pool. A long brass light fixture ran across the length of the room, the cool light source smearing the faces of everyone who sat below. The light stayed steady; at least this far into the interior of the Homeland, Lorrie thought, they could still keep the power on.

The dining hall was full. Most of the women seemed to be around her age; the men, of course, were all much older or younger, with a few shining or hellish exceptions. Even so, there were barely any of them, one for every five women or so, a grand majority of the men wounded vets from well-to-do families. It wasn't hard to make out why there were so few men around. The Registry, rumor had it, was now taking almost everybody. Twenty-two years into this war and they needed whomever they could get, no matter how feeble their sanity.

"Sit here," one of the uniformed men pointed. She slid in between a bewildered-looking woman who was whispering into her watered-down orange juice and a ridiculously tall young man with a poorly stitched together facial wound who immediately turned toward her with an extended hand and introduced himself. She shook it heartily.

"You have a firm grip for a woman," he said. His teeth were stained with a bright brown juice that dripped steadily from the bottom of his chin onto his lap. A light piece of bark glinted against the back of his teeth.

"What's in your mouth?"

"Turtle root," he said. "Keeps me from becoming violent." He smiled. "Lowers my blood pressure, too." He had a theatrical tone to his voice, little flourishes and well-placed breaths and pauses that snaked around his words. "You'd want to be violent, too," he added, "if you had been in the jungle."

From the large basket of fruit that sat in front of them, Lorrie grabbed a mottled apple that must have once been red. Even old fruit was a treat, and she wanted the taste. A few day-bugs fell from her hand as she reached out, and she looked to either side, wondering if anyone had noticed. She took a bite of apple; its flavor only vaguely rested against the edge of what fruit could be. No one spoke, though the man with turtle root juice dripping down his throat darted his eyes about crazily. A day-bug circled the bones of Lorrie's wrist.

"I believe I'm hallucinating right now, in this very moment," Lorrie told the man next to her. They didn't speak for the rest of the meal.

The plates were paper, the knives were plastic. A few people yelled random accumulations of words, but for the most part there was only the silent sound of hasty chewing. No one was allowed to stand up until everyone else was finished, so Lorrie and her once-useful fellow citizens stared at the walls until the eating period was officially over. Right before the meal was scheduled to end, the bewildered woman next to her who had previously only spoken in low whispers to her orange water threw back her neck and shouted a passionate and incomprehensible prayer to the ceiling before tossing her soggy plate of cold, tasteless food at the nearest wall in sacrifice. Lorrie watched a saucy piece of frozen cauliflower slide to the floor like a hurried garden snail, a slimy trail of cheese tracing its path. Perhaps her offering was a signal, as the uniformed men began to lift the more sluggish by their armpits and herd them back to their beds. Just as they began to drag people from their chairs, a sharp buzz followed by a connected series of jerky crackles echoed throughout the dining hall. The long brass fixture above clicked off abruptly. Patients walked to their rooms—or had the walking done for them—in complete and utter darkness. *I was wrong,* Lorrie thought. Even here in the vast rural emptiness, the Homeland still couldn't keep the lights on.

"Take these," a man in a uniform told her. All the patients slept in a large dormitory, a long, drafty room, the walls lined by their narrow and adjustable beds.

"What are they?" She had already tucked herself in.

"They're the pills you're supposed to take." The uniformed man held out a low paper cup, a medicinal salad of blue ovals, oblong lime-green tablets, and a bright red pill in the shape of a diamond. One hand extended, he stood over her, arms flexed and veins popped as though in a show of strength. War age, there was no doubt about it; his face had only the slightest presence of frown lines, and Lorrie wondered what was wrong with him. A healthy man under forty, she knew, had very little chance of being able to be in this place. Maybe, just maybe, she thought, this sick job of stuffing pills down young women's throats was his reward, the treasure received for multiple calls to the Point Line.

"I need to know what it is you're trying to give me." To Lorrie, the only vulnerable aspect about the uniformed man were his rimless glasses, which had slid too far down his longish nose.

The man glared at her through their lenses and laughed. "Take them," he said. "Now."

A glance to the right to see who her neighbor was, to determine whether this person was witness to the scene, the type of neighbor whose eyes might contain some compound of daring and virtue that would allow Lorrie the power to resist whatever these people wanted to give her.

The neighbor was snoring.

"Fine." Lorrie grabbed the paper cup out of the hand hovering in front of her more viciously than was necessary. The pills slid down her throat and into her stomach. That night, the itches grew worse, and once again night-bugs crawled all over her, in and out of her nostrils, up and down her spine, burrowed below her nail beds, anywhere they wanted to. Night-bugs were the worst kind.

❖ ❖ ❖

"Up!" yelled the man in uniform, the same man as the night before.

After hours of restless scratching with the bugs feasting on her nerves and tendons, she had only just gone to sleep. "Up?" she cried. The reddish light resting on the man's face told her the sun had yet to fully rise. Before arriving, Lorrie had pictured herself strolling through gardens, becoming reacquainted with the fine old books that she had long neglected, taking up some sort of craft. Now it was barely sunrise, and a man in uniform was nodding his head and yelling in her ear.

"That's right, out of bed with the sunrise. Who knows how much power we'll get today!"

"But it's barely light out."

"Get up anyway." Clearly the orderly was not a Registry-runner. People who were underground, Lorrie knew, had compassion. This man's blood was spiked with additives of rage and sandpaper.

"What for?"

"What for?" the man sneered. "For you, that's what. For you and the Young Savior."

The Facility, Lorrie soon found out, was a pious one, overseen by some obscure offshoot of Homeland Religion that had curious and ill-defined ideas regarding shame, redemption, evil, and the true age of the Young Savior. Evil, she soon learned, consisted of Ideology Five, that Foreign doctrine that the prime minister had long claimed would, if left unchecked, threaten the very existence of the Homeland. All the patients in the Facility seemed to feel the institution's strange devotion to ideals they didn't understand, whether they knew it or not.

Lorrie dressed silently and was led to a small room with folding chairs arranged in a circle. After a few minutes, other patients wandered in and took their seats. On the white walls, an old depiction of the prime minister, his face not yet ravaged by the thinning of the skin that accompanies life in its ninth decade; next to the portrait was a pushpinned sign: "Without the Young Savior, we are merely objects filled with shame and disgrace."

The distraction of her own judgment annoyed her. *Don't just listen to this stuff and make fun of it,* she told herself. *Breathe it in.* Besides, she would have to learn the values of the place if she was ever going to get out.

At the center of the circle, a short fat man with no hair and a soft, youthful glow introduced himself as the group leader.

"Welcome to talk group," he said. "Seems we have someone new today." His high and raspy voice pinched her nerves, the sound of someone who needed to clear his throat but couldn't. *The guy can't even burp himself,* she thought. *He's like some sort of grown baby.* Though his face was young, a closer look showed that his ears, his hands, and his loose and ragged tongue all behaved like that of a man much older. This man, she saw, was aging completely unsystematically.

"Let me go over the rules for our newest member," the baby-leader began. There were punishments for misbehavior, it became clear, but no incentives for sanity and adherence to a standard social contract. Though the guidelines were confusing, Lorrie did her best to turn off the distracting patter of her own judgmental thoughts.

All sorts had made their way to the talk group: a wounded vet who refused to speak on Wednesdays and Fridays, a middle-aged woman who was already sobbing quietly, and a handsome man with an actor's face, his clothes all black, the sleeves of his shirt pushed up and exposing an intricate network of silvery cuts and scars that ran from his wrists to his elbows.

"Let's talk," the baby-leader continued, scanning the circle, "about shame. And about the Young Savior. I would like us to talk about the Young Savior and shame, together. Now who'd like to begin?"

For Lorrie, the Young Savior was a bore, with little to offer. A peaceful life, free of bugs and awful men—now *that* was a pleasure worth reaching for.

"I'm convinced the food industry is destroying my brain," said the wet-faced woman across from her. "And I'm ashamed that the Young Savior has let this happen to me."

"What have you been eating?" asked the usually silent vet. "Have you been eating too many oats? Oats are not a good thing to eat."

The woman burst into loud, hungry sobs.

The people in her talk group were crazy, Lorrie decided, twisted-up people trapped in horrid worlds they couldn't escape. And so she listened, surrounded by the most sapped-out citizens in the Homeland, people she was sure had wasted their entire lives, their minds dazzled by misapprehensions, by all the wrong things. The oatmeal woman had snorted some new Substance derivative and burned her kitchen down; the angular man in black was an artist who had ripped off his skin and tried to stretch it into canvas—a disquieting thought, it seemed, for the Registry as well. Lorrie massaged a temple with an index finger. These people were a mess.

"How about you, Lorrie?" the baby-leader asked. "What are you ashamed of?"

"Ashamed?" she said. "I'm not ashamed of anything."

"Of course you are," he said. "You just don't know it yet."

Heads bobbed up and down the circle in agreement.

"You see," he began, addressing the group but looking at her, "reducing your levels of shame is the key to liberation, to freedom, to a successful existence in which your actions have purpose and meaning. Some of you"—a hard stare in Lorrie's direction—"have locked all your shame away. But somehow it always comes out. Shame changes, it squirms, it evolves, and you can't get rid of it in a sideways manner, no matter how hard you try."

What did this baby-leader know? What kind of training had he had in order to make his evaluation? "I had bugs," Lorrie told the group leader, "not shame." Saying she *had* bugs in the past tense seemed faintly healing. Just then a trail of flat-bodied arthropods scuttled across the knuckles of her left hand, their tiny segmented bodies following one after another, antennae first. Day-bugs. Much more manageable. She closed her eyes, clenched her fists, and did her best not to scream.

A few people in the circle shook their heads, saddened at her resistance.

"Wrong," the baby-leader said. "You had bugs because you were ashamed of something. You shut that life of shame away, locked it up tight in a box, and stuffed it beneath your feathery little mattress." The baby-leader crossed his legs and then uncrossed them. "Now it comes out as bugs instead."

"Exactly," nodded the crying woman.

"So true," said a barely teenaged boy on his fourth suicide attempt.

"Wild," said the artist who had skinned himself with a paring knife.

"How exactly do you mean?" Lorrie asked. She felt an awful tingle below her skin.

❖ ❖ ❖

The next morning, the uniformed man with the rimless glasses woke her at first light. Again the two of them began the same routine as the day before.

"Pills?" he said, pushing the low cup in her face.

She watched him. This was a test, his attempt to see if a full day and night in the Facility had broken her. "Pills," Lorrie answered. Let him win today, she decided. Give him the feeling that he's in control.

The uniformed man smirked.

That control he felt, Lorrie knew, was the emptiest of all emotions. She was a wind-torn cloud, and this simple man in uniform would not be able to grasp her.

Through the window, Lorrie watched a rise of air shake the branches of a small, scaly tree. The Facility was meant to operate on a loop, she realized. The sooner she accepted her place in the wheel, the easier it would be for the people who wanted to turn it. Without resistance, each day would be the same.

Swinging her legs over the bed, she pressed the undersides of her feet against the cool grey-green tile. A small red bug made quick slaloms between the crevices of her toes. But one little day-bug was nothing. And why should it be? Every day would be what this day was: more pills, more bugs, more shame, and more of the Young Savior.

Only, today was different. The baby-leader directed the group away from shame, away from the Young Savior, and toward, he said, the few things in their lives worth feeling good about. Lorrie studied him, eager to make sense of his mismatched jumble of parts.

"What do you *care* about?" he asked the circle. "What do you do, what *can* you do, that when you do it you feel as though you could have been doing it all your life?"

Lorrie leaned over to itch her elbow. *So much doing,* she thought. What she needed to do was get the hell out of this haunted countryside and back to civilization. The war was still raging, right now, in this very moment. Didn't these people understand?

"Lorrie?" the baby-leader asked. "How about you?"

"The fight for justice!" she yelled. "Answers from our leaders! Freedom!"

Standing up, the baby-leader hobbled toward her, raising his voice. "Those are just words, and those particular words don't mean anything here. Freedom, how? Justice, why?" The baby-leader loomed over her, waiting for a response.

Every skin-grazing bug on her body froze as though under a spell. Perhaps they, too, wanted to listen.

"So tell me, what are you talking about, Lorrie?" the baby-leader yelled down to her. Spittle poured from his mouth and drilled against the top of her head. "Say something real! What do you *mean*?"

A silence fell over the room. The day-bugs paused from engaging in their frantic scratches; the speechless vet pressed his slender fingers together and rested his nose on his fleshy fists. The crying oatmeal lady cupped both hands over her heart. The peeled-skin artist pushed his tongue against his cheek, thoughtful. The baby-leader was waiting, the talk group was waiting, the bugs were waiting, and most of all, Lorrie was waiting, too.

Closing her eyes, she felt the broken people of the talk group shoot the breath of life right into her. The shock of realization was instantaneous. How long, she wondered, had her focus been so diffuse? Years of work, and all of it for nothing. The answer entered her, bouncing around her insides. Of course. She could not stop the war. No more sniffing aimlessly around its edges; it was too big, too powerful. But she could, at least on a small scale, stop the suffering. And so it was clear. Forget the war. Find a way to save the men, one by one by one.

"Anything?" the baby-leader asked.

"Nope," she said. Not all truths are for sharing.

Even so, everyone in her circle was a witness. Even so, they still scared her, the members of the talk group. When they smiled, their grins looked hideous, the muscles deeply rusted and out of practice.

Only the artist with the peeled skin, the man in black, had features that approached a level of balance and normalcy. He appeared by her bed that night after curfew. They sneaked off to the roof.

❖   ❖   ❖

The tar and gravel cut into Lorrie's back uncomfortably. Though Lorrie knew the artist was marked, had scarred himself, in the darkness she could only see the outlines of his body, none of the details. The artist was a blur, and she lay back and watched as he put a leg on either side of her. His bottom rested on the lower part of her belly. After a moment, he stood up.

The artist seemed nervous. His thin chest heaved and shook, and he began to undress her as though he were following the steps of a manual. Shoes first. Left sock, then the other, the zipper of her pants, followed by the button, both hands pulling down slowly, methodically. He was not Lance, and she pushed out all thoughts of the pure, sloppy joy the two of them had once shared. Where was Lance now? Had the Registry gotten to him? A lone night-bug emerged from the underpart of her thigh and shuffled aimlessly into the night as the artist tossed her jeans aside. There was no urgency to the way the artist removed her clothes. Maybe, she thought, his passion had been all used up when he skinned himself.

"Take off your shirt," Lorrie called up to him.

He paused.

"Now," she said.

The artist gripped his collar with both hands and lifted his shirt over his head in a single, smooth movement. The light was dim, but she reached her hands up and placed them on his belly, on his chest. Small, prickly bumps of raised tissue met the tips of her fingers. Long vertical lines like tiny corduroy wales ran from the base of his collarbone to the bottom of his ribs. His chest was hairless, but her fingers could feel everything: he had not left one part of his torso unpeeled.

"Please," breathed the artist, his neck arced. Wisps of steam rose from his nostrils and circled in the air: a fragrant mix of fear and pain and other ingredients she couldn't identify.

Her fingers ran over the vertical ridges of his chest. "You did this for art?" she asked him in a whisper.

"Yes." He opened his eyes and looked down at her.

"Really?"

"Yes."

"For art?"

He was quiet.

"Not for the war? Not to escape it?"

He placed both hands in a triangle in front of his nose. "Yes," he said.

Clouds blocked most of the moon, though a thin strip of grey light cut through to shine on the artist's face. He leaned forward, the creases in his belly folding over one another to make long, horizontal lines that ran from one hip to the other. Lorrie poked a finger inside one of the folds. There, in that small, warm space where skin doubled over skin, she found a pristine patch of smoothness, the one part of his body he had left untouched.

Clouds moved, bright dots of light made slow arcs across the sky, and Lorrie let her head fall back. The artist leaned forward, his legs froglike, splayed to the side and fully covering her. Each of his breaths was hot and labored, and he burrowed his face into her neck. They did not kiss. Lorrie waited, not knowing quite what she was waiting for. The artist lay there, softly crushing her. Suddenly, without warning, he lifted his head, stretched back his neck, and from deep within, the artist released a sad, strange howl of wordless words, less-than-human babbles that sailed up to the highest points of the dark sky above.

After a few minutes, he sat up, still on top of her. The artist studied her face. Perhaps he thought that his howl showed evidence of some deep hell overcome. Maybe, Lorrie thought, he was just looking to see whether she'd still have sex with him.

The artist shifted down her body, placed his hands on her hips, gripped the fabric of her underwear in two tight fists, and tugged downward. Before Lorrie knew what was happening, the artist had buried his face between her thighs. A loud pop leapt into her brain, and she stretched her eyes wide open in the half darkness as the questions piled up: *What am I doing? Who is this man?* She had not prepared for this, had not tamed, shaped, showered, and groomed in the ways she wanted, and now a strange man with shaved skin and a beaked nose had his parted lips on her, in her, all over her, spreading her as though she were in an exam room, panting and slurping and lapping in her general direction with a stretched tongue as though he were some starved hunter-gatherer who had just had his first kill in days. The artist licked her in all the wrong places, he was off-key, too ravenous; he plunged, dived, and explored erratically when all she wanted was a slow sense of rhythm. Lorrie wondered if his tongue was staggering away from her in some sort of subtle protest. But no. Two showers, she told herself, she had taken two showers that day, one early in the morning, another after the difficult talk group in the late afternoon. The hot water had left her during the second shower; war years, Lorrie knew, meant that any warmth in the water at all was a lucky break. The problem, she saw, wasn't with her at all.

"Wait," she told him.

The artist looked up, cheeks glistening, and under the big night moon, Lorrie saw his tiny eyes.

"Go slow," she said. "Much slower."

As she watched the scarred man in the blue light do his best to let her feel something, Lorrie told herself that these were certainly war years. Her eyelids shut, the artist slowed down. She had hoped that the artist might help her escape, if only for a moment, from the rhythm of her thoughts and the drab, inner scolding of her mind. Insects that were not in her head buzzed around her ears, and Lorrie allowed herself to surrender into his touch.

His touch was nothing special.

All his intensity had been howled out, she saw, maybe by his failed art, maybe by his fear of war. Whatever it was, it had eaten up all he had. The artist had been emptied. There was no way this hollow man could empty her, not even for a moment.

Even so, it had been too long since she'd been touched, and though the artist was mechanical, he was warm, he was a person, he was the first contact with her skin that was not from a bug but an actual human being. Her first caress after a million years spent alone.

With both hands Lorrie reached down, grabbed his ears, and pulled him up. Once the artist was inside her, she laid her head back and looked at the stars. A deep breath, a gaze at the moon, at the small points of light that dotted the sky, the grunts of the artist in her ear. A real person, she thought, a good, though damaged person, was touching her. The artist placed a hand on her face that blocked her view, so she gave a sharp bite to his finger, and once again, Lorrie could see the stars. The slowly turning sounds of night swept across her eardrums while bright red spots laced and twisted themselves in front of her eyes. Lorrie felt sure these small, moonlit moments were the gateway to a less poisonous season of life that lay ahead. Finally, as the artist continued to unroll himself into her, a welcome emptiness took over. A perfect nothingness. But then, he was finished. She kissed him good-bye and tiptoed down to bed. That night was her first without bugs, her only invasion-free sleep in months. Her dreams were empty, and she loved it. The day had not been the same after all.

❖ ❖ ❖

The next morning, the uniformed man with the rimless glasses shook her awake. After a night free of insects, she could already feel her heart expanding. Lorrie could not take it for granted that she was able to wake up in her own skin.

Readings were assigned for the talk group, and that morning she charged through them, not once feeling the need to itch. No bugs made themselves visible, so she took a victory walk in the garden, strolling triumphantly among the black haws and low bushes. Spotting the artist, she gave him a sign, and the two of them slipped into an empty broom closet.

"Do you understand?" she said to him. "How huge this is? I didn't itch at all last night."

"Oh," he said.

He didn't seem to get it, she thought, and why should he? Just because the guy had placed blade against skin and pushed down smoothly until he had seen the pink and the blue of his tendons didn't give him some paranormal ability to understand her.

The artist burst into tears.

Lorrie told the artist good-bye and slinked out of the closet. Stepping into the light, she watched as the jagged wings of a day-bug flapped slowly on her wrist. Quickly she blinked the vile thing away. The yelps of the baby-leader, the readings, her shame acceptance, a night with the artist on the roof—she had thought any and all of it had scared those bugs off for good. Still, there had only been one, she told herself. One was nothing, a mere day-bug. Lorrie left the artist in that closet, crying softly for all of them, alone in the dark.

❖ ❖ ❖

"Today," cried the baby-leader, "a special session, with even more focus on shame!"

"Oh boy," Lorrie murmured, mostly to herself. She would have liked the artist to hear it, but sex with other patients was prohibited, so they sat on opposite sides of the circle to be discreet.

"Did everyone read the passages?" the baby-leader asked.

Heads bobbed up and down as the white sunlight poured across their faces, a fortunate occurrence as the lights had been off all morning.

"I liked the jokes," said the speechless vet, who was having a speaking day. "I liked that even this book can be funny. I laughed out loud twice."

"Jokes?" said the baby-leader. "There weren't any jokes. The Young Savior doesn't make jokes. You read the words wrong."

"Oh," said the vet.

"We're talking about shame and sin here," said the baby-leader. "Nothing funny about sin."

A few of them giggled, because they knew that this statement was completely untrue. As the baby-leader delved into the virtues of shame reduction, Lorrie did her best to ignore him. Even so, the lectures and readings seemed to help the talk group. The pervert said he was less perverted. Prime Minister Four's great-great-great-granddaughter felt she might slide out from the smothering weight of her ancestor. But for Lorrie, nothing in that book had touched her. She wanted to yell at them that the prime minister would soon be ninety-seven, that the war would soon be twenty-three, along with any other dispiriting numbers she could think of. Just one day without the bugs, she decided, and she was out of here.

Without access to her many newspaper subscriptions, with no television and no radio, the outside world had hardened into an even more polished, shinier version of itself. Were the Foreigns still playing their successful games of cat-and-mouse in the distant jungles? And closer to home, were attacks on the Homeland still occurring with terrifying frequency? Before, she had been obsessed with following the reports on each new piece of violence: Did the latest rounds of domestic hostility emanate from utterly crazy Fareon folks? Or were hidden sleeper cells of Foreigns behind it all? There was plenty of speculation that everyone's worst nightmare had come true and that youthful Homeland citizens, drawn by the sparkling ideas of Ideology Five, were attacking their fellow citizens in solidarity with the Foreigns. And now, just as Lorrie was put away, the attacks had begun to alternate between the deadly and the absurd. First, the stolen Registry trucks, found abandoned and full of charcoal. On the drive up to the Facility, a radio announcer had reported that the pilfered uniforms had popped up on department store mannequins in several Western Sector cities, the fabric cut and sewn into fashionable skirts, shirts, and dresses. What did any of it mean? No one, it seemed, stopped dying just because Lorrie was in some rural nuthouse. It was time to get out of here.

"I think the bugs are gone," Lorrie told the baby-leader. "They just up and left." This was almost true, so it felt fine to say it.

"No," he said, both hands smoothing his shiny head. "Your bugs are in the same place they've always been. The shame. That's what's gone."

Or that's what she thought he said. She still couldn't hear well. Ever since Lance had knocked her around, sounds entered her left ear in a pitched and murky way that forced her to angle the right side of her head toward whomever was speaking.

"See, everyone?" the baby-leader said. "The passages have cured her! The teachings of the Young Savior have brought her back. She said so herself." He rotated his head so the entire group could see the triumphant light in his eyes.

Lorrie turned her good ear away from him, letting his words become mush. She was ready for her second act, her chance to unleash a new downpouring of effective resistance on the Homeland. But she was still here in the Facility, stuck in intermission.

"You folks are here because your toolboxes are weak, empty," the baby-leader went on. "You've got plastic wrenches, aluminum pliers, but our work here is to trade those in for some high-quality Homeland steel. And we've got a whole new set of sockets for you, one for every situation you're going to encounter out there. Because, get this, the future of humanity depends on not just being able to determine what's wrong and right, what's good and evil, but the knowledge that this determination is superior to all others. That's the message. And the Young Savior is the tool, a prophet who has departed our world but has left behind complicated puzzles and hidden messages, all in the service of helping you figure it out."

Everyone nodded, but for reasons Lorrie was sure were different than her own. *My tools* are *wrong,* she thought, but so were the ones the Facility wanted to hand over in their place. It had been days since she'd itched. She knew what was wrong, and she knew what was evil. So when could she leave?

❖　❖　❖

Lorrie looked for the artist so she could say good-bye. He was usually in the garden, but now he wasn't. An orderly said they had seen him hop into a closet. In a utility closet beside the garden, she found stacks of reproduced paintings of the Young Savior. There was no doubt that these were new portraits. The high-quality finish of the frames and the glossy paper made it clear that the piles in front of her were meant to replace the limp and fading vision of the Young Savior that hung in every room of the Facility. Even in the one-bulb light, Lorrie could see that these paintings were different. This new incarnation of the Savior looked sharper, less dreamy—angry, even—but mostly, more than any likeness Lorrie had ever seen, this new Young Savior was much, much younger.

But Lorrie didn't want the Young Savior. Never had. She wanted the artist, and she kept flinging open doors hoping she'd find him. Outside, leaves were falling in slow circles. The artist wasn't anywhere. Some stories, it seems, don't have a clear beginning or end.

Standing in the hall, she happened across the baby-leader.

"It's hard to leave, I know," he said, wrapping his elderly arms around her. Standing in his weak embrace, feeling his hot breath and hearing the cool rattle of his ancient lungs, the thought again snapped into Lorrie: this young-looking man was unnaturally old.

Though the simplistic Fareon plots of the antiwar movement had never appealed to her—ridiculous, the idea that the complexities of war could be reduced to some simple scheme in which the prime minister did not want to die—Lorrie found herself unsettled by the indeterminable age of the baby-leader. But no. His wrinkled hands and smooth face were not proof of a sinister plot perpetrated by the highest echelons of government. If anything, simply being exposed to the ridiculous ideas about the prime minister and his need to live forever must have accentuated her thoughts that there was some misalignment with the gentle man wrapping her in his embrace. That must be it. After all, one man aging strangely did not mean that all aging men were strange.

In the holding room, her parents hugged her tightly and filled out the discharge paperwork.

"Western City North made me crazy," she told them in the car. "Everything will be different now." A solid respite in a centrally heated facility in the middle of the Homeland had washed the bugs away. She could now see that the people she had known in Western City North had not been the people she thought they were.

"Damn right," said her father, his eyes on the road.

I have a plan, she wanted to tell them. *Well, maybe not a plan, but at least a vision.* Just as she was about to do so, her father slammed on the brakes, swerving to avoid a yawning pothole that had seized an entire section of road.

"In the paper the other day," her mother said, turning around to face her, "they said a new legislator joined up with those Coyotes."

"So what does that make now, three of them?" her father said.

Her mother giggled.

Lorrie slapped at a day-bug that was biting her neck, but softly, so her parents wouldn't see a thing.

❖ ❖ ❖

Back with her parents in Interior City, Lorrie discovered that the hearing loss in her left ear was permanent. A doctor placed a set of headphones over her ears and determined that full, sharp sounds would never return to her left eardrum in the manner they were supposed to. But Lorrie got along fine. She knew that her busted ear was just another reminder that she wouldn't be going back to where she came from.

The lack of crawlers cleared her head. In that freeing of space, Lorrie began to rediscover what it was she cared about in the first place. There was more work to do than ever.

Lorrie's parents had never liked Lance, and when she told them he had hit her, they liked him even less.

"I do believe I'll kill him," her father said upon hearing the news.

The family sat around their large candlelit dining room table. Blackouts were hitting Interior City with increased regularity, and good candles were in high demand. Lorrie's parents had used up all their quality candles and were on to the cheap kind that dripped heavily and gave off a disagreeable smell. Her mother stood to clear their finished portions of deviled crab and beef stew.

"Stop it," Lorrie said.

"No." Her father stood as well, removing his napkin with two fingers and placing it on the table. "I'm quite serious. That's the wrong boy for you, and he's roughed up the wrong man's daughter." The smoky yellow light lit up his features.

Lorrie could not determine how much of her father's anger came from love and how much from simply feeling that he had been a victim of property damage. With her thumb and forefinger, she kneaded the lobe of her bad ear. Her father's face was pained and twisted, his mouth low and stuck in a frown. He wanted, she saw, to erase that whole part of her life.

"Fine. I'll call the Point Line. Surely that boy is out of compliance with the Registry."

A slow and flickering joy crossed her mother's face.

"No."

"Why not?" asked her mother.

"You will not call that awful Point Line." She started up the stairs to her old room. "I'm not kidding," she called over her shoulder, her body desperate to not convey her fear of speaking to her father in such commanding tones. "Don't you dare do one little thing." She shut the door gently. Lorrie wouldn't be responsible for the sacrifice of another man, even if that man was Lance. Not now, she told the day-bugs, and all but two stayed away.

❖ ❖ ❖

In her room, she wrote letters. *Please do not to mention Lance or his whereabouts to me,* Lorrie told her friends. He could be anywhere, but she didn't want to know, couldn't. Even the slightest slip-up, and her father might call the Point Line. The less information, the better. To her friend Rebecca, who was, she had heard, zooming around Homeland Indigenous Districts, she wrote an apology to the last address she had, telling her she was sorry for everything. *I was not myself,* Lorrie typed.

Borrowing the Currencies from her parents, she restarted her subscriptions to all the important newspapers—at least fifteen of them, she had decided, were essential. No more side issues, she promised herself, no more tangential causes. If vets needed free breakfasts, it was because of the war. If certain professions lacked adequate numbers of women, that too was a result of the war. The war was sucking up all the boys, but she would be the one pulling on their ankles.

Her dreams cursed the geriatric prime minister and remained, for the most part, insect-free. In the coffeehouses around town, Lorrie started asking people whether they knew about any anti-Registry centers in Interior City. Preferably, she added, a place uncorrupted by the infiltration of the Fareon folks.

Imagined scenes from her future life: stacks of dinnerware stripped clean save for a few small hunks of torn bread, Lorrie having offered to cook for the other volunteers, nice people her age, disgusted but not too overwhelmed by the breathtaking machinery of the Homeland, all of them passionate about a world with less war, but all able to fully comprehend the seesawing existence that often called for a nice wine and long, wavy curtains.

"But what should we do about this, Lorrie?" they would ask her. After holding forth, a brave soul might have a follow-up: "But what about that?"

When she talked, they would listen. Clinks of forks on plates would subside, and all eyes would be upon her. Sure, they would make cracks about how neat her place was, how the forks and knives she served them with were probably worth three months' salary, but none of them would ever decline her coveted invitation. *We would be a new sort of family,* she thought. Now all she had to do was find them.

IO.

Keep Benny near. For Joe, the world was not some random accumulation of cause and effect; each action was related to the next. By keeping close to Benny now, he would keep Benny close in the future.

Another turn, and Joe saw that Benny had led them into the theater district. He knew this part of the city. To his left, a wraparound marquee advertised a movie that was three years old, maybe more. Across the street, another theater, this one smaller, with a cracked stucco exterior, advertising an afternoon showing of *Breath Rises!!!!* So sad, but funny, too, in the way that rotten things often were. Joe had seen this film years ago. It was clear that the accompanying punctuation had been added by some anonymous employee in the hopes that a bit of enthusiasm might replace the staleness of the product on offer. Movies, Joe knew, hadn't always been like this, but then again, neither had war.

Twelve minutes after Joe started following him, Benny stopped walking, pausing in front of the theater with the exclamation points. Joe stopped, too, and leaned against a telephone pole. After a moment, he saw Benny squint and gaze toward him. Quickly Joe jerked to the other side of the telephone pole, the fear of exposure jumping his chest so hard he had to clench his teeth. Had he been spotted? There would be no way to explain himself.

Instead, he saw Benny pay at the ticket booth and head inside. Though he knew Benny's Currencies were low, he also knew that movies were unpopular enough as to be nearly free these days. So why was Benny headed to a movie when he was supposed to locate a hard-to-find book that would save them from the Registry? Just hours until he had promised to meet Joe at a bus stop and this is how he wanted to spend the time?

A few minutes after Benny entered the theater, Joe walked up to the ticket booth and asked what time the movie let out. The outbreak of unstructured time came as a surprise; following Benny had been hard work. There was time to kill, and he was just a block away, so why the hell not?

He walked around the corner to the apartment he knew well and pressed the buzzer. An unwelcome quote from the Young Savior on the moral breaches of lust pushed its way into his thoughts, but Joe forced himself to focus on his task, not his feelings. Three floors up, a face poked out from a window, registered the familiar top of Joe's head, and, along with the body attached to it, leapt down two flights of stairs, flinging open the door to greet him. Of course. Ronald was always home and always happy to see him.

Bringing him close with his one arm, Ronald gave Joe as tight a hug as a one-armed man could muster. Inside the apartment, the air, as always, was warm.

"You came," Ronald panted.

Always so eager. Joe found himself staring yet again at the stainlike scar that extended across Ronald's neck and below his collar. "I've only got a few hours," he said.

"Excuse me?" Immediately Ronald's lower lip pushed upward into a sulky pout.

"Look," Joe said. "I'm up on First Tuesday, I'm not sure what I should do. I've got a few hours and was in the area, so I figured—"

"You're up on First Tuesday? Why didn't you tell me?"

"I don't want to talk about it."

"But, Joe, I thought that we might—"

A surge of blood pushed at the edge of Joe's wrists, and he leaned forward to kiss him. Whatever it took to shut that beautiful face up. As always, with his eyes closed, he could make Ronald into anyone.

After they were finished, the ever-predictable Ronald made his final pitch. Joe sat there, listening, but it was too late. Now that they were done, a fast-growing weed of regret had already sprouted inside him. Ronald and his large round eyes had nothing to offer him but the empty consolation of his unwanted love.

Down the block, Joe waited, one eye on the theater. Though Ronald's furry thighs and taut chest swam beautifully through his thoughts, Joe understood that the Young Savior would demand the drowning of all such images. No beautiful balls or shimmering shoulders, not if the Young Savior was going to stick around. It was one or the other, plain and simple. Only it wasn't, as Joe was not willing to let either go.

After a while, Benny emerged from the theater. A slim woman with broad shoulders walking by tried to chat him up, but Joe watched as Benny quickly blew her off. No surprise—Benny was pickier than ever these days. Again Joe stayed half a block behind him. The bus station wasn't too far from here. But immediately it was clear that Benny was not headed toward the bus station.

Three lefts, and Joe stayed on his tail. He followed as Benny headed down a particularly grimy block. Practically every other car was perched on cinder blocks, the decrepitude on proud, stately display. Probably this was a neighborhood of mangled vets. How awful, Joe thought, to be surrounded by people whose lives had gone in the very direction he was so desperate to avoid.

Using the raggedy bushes, Joe did his best to stay outside the airy edges of Benny's vision. A shadow spread over the block, and he saw Benny stop and look up. Joe ducked behind a car and looked up, too. As he did, he saw a strange sight: a thick, sludgy cloud had scooted across the sky and blocked the sun completely.

Again Benny was on the move. *I love you,* Joe repeated to himself, to Benny's back, to the dark cloud above. He was struck by the sense that people could live whole lives and never find another person they cared about so deeply. After the third repetition, the thick sound of Homeland Religion church bells splashed through the air. An instant sign of disapproval from the Young Savior? Ridiculous; of course it wasn't. But he also knew that old ideas never have the grace to slither away quietly.

Just then he watched as Benny gave an obvious, lustful leer to a girl who couldn't have been more than fourteen. Even from a distance, he could see the unfortunate girl grip her father's mangled hand even tighter. Out of instinct, out of jealousy, out of common decency, Joe wanted to rush at Benny with a roar, shake him by the shoulders, and ask him what he thought he was doing. But Benny kept on walking, and Joe allowed the quaint notion of himself as defender of the innocent to die a small, insignificant death.

Finally Benny seemed to choose a house. Joe watched from across the street as Benny knocked. The door swung open, answered by an unshaven man with a strong resemblance to a mountain goat. Too far away to make out any words, Joe watched as Benny and the goat-man had a brief conversation before Benny entered the house, shutting the door behind him. Perhaps these were the people with the book that would save them. The goat-man who answered the door didn't look so awful. So why had Benny excluded him?

As he was pondering this unfair exile, an armored truck with Registry markings pulled in front of the house. Joe backed away, positioning himself behind a parked car. Two men emerged from the truck, both clad in khaki uniforms, both of them carrying wood-gripped rifles. The moment they banged on the door, the house began to belch up men.

One jumped from a second-story window. Another, his face lost in a memory, burst through the glass of the front room, pausing only briefly to remove some of the toughest shards that had stuck to his skin before he raced down the street, unending streaks of blood marking his path. A third emerged from the side of the house, shimmying down the plumbing pipes, his lips moving softly, probably reciting some long ago memorized prayer to the Young Savior. He landed on two feet in the front yard, looking around for more men in uniform before scurrying away. In the distance, the faint yelping of bothered dogs.

Every few minutes, the two uniformed men would emerge with an unconscious, limp body, open the back of the truck, and toss it in. More men jumped from more windows, a few screaming on their way down. Most escaped easily; clearly, this was not a well-funded operation. But where was Benny? Why hadn't he jumped? Another motionless man was being carried out, and at first Joe was sure this was Benny, but then he caught another angle. This dangling man had short-clipped hair and looked nothing like Benny at all. Perhaps there was a back route, some other way for Benny to get the slip on the men in uniform. Joe watched from his perch across the street. The tips of his fingers felt as though he was being forced to hold them over an open flame. *Hurry up, Benny,* he whispered. *Get the hell out of there.*

The men in uniform tossed another barely stirring body into the back of their truck and returned to the house, looking for more.

II.

The feeling came, and Benny couldn't help but let it wash over him: little teeny angels sprinted through his poxed leper veins and healed him. So much time had passed since Benny had heard the frequency, he'd forgotten the sound.

A man in an old coat, one of the dealer's crew whose name Benny hadn't caught or couldn't remember, struck a match while another hand held a small spoon of liquid. After studying the setup for a moment, Benny realized that the hand grasping the spoon was his own. He wanted to be stuck. He was ready for the voltage. *My eyes have never been wetter,* he thought. His legs were crossed over themselves on the planked floor; the man with the match was squatting down beside him. The flame raced down the wood of the match and kissed the tips of the man's fingers before he flicked his wrist.

As the divine odor filled the room, Benny's closed insides opened. He decided to lay his head on the floor and let his eyelids fall shut. As he did, a little river rushed inside his head from one ear to the other. Milky brain fluids sloshed to parts of his mind that should have been hot and dry. There was enough water in his head for everyone in the world, ten thousand times over. No one would ever go thirsty again.

How sad that the people closest to him would never experience such a beautiful chain of eruptions! Joe, of course, would have been too scared, too judgmental to join him. The meek were never free.

Leaving all thoughts of Joe behind, Benny spread out his feathers and traveled to worlds both vile and flawless, all at once. The bus that would take him up to his uncle's cabin would idle in the station; he could hold it there until he was ready, all with his mind. Muck around the wheels, old gasoline, a puncture in the back tire, Benny created it all. Power piled on power. The bus would wait; there was time for everything.

An angel came to him and asked for his papers, questioning his right to travel around this holy place. Benny stuck a hand into his pocket; his passport was no longer there. This loss was devastating, as he had thought he might stay, but the angel told Benny that everyone in this world to come had to have papers.

Shoes slapping wood, fearful yelps—the sounds seeped slowly into his consciousness. A musky, stale scent floated into the room. Then, a strange burrowing feeling just below the final arch of his lower rib—a shoe, nudging him—and he opened his eyes and saw two men standing over him. Or maybe it was three.

Benny tried to lift his head from the floor. He couldn't see the men's faces, maybe because his ears were all wet from the inside and the moisture was mucking up the backs of his eyeballs. The nerves were loose, the sockets must have expanded, and now Benny saw that his eyeballs were too wet, an impossible pressure behind them. Soon the little balls he used to see with would pop from his skull and roll onto the floor, and all that water would spray from his eyeholes like a busted hydrant. Benny thought about his uncle's cabin, that beautiful rounded lake with a narrow middle, piped by snow-capped mountains. That lake was the right amount of wet.

Again he tried to lift his head, to stand up and greet the two or three figures looming over him. The weight was too much. He would have to contend with studying their loose and floppy features from below. Perhaps these weren't men at all, but angels. Though he couldn't make out lips or teeth, Benny still knew that these shadows were smiling. Perhaps this form of faceless communication was how it was with angels: they were just dim amalgams of emotion, and Benny didn't need cheeks or frowns to know it. One of the angels picked up his coat and held it up next to his own. Benny found himself deeply touched to see both coats side by side, one from the firmaments, the other from the thrift store. He let out a laugh. How to ask them if he could stay in this new place instead of back in that dead land of order he had come from? But the angels were too pretty to complain to. Benny's mouth opened wide, and he heard a rattle, a happy moan of joy that arose from the back of his throat. "That's everything that ever moved me," he croaked up at them. "I have nature in my head and brotherhood right in front of me."

These angels seemed to have outfitted themselves in matching khaki uniforms. One of them was far taller than the other. A mouthless voice spoke down at him with a commanding spiritual swagger as it pulled a piece of paper from Benny's pocket. "What you've got is a bus ticket for Rural Sector M leaving in about an hour," the angel said. This angel had the airy voice of a child. The snow in his head sung itself into water. The sound was stunning.

"And twenty Currencies, he's only got twenty Currencies."

"Not a lot for a runner."

Benny hadn't known angels dealt in such earthly matters. Their voices were whispers from the far end of a long tunnel. One of the angels continued to inspect the pockets of his coat.

"Let's purge our sewn clothes," Benny called up to them. "Let's have an upsurge of wildness." The trees at his uncle's cabin were kind trees, trees that helped a person solve problems, trees that showed a visitor a good time and let you be exactly the person you were. There weren't trees like that around here, not anywhere. Benny tried to tell this to the angels.

"Does he have any idea?" said the first angel.

"Why do we even want him?" said the second.

"I'm worried that we do."

Benny didn't like that the angels didn't like him. "Hey," he said. He would plead his case, replay this scene, and turn it around. But before he could form the bits in his head into a defense, the angels stopped being angels and turned into faces, converted themselves from messengers into men, both of whom, Benny saw, seemed to have some sort of writing in a patch on their shoulders.

"Hey," Benny said. "Welcome back to the brotherhood of humanity."

One of the men twitched his lip, the other frowned, and Benny saw a moment of understanding pass between the two of them. Before he knew what was happening, Benny felt a terrible sting in his jaw, and the men's faces disappeared into black. Darkness everywhere, and his own face on fire. Benny could feel the world again.

It hurt. Badly.

12.

Lorrie's mail had piled up: newspapers and magazines that Lance stacked against the back wall of his kitchen. As Lance dropped another day's paper onto the teetering pile, he glanced at the sickly, disembodied words. The next First Tuesday, a headline told him, would also be the twenty-third anniversary of war. One column over was news of more attacks, this round stranger than the last. A Homeland Religion church defaced and a historic statue of the Young Savior altered; the Holy One himself—blessed be He—was now clothed in a Homeland Army uniform. Below the marble was a small bomb that had not gone off, buried in a huge sack of charcoal. Why charcoal? a columnist asked. Foreigns don't even barbecue.

Lance shook his head. Just another newspaper on the stack.

Reaching down, he grabbed his sketchbook and began to draw. Irises and pupils, he decided. After a few passes, he realized that the eyelids on the paper contained no hint of life, nothing of Lorrie's spark. The air sagged around him, and he tossed the sketchbook away, smiling as it hit the floor with a loud slap. When he heard the knock at his door, he had not stood up in nearly fifteen hours.

"Apple?"

Standing in his doorway was his neighbor Tim, a bright green apple in his palm. "Haven't seen you around," Tim said.

This was true. Lance called up the glittering sight of Tim's girlfriend Rebecca in his apartment, the two of them visiting during some long ago dinner party, warm wind filling the air, her lips wrapped around a Substance Q cigarette. "How the hell did you get an apple?"

Tim smiled sheepishly. Though Lance could not remember the last time he had bitten into an apple, he knew that had he come across one, Tim was low on the list of people he would think to share it with.

"So?" said Tim. The apple, it seemed, was just the beginning, an offering so Lance would allow him over the threshold and through the door. Lance shrugged and stepped aside. He took the apple from Tim and placed it on the counter. Finally, something to look forward to.

Lance knew his apartment looked blank, as though some permanent sense of home had been sucked out of all the objects, but now he saw the place through his visitor's eyes. A stale smell coated the room, and a thin film of dust rested atop every surface.

"I'm sorry about Lorrie," Tim said. He sat across from Lance on a low ottoman that he squeezed with his thighs.

"Yeah," said Lance. Tim's acne scars—or maybe it was razor burn, who could tell?—rode down his cheeks in staggered strips, deeper and more lurid, Lance thought, than the last time he'd seen him. Lance looked around some more, if only to not have to stare at Tim's face. "How's Rebecca? Sorry my place looks like shit."

"Rebecca," Tim snorted. "She's gone, zooming around specially zoned Homeland Indigenous Districts. Says she's three twenty-fifths Group F or something so she's called to fight the quotas." His smile was a shadow, left over from some earlier, happier time.

"What quotas?"

Tim shrugged.

"When's she coming back?"

Again, his shoulders rose and fell.

Lance was shocked. Though he knew Tim and Rebecca had their problems, he had considered them a stable force, a repudiation of the idea he often heard other people say: that young people in these tumultuous times were finding love and stability to be an impossible combination. Incredible, he thought, that some half-dreamed conception of Rebecca's past allowed her to disappear into the most rugged sector of the Homeland.

"How did it—"

"Forget it," Tim said quickly. He rocked back and forth on the ottoman, fingers tapping against the sides.

Through the large rectangular window that looked onto the street, the downtown towers glimmered in the distance. It was a beautiful view, tempered only by a few of the low-lying dark clouds that Lance vaguely remembered reading were acidic, or toxic, or perhaps not clouds at all, but massive puffs of carcinogenic vapors.

"I'm going, you know," Tim said quietly. "The Registry got me."

Lance shifted his head away from the view and back to Tim. "And you're really going?"

"And I'm really going."

The two of them sat there, Lance sunken into the excessively soft couch, Tim on his backless square, posture slumped. After a few moments of silence, Lance offered coffee. In the kitchen, he opened a few cupboards before returning to the living room apologetically. Of course he didn't have any coffee.

"You really are going?" Their departed girlfriends, who had both opposed the war so viciously, added a special layer of quiet to their conversation.

"I am." Tim's look was blank, protected. "Do you hate me?"

Lance thought a moment. "No," he said. He stared at the dark clouds. "To be honest, I can't say I care."

Tim said nothing.

At a point like this, Lance had thought it would be different. Had Lorrie been by his side, he might have been moved to stomp and storm. He would have meant it, too. "I don't mean that to sound like it just did," Lance said. "I just can't find anything else in me right now. My instincts tell me it's a pretty bad choice you're making, but every other part of me is just screaming that it just doesn't matter."

"That's what I thought," Tim said softly. "I thought so."

"What any of us do, really." Lance wished he still had it in him to call Tim a puppet of the Homeland, a baby killer in training. He dug hard within himself, searched for any sort of burn, for that anger that arose from certainty. Instead, he breathed out a hard exhalation of emptiness.

A dampness took shape in the corners of Tim's eyes. Perhaps, Lanced hoped, this meant they would not have to talk about the war or the Registry any further. He thought about offering a Substance Q cigarette, or two glasses of whiskey. A good smoke or a heavy drink, anything so they didn't have to get into *that*. They'd have a few drinks, he'd pat Tim on the shoulder and tell him good luck, shut the door behind him, bite into that apple, and never think about the guy again.

But such a world was not to be. Tim declined the Q, said no thanks to the whiskey, and instead sat in front of Lance silently, his shoulders low. Even the toxic clouds hovering outside the window seemed more upbeat than the two of them. Time to get rid of this guy, Lance thought. But just as he opened his mouth for some sort of closing statement, Tim began to speak.

"I've thought the war through," Tim said.

Lance cocked his head and listened as Tim began a long monologue in which he spoke nothing of the struggle against Ideology Five—still after so many years the stated purpose of the war—and everything of helping Foreign villagers who could not help themselves. He spoke of moral duty and purpose, of a transfiguration both mental and physical that would catapult him into realms where lesser men feared to tread.

He said he hoped to stand firm against indifference and hate, to know when to object and when to flee, and that any fear he had was weakness. The key, he felt, was to not deny the fear and to not deny his weakness. This, he was sure, would translate into a valor that would drag him from the life he currently led, in which there was little to fear because there was little he cared about. He hoped to be assigned to a light infantry brigade.

So the guy wanted to share what he was about. Fair enough. Besides, it wasn't every day someone offered up their own brutal truth: *Here was a story about how people thought about fighting in war.*

Such a story had always been withheld from those closest to him. As each brother had left, there had been no recognizable pattern of fear or desire, no narrative of how or why. Instead, each one had simply known it was his turn, accepted this as fact, and then departed.

"Just a handful of days," Tim said. "Then I have to get myself to the induction center. Didn't make that First Tuesday cutoff, though. I guess it's too crowded or something."

Only then did the spinning realization come to Lance that compared to him, Tim's handful of days was a quiet, blue-winded paradise, whereas he, Lance, looked out at life from a barren rock stranded in an empty ocean. A handful? That was a lifetime. Lance had forty-eight hours.

A siren screamed down the street, its screech echoing into the distance. Both of them turned toward the sound.

"Hey, have you heard from Lorrie?"

Lance looked at him, but Tim had spoken to the window.

"Do you know where she is?"

Lance shook his head.

"Do you want to know where she is?"

Lance couldn't tell if Tim was offering information or inquiring into his state of mind. "What do you mean?"

"Could you find out where she was if you wanted, but you haven't tried to find out? Or could you not find out, and so you haven't tried to?"

"I don't know," Lance sighed.

"Because I was thinking, maybe I could write her. Just say hello, tell her how you're doing, fill her in on what you're up to, if you want. It might be nice to hear from a neutral friend."

"Okay."

"But?" He saw Tim wipe his palms on the side of the ottoman.

"But I don't know where she is," Lance said.

"Right."

"Soon, though, I'll know."

"You'll let me know when you find out?"

"Is that why you came here?" Lance said. "To talk about Lorrie? I think about her enough as it is." From down the stairs, the wheezy asthmatic neighbor coughed a series of chalky coughs. After a moment, he added, "She probably wouldn't want to talk to a soldier anyway."

"Maybe so," said Tim. He had a look in his eyes as though he had suffered the same kind of gaping loss despite the fact, Lance thought, that he had imparted the story of Rebecca's departure with spectacular indifference. "You might be right."

Lance stared at Tim, trying to grasp whatever thoughts were doddering around his brain. He felt unclear about what, in fact, he was seeing. "Whatever. I'll tell her to write you when I see her," he promised. "Not too long from now."

Tim nodded his head and started talking, this time faster than before, again rocking back and forth on his ottoman. "The war would be a good thing for you to find out who you are on your own," he said.

The overhead lights buzzed and turned off, and as they did, Lance's thought that he should discuss his own impending induction passed. No, sharing that he was going to run would be absurd. People who thought war was good for themselves were quick to pounce upon those who didn't. If he told Tim he wasn't going, the guy would point him the second he left. Tim, he could see, had invented for himself the role of the soldier, and now he thought everyone should play it.

Lance closed his eyes and pressed down hard. Already Lorrie was being erased from his memory. Her nose, her dry lips, that was all there, but what about what she might say to him right now? He opened his eyes, but his world was still black.

"Just one more thing," said Tim. "Not about the war." He stood up, so Lance did, too. "I am so, so sorry about Lorrie." Tim leaned over and hugged him. At first, the touch was shocking, a bright green surprise in the darkness. Lance could not recall the two of them ever having had more contact than a handshake. "I know how much you must miss her," Tim said. A few deep sobs, and Tim dug his fists into Lance's shoulder blades. If Tim meant for something to be passing between them, Lance couldn't feel it. They had become different, too different, all while sitting across from each other in Lance's small apartment. As the embrace went on, all Lance could feel was deep embarrassment for the two of them. Why was Tim crying *now*? He had remained sober and dry-eyed as he imparted the story of Rebecca's departure. Following the story of the annihilation of his relationship, he had slipped in his decision to go to the bloodiest war in Homeland history in a sturdy, assured manner, and now, at the mention of Lance's departed girlfriend, of someone else's love having vanished, at the two of them clasping together for a touch, only now did Tim's eyes swirl in their sockets and drop sloppy tears onto the floor. None of it made sense, and a vague uneasiness crept over him.

"Enough," Lance said, peeling himself away.

Perhaps, Lance decided, it was impossible to have his own grief lessened by a man on his way to the jungle, a man, he was sure, who was about to die.

13.

Each Sunday, Sally and Mr. Dorton drove three hours to see Daniel at the military hospital, and each time they did, the doctors told them he was closer to release. For the first time, they were frisked upon entering.

"New policy," said the guard at the checkpoint. "Just the other day, there was a failed bombing of a military hospital up in Western City North."

"No one was hurt I hope?" said Sally.

"No, ma'am," the guard answered, though he only looked at Mr. Dorton. "They filled two ambulances full of charcoal, stuffed them top to bottom, and tried to light them up. Didn't work, though. These damn Fivers are probably planning something for the twenty-third anniversary. Especially considering it's a First Tuesday and all."

"Oh my," said Sally. "How can people be so awful?"

Mr. Dorton had no time for small talk. "Can we go in now?"

To get to Daniel, they walked past rows of damaged men, missing fingers, popped-out eyeballs. Even so, those boys didn't mean much to Mr. Dorton, not right now. The doctors claimed Daniel would be ready to go home soon, complete with two arms, two legs, and three medals. And his Benny didn't know any of it.

❖ ❖ ❖

On the expressway now, headed home, after another silent hospital visit with his boy. In the side pocket, a crumpled pamphlet handed to Mr. Dorton from the split-springed bed of a mangled young veteran he did not know. "Take this," the boy had croaked as Mr. Dorton passed. The outstretched arm was impossible to avoid as the anonymous boy was parked in the hallway, another one of the overflows.

Never one to refuse a veteran, Mr. Dorton had obliged, taking the pamphlet. What he read shocked him. The good prime minister, so resolute in the war against the barbaric Foreigns, so patient in his determination to rid the world of Ideology Five, slandered not for his policies, but as a driver of an occult agenda to immortality.

"What in the hell," he asks his wife, "is Fareon?" They drive slowly. The roads are not good.

"Never heard of it," she shrugs.

"Can you believe this thing?" Mr. Dorton can feel the blood rising to his face. "Just because the prime minister is getting on in years, just because some soft mineral or what have you is only in Foreign hands, it's just—"

"Daniel seemed good today," she interrupts.

But Mr. Dorton isn't finished. "Never die? People on this Fareon never die? Do they even realize how ridiculous that sounds? It's people like this who are blowing up our buildings."

"I thought it was Ideology Fivers."

"The idea that the secretary of the interior fathered a child in his eighties," Mr. Dorton continues. "None of my papers mentioned such a thing, not to say—"

"I think Daniel was excited to see us. Don't you?"

Mr. Dorton takes the hint.

The visit had been no different than any of the others: Daniel stares at the wall. Sally stares at Daniel as he stares at the wall, Mr. Dorton gets so he can't take their unmatched gazes and his son's cruel silence, so he stomps out toward the nurses' station and tells stories to the ones who will listen. Only the old and wrinkled do. When Mr. Dorton leaves the room, Sally reports that Daniel shakes and cries.

Back on the expressway, Sally keeps her eyes in front of her, doesn't shoot them Mr. Dorton's way, he notices.

"How about," he asks her, "you ask your brother up there to go around Western City North and take a look for Benjamin?"

"He lives on the outskirts, though, across that big bridge. He wouldn't know the first place to start looking."

She's right. Her brother is an odd one, Mr. Dorton thinks. He has a small shack in some rural sector a few hours from Western City North, a pitiful little house really, diagonal floors and rusted pipes that he escapes to when the city becomes too much for him.

"Besides," Sally says, finally giving him a quick glance, "Benjamin would never be anywhere obvious." She slows down to avoid a dramatic pothole.

Right again. His Benjamin is a boy who understands, no matter how backward that understanding is, that this world could still be one of large possibilities.

Ahead, the expressway is jammed, the shoehorned cars bumper to bumper, more holes in the road ahead, no doubt. "You could," she says slowly, "ask Craig Camwell whether he's heard from Joe. Try and put in another request, in case he talks to Joe, for Benjamin to call."

Even after two decades at the prison complex, Sally, he realizes, still thinks that the place is some sort of gentleman's club where all the employees share cigars and clap one another on the back and shoulders. "I never see the man," he tells her. "He's in food services, for god's sake. I don't deal with food services."

"What about the poker game?"

And yet, Sally knows his life well. Occasionally Craig Camwell subs in at Mr. Dorton's regular game. The Camwells are religious people, not to say that Mr. Dorton doesn't go faithfully each Sunday morning, but the Camwells are different. The church Mr. Dorton and his wife attend is a small and classic Homeland Religion–style building with clapboard siding and a tall spire at the end of an empty road. The Camwells do their Offshoot worship in an unadorned storefront near the hardware store on a busy street full of horns and traffic. Neither Sally nor Mr. Dorton has ever been, but there is talk that behind the drawn curtains transpires prostration, breast-beating, and worship of a Savior so young as to be unrecognizable.

"Fine," Mr. Dorton says. "I'll see if he shows up at poker."

"But you did ask him before, right?" says Sally, eyebrows lifted. "To tell Benjamin to call us."

"Yes." This is true, though he doubts whether Craig Camwell remembered his request. To be sure, the man has things to talk to his own boy about, and passing messages along for Mr. Dorton is, in its way, humiliating for all parties involved. It pains Mr. Dorton that he is even worse at keeping track of his boy than the breast-beating, baby-worshipping, food-services company man, Craig Camwell.

❖ ❖ ❖

"At least Daniel seemed better than last time," Sally says. The two of them sit across from each other in their kitchen. Sally has fixed their regular Sunday lunch: frosted meatloaf with sour cream, though in times past they might have had an orange wedge on the side. The loud, dull sound of faraway thunder crashes around the house, but there is no rain, at least not yet.

"He did seem well," Mr. Dorton agrees, though in his opinion, the silence and shivers of their morning visit were hardly a cause for happiness and hardly a change from before. Shreds of cheese disappear into Mr. Dorton's meatloaf, and he pushes it around his plate.

"I wonder if he's making friends in there," Sally says.

"Oh, I'm sure of it. That's just the place for making friends. They sit around, swap stories. They've got plenty of tales to go on about, I just know it." He just better stay away from that Fareon freak with the pamphlets, Mr. Dorton thinks. How many of the recently returned boys actually buy into this stuff? Because he knows he must, Mr. Dorton forces a small square of meat into his mouth. His absent sons guzzle up the flavor from even his favorite dishes.

"I'm sure you're right." She smiles, and Mr. Dorton smiles back, a grin so big he thinks he might look insane.

"It's just us." He plops another hunk of meat in his mouth and gives a large swallow to push them down his throat. "That's how boys are with their parents, you know that. I'm sure he's a regular chatterbox with the other fellows in there. If you ask me, it's completely understandable. Why be a motormouth with us when he's been jawing all day to the other boys?"

"Yes." Sally clanks her fork and knife down, stands, and begins to stack and clear the dishes. "That must be it."

"Even so," Mr. Dorton says. He places the thought on a platter and offers it up to his wife. He knows he does not have to articulate the bitter question in both of their hearts: *What did he see over there? And why won't he talk to me?*

❖ ❖ ❖

Mr. Dorton looks for his favorite newspaper. Sally has hidden it from him, he guesses, shredded each page into the upstairs bathroom garbage can. With great care, she would have crumpled the accounts detailing the torrent of tears that their local representative in parliament, a man both of them had voted for, had unleashed at a press conference. From now on, the lawmaker intoned, he would be voting with his conscience. But what does that mean? the gaggle of reporters had shouted. Yes, Dorton's own man in parliament is now a Coyote. Mr. Dorton subscribes to more papers than his wife is able to destroy.

Why hasn't Benjamin called? What kind of son is he? Mr. Dorton sits by the phone in his living room and smokes one cigarette and then another, considering with each inhale whether he put too much emphasis on his youngest son being well scrubbed on routine and commitment, on all of the simple truths that he was sure would add up to success and dignity but now seemed to be thrown back at him in disregard by the boy's disagreeable absence. The phone stays silent. What did Daniel see over there? A third cigarette, and an ache pops into Mr. Dorton's chest and loops the lining around his heart into sharp little knots. Mr. Dorton unscrews the small plastic bottle he keeps in the front pocket of his cardigan and places a small tablet of aspirin on the edge of his tongue. *I wish I knew Benny's life better*, Mr. Dorton thinks, *so as to have an idea of where he might go.*

"Enough, dear," says Sally. She sits beside Mr. Dorton, hands folded on her lap.

"He'll call tonight," he tells her. Two more hours and a half a pack of cigarettes pass. Outside, the hard thunder hurls itself against the windows. The rain slams itself against the glass, sharp and cold. His silence takes forever.

14.

His time was up. *Go*, whispered Lorrie. *Don't just run. Tell them why. Make it official.*

And now, on the advice of the invisible Lorrie in his head, Lance found himself in this forgotten industrial corner of the city. Rows of men were posted in front of the induction center, hands on their rifles. Each man faced outward, the engagements of their minds dark and shielded.

Lance walked up the steps and presented his papers. Of course security was going to be tight; every nut job in the Homeland wanted to destroy this place. Because it was not a First Tuesday, he had assumed there wouldn't be much of a crowd. But First Tuesdays, it seemed, were just a media show put on by the Registry, a day when the appetite for men was only slightly stronger. Long lines of them waited to report, the most hard-bitten arriving alone, others accompanied by red-eyed mothers, wives, and sisters.

Once he was cleared, Lance was sent down a long, narrow hallway. At the end was a metal door. Pulling it open, he spotted a pretty, young secretary at a large oak desk. Behind her, a massive portrait of the prime minister with a small brass plate below indicating it had been painted twenty years ago. Funny, Lance thought. He still looked exactly the same.

"I'm here to refuse," Lance told the secretary. The smug prime minister smiled down at his story.

"Not here," she said, handing him the number of another room. Lance took a sharp left turn down the long hallway, followed by two rights and another left. Framed photos of the prime minister hung in short intervals along each wall. The hallways were lined with men, some sitting on the brown slate tiles, others standing.

What do you think? How am I doing? he whispered to Lorrie. As the Lorrie of his mind was composed entirely of Lance's own memories, she had been very supportive as he had left his apartment, hopped on a bus, transferred, twice made wrong turns on foot, and finally located the building that had been packing men off to war this year, the year before that, and the years before that as well. Of course Lance knew that this cleansed, sanitized, and uncomplaining Lorrie whom he could not touch, whose dry lips he could not see, was not the real Lorrie. But as the real Lorrie had been so completely removed from his life and he so immersed in absolute loneliness, just to sense her, he was sure, was a salve against his own self being ripped apart completely. Besides, once all this was done, he would replace her with the real thing. This whole ordeal was just one more story to share.

Taking in the room in front of him, Lance saw several dozen uncomfortable-looking chairs jammed too close together, the lightly padded seats all occupied by men in a similar age range. One of the men read a magazine. On the cover: "Homeland Indigenous in the Service." And below, in smaller print: "Group F Does Their Part."

We talked about that, he whispered to Lorrie. *At the beach.* She nodded her ghost chin up and down. *We sure did, baby,* she whispered. Lance appreciated the affirmation but found himself increasingly troubled by how little Ghost-Lorrie sounded like her real-life counterpart.

The line moved slowly, the dejected men crowding the hallway, their heads low, their dreams full of girlfriends or safety, or whatever it was that these men dreamed about. Finally, Lance reached the auditorium.

To the back of the room was a low stage with a podium and thick red curtains. No windows. The overhead lights were sharp and bright; if any building was exempt from the rolling blackouts, surely it was the Western City North Induction Center. Watching the officers, memories of high school pre-army classes flooded into Lance: the tall man standing stage left was a sergeant; the thick man beside him with the raspy engine voice had shoulder insignia that showed him to be a captain; the third official was a second lieutenant who looked like he didn't want to be there any more than Lance did. On the floor below the stage were eight inductees in two rows of four. Lance chose the second row, not the first. Eight more men were outside the door awaiting the next round. Behind them, eight more, and another eight after that. Lance felt his blood rise to the surface and threaten to burst from beneath his skin and stain the carpet below. This was it.

Hey, he whispered to Lorrie.

Silence.

He looked around the room frantically, at the stage, at the other inductees, at his dark brown shoes. Lorrie, it seemed, could not follow him here, into the bowels of the Registry.

"Each man will repeat his full name," the sergeant barked, "after which I will follow with the phrase, 'new inductee of the Homeland Army.' Understood?"

The men nodded.

"Once I have called your name and spoken the aforementioned phrase, you are to take one step forward. It is this step"—the sergeant paused and stared at each of them before glancing back at his clipboard—"that will officially conscript you in your service to the Homeland."

The thought came to Lance that it seemed silly to officially refuse, that the symbolism of not putting one foot in front of another was inconsequential to the handful of people in attendance. Why now, he thought, why say no now? He had not said no to Lorrie's parents, he had not said no to her obsessive need for hot wash; instead, he had gone along with all of it. Every tactic he tried, each word he had said and strung together with another one, all of those words had failed to debug her. None of his words, he realized, had worked. The thought struck Lance that he knew Lorrie didn't write or call because he had hit her, and he knew he had hit her because his words hadn't worked.

The sergeant called out a name, and a man in the front row stepped forward.

New inductee of the Homeland Army!

One small step to determine all his possibilities, to narrow them into one. Lance worried that his body might refuse to obey, that his arms or bladder or legs might decide to perform some action that his mind didn't agree with.

New inductee of the Homeland Army!

They were on his row now.

"New inductee of the Homeland Army!" the sergeant yelled, grasping the hand of the young man who had walked across the stage toward him. More names; another repetition of the six-word phrase. Suddenly the man next to Lance was pronouncing his full name for the sergeant as though it was the first time he had heard the words. One name away.

All Lance had to do was repeat his own name and then step forward. He knew that if he stood in place and didn't say anything, his life would get even worse than it currently was. The world was closing in on him. But so what? His heart was still open.

"Lance Sheets," called the sergeant. "Please say your name and step forward."

Lance's life struck him as a salt-kissed wound, open and bloody and with no relief in sight. The room was warm; his skin was damp and salty.

"Ahem!" yelled the sergeant, louder than before. "Lance Sheets." The name bounced off the faded walls around him; his eyeballs showed him nothing but black air and clouds. Each of his fingers was twisted around the other. New inductees of the Homeland Army bent their necks to look at him.

If to step forward was the army and to stand still was prison, neither option contained freedom. But, he reminded himself, there was always a third way.

"Lance Sheets?" the sergeant called again.

He blinked his eyes clear. More heads turned his way. His knees sizzled, bouncing up and down in their sockets. He bit his teeth together to try and force them still.

"You're sure?" the staff sergeant said to him. "You have to be sure."

Each limb was soft, gelatinous. He felt near collapse.

"Just step forward," said the second lieutenant. "It's that simple."

The second lieutenant looked at the captain. The captain looked at the sergeant.

The sergeant tapped his foot. The captain sighed. All of them looked at Lance.

"Step forward," said the captain. "Now."

"You're going to have to step forward, son," said the second lieutenant.

"We don't have all day," said the sergeant.

All the days since Lorrie had gone were one long day in which yesterday and last week could just as easily have been tomorrow or a month from now. How exactly he had arrived here seemed an infinitely small series of events, each one impossible to pinpoint.

"What's that?" the second lieutenant said.

"Speak up, you coward," the sergeant growled.

"No," Lance said. "You heard me the first time."

15.

Back in Western City North, Lorrie's mind had been full of misapprehensions, dazzled by all the wrong things. Now, in Interior City—that land of traditional, bighearted, and ruggedly individual Homeland citizens—she could finally focus. She would stop the war by blocking its supply.

As it stood, the war showed no signs of ending. Two attacks on the Homeland's Strategic National Stockpile just within the last two weeks. *Leave us alone,* scientists on television pleaded, their appeals broadcast on hundreds of channels, their words reprinted in thousands of newspapers. *We're warehousing vaccines, antidotes. This is a place of medicine. That's it.*

Though most major newspapers preferred to refrain from even printing the word, everyone knew what those terrorists were looking for. And now, Lorrie guessed, the prime minister would stomp all over the Coyotes and use the attacks to justify another surge. With so much to do, she was worried about time.

I need, she thought, *to live forever.*

Asking around, she had discovered an anti-Registry center in the southeast quadrant of the city. A place that counseled men about their options and whether they had any. The official name of the place was the Registry Assistance and Counseling Center (RACC), but after a day it was clear that everyone just called it "the Center."

Her first day made her nervous. Even going to an anti-Registry center in Interior City was more weighted, more fraught than Western City North, where opposition to the war had started early and was easily anticipated by anyone paying attention. Interior City, on the other hand, was a small town clothed in big-city trappings.

In other parts of the Homeland, the general wisdom was that the Foreigns perpetrated attacks that maximized casualties, whereas some faction of antiwar Homeland citizens carried out attacks that minimized them. As for the recent round of weird attacks—the Homeland Army uniforms sculpted into skirts and dresses, the armored cars filled with charcoal—no one in any part of the Homeland had any ideas about that. But in Interior City, most found discussion of the so-called "weird" attacks to be an uninteresting distinction. This was not a region that had elected any Coyotes to parliament. In Interior City, an attack on the Homeland was an attack on the Homeland.

That first day, Lorrie wore long sleeves and an ankle-length skirt to cover the scars and scratches imprinted on her limbs. The Center occupied the bottom floor of a decaying four-story building that was home to several families who had escaped from the Foreigns just before the Old War. The building was badly in need of repair, as were most of the two-family bungalows on the block surrounding it. After a late-night assault by pro-war patriots, a window in the back room of the Center had been clumsily boarded up with plywood, a shoddy repair job that sneaked wisps of cold air into every room. But the Center—despite its mysteriously shifting roof leaks and rickety foundation—was the locus of anti-Registry action in Interior City. To be sure, Lorrie heard, there had been other centers. But those others had been harassed by neighbors, raided by the Registry, fallen under the glistening spell of the

Fareon folks, or simply lacked the funds to operate. For anyone opposed to the war in Interior City, the Center was all there was.

Eric was the leader, a role Lorrie could spot immediately. His hair was styled and fashionable, he wore motorcycle boots, and his face was arranged in a way that implied that once he reached middle age he would look like the kind of man who had been very handsome in his twenties. She was unclear on why the Registry didn't yet have him. From across the room she watched as Eric finished a plum and spat out the pit in the garbage. A plum! Nobody had those anymore; the mere fact of possession set him apart from the rest. Lorrie hadn't seen one in years.

By late morning, all the volunteers had shuffled in and taken seats on the metal folding chairs in the back room, spines erect and shoulders level, all of them ready for an inspirational morning speech. Something to rally the volunteers before a long day of informing desperate men of their slim chances.

Eric rose and exited the circle, a movement that forced Lorrie and the rest of the group to rotate their heads in order to see him.

"We do not hope for an overnight revolution," Eric began. Most of the volunteers closed their eyes or looked at their laps; a few followed Eric's movements and placed a flat hand over their brows to shield their eyes from the brightness of the sun. His voice was indistinguishable—not an Interior City accent, but not identifiable as originating from some other sector of the Homeland, either. "We are not fools. We cannot be childish enough, naïve enough, to think the war will end tomorrow, that if we just march hard enough, often enough, we have done our work."

Don't mention Fareon, Lorrie thought. Already she liked the place, could imagine herself working here. But one conspiracy theorist was all it took to turn a group on itself.

Eric went on, walking faster around the outer edges of the circle now, his red gingham shirt leaving trails of leftover morning light as he passed. "A true revolution reaches far," he was saying, "and is the completion of a course. Our course"—he paused—"is far from over. Our course has only just begun."

Susan, the only other woman Lorrie's age in the room, nodded her head. She wore a bright yellow minidress with a big zipper up the front. Nothing special. But when Susan crossed her legs, Lorrie saw half the volunteers move their eyes over the faultless curve of her thighs. Beneath Lorrie's long, heavy skirt lay two limbs pocked with fist-sized sores, the dark blotches brought on from her months of obsessive scratching. Susan and her perfect shiny legs made Lorrie feel like some sort of animal.

"Any questions?" Eric asked.

Immediately people began to argue.

Nobody at the Center, it seemed, could ever agree on anything. Even official statutes of the Homeland were often unclear: Were there really any antisodomy laws on the books? What actually happened when you called the Point Line? All could agree that the Homeland obscured the rules, but deciding what to do about those hypothetical rules was much more difficult.

"We need to vote on our Fareon position," said one man.

"I've already drafted a manifesto of support," said another.

"Of support?" came the cry. "How can you support something that doesn't exist?"

As one volunteer stood and spoke in an attempt to cajole the others into the embrace of adopting some stance, another person would immediately disagree. Any plan orbited a set path only for a moment until banged off course by counterproposals, cuts, deletions, and amendments.

The position paper on Fareon was soon forgotten as others wanted to discuss a legislator from some distant part of the Homeland who had joined the Coyotes and given a timid speech from the parliament floor detailing his hope of drawing down troop levels by as much as a quarter in the next five to seven years.

"We should send a letter of support!" cried one member.

"Capitulator!" came the response from across the room.

Up next, a local elected official, asking the anti-Registry center to officially denounce violent opposition to the war.

"Just the attacks where people die," someone said. "We only should condemn those."

"Just these new weird attacks," another argued. "We condemn violence, but we like it when they fill Registry trucks with charcoal and dress up mannequins in Homeland Army miniskirts."

"Sellout!"

"Militant!"

Words as sharp as the points of diamonds hurled from one volunteer to another, until finally: "That's Homeland Ideology!"

The ultimate insult. No one wanted to be accused of dancing anywhere close to the governing principles of the Homeland. All of them, they were sure, had shed that dead skin.

What the hell was Eric doing? Lorrie thought. This place needed a leader, not just some guy giving vague speeches before crawling into his shell once reality poked its head through. In some ways, though, she understood the challenges of containing such an unruly mob. Clearly, as soon as a volunteer established himself, he would be snapped up and have to go on the run. These men shouting out ideas were probably in their first or second week of attendance. The men of the Center, save Eric, were on a steady rotation. Yet another thing, Lorrie saw, that needed fixing.

After the talk, Lorrie went up to Susan and introduced herself. Though she just wanted to talk, she felt blazoned, on display, as though her mere presence as a woman in this place was a barely tolerated trespass. And now the only two women were talking? Ridiculous. Women were the only ones who could stick around. *Let their teeth clatter,* Lorrie thought. *Soon there will be more of us.*

Lorrie and Susan faced each other in the small back room as the men filed out to counsel.

"So, Lorrie. How many words per minute?" Susan's large eyes were a peculiar shade of grey.

"Pardon?"

"How fast can you type?" The large grey eyes were fixed on her. "Eric wants these notes typed up for our leaflet by the end of the day. I can't do it all alone."

"Well—"

"Look." Susan gestured around the room. A volunteer named Doug was having trouble twisting the top off a pill bottle; another young man with an old face sat at a small table in the corner attempting to tune the radio. Lorrie could see he had the sort of quivering hands that just might keep him from the Registry, and she noticed his stomach was pouched like that of a small boy. Maybe that counted for something, too. "These guys have things to do," Susan said. "Doors open in a few minutes. Are you going to help me or not?"

"You don't counsel?"

Susan looked as though she wanted to run the other way. "Counsel? Me?"

"Have they not trained you yet?"

"Oh no," Susan laughed. "Eric and the rest of the committee believe that to truly understand someone's plight, you have to be able to experience it."

"I see," Lorrie said. An obstacle she had not foreseen. The only question would be determining the most efficient way to remove it.

"Good. Let's go work in the back. We just distract them when we're up front anyway." Susan laughed a huge laugh, too large for her frame. Lorrie didn't smile.

Susan and Lorrie headed to a musty side room around the corner from where the men were counseled on their chances. Every now and then, vague sounds from the sessions consolidated into words in the air around them: *Run. Hide. Pay.* Mostly the sounds from the counseling room weren't words at all, just sobs and pale, desolate moans.

From opposite ends of the small, windowless room the two of them pounded away on their antiquated machines, battery operated so as not to be affected by the blackouts. When the lights finally did go out, they lit candles and kept typing. The buckling springs beneath their keys made for a constant racket, and often Lorrie had to ask Susan to speak up; her bad ear muddied sounds. Susan, she learned, had refused to break off her engagement to her fiancé, who was currently on the run. Her parents were upset, and she hadn't heard from the fiancé in weeks. When Susan shifted the conversation and asked how long Lorrie had been in Interior City, Lorrie added the time she had spent in the Facility to her answer.

"I just can't believe anyone would move here from Western City North," Susan said.

"It was actually kind of terrible out there. It's just so crazy in that place."

"But so vibrant, they say," Susan said, exhaling. "Western City North. Popping and jumping. So wild."

"Too wild."

Susan laughed her huge laugh once again, and Lorrie turned around and watched her shoulders tremble, as though "wild" was just some inventive wordplay and not a state of mind that was much, much more than anybody should ever have to endure.

Lorrie decided that she was not willing to put up with this typing shit for much longer.

But how to get Susan on her side?

❖ ❖ ❖

"War is a fiction," Eric began. The volunteers of the Center were circled around him for another morning inspirational, words to inspire before the counselors counseled and Susan and Lorrie typed and filed. "A false need created by individuals."

By now Lorrie could see that the ruddy shore of Eric's leadership would soon be completely washed to sea. Brash when the situation called for timidity, clear as a ghost when a spokesperson was called for, the man was a disaster. Sure, he was attractive in a generic sort of way. But what the Center needed, Lorrie knew, was a manager who could marry a tacit understanding of the operations the Center already had under way with a vision of how to improve them. Instead, the Center had a guy who liked to listen to himself talk.

"We expose the system," Eric was saying, "in order to reveal that the entire structure designed to protect us is actually causing us harm."

How much longer was Eric going to drone on? Lorrie massaged her fingers and wondered if she should get a skirt as short as the tight-fitting olive-green one that outlined Susan's perfectly proportioned hips. No way. Besides, even if she did have the figure to pull off an outfit like that, there were still the scars. Always the scars.

Eric went on, slipping through the chairs of two volunteers in order to pace behind the circle, hands waving, his unsparing voice hovering above their heads. "Why are people so scared to come here? Yes, we've all been harassed by the Registry, had their agents knock on our doors on day one to warn us, day two to cajole, and the day after that to threaten. But what are the results for us when people attack the Homeland? It doesn't matter whether it's a serious attack that kills people or one of those weird ones, like filling an unguarded tank full of charcoal. The point is: all this terminal havoc serves to convince people that opposing the war involves some sort of miserable sacrifice."

Sure, Eric had some interesting points, but what was he doing to help anybody? A whole lot of nothing. Lorrie directed her gaze to Susan's skirt. Her legs really were perfect.

Eric, still speaking, came to a stop directly behind Lorrie, a rise in his voice. Drops of spittle rained down on the crown of her head, and for a moment Eric was the baby-leader and Lorrie was whisked back to the Facility once again. Bugs, shame, and the Young Savior, Eric/baby-leader said. Bugs bugs bugs.

The lemmings around the circle began to clap.

"Tom? Jane?" Eric looked to his parents. "Anything to add?"

Young Savior help me, Lorrie groaned to herself. More talking.

Both Tom's and Jane's faces were pasted with ecstatic grins. She had heard that Eric's parents often dropped by the Center and that his relationship with them was showy and alluring. All of the other volunteers, Lorrie was sure, wished that their mothers and fathers would use words like "Homeland" and "tyranny" as close together as did Tom and Jane.

"Tom," Eric would say, "can you help me out here? How to better articulate that if you just want to be pure of heart and sacrifice yourself to a cause, well, you're a good martyr, and that's nice and all, but you're in it for yourself and not the rest of us. Do you have a way you could help me put that, Tom?"

Lorrie had never known a person to speak to his or her parents like this. Of course her parents loved her, or so they said, though infrequently. Mostly those words had come upon her break with Lance and a few more times after she was let out of the Facility. Not that having parents who opposed the war changed anything. Tom droned on, repeating much of what his son had just said.

The mother was different.

Jane's face was gentle. She had neat, greying hair and wide, welcoming cheekbones. Unlike her son, Jane spoke from in front of her chair; no need to crane necks or rotate eyeballs to see her. Though she had no official position, Jane was the only woman at the Center with any sort of power.

"I want to talk today," Jane began, "about aesthetics. How is it going to look, men, going into Quadrant Four with hair combed so far away from the scalp you have to duck under a doorway? And, ladies, knocking on doors with no brassiere?"

A group of faces turned toward Susan, who immediately began to tug at the sides of her skirt, her pitiful action completely ineffective against the small amount of stretchy fabric. Jane avoided eye contact and continued. "Think about how you look before you go down to some quadrant where angry out-of-work Majority Groupers who can't sell their homes are just about to boil. You think they'll crack a screen door for one of you with your hair greased up and stinking? You think they'll want to hear what you have to say?"

Poor Susan crossed her legs, then uncrossed them. Jane seemed not to notice.

"Now, ladies," Jane continued. "We're barely in this. It's our men who are on the line, who the Registry wants, so we're lucky to even have a seat at the table. With that in mind, don't look cheap. Don't come with wild hair and your flesh showing this way and that." She clasped her hands together. "I'm not saying it's wrong or right, I'm not passing judgment, but think about who we're dealing with. You'll set the words off in these men's minds, you'll hand the insults right over. Look like someone they know, remind them of their mother or sister. Good? Good."

More shame, Lorrie thought. This woman was an expert shamer. There had been no mention of the Center's long wait times, nothing about the marginal benefits the Center actually offered to those who could access its services, and a complete dismissal of the fact that many of the unruly counselors seemed to be poorly trained. Who cared what any of them were wearing when what they were doing was nothing more than chanting silly songs in the rain? Even so, Jane seemed to possess an accessible, ever-ready passion. She was already wound up, Lorrie saw. She would just have to point her in a different direction.

While Jane talked, Lorrie watched as Tom bit into a peach and her son popped a cherry into his mouth. The First Family of the Center, it seemed, had a line on impossible fruits. No one, Lorrie noticed, was invited to share them. But then again, had anyone ever asked?

Lorrie made her way over to Jane. An older woman in a predominately male environment, she knew, should be eager to take on a humble apprentice, provided the flattery was subtle and light. But before she could get to Jane, Susan stepped into her path.

The moment Susan opened her mouth, the lights went out. Even so, the Center was still open for business, ready to offer advice to any of the slope-shouldered men who walked in the door. No power or electricity was necessary; any of the counselors could light a candle and see the sad faces of their clients in the dark.

"Let's do this," Susan said.

A blue ribbon of rage ran through Lorrie, but she quickly swallowed it. The more people on her side, the better. *Take your time, Lorrie.*

"You know, about what Jane said," Lorrie began. "I really don't—"

"Just forget it and help me out, okay?" Susan said. "Didn't you see those lines outside? We're slammed."

The two of them headed to the side room with notes from Eric's latest lecture, ready to transfer the handwritten words into printed ones. The typewriters—heavy manual orbs kept around for their ability to ignore the frequent losses of power—came in handy that day. Over the din of their clacks, Lorrie could hear the counselors counsel. Lately it seemed men just came to the Center to cry.

After each visit, a counselor would come around the corner and hand Susan or Lorrie his notes from the session. The charting was inconsistent and depended on the counselor. There were, Lorrie saw, few quantitative measures in these scribblings. How they could help people on a mass scale by jotting down feelings was beyond her.

"Here's my latest." A man with a sloppy smile and browned teeth handed her a folder. Lorrie struggled to remember his name. Upon opening the folder, it came to her immediately. This was Doug, a counselor so twisted off Substance Q or some harder drug that his notes were made up of strange scribbled labyrinths that blurred Lorrie's eyes if she looked too hard. Lorrie couldn't imagine he was helping anybody avoid anything. She thanked him for the notes and returned to her filing.

Inside the musty room where Lorrie and Susan typed, newspapers were stacked everywhere. Though no one could remember who had come up with the idea, the Center had a subscription to every underground publication that could be found. Each day, the long-suffering mailwoman dropped off several crates that Lorrie stacked against the back wall. But what does it matter? Eric had said when Lorrie asked about the unread papers. If there were any sound theories about how to go about doing things in those papers, Eric said, the Center was probably already practicing them anyway. *Ridiculous,* Lorrie thought. But Eric, it was clear, did not play the learner, only the learned.

As a possible ally, Susan was proving disappointing. She kept a large, old-fashioned radio on her desk tuned to loud, instrumental music whenever the power allowed it. For Susan, there seemed to be a power in transcribing the pain of these men. Perhaps, Lorrie thought, she was wishing their souls into safety as she took down a record of their fears. But Lorrie didn't want to wish. With no one else up to the task, it was clear she would have to change the Center by herself. Not that it would be easy. There were no scripts for this type of takeover.

Her thoughts were interrupted by the return of electricity. The sudden clamor of a fast song pushed into the room. A woman sang of her last memory: a smudge of makeup on her lover's cheek as she kissed him good-bye.

"Here," said Susan, adjusting the volume of the radio and twisting around to hand her a typed sheet of paper. "Can you give this a once-over?"

The notes were from an Eric lecture a few days ago on whether a government that claimed roots in participatory democracy could even legitimize the concept of the Registry. Basic stuff to their counterparts in Western City North, Lorrie thought, but at least he wasn't leading them into a cherry-picked world of ill-sourced Fareon facts. Even so, the underground papers—at least the ones Lorrie read—were jammed full of the kind of stuff that Eric was presenting as new and radical. Lorrie knew that resisters throughout the Homeland had tried to make similar arguments in court only to have judges strike down this line of thought en masse. But because the volunteers around her seemed so excited— "someone will *definitely* want to reprint this soon"—Lorrie dutifully did as she was asked and circled a few places that needed commas, made note of a dangling modifier, combined several sentences with participial phrases, cut down on one too many conjunctive adverbs, and changed an "affect" to an "effect."

"Whoa," said Susan when she handed the paper back. A frown hung on Susan's face, and her forehead was puckered.

"What?"

"This isn't what I was asking, Lorrie." Susan stared into the paper. "This is a joke, right?"

"What do you mean?"

"Ideas, Lorrie." She waved the paper over her head. "I wanted to know what you thought about the logic, whether the ideas progressed in a reasonable order. You know how Eric is: introductions at the end, conclusions in the beginning."

"Oh." Lorrie reached out her hand. "As a matter of fact, I do have some thoughts in that regard."

"I don't know." Susan made no move to return the sheet. "I really don't like what you did here. This is not an attitude I like."

"Grammar?"

"That's exactly what I'm talking about, Lorrie. You've really got to drop all this stuck-up crap."

Lorrie knew she shouldn't get drawn in to a battle on this. Intelligible messaging was the least of the Center's problems. She took a deep breath in. "I'm just trying to understand. You think it's stuck-up that I repaired a sentence or two?"

"Repaired? Listen to yourself! It's like you think you have some sort of patent on speech."

Oh boy. Larger goals be damned, Susan needed a quick refresher in basic communication. "The sentence you're talking about barely meant anything." Lorrie wheeled her chair closer to Susan in order to point out one of the more egregious errors. "It was near gibberish. Listen: 'After counseling resisters all day, a soft bed seems a welcome sight.' It's a dangling participial phrase. It should read—"

"Just stop." Susan rolled her chair backward, clutching the paper to her chest. She breathed in, pushed out her cheeks, and sucked them in again. "What you're doing right now, this is Homeland Ideology in action."

The most hurtful insult one could speak at the Center, and Susan had spoken it to her. A white-hot accusation, a slash to her cheek with a sharp blade. "Communicating clearly is Homeland Ideology? Understanding each other makes me a Homeland representative?"

"The message isn't in the construction." Susan had rolled as far away from Lorrie as she could, back toward her desk. She grabbed a blank piece of paper from a stack piled in front of her and began to write rapidly. "Here," she said, extending the paper toward Lorrie disdainfully.

broun doun renoun toun hewed

"What? I can't make any sense of this."

"Fine." She grabbed the paper back, hunched over, and scribbled again.

Tear tayre tare

"I don't understand what you're trying to tell me."

"Don't you get it?" She peered at Lorrie with wet, frustrated eyes. "Way back when, back before all this, before the Homeland, when someone wanted to write a book, they just took some old sheepskin and printed whatever they wanted in whatever way they felt like. And people understood, you know?"

"So?"

"It's all just another weapon, these rules of yours, in the name of propaganda and obtusification."

"That's not even—"

"Just look at the history," Susan continued. "Rich people buy up all the land, print up dictionaries, and lo and behold, Homeland Ideology."

"You don't even know what you're talking about." Lorrie's fists were clenched and her skin felt hot.

"How dare—"

"Ladies, ladies," Lorrie heard Eric say. It was lunchtime, and he wore his high boots, pigskin gloves tucked beneath his armpit. "Wow. Look at you two go. Did I interrupt something?"

Immediately more heads poked around the corner. A small semi-circle of counselors on break shuffled into the back room to see what the commotion was all about.

"I was just trying—"

"The girls are at it again," said Doug. His eyes were glazed and messy.

"Caged heat," said a scratchy-voiced counselor Lorrie had never spoken to.

Susan gave a hard look to a worn square of linoleum beneath her feet.

"Fuck off," said Lorrie.

"Calm down. I just wanted to ask you girls a question," said Eric.

"Yes?" Lorrie said.

"Fire away," said Susan.

"But maybe I need to let you relax first."

"Ask the fucking question, Eric," said Lorrie.

"Maybe you two could kiss and make up," said Doug. "A nice big tongue kiss to tell each other you're sorry."

The flock of counselors swayed and tittered.

"Yeah, kiss!" said Scratchy Voice.

"Damn the sodomy laws!" said his friend.

"There are no sodomy laws," cried another. Laughs all around.

Lorrie could recognize she was in the thick of a singular moment. There was an opening here, an invitation to act in a manner that would enlighten the men around them, de-escalate the situation, and bring her critique of the Center to the forefront. But before she could act, she watched as Susan leaned over and yanked the cord of her massive radio from the wall. Bending her knees and lifting, she wrapped both arms around the heavy machine. "All I was doing was trying to help!" Susan screamed.

"What the fuck?" said Eric.

Susan released her grip. As the radio crashed to the floor, an explosion of parts scattered on the stained tiles below. Susan turned the corner, walked through the lobby, and stomped out of the double glass doors.

"Whoa," said Doug. His pupils had expanded ferociously, the dark circles dull and flat.

"What's the deal?" said the scratchy-voiced counselor.

"She'll be back," said Eric, his round head shaking. "Some people."

"That was a good radio," another voice said.

"Crazy bitch," said Doug.

Everyone laughed, and Lorrie heard herself joining in. The sound of failure.

As the counselors shuffled away, Lorrie went and got a broom and a dustpan. There was no way anyone could fix that radio, so she just tossed the smallest parts into the trash. Most of the insides had fallen out, so she left the husk to rest in the corner where it wouldn't bother anyone. Her stomach told her it was lunchtime, but Lorrie knew there would be a line of men in front of the Center, all of them with no idea what to do next. Was anything in this place helping those men?

She tried to push the question away, but some part of her knew that if a question was worth asking in the first place and no answer came, wasn't it worth it to ask again?

16.

The dance is tonight. Not one girl from the sister school has agreed to go with Alan, but then again, he had not managed to ask anyone, either. He reminds himself that people who have not challenged themselves should not be disappointed when their goals stay unmet. Nonetheless, he is.

Tomorrow, all fourth-years will receive their assignments from the Registry. The boys will hold their sealed envelopes up to the light, a few of them drunk from some homemade cider they have saved for just this occasion, their eyes squinting in the shafts of sunlight, all hoping that they are the ones offered a job as a cook or driver. But that day has not yet come. For there is still tonight. And tonight is a dance. And at a dance, anything can happen.

Months ago, the boys filled out their forms. For those in Majority Group, Alan has read, the Registry form is a paper of possibilities. Maybe you'll be lucky, the form says to these boys, maybe you won't have to fight. But the pamphlets have spoken to him, and now he knows: for Homeland Indigenous, for graduates of the School, the form is different, not a matter of *if*, but instead a circling shark, hungry and biding its time, sure to strike just as soon as it's ready.

From his bed, Alan had watched as Gad's pen attacked the thicket of printed boxes. Weight. Height. Few of the questions on the paper left room for possibility. And then Gad paused. *Name and Address of Person Who Will Always Know Your Address.*

Gad had looked at Alan. A slight nod.

Both of them knew then what they know even better now: the real is getting closer.

❖ ❖ ❖

Priests and nuns roam through the crowd, demanding light and space between dancers and catching each other's eyes in glances that say they hope these kids aren't the future. From Alan's perch on the wall, he spots Gad, toes pivoting, heels rising, his entire body gliding above the gymnasium floor in perfect agreement with the music. A glistening nun slides a wedge beneath the steel door; the burst of warm desert wind passes over the sweaty crowd unnoticed. Gad sways, flows, and bounces, looking truly comfortable as he twirls the girl in front of him around. *The one place*, Alan thinks, *where Gad has more power than me.*

The generators are fired up; no loss of power can ruin the end-of-the-year dance. While the younger students sway and shuffle, Alan sees that the boys who are due a letter from the Registry in the morning dance with the most abandon. Except for him.

Inches away from Gad, a girl Alan has never talked to but now realizes he has always loved does the same wild steps right back. The song rises to a scream, followed by a pause—a gap in sound that Alan is sure that every dancer on the gymnasium floor but him seems to have anticipated—until a blast of horns replaces the silence and every one of his whirling classmates lets out a joyful shudder that races up the length of their bodies until the entire crowd throws their heads toward the rafters and howls along.

Other kids are with him, involuntarily pressed in a row against the wall. None of these boys are halfies. They're all full-blooded Indigenous, no exceptions. Girls, it seems, even the Homeland Indigenous ones, find half-breed features irresistible. The thumps of Alan's heart are unreasonably hard. *Why can't I just grab a girl and get out there?* In every area of his life, he is strong, powerful, a leader. Only now, when girls and music are involved, does the world become lopsided. Small skirts, swaying thighs. On every female face he sees a smug look of separation. Their deepest desires are all aimed elsewhere.

Across the gym, three girls sit in folding chairs. These girls are, Alan knows, the leftovers. The few erotic model types that dampen the socks of everyone are spoken for, their feathery bodies floating high above the dance floor. These final three are the clumsy, the uncomfortably zitty, and the thickly bespectacled. But through the crowd, Alan sees a fourth girl has joined them. He has spoken to her before. She is pleasant, she has a pretty smile on her longish face, and she is, he realizes, the deliverance from all his problems.

He angles his way toward her, passing through waves of dancing couples, his throat dry, the five words forming in his throat. It's not hard, he tells himself. Five words and she can end the misery.

Closer, only steps away. *Would you like . . .* The words are there, ready. Two more steps and he'll be right in front of her. *Would you like to . . .* He will need to be close for her to hear him over the music. He will need to lean in. *Would you like to dance?* Easy. And then, slanting in from a sharp angle, a much shorter boy steps in front of him. Whatever magic collection of words this tiny idiot speaks, Alan cannot hear. He watches the long-faced girl extend a shockingly perfect hand as he leads her toward the dance floor. Alan lets out a deep breath. Perhaps he can continue exhaling, he thinks, and deflate himself right into a pile of clothes on the floor.

His face raw, he runs to the bathroom. Catching his reflection in the mirror, he cannot recognize the dainty, weak boy before him.

Without thinking, his fist bursts out, hurricane-like, and smashes into the mirror. He can barely hear the shatter of glass over the music.

Back in the dormitory, the murky, unnatural rhythms are still easy to hear, and he wants desperately to escape the heavy bass rising up in the chilly desert, bouncing his failure from one old building to another. Yes, that kid was an idiot, but such knowledge still leaves Alan's insides pickled and hopeless, because that idiot also has a girl to dance with, a girl who despite her greasy face still has hair that shines under the bright light, tapered hips that accommodate a pair of hands perfectly, and heartbreakingly long legs that Alan has only ever glimpsed from knee to ankle. And she chose to dance with that half-breed mother-raper? Maybe Alan had made his approach from too far in the shadows. Maybe it was he who she had truly been looking for.

Yeah, right. Logic, he sees, is piss-poor at sending shame on the run.

❖ ❖ ❖

On the hard bed of the empty dorm room, a woman comes to him. But it's not any of the girls from the dance, all of whom had avoided eye contact as they awaited their chance to grind against someone with an appropriate percentage of Majority Group features. All those girls waiting for anyone, Alan thinks, but him.

The Majority Group lady appears, and he talks with her.

"How major?" Alan asks her in a whisper. He drapes the fleshy front of his elbow over the bridge of his nose; the more darkness, the better.

"Incredibly major," she says. "Make it wild. Show them who you are. You're about to ship out anyway."

In the darkness, he can see small spins of color on her lips.

"No one has to get hurt," she says. "Not if you do it right."

"Gad should help me."

"He won't understand. Gad's a halfie, you know that."

Alan sits up. "Yeah, but you're full-on Majority Group."

No answer. The woman is gone. Everyone else is still at the dance, swaying ecstatically around the gym at varying speeds. Now it's just Alan and Hazel the guinea pig, the tiny rodent squeaking pitifully, both of them biting at their cages. Time to make it wild.

17.

The cabin was small. Fungus had begun to eat away at the wood where the logs scribed. After a few circles around the house, Joe could see it was a solid structure with good bones. With Benny in the back of a Registry truck, Joe had no key. Without Benny, there was no clear way in.

He did a quick few paces around the perimeter. A moment of fierce relief that he was in a place where he could feel the wind and smell the dirt. All the windows were shut tight, locked. On the west end of the cabin, hidden from the lake, he came upon a small apple tree. The stalks were thin, dying even, and most of the apples had fallen to the ground, but there was one still on the branch, ripe and ready to go. A dazzling red globe with a small thumbprint patch of yellow, Joe stared at the apple with a violent, motherly love. No one would hurt this apple. He would not pick it, he decided, until Benny was here and the future was a vivid bloom. Only as he turned to walk away did he remember that Benny was in the hands of the Registry. The vision of the two of them sharing that apple faded as quickly as a morning dream. He left the apple untouched and went back to the front of the cabin.

The door was solid. Joe gave it a few light kicks, then some harder ones. Nothing was working. Joe thought about his mother and father, harmonizing in church with their supreme confidence at the mysterious order of human events, the Young Savior smiling down at them. They exhibited a faith that didn't allow for the loneliness and confusion he felt, and it crossed Joe's mind that a state like his own would vault their heads off. They had never been placed in a situation beyond all doubt. Though they thought they had all the answers, they had never truly needed them.

Food, books, earmuffs, gloves. These were the things Joe needed. He looked around the lake. The lake was it. A lake and some trees. Mountains and rocks, stumps and leaves. And no Benny. As the stars emerged, the squawks of strange birds stabbed through the air. The chiming voices of the forest had, up until now, been soft and welcoming. But now, with the cold rising, the place began to reveal its true self.

Benny hadn't mentioned how cold it would be. A burst of icy wind clawed his face. The weight of what was happening was fully upon him. He could not get into the cabin; at this elevation, he could not stay outdoors for the night.

A dark mass of clouds floated across the sky to take away Joe's last rays of light. He put a hand in front of his face and watched the colors of his palm slowly dim to a fuzzy nothing. Thick coffee and warmed milk, a hot mug to wrap his hands around, where was anything he had ever wanted? Darkness settled in, and soon the objects around him faded. With the air cold and metallic, Joe went down to all fours. It was time to break a window.

Knees steering, Joe kept his hands flat in front of him, palms in the dirt, and lightly tapped the ground in search of a good-sized rock. Frozen mud and flat grass slipped between his fingers, and for a brief, pleasurable moment, he saw himself as a little boy in his parents' backyard, dragging his body over the soil of his mother's peonies until his present life thrust itself forward in the sharp slice of a rock across his palm. A surge of blood poured from his broken skin. It hurt like hell. One palm was bloody, the other numb with cold. In the distance he saw a streak of light hurtle through the sky: a shooting star.

Nobody knew Joe was out here but Benny, and Benny was gone, disappeared when he was needed most. The two of them had never been apart.

In his animal position he could smell the wormy odor of the dirt beneath him. A picture of Benny's head entered his vision, and Joe saw himself kicking it. Ten imaginary kicks to Benny for being himself, and five more to his flat head just for being someone Joe needed so much. *Young Savior, help me.*

The swaddling chill felt gigantic. His fingers jingled with the pricks of ten thousand tiny stones, or whatever the hell was driving upward into his hands from the ground below. Still on all fours, Joe had yet to find a good rock to break a window with. He kept crawling, unsure if he was going in circles or not. The cold air stuck to his lungs like a plaster cast. A lump formed in his forehead, an understanding that his own stupidity and hopefulness was the reason he was on the black ground at all.

The lump pushed itself behind his eye. The picture window along the side of the cabin. That was the one. The lump slid down to his throat. A flash of blue before his eyes, along with the fallen notion that for every person there was a glistening other to alleviate the loneliness of being. His left knee bumped against something promising, and Joe reached back and felt a stone the size of a fist. Gripping it, Joe stood up, dropping the lump down his gullet. A small bubble exited his nose and fell to the ground. His chest felt like he had swallowed a razor.

A cloud must have moved and allowed the moon to show up, yellow and round, lighting the surface of all the objects around him. Silhouetted trees jumped off the large window of the cabin. Joe looked into the night before him, and from low in his throat, unbidden, his body released a sound.

A thousand trip-hammers pounding rapidly, a million percussive drills shattering dense rocks into crumbs. The sound from his throat was terrifying, a baleful chorus of all the evil creatures trapped inside him. Where was Benny when he was needed most? The stone in Joe's hand felt impossibly smooth, carved and chiseled to a fist-sized globe, perfect for his grip. Arm whirling, Joe's voice raising high, he knew that the trees would swallow his cries.

Nothing will stop just for me.

Louder and longer, arm windmilling faster with each revolution, Joe pushed out air, the pitch of his scream growing until he finally heard a tremble in his voice. Joe let up his grip on a downstroke. The rock sailed through the glass of the front window, vanishing the lump in his grand noise that was piercing the blackness around him. The hole wasn't large enough. He would have to throw a few more rocks. He did, until the space was big enough to crawl through. As he snaked his body into the window, a small shard of glass cut his shoulder and left a long, deep slice in his skin. But Joe didn't care. He was inside now.

The cabin was entirely dark and completely still. Joe's head bumped against a low-hanging lamp. A short-legged table knocked against his shins. He rushed to the tap, desperate to run hot water over his tender hands, but the faucet let out nothing but the slow hiss of a deep sleep. If he was going to miss his induction, he needed to plug the hole he had made in the window. And get food. All by himself. Benny had been swallowed up. The only question was whether he would let himself be swallowed, too.

For now, he found a cold bedroom and slept.

His dreams were gruesome. Over an impossible connection, his mother yelled: there's a plan for you, a destiny! But even in the dream, Joe knew that when unrolled, her insipid shouts were parts of a story she hadn't thought to read to the end, her own advice ignorant of the fact that the Young Savior had slipped away early, that the carefully plotted diagram of Joe's life and purpose was stacked in a high pile of papers rotting on an untended desk. At least he wasn't alone; thousands of other destinies lay below and above, all of them left to languish while He enjoyed His eternal lunch break, a hundred First Tuesdays passing by in the blink of an eye. *A little help?* Joe shouted into the treetops. No answer, of course; his words fell into a bottomless mass. There was nothing for Joe to soak himself in, not even a drop of His old bathwater.

In the morning, the cold sun poured through the window onto the bed, warming his legs and feet. A yellow dust coated all the furniture and countertops, the tiny motes making small tornado swirls through the air as if disturbed by Joe's presence.

❖ ❖ ❖

The light of day allowed Joe to make a survey of his new surroundings. The cabin consisted of a kitchen with a bar that bled into a living room, a small bathroom with no tub, and a large, rectangular bedroom. Knotty pine for the walls, oak for the straight-backed chairs, and no personal touches to the place except for a dusty vase with some long-dead flowers on the heavy elm table in the dining room. No generator for blackouts. Mice droppings bordered the edges of the walls. Light jumped off the little pieces of glass from the front window that Joe had shattered the night before. The shards were everywhere, and he made sure to keep his boots on.

The light on the stove was beyond dead. In the bathroom, as Joe slid open the shower door, a team of roaches burst into life and skittered down the drain. When he turned on the water to drown them out, the liquid oozed from the showerhead mealy and brown. Benny's uncle had stocked the kitchen well. Joe ran his fingers over the cold metal cans and did a quick survey: boneless turkey, pork chunks, cooked ground beef. The bookshelves were empty except for a massive, ripening stack of old newspapers.

For the next few minutes, Joe picked up the rocks that were scattered all around the cabin. They had rolled everywhere: under the couch, into the fireplace. He needed to talk out loud; without the sound of his own voice, there was a complete absence of human life. "How'd you get here?" he said to a rock that sat in the bottom of an empty wastebasket.

Poking around for more wayward stones, he found a crackled pamphlet demanding answers in regard to the aging of Homeland leaders. The anonymous author detailed the lives of a series of cabinet members who had become fathers in their seventies and eighties, all of them allies of the prime minister. Thanks to Fareon, the pamphlet claimed, these jubilant men were thriving well past their expected expiration dates. The pamphlet struck a tone of conquered spirit, of hope burned and flattened. What power, the pamphlet asked, might a few timid antiwar legislators, the so-called Coyotes, have against these men who could live forever?

After a few minutes, Joe tossed the yellowed booklet aside. He hadn't heard of these statistics, hadn't read before about these old men and their babies. But even so, there was no time to think about the wide chasm of life expectancy between the prime minister's cronies and everyone else, no time to think about why these old men weren't dying. All the days he had ever lived were rushing toward one: First Tuesday. Joe needed to make a choice.

Whatever happened in the next stretch, he knew his decision needed to be sharp and unbreakable. Instead, all he had was a dull and gnawing doubt. *Young Savior, help me.*

In a closet, he pushed aside more old newspapers until he came upon a toolbox. He decided to cover the smashed window, a reasonable gesture, he thought, whether he stayed or not. From that same closet he grabbed a heavy jacket with mold-stained sleeves, shook it, and went outside. Laid against the back of the house were three large sheets of plywood. There were nails in the toolbox, as well as a short saw with long, sharp teeth. After measuring the size of the window and marking the dimensions on the wood, Joe found two flat stones and laid a plank across them. As a makeshift sawhorse, it would have to do.

The saw's teeth bit into the wood. Like anyone else, Joe had seen pictures of Homeland hospitals with rows of torsos, bodies chopped at the waist, humans cut short, their structures flipped open. His sawing was smooth and clean, and the wood didn't splinter. As he worked, the world above him poured out blue birdsongs he couldn't understand. But Joe also knew that in this same moment, with each stroke of the saw, coffee was being served piping hot at the Unicorn, wild-haired men were being trimmed and trained and boarded onto buses, and that the solid earth still spun on its axis even with him up here all alone and not witness to any of it. Even though the air was cold, Joe broke out in sweat. He finished sawing, and the wood was cut down to size.

Picking up the plank, Joe listened as the leaves crunched and rattled beneath his feet. His parents would have liked a call, Joe knew that. First, his mother would ask about church, followed by a fatherly monologue about how the door to a respectable life started and stopped with Joe showing up at the induction center and coughing on command for the Homeland. Joe thought back to the religious classes he had faithfully attended each and every Sunday of his youth. The prophets, he knew, when they needed to think on something, to locate the ultimate origin of a problem, would go apart from their towns and live for a time in agony and solitude. So far, so good; he had that part down. But that was it. Ostracism and exile were all he had accomplished. What was the next step?

The whole forest is chattering, Joe thought, *but there's nothing I can take from it.*

With a final heave, he lifted the plank to the window frame. Immediately he recognized that he had miscalculated. His measurements were off, and the plywood had been cut far too small for the inset of the window.

It was early; the sun was still plenty high. If he wanted to leave, to surrender himself to the Registry, he had to decide soon. A bird called down from the trees. He checked the measurements of the plank and tried again, lifting the wood against the frame. It still didn't fit. His sawing, his measurements, something had been off. All alone, Joe thought, in the earthly beauty of the forest, true isolation, just vast swaths of wilderness, a wide and empty landscape, devoid of the one person he wanted to see. Or anyone, really.

It felt like a prison.

18.

Benny knew he was moving before he opened his eyes. A sightless survey of his surroundings: on his shoulder, a damp and unidentified pressure, seeping through the fabric of his coat. Below him, a mechanical hum vibrated the floor. None of it felt right.

Mostly he was confused. His coat was damp, but the revelation that he was wearing a coat at all was much more of a surprise. Someone had been inspecting this very coat, that much he was sure of, but how and why and how long ago all that had happened, his ragged thoughts could not figure. All he knew was that his shoulder was wet and that, somehow, he was moving.

Thoughts came in small, heavy slices, and though waves of pain rolled throughout his body, he did not think to open his eyes. Another bang, that was what he needed, just a sniff or snort to clear his thoughts. But the humming floor, the angled dampness on his shoulder, the swinging ache in his jaw. Something was wrong, and so, Benny thought, he would keep out the world, if only for a few minutes more.

But the world kept coming. Thinking clearly was difficult, as he was sure a small hammerstone was battering the thin bone behind his forehead, an internal pounding that dragged each brief spark of a thought immediately to the guillotine, an endless cycle of quick birth and death. No idea stuck until, finally, one did: Touch a finger, this cognitive survivor told him, to the wetness of your shoulder. Yes, he decided. To find out why his shoulder was wet was important. Just as rapidly, this thought, too, gave way to another: Why am I not able to touch my shoulder? Followed by: Why are my hands tied? And finally: How about I open my eyes?

Yes, Benny. Open your eyes.

Instantly, that rare life phenomenon: an immediate answer. The wetness on his shoulder was saliva. A strange man was resting his chin against Benny's shoulder, the banks of his teeth pouring forth a rushing river of drool. The man's eyes were closed, his breaths slow. Answer two delivered itself just as rapidly: the vibration beneath him was the slow hum of an engine, and gradually the scene before him took shape: he was on a hard bench, in the back of a truck, a man next to him semiconscious and drooling on his shoulder, his hands tied with some sort of thin cable. All around him were more men in various states of alertness. A softly fermenting smell of sweat coated them all, and Benny found the thick stench that had invaded his nostrils hard to bear.

"What is this?" Benny asked to no one in particular. His voice hovered over the truck hold. One man was snoring hard, the deep sleep of a Substance-smasher. No one answered. "Where are we?" Benny asked again, his voice pinched and rising.

"Not so loud!" a man from the far end of the bench yelled, far too loudly.

Benny understood. Simply speaking those three words had sent waves of pain through his fragile skull. To pull oneself so radically away from a planned day of Substance smashing was to dry out a small plant in desperate need of mere drops of water. From the looks of the men in the truck, they, too, had been snipped from the tree much too early.

Again he spoke, softer this time. "Does anybody know where we are?"

The same man answered, offering only the side of his face, as if to turn toward Benny was too much. "The Registry, man. This is the Registry."

"What?" slurred Benny.

The unhappy man seemed to gain strength from Benny's ignorance. They were, he explained, in the midst of what he had heard was called Operation Lowlife, though he had also heard many other names and doubted that one was any more official than the others. "They raid the drug houses," the man explained, "pick up whoever they find, hold us till we're clean, chop our hair off, and toss us into the jungle. Fast track. I didn't know it was true, I'd only heard stories, but look around. It is true, it must be. They say they pull up at a house, scatter or catch the dealers, and grab the users. Now look. That is just what has happened."

"I'm not a user," said Benny.

"Right," the man said.

"Maybe every now and then," Benny mumbled.

The slow hum of the engine disappeared.

"What's that?" Benny asked the man, the only one, it seemed, who could talk.

"That's the next stop."

"The induction center?"

"Oh no. You don't go straight there. They hold you in these detox zones, make sure you're all clean and that the stuff is out of your system."

"But tomorrow is First Tuesday. Why take us today?"

"Was it your turn?" the man asked. "Were you really going to go?"

"Maybe," Benny said. "So you think we're at some detox place?"

"Nope. Take a listen to those screams. We're at another drug house. They need as many of us as they can get."

And though this made sense to Benny, and though he knew on some level that he was included in their numbers, for a brief and unre-deeming moment, he, too, felt worried for the Homeland. *What has it come to*, he asked himself, *if these men surrounding me are the type of men we need to win our fight?*

The man who had been drooling on his shoulder woke up and promptly vomited onto the floor. Benny, who now understood the terms of the world he found himself in, passed out, the Substance still smashing its way through his system.

❖ ❖ ❖

A slash of light bored into his eyeballs as the back door of the truck was ripped open. Benny blinked rapidly, snapping his eyes into focus. Through the slant of the door he saw a tree-lined street. Two familiar-looking uniformed men clad in khaki stood by with large rifles slung over their shoulders. Though bothered by the light, Benny could make out the wooden grip on the shorter guard's rifle, the only part of his long weapon that did not catch the sun. The taller guard was shoving in one man, then another, both of them barely able to walk, the first barefoot, the second with twig arms and legs attached to a skeletal frame. Once shoved through the doors, the barefoot man made the slow effort to crawl toward an empty space on the bench, inching along on his stomach, as his hands, Benny saw, were bound behind him, knotted with a slim spiral of plastic. The other man, no power left, simply closed his eyes and lay on the floor, breaths distant enough from one another that Benny was worried his lungs might simply be forgetting to draw in air.

"Hospital!" Benny croaked. Speaking was still difficult, yelling even more of a challenge. "Get this man to the hospital."

But the doors had already been closed, and with a small shake of life, the truck was once again on the move.

"Grab onto my ankles," Benny said to the man on the floor, extending his feet toward him. It took a moment for Benny to remember that just as his own hands were bound behind his back, this man's were, too. Time for a new tactic. "Slide forward a bit," Benny told him, "and I'll hook your armpits with my legs and pull you toward the bench. You don't want to stay down there."

Indeed, a curling stream of liquid was winding away from the minced heap of vomit piled on the floor, a braided path sliding down the bed of the truck. But the man just looked up at him, smiled, and closed his eyes, placing his cheek flat on the floor.

"Don't you even want to try?"

But the other men, still in their own small worlds, hissed at Benny to be quiet, and the man on the floor lay silent and still. Watching him, Benny could see that it was far too easy to stop living long before you were dead.

Slowly, a routine began to take shape: the truck would stop, fists would bang on doors, yelping men could be heard scattering, followed by the back doors of the truck swinging open to allow two or three more—always those who had been most overrun by the flood, the ones who could barely walk, the men who had not run because they were not able to do so.

It became clear that this was a small, poorly funded, and modest operation. From the dim sounds of each stop, Benny gathered that the driver and his assistant did not chase anyone, only grabbing those Substance-smashers who had drifted too far into a melted mix of inner light and shadows. These smashers, the ones who had not moved, were unprepared for the event of being ripped from their pleasant and hallucinatory world and pushed into a very unpleasant arrival in the real one.

After a few hours, the truck was full. Several of the men were shirtless, or shoeless, or some combination of the two. More hours passed, and Benny heard the motor cut once again, but this time the back door did not open. Instead, they sat, the deep darkness smearing across their thoughts.

"Where do you think we are?" someone asked.

"Downtown," another man answered. "Listen to those sounds."

The man was right. Horns, a drill shattering concrete, crashing cityscapes, the earthly sounds of clustered Homeland citizens moving through the afternoon, living their lives.

And then the muffled voices of what could only be the driver and his assistant arguing, raised speech loud enough to be heard through the metal walls of the cargo hold but stripped of style and meaning. A few of the more alert men pressed their ears against the wall.

"Something about a kid's birthday," the man reported back to them.

But the others shook their heads, accused him of still being in the obscured state of withdrawal. Kids? Birthdays? That's not what these men with inkblots on their hearts talked about. The eavesdropper shrugged, and before long the truck began to move again.

After a while, the loud city sounds died away. A few of the men told stories of the detox zones. Some said they were far from the urban areas so no one had to hear the screams of the unwillingly sober. Others claimed these detox zones were simply short stays in established prisons, the Substance users thrown in cells with the worst the Homeland had to offer. Everyone in the truck, it seemed, had a story, but none of them had the truth.

An hour later—was it really an hour? Benny could not tell—the truck again stopped. Almost all the men were awake now, returning to consciousness and slowly inching like earthworms onto the long rows of seats or benches. Even so, there was not room for everyone, and the latest arrivals were forced to occupy the floor.

With sudden force, the hinged doors swung open. Though the light was bright, it was not hard to make out their location at the entrance to some sort of detention center, watchtowers and heavy gates slathered in barbed wire the only view. Benny noticed they were not inside this prison, but rather parked out front.

"One of you," the guard said. "That's all they've got room for."

Benny looked away, twisting his ear into his shoulder. Eye contact, he knew, could only hurt him. The other men did the same. But burrowing into himself like a frightened ground mole was not, he decided, in his nature. One must act, he told himself, in order to live. "Him," he told the guard, pointing to the barefoot man who had been unable to summon his own strength to move from the floor. "He'll go."

The tall guard nodded and began to pull the man by his ankles. Awakened by the movement, he opened his mouth and moved his lips rapidly. When he realized that no sounds were emerging, he narrowed his eyes, locking them on Benny as he was dragged away. In the subtle language of silence, he put forth the question: *How could you?*

The men looked at Benny, some grateful, others thick with resentment at his brief entanglement with the enemy. But that barefoot man was being dragged to some unfriendly detox zone of a prison and he, Benny reasoned, was not. The stares of the other men slid off him easily. Was not freedom the only dimension of life that made it worth living? He shrugged at a man glaring at him from across the hold. Staying free meant staying ready.

As the door behind them closed, they heard the tall guard say to the shorter one, "Where the hell are we going to take the rest of these guys?"

"Anybody catch where we are?" Benny asked the group.

"I saw a sign," came the answer. "Prison Complex J."

"That wasn't a J. That was a T!" came another voice.

The two men argued, and the truck drove on. Such a cruel joke, Benny thought, that this harsh, stinking cage had carried him past his childhood home. The depth of his own fall was stupefying.

More hours, more driving. Again a stop, and again the muffled sound of an argument coming through the truck walls.

"You must take these men!" they heard one of the guards yell.

The response was captured by the layer of metal between them, but a few phrases shone through: insufficient staffing, lack of provisions, and, finally, not enough beds.

"Wherever we are," one of the men in the truck whispered, "this place is too full to take us."

Another man slapped him on the side of the head for stating the obvious. Outside, the muffled negotiations continued. On edge, each man was silent, and then the doors opened and the guards again appeared.

"One more," the tall one said. The short one stood shaking his head.

All the men again looked away. Benny pondered telling them to take the man who had not stopped eyeballing him since he had suggested the last prisoner. But it was too risky. Nothing could make him more vulnerable than another show of strength. Better to stay quiet.

A long line of silence followed until one man, his clothes ripped and askew, leapt to his feet. "Go ahead!" he screamed. "Take me. Take me away!"

And so they did. But there were still quite a few of them left. And as they again began to drive, a creeping knowledge climbed into the men that they were driving for so long, one detention center to another, because there was no place to put them, that the terrible worlds behind the barbed wire were full and spilled over and that in a country the size of the Homeland, either they would drive for quite a long time or someone in some official capacity would have to start construction very, very quickly.

No wonder they were burying the men in military graveyards vertically now, their coffins upright and standing. There were too many dead, they all knew that, but it was in this moment they realized that there was also not enough room for a good chunk of the living.

❖ ❖ ❖

With the Substance seeping out of their bodies at varying rates, as the more experienced among them knew would happen, the men become very hungry, very quickly. The hunger, though it hit each man on his own internal clock of bruised sobriety, was, upon its arrival, otherworldly. A stomach outside of itself, first a gentle murmuring followed by a heavy rumble that soon gave way to a shocking ache, a protruding message given to the men, few of whom had ever heard anything so clearly: feed me.

Soon the men were pounding on the wall behind the driver's seat. But the truck stopped for no one. From the cab, the garbled snarl of the two guards' voices. Finally the back door swung open. Benny blinked, adjusting his eyes to the new light. High-rising walls of rock hemmed in a two-lane road that seemed to be cutting through a narrow canyon. Wherever he was, it was not somewhere he had been.

The sun was setting, the light in the sky a brilliant mixture of tinged pinks and blues. Though he was tired and hungry, Benny could not help but pause to look up at the majestic colors outlined above him.

"Are you trying to kill us?" a man shouted, breaking the mood. "Give us food, let us use the bathroom, give us water!"

The short guard looked at the tall guard. Both crinkled their noses, and Benny heard the tall one curse the Young Savior for the smell wafting toward them.

"There's a store not too far away," the short guard said. "We can get you a small bite."

"With whose Currencies again?" grumbled the tall guard.

"A small bite?" cried one of the men.

"Shut up," the others yelled, grateful at the promise of anything.

"Let us go to the bathroom?" asked another man, hopefully.

"Fine," said the short guard.

"And unclip their wrists?" said the tall guard.

But unclip they did, the short guard fetching a curved pair of shears with a rusted blade and snapping their zip ties one by one.

Slowly those who were able to walk were allowed, one at a time, the rifle of the tall guard trained on them, to relieve themselves on the side of the road. Once finished, they were again freshly zip-tied behind the back. Zip ties: the one thing the Homeland seemed to possess in plenty.

When it was Benny's turn, he leaned in toward the guard. "Please," he said in a tight whisper, feet on the empty road. "Can't you give me even a sip of water? You must have something."

The mouth of the short guard sagged, and he grabbed Benny by his elbow. "Now listen," he said, his voice low enough for only Benny to hear. "Do you see all those people in the back of this truck? Do you see them? I am just one person, do you understand, one person with a job to do and an angry partner. My own Currencies—not the Homeland's but mine—that's where your small portion of food is going to come from. If I did know what to do with you, where to take you, how to really feed you, I could not do anything different for you than I could do for any of these men. All of them are hungry, same as you."

The men waiting in the truck to use the bathroom began to yell that Benny should hurry up, but the guard continued his rant. "This was not how I was supposed to spend my day. My daughter's birthday was this afternoon, and I have already missed it. Just so you know, I voted, and I voted for a Coyote, a fact that my partner is aware of and frequently chides me for. For the last five hours I have been arguing with him over my choice to spend my own small paycheck to get you men something to eat. Every place I try and drop you, I am told by the warden that it is too full, that we must keep on moving. I am just one person, and I cannot take the miserable choices you have made with your life and make them any better for you. Now get out of my face."

As Benny climbed back in the truck, a leftover quote from some old religious class of his youth came to him; perhaps they were even the words of the Young Savior himself. Either way, he saw their truth: *each of us has his own rhythm of suffering.*

While the two guards conferred, the men waited. All were, of course, ravenously hungry, but with the doors open, Benny's hunger was replaced by the small pleasure of fresh wind on his face.

The tall guard was holding a thick binder. "It says here"--he pointed—"that we are obligated to take them to the next available detox zone before we end our shift."

"But we've taken them to the next available, and the one after that," the short guard said. His voice was nearly a whine.

"Well, whatever holding center we haven't yet tried is the next available."

"You expect me—us—to drive around forever, looking for a place for these men?"

"There must be a place for them somewhere."

"But how long until we've been to every possible location? Should we drive halfway across the Homeland, looking for the next available center, until the last of them has been interred?"

"It's in the book," the guard shrugged.

❖ ❖ ❖

The men felt the truck turn around and head back the way they had come. Though the promised snack had done little to fill their stomachs, the small portions of soupy porridge the short guard had purchased for them had calmed the fire within.

Ever attuned to the movements of the truck, the men felt the jostling motions of a three-point turn. Minutes later, a U-turn, and they were again headed in a new direction. A few minutes after that, another turnaround, and the truck was lumbering, the men were sure, back toward Western City North. The dim light from the crack beneath the doors slowly faded into blackness. Leaning against the back wall, now well acclimated to the thick air and dense stench that surrounded him, Benny closed his eyes and let his head fall to the shoulder of the man next to him. Soon, most of the men drifted off.

A loud and unmistakable bang awoke them, followed by the swerving and swaying of the truck. With hands unavailable for grip and balance, the sharp movements tossed the men to the hard metal floor. The truck skidded to a stop. In the dark, they disentangled themselves from one another. As Benny slid from under another man's shoulder, three more stuttering pops sounded from the cab of the truck.

"Those," Benny said, "were gunshots."

"You don't know what you're talking about," said a voice down by his ankles.

But everyone yelled at that man to be quiet. Because coming through the metal separator of bed from cab, they were sure they heard another noise, a new one: the muffled sound of one man crying.

❖ ❖ ❖

Go, the short guard had told them, lining them up and cutting their zip ties once again. Get out of here. He was heading home to his wife, he said. To his child. He had not signed up to drive around sick, morally pale men for hours on end, and there was, he explained finally, no place to put them.

But go where? It was dark, and none of them knew how far they were from the city. A nighttime chill pushed its way through the open doors of the truck, and a few men attempted to climb back into the truck. The shaken guard lifted his rifle and gestured that no, these men could not stay.

Soon all were gathered on the asphalt of the two-lane road. A swarm of dragonflies buzzed Benny's ears as his eyes struggled to adjust to the clumps and shadows all around him. A heavy wind pushed against his back. Above, the sky was bare and grey; an unending sheet of clouds drowned out even the closest stars.

His hands finally free, Benny plunged them into his coat, where his fingers encountered all sorts of small objects and strange papers floating around those massive pockets, relics of who he was only a handful of hours ago. His eyes adjusted to the landscape around him. Large trees, most of them scarred by fire, surrounded the road. He was tired, he was hungry, his throat was dry and tight. But as Benny looked at the ragged trees around him, a slow, comforting warmth spread upward from his toes. *I am still free,* he thought.

"You have not seen me!" the guard called to them. "It would be better for me to shoot you all right now. Sadly, I cannot bring myself to do it. But let us be clear: none of us will see each other again!"

"How far till the city?" they pressed the guard. "Which way?" But the guard only shook his head and hopped back in the truck, speeding away.

A few of the men felt their way to the side of the road and curled into sleep. But not Benny. He started to walk, the tiny red taillights of his temporary prison falling further into the night.

19.

Lance's trial lasted twelve minutes. His volunteer lawyer sputtered vague philosophical arguments and obscure interpretations of lesser-known Homeland documents that she claimed proved the invalidity of the Registry, while a disgusted jury of Homeland Army veterans and their wives looked on. As the lawyer for the Homeland made her case, the elderly judge nodded his head. There were no peers on the jury; Lance's peers were all in the jungle.

Ideology Five, he saw one juror mouth to another whenever his lawyer spoke. Next to her, another juror ignored the proceedings completely, her head buried in a cheap magazine that devoted most of its print space to aging movie stars and the rising ages of the leaders of the Homeland.

He had thought news of a trial might bring Lorrie back. She would watch quietly from her seat in the courtroom balcony, her eyes fixed as she followed the defense's argument, disgusted at the whole charade and more proud of Lance than she'd ever been. But who was he kidding? Every day there were thousands of trials. Only a few of the papers covered them, and most got only an inch or two at best. Today, the big news was the discovery of yet another unexploded charcoal bomb, this particular one smuggled into the luggage compartment beneath a bus of newly drafted soldiers. The judge had mentioned the story from the bench, repulsed; it was not a good day to be tried for resisting.

"Lance Sheets, please stand," said the judge.

Why should he have to stand? He did not stand.

"Stand!" yelled the judge.

"Please stand," whispered his lawyer.

Lance gripped the edges of his chair and did not let go.

"Stand up!" yelled an out-of-order juror whose face was round and pretty.

Lance looked over at the observation seats. Empty.

"You will," the judge intoned, "stand for the Homeland."

Lorrie could be anywhere.

Two uniformed women came over and jerked Lance to his feet. Lance's lawyer buried her head in her hands.

The judge spat out a sentence. The jury clapped and cheered. A smile from the prosecuting lawyer, a shrug of apology from his counsel, apathy from the empty observation seats.

Nine to twelve years in a Homeland penitentiary.

An officer of the court moved in with chains the moment gavel struck block. Lance was pulled downstairs to the detention center beneath the courthouse, the guards dragging him through yet another series of long halls that ended in a square office with a metal desk and two sagging chairs.

But it was all for show. Away from the popped eyeballs of the seething jury, one woman uncuffed him while another asked him to fill out some forms and return tomorrow.

"Tomorrow?" Lance said.

"Tomorrow," grunted the officer. "There's no room for you yet."

Like so much in life, the loss of freedom, the officer explained, happens in stages. Lance would be followed, undercover agents would track and surveil his every movement, but until a space opened, he was still, in the slimmest sense of the word, free. As he walked out a side door and into the sun, Lance knew that tonight he would set off into the Homeland. Now was the time to find Lorrie. And to his own surprise, he knew just where to start.

❖ ❖ ❖

Back in his building, he banged his fists against Tim's door. Was he too late? How long till Tim said he was shipping out? An outline of a phrase came to him. *A handful.* But what actual number filled that small amount? Perhaps he was too late.

But then a shuffle from the other side of the glass. The moment his neighbor let the door crack, Lance rushed through, breathing heavily. With both hands, he grabbed the collar of Tim's shirt and shoved him against the wall. Tim, startled and smaller, his hands pinned, could not escape.

"Where is she?" Lance growled.

"What?"

"Where is she?" Lance repeated. He tightened his grip around Tim's wrists, pressing them hard against the cracked wall. "You know who I'm talking about."

"Lorrie?" Tim squeaked.

Lance released one of the wrists and angled his forearm across Tim's hot throat.

"I don't know."

More pressure, Tim's neck contracting and expanding in quick bursts just below Lance's arm. Tim was shaking, eyes open wide, knees trembling. How would this guy ever make it in the jungle?

"I said I don't know!" Tim gasped.

Letting him go, Lance walked down Tim's hallway, into the kitchen. Immediately his eyes fell on a slotted wood block, the black handles of several knives swaying seductively.

"What is this, Lance? What are you doing?" Tim had followed him, protesting his presence in this place where he did not belong. "Is this about the trial? It's still not too late. You can always—"

Reaching for the knife, Lance pivoted.

"Okay," Tim said, his hands rising immediately. "Okayokayokayokayokay."

Lance stood there, knife pointed. With a lift of his eyebrows, he made it clear to Tim that now was the time to start talking.

"But I don't know where she is!"

With a shake of his head, Lance rotated the blade belly up, gripping the handle hard. In the apartment across the hall, the asthmatic coughed so loud her throat seemed to split in two. After a few loose swipes through the air, Lance rested the sharp tip of the knife against the soft tissue of Tim's nose. This final act seemed to increase Tim's desire to talk.

"She wrote me once, okay? You happy? She's in Interior City. I don't know where she lives. The return address was some anti-Registry counseling place."

Lance dropped the knife, its flat spine slapping the floor. Outside, two long blasts from a train whistle, the type of train that no longer took passengers, only conscripts and their weapons. *I love you,* Lance told the Lorrie in his head. *I have loved you always, and I will continue—*

"Please," Tim was saying. "Just go."

Lance nodded.

"By the way, I leave tomorrow," Tim said. He was breathing hard. "For the jungle. Shipping out. It's my last day here in—"

"Not my problem," Lance told him. Only when the door closed behind him did he realize that he truly meant it. Caring about yet another dead guy was a sensation that had long been lost to him. Time to keep moving.

20.

Across town, Lorrie had heard, another anti-Registry shop had opened. Fareon freaks, people said. A few counselors from the Center had gone there on an undercover mission and returned to report tales of cocky lectures on the impossibility of geriatric health as sharp as the prime minister's. Desperate, sobbing men were sent away with detailed descriptions of the supply line of Fareon from solar evaporation ponds deep in Foreign jungles right into the bloodstream of the Homeland's most powerful.

But what about me? these men would ask. *What should I do?*

Thwart and expose the endeavors of the prime minister, these men were told, and you thwart the war.

Great, the men would say. Another way of saying nothing.

Hearing these stories only assured Lorrie she was on the right track. How sad, she thought, that the Fareon folks and their way of thinking was gaining ground. "Two attacks on the Strategic Stockpile?" smirked a headline in one of their newspapers. "Just you wait."

On most days, Lorrie's plans to make the Center more effective felt maddeningly slow. She had no revolution in mind, no usurpation of power. Eric's leadership was too ensconced for that. Instead, she would influence his influencers. She would use his mother.

In service to the plan, Lorrie had begun offering Eric's mother, Jane, fresh little confidences, pieces of her life that she knew the older woman would interpret as admiration. Not that there was much competition for female companionship. Susan had not come back since her radio-shattering exit, and though a small handful of other women volunteered, thanks to Lorrie's stubborn persistence, Jane had recently begun asking her on daily walks. Though Lorrie felt guilty leaving whatever other girl had shown up that day to file and collate, becoming a bright and blooming presence in order to win over Jane and convince her of the need to restructure the Center was the highlight of Lorrie's day. It turned out that pretending to be interested in someone could actually lead to the real thing.

At first their walks kept to the blocks immediately surrounding the Center, but soon the two of them ventured out farther and deeper. From sprawling neighborhoods of vast and manicured houses to gridded complexes with harsh angles and an abundance of concrete, Lorrie and Jane walked and talked.

"We don't just save men's lives, you know," Jane told her. She wore a thick headband that covered most of her hair. "The Foreign women, doused in those chemicals we're spraying them with, they're mothers. By stopping this war, we're trying to save those women over there, those mothers, too."

"But do you think that the Center's operations are as effective as they could be? As efficient?"

Up a narrow street that seemed to be reserved for bicyclists, they strolled through a park shaded with trees, past a group of missing-limbed men shouting and playing speed chess. Lorrie waited for Jane to answer.

"Let me tell you a story."

Though it was not clear exactly how the anecdote related to the bloated and redundant structures of the Center, Lorrie was nonetheless intrigued. Decades ago, Jane said, she, too, had been in Western City North, fighting against the proposition to allocate no-strings governmental funds to any huckster that wanted to start a newspaper.

Lorrie had not known there had ever been such a battle.

"Well, we weren't successful," Jane said, and though her smile was sad, Lorrie could see there had still been some joy in the fight.

Jane, Lorrie was convinced, had lived her life fully. Lines of delighted tension crept across her face with each shared memory. A soft wrinkle appeared as Jane recalled her national campaign to send Mother's Day cards to Homeland legislators demanding an immediate stop to the war for the sake of mothers everywhere. Sometimes, when Jane was recounting a particularly important moment, she would reach over and give Lorrie's hand a squeeze. Few people had touched her like that. *There is no one else*, Lorrie thought, *who could become so excited about upending our sick world that she has no choice but to reach out and grab my hand.* With each squeeze, Lorrie loved her harder.

Arriving at a small lake, the two of them silently agreed to take the path that ringed the water. Jane went on. In addition to her duties at the Center, she was vice president of the Interior City branch of the Women's League for Freedom and Justice, she said.

"WLFJ?" Lorrie said, laughing.

Jane blinked and laughed, too, said she knew it rolled odd off the tongue, but told Lorrie that the name was stuck, that WLFJ had been founded many decades ago and was the oldest pacifist women's organization in the history of the world. *"Willffij,"* Lorrie said, giggling.

"I think I can tell you this," Jane said. "I feel as though you'll understand me."

Lorrie nodded.

"The Center, our tactics. We're not winning."

Here it was. Lorrie didn't need to bring Jane to her side. She had gotten there all on her own.

"Our edges are too rough," Jane went on. "We've alienated the mothers, the lawmakers. They associate us with violence, with attacks on the Homeland, with weirdos cutting up their sons' uniforms and putting them on anorexic mannequins. Ideology Five, our detractors say. Not that any of them have ever bothered to learn any of that system's most basic principles. But even so, we're part of the problem. Think about our counselors! They scan a few of the five thousand newspapers we subscribe to, eyes zigging and zagging over the pages for some elusive key idea. Once they think they've attained that, they crumple that paper and discard it for the next. But that's not how knowledge works, right, Lorrie? You know that. A person needs to understand how one concept relates to another. Instead, so pressed for time to stop this war, they've taken the easiest parts of a thousand complex ideas and formed them into some new, shallow theory based only on a misconception of other theories. All those Coyotes in parliament, they want to put an end to this thing just like we do."

"But there's only, like, five of them."

"Oh no, don't believe that for a second. I have it on good authority that quite a few more are in the process of declaring publicly. Each new attack, though. It's a setback. But these legislators, they can help. We've got to change our path."

"I know!" Lorrie said. "What I've really been focused on is our work flow. Our training. Our organization as a whole."

"Honey," Jane said brightly, "I can't tell you how much I agree. I've been meaning to talk to my son about this. But if you have any ideas, I'd love to hear them."

They paused in front of a large shrub. Lorrie noted the beauty of its slippery shade of green. "What about letting women counsel? We train the men who volunteer, and in two or three weeks, they're gone.

At least with women, we could stick around. Have some continuity." As she spoke, she reached out absently to feel the leaves in her fingers.

"Don't touch that one," Jane said, gripping her wrist. "It's poison."

Lorrie drew back her hand.

"I don't know why it's here, around a lake in the middle of the city," Jane said, making a sour face. "Touch just one leaf and you'll swell up severely. Oozing, crusting, anywhere it makes contact with your skin."

"I'll be sure to stay away," Lorrie said.

In that moment, Lorrie wanted to tell her she knew what it was like to hate your skin, when two men approached them. Both wore snap-brimmed hats, long, drab coats, and brightly polished loafers.

"Ma'am," one of the agents said. "We need to talk to you. We're going to need you to come with us."

And before Lorrie could speak, Jane was being dragged away.

❖ ❖ ❖

When she was sick of typing and filing, Lorrie sat in the front room and watched the counselors. Without Jane, she felt more alone than ever. Surely she would soon be released, Lorrie told herself. But there was no getting around it: her ally was gone.

The first drop-in was easy. The kid clearly had money, so the counselor sent him to a "Respected Doctor" who was secretly sympathetic to the cause. Not that such beliefs came cheap. For a thousand Currencies, that doctor would write anybody a note for anything. Only Respected Doctors could grant deferments now; hence the deliriously high pricing. Not many Respected Doctors were left.

Two more boys came in, and Lorrie watched them head toward Doug. Poor kids, why did they have to land on Doug? There should have been a warning sign above his desk informing the helpless about the shoddy, ill-informed counseling they were about to be subjected to. Lorrie leaned in close to hear what he had to say.

"Hold on, let's talk big picture," Doug was telling them.

"Big picture?" one kid said. "But what should I *do*?"

"No, no. Big picture first." Doug turned his head sideways and gazed at something in the distance that Lorrie couldn't see. "Ending it."

"Ending the war?"

"No, man. *Big* picture. Ending the army."

"Oh."

"Yeah," Doug said, his voice rising. "The end of the Homeland Army. You guys ready for that?" He sniffed and squeezed his nostrils with his thumb and forefinger.

The two boys did not look ready for anything.

"How about taxes?"

"Taxes?" The boys looked at each other, confused.

"Yeah, taxes, you paying 'em? You shouldn't be. Don't support the machine."

Doug was completely twisted, she realized, a real Substance-smasher simply trying to endure his time between fixes. As for the two boys seeking help, the kid who asked the most questions kept slumping his shoulders lower and lower. Another minute and he might melt into a globby pool of guts and bones, a small stain of liquid on an old chair ripe for a gnat swarm. Doug looked like he wanted to go to the back and sniff up some more of whatever he was taking. The boys tried to appear casual, but Lorrie could see that they were devastated.

"Thanks," they mumbled to Doug on their way out.

Two more casualties.

She followed the boys out the door.

"I can help," Lorrie said.

The three of them stood in the parking lot, the boys with their short, spinning waves of hair neatly trimmed, Lorrie readying herself to hear their story.

"Who are you?" the taller one asked.

Lorrie examined the boy's face for a fear of death, unclear on which one had problems with the Registry. The tall boy looked blank and thoughtless, but without fear. "I work," she told them, "for the Center."

The boys gave each other sideways looks of distress and confusion. "Great," said the shorter one, softly. He was the one who had done most of the talking.

Lorrie understood his disappointment. How could she not? The man he had put his faith in was probably Substance smashing in the bathroom at this very moment. He had treated their desperate lives as some sort of monumental game. "No, really," Lorrie told them. "I can help." She felt frantic to see someone so young and vital accomplish something, even if that something was simply not to die.

The shorter one shifted his weight from one foot to the other and spoke. "Just me," he said. "My friend is safe. For now."

"Have you got any Currencies?" Lorrie asked.

"Some."

"One thousand Currencies, and I can get you a Respected Doctor who will swear you have any disease you want."

"I don't have a thousand Currencies." Across the street, a motor struggled to start.

"Are you close?"

"Not even," the tall friend replied.

Lorrie thought she saw a smirk. Maybe the friend had already accepted his own early death in the jungle and wanted everyone else to be dragged down with him. Loud ticking, metal grinding on metal, and a high pitch of unpleasant sounds all melded together. Someone's car was fucked.

"It doesn't matter anyway," said the friend. "I read that the prime minister has a secret stash of some crazy Foreign mineral that keeps him healthy. You think he'll give that up? There's no stopping this. It's just a matter of when we go."

"That's not true!" said Lorrie. Turning to his friend, she asked, "Do you hear how crazy that sounds?"

"Just because something sounds crazy doesn't mean it's not true," the tall one responded. "Besides, how would you know?"

"Don't you think if this whole war were predicated on some search for a secret mineral, someone would have spoken up by now? How many people would it take to pull something like that off? How would the supply chain work? Somebody would slip."

The tall friend shook his head. "Of course they wouldn't slip. They're probably paid in small amounts of the stuff themselves. The whole point is that the prime minister is organized, that he has all the power. He created a war; you think he can't create a cover-up?"

"He may have started the war," Lorrie said, "but this war has been going on for almost twenty-five years. We elected him. Every time."

"But back to my induction," the short kid said. "You said I had options. Is that really true?"

What did she think she was doing, talking to this kid? "I'm sorry," she told him. "If there are any real options, I don't know about them. Not yet." She made sure not to look at his face as she walked away.

21.

The search for Lorrie. Three options, the ticket lady told Lance, three ways to begin: option A, a seat on the first-class luxury special that would deliver him directly to Interior City—one piece of fresh fruit included—option B: a regular ticket accompanied by plenty of stops and transfers. Or, she said, the power draining from her voice, a third option. Option C. Our most reasonably priced option.

Go on, Lance told her.

The ticket lady paused, frowned, and leaned into the glass window between them. "The Broken Bus."

Though he had never before heard the term, it was easy to decipher. *Broken* did not refer to the bus itself, but to the people inside it. A bus of vets. And why not? There was, he knew, no better place to hide than right inside the monster's heart.

"So?" said the ticket lady. She quoted him a price.

The Broken Bus was cheap enough that Lance could now arrive in a strange city with a few extra Currencies in his pocket, expenditures for a new life he would resume with Lorrie, a life in which their reunited love would overtake his lack of money, or perhaps make him so happy he would fail to notice the poor state of his finances. The Broken Bus it was.

In he went, deep into the dark belly of the bus depot, down the concrete walkways lined with small kiosks stuffed with racks of newspapers and the catcalling women selling them, through puddles that stank of piss and various alcohols, beneath archway billboards advertising the Point Line, past a young woman with a desperate smile selling hard-boiled eggs and raw browned turnip tops. Finally he arrived at the gate, a lifeless part of the terminal fallen into disuse. There were no other buses besides the run-down vehicle with rusted rub rails and crooked windows that would chug him across the Homeland. No one, it was clear, wanted to see these men.

The bus itself was unmarked. It made sense; after a series of attacks on Registry buses, everyone was being careful. How perfect, Lance heard a vet remark, would it be to make it out of the jungle only to be killed by some Ideology Fiver back on Homeland soil? At the entrance door of the bus, the driver laid a tilted ramp over the small steps. Up the ramp shuffled the monsters: braced and twisted knees, swollen necks, scarred faces, leaky ears, exploded noses, all exposed and naked in the exhausted light. Men like this could have been his brothers, Lance thought, if any of his brothers had been blessed with just slightly more luck.

Lance boarded last. On the way to the bus station, he had taken seriously the warning that undercover agents were following his every move, but after a series of dramatic loops and turns, it was clear no one was watching him. Of course the Homeland couldn't monitor every single person it didn't have room for. As he stepped onto the bus, he could feel the break of the invisible chains that had controlled him from afar. Yes, the pleasure of exposure was sweet.

To form a cover story, he had picked out a newspaper at random, turning straight to the news of a recent jungle skirmish. A quick scan and he now had a military unit, a subtle infirmity, and an area of Foreign territory he hoped he could pronounce well enough to have credibly been in battle in. Even this tactic worried him. Perhaps being able to pronounce the name of the place you had fought at was a sure sign of not having fought there.

Luckily no one on the bus seemed interested in talking. Instead, they just stared at his two arms, his functional, healthy legs, and, he was sure, hated their disproportioned selves even more. Once seated, he let out a few naked yelps and thrust his tongue out at a far angle, just to show these vets that while his body might be intact, it was very possible that his mind was not.

Surrounded by young men in misery, he could not look at any of them. Why would he? Once the Broken Bus stopped, who would be waiting for them? There was no doubt in Lance's mind that Interior City was the dawn of his new life—which was really just his old life resumed in a new place. Alive and healthy, he was ready to find Lorrie, ready for her to love him again. A small smile crossed his face as he leaned against the window.

A few hours later, a picture of a woman floated before him.

"This is her." The kid behind him was talking, having seemingly started a conversation without any of the normal formalities or introductions.

Groggy, Lance took the picture from between the kid's thumb and little finger, the only digits he had available.

"Nice," he said.

"We were married two days before I left."

"Okay."

"Just me and her, no one else at the wedding."

Lance nodded, and the kid continued.

"Her family was all spread out after First Aggression. Not a lot of them made it out."

"Common story," Lance said. Night was giving way to morning.

"You know, it's the first time I'll be seeing her." The kid let out a self-conscious smile. "Sure, my fingers don't work much, but everything else does."

"Good to hear."

"You got a girl?" the kid asked.

"Yeah."

"That's where you're headed?"

Lance nodded.

"I'll bet she's glad her man's all in one piece."

"Hope so."

"I'd bet my life on it. Strong guy like you? Just showing up at her door will have her shouting up thank-yous to the Young Savior."

Shouting, yes, Lance thought, but perhaps to the Point Line instead. After a while, the kid got tired of telling his story and leaned back in his seat. In the early light, Lance watched as the dense streetscapes of the city gave way to the endless ripples of fallow farmland, the expressway parallel to a set of tracks, old Homeland trains hauling grains, armaments, and chemicals for the war. Only once had Lance been on a train—he and his father and two of his brothers had gone to visit his grandfather. Now, not so many years later, Lance thought, his father had disappeared, his brothers were killed in action, his grandfather was dead, and the trains were closed to passengers.

In ravines by the side of the road, Lance saw grass-stained washing machines, pyramid stacks of bald tires, and heaps of rusted televisions, all silently blaring the fact that either people could no longer afford to pay to dump their trash or that they could still pay but did not want to and no one was around to catch them. "How much longer?" he asked a guy across the aisle with no flesh beyond the stumps of his elbows.

The man lifted his leg and gestured to the watch around his ankle.

Lance allowed himself another smile, not caring who saw. Nine hours till Lorrie.

22.

Benjamin still hasn't called. And Daniel still hasn't spoken.

Mr. Dorton drags himself over to the poker game at his friend Lambert's. Though it's unlikely, he hopes one of the regulars will take sick and call Craig Camwell to sub in. Camwell is no good at cards, but Mr. Dorton wants to see him. He wants to make sure Camwell tells his boy Joe to tell Benjamin to call. And why not? No matter the indignity, it was still worth a try. Benny and Joe, they were always together.

Lambert's kid opens the door. Mr. Dorton can't even remember his name. His age, if he had to guess, must be somewhere between his oldest son, Daniel, and his youngest son, Benjamin. Everybody in the complex, Mr. Dorton included, knows Lambert's kid is fresh back from another fourteen-month stint: Lambert never stops yakking about his kid's five tours in the jungle. Practically the whole prison complex has heard Lambert recount one of his son's all-night jungle shootouts. Each battle is stretched and amplified with every retelling. But so what? A son's bravery doesn't bother Mr. Dorton; his Daniel has two valor medals and a bronze Illustrious Hero bar.

The Lambert kid grips Mr. Dorton's hand tight and welcomes him into the house. His father, he tells Mr. Dorton, is running late, but can he get him anything? Just a whiskey and some water. The kid comes back to the living room and presses a lowball glass into Mr. Dorton's hand. He doesn't offer a seat, and Mr. Dorton doesn't take one. The Lamberts have installed wall-to-wall carpeting, and Mr. Dorton watches a piece of moisture fall from the rim of his drink onto the thick pile. Lambert's kid doesn't notice.

Instead, the kid talks weaponry. The rifle he used, he says, was truly something. Mr. Dorton can see in this kid's eyes that he misses that rifle. It's like a bad breakup; Mr. Dorton knows how these Homeland armed services kids get: you watch that rifle at all times, she sleeps in your bed, you anticipate the upward kick each time she sprays her tapered bullets. Letting anyone hurt or even touch her is incomprehensible, and then one day you've got your discharge papers and she's gone.

"Thirty-six hundred rounds," the kid says. The two of them are still standing.

Mr. Dorton has stopped paying attention for a moment, thought the kid had moved on, but no, the kid is still explaining the intricacies of his combat rifle. Thirty-six hundred rounds a minute, he says again, effective kills at some ridiculously large number of distance-units, a sporting shot from even farther. Next he shows Mr. Dorton a few scars and describes the origins of each. With thick, steady fingers, the kid rolls up his left pant leg and motions for Mr. Dorton to lean in for a better view. First stop: a blotch the size of a fried egg, from a leech, the kid explains, that had fastened to him during a stomp through the jungle on an intelligence-gathering mission outside a Fareon pit.

A what? Dorton is about to ask, but the kid is onto the next destination, pushing up a sleeve and exposing a bicep. The skin over the kid's muscle is thin, the result of some sort of jungle infection that went untreated after too many days in the bush. What's next, Mr. Dorton thinks. Will the kid unbuckle his belt and drop his trousers in the middle of his parents' living room? Instead, the Lambert kid asks about

Daniel, which, Mr. Dorton gathers, means he is closer to his older son's age than his youngest.

"We played varsity together, you know," the kid says.

Daniel was on three varsity teams, but Mr. Dorton doesn't care to know which one of them had been with this kid.

The Lambert kid is all big smiles and ragged grins, even when he talks about the boiling heat of the jungle, where before the day is even started, a layer of sweat covers you from your toes on up, but that's how you want it because when a breeze finally does come your way, the sweat cools you down even faster. Such new and intimate information about the fighting, Mr. Dorton thinks, should not be given to him by a stranger. A story like this should come from his son.

Mr. Dorton finishes his drink and desperately wants another, but the kid is on a roll. Thirty-six hundred rounds per minute, he tells Mr. Dorton a third time.

"But what's next?" Mr. Dorton asks him.

Corrections, the kid says. His father is going to help set him up with a job in the prison complex. A growth industry, he jokes, what with all these dodgers. And then more seriously: provided the prime minister stays healthy. Can't let these Coyotes take over now, can we? But you and me, the kid says, we'll be colleagues. How about Daniel, he asks, touching Mr. Dorton's elbow. He have a good time over there?

Daniel is silent and bed-ridden—maybe it's the pills that have him all clammed up—and Mr. Dorton has no idea what he laid eyes on over there because he won't say a word. Daniel had a great time, Mr. Dorton says. He's sinking into the carpeted floor, and this kid is getting taller and taller.

Lambert's kid goes on about the strange, flat fauna that make a dangerous thicket of the jungle, from gigantic, gnarled trees slathered in deformed flinty bark that send out wide roots to curl around your ankles and bite at your skin to bushes whose berries are so sour just one lick would salt your throat for a week. Then he moves on—Mr. Dorton doesn't know how, can barely follow—to stories of his unit's mission as sample gatherers, entering deep into Foreign territory late at night with special scoops and cores, their chrome-plated tools probing the strange soil. What the hell the Homeland needs with Foreign soil samples, Mr. Dorton has no idea, but the kid keeps moving. Somehow, he has transitioned into a story about rules.

If you wanted to stay alive, the kid smiles, you had to break the rules.

Mr. Dorton sinks lower and lower into the Lamberts' living room carpeting. His Daniel never talked about trees that bit the skin or soil samples, and he never talked about rules, either. No, this Lambert kid was not the right boy to be telling him these stories.

Follow the rules, the Lambert kid says, and you're dead.

Enough. *How,* Mr. Dorton thinks, *do I get this kid to talk about something else?* "You have a car?" Mr. Dorton asks him. It's a stab, a nothing remark, but the kid bites.

Eyes wide, the kid says he's been saving up for a Brand 42, a real sensible choice, doesn't Mr. Dorton agree? Seventeen different newspapers, the kid says, voted the Brand 42 as one of the best cars in the Homeland, so what could go wrong? What kind of car does Daniel want? the kid wonders.

Mr. Dorton feels just about ready to set this kid's teeth on edge. Can't they just talk about cars?

"Brand Thirty-Seven!" the kid says. "With the big grille in front? I bet Danny is a Thirty-Seven type."

Daniel has become a different type entirely, a type who doesn't just cry, but now weeps, heavy, bitter wails that push through the polyester curtain ringing his bed and run all around the hospital.

"How'd you know?" Mr. Dorton says, smiling. "A sleek little Thirty-Seven. That's what he wants."

"Turbo or regular? I'll bet Daniel wants that turbo."

"I'm troubled," Mr. Dorton tells the kid, "by these Ideology Fivers. Not the Foreigns. We know they hate the Homeland, but the converts, the ones hiding among us."

The kid nods up and down so vigorously Mr. Dorton thinks his head might pop off. "Last week's attack was the most messed up yet."

"The military hospital? The ambulances full of charcoal?"

"No, even more recent. Up in Western City North, they hung an effigy of the Homeland."

"You mean the prime minister?" Mr. Dorton's papers have not covered this event.

"No, like a dummy that was labeled *Homeland*. If I could just get my hands on these mother-rapers."

"Was anybody hurt?"

"If I'd have been there. But no, there was a bomb, but it didn't go off."

"Who did it? Foreigns?"

"Nobody knows. But it doesn't seem like it. Two of the papers said there was a note next to the dud bomb. *If the culture is killing us, then why not kill the culture?*"

"That's the most asinine thing I've ever heard!" Mr. Dorton says.

"Right?" says the kid. "These idiots can't even build a bomb right."

"But the idea," Mr. Dorton presses, "that these attacks could be perpetrated by Homeland citizens. It's simply not possible. It's—"

"It's the times we're in," says the kid. "Doesn't matter, though. Once we finish the Foreigns, these people will have to find something else to complain about. And I think we've got them on the ropes. Year twenty-three is our year, Mr. Dorton."

Ten minutes with this kid and Mr. Dorton has heard more from him than a month of visits with his own boy. Finally Lambert walks through the door, and the other men arrive as well. Everyone who is supposed to come to the poker game does, so there is no need for Craig

Camwell to sub in. Mr. Dorton won't be able to ask him if he's heard anything about the whereabouts of his Benjamin.

Mr. Dorton shakes the Lambert kid's hand and gives him best wishes. The kid's grip is so strong, his smile so thick, that Mr. Dorton doesn't want to let up. He holds on for as long as he can, soaking all that vigor up until he is over capacity, a little bit left to pass on the next time he sees his Daniel.

❖ ❖ ❖

"We're so glad he's ready to come home," Mr. Dorton had said to the doctor.

"About that," the doctor had said.

As the doctor spoke, it became clear the decision to release him was based on factors completely unrelated to Daniel's health. "Space," the doctor had mumbled. "Overcrowded corridors, psychological consequences. New boys just keep coming."

Now Mr. Dorton sits in a reclining chair in his den, his feet extended on the small footrest before him. He leans forward, places a pillow behind his head, and pushes down with his feet, setting the chair in motion. Even in this room, he thinks, his room, he is unable to find comfort.

Ever since Daniel has returned, the house has been cross-sectioned into territories, private areas and alcoves for each member of the family. Only now, an area is under dispute. Mr. Dorton finds the conflict tremendously depressing and finally stands and walks into the living room, his wife's domain, to address the issue.

"Let's help him clean out his bedroom," he says to his wife. She lifts her eyes away from the television and up toward him. "Daniel doesn't want to be surrounded by those boy things."

But Sally responds with notions of familiarity, comfort, and free will. If Danny wants to take down his old pennants and posters, she says, then Danny will do it himself.

She's a coddler, Mr. Dorton thinks, buying their son the fresh fruits they can barely afford, offering a hot breakfast each morning the moment the boy awakes. Sure, Mr. Dorton keeps a few strawberries in his office, but only for appearances. He slinks back toward the den, shoulders low, and leaves his wife to the living room. Removing a bottle of aspirin from his coat pocket, he pops three of the dull white pills into his mouth. The pills go down hard.

On Daniel's first night home from the hospital, the boy had stayed up late, the two of them staring at the television until the sky had gone completely black. Another failed attack on the Homeland's Strategic National Stockpile, a reporter tells them. *It's just a warehouse for flu vaccine,* an official pleads. *We swear it!* Daniel watched silently, saying nothing. Outside, the stars were densely packed; almost no space remained between the pinpricks of light. Daniel had announced he was tired, the first words either of them had spoken in hours. Once he had stated his intent to sleep, Daniel stood and walked up the stairs to his old room. Mr. Dorton had wondered whether his son's familiar trappings would comfort him. But then he stepped through the door into his old room and vanished.

He did not come out for three days.

"Substance Q? Something harder?" Mr. Dorton asks his wife. The two of them drink decaffeinated coffee around the kitchen table, a neutral zone. "Some of them fell into all sorts of stuff over there, new Substances we haven't even heard of yet. I saw a report on a few of the news shows."

"When was the last time there was something true on a news show?"

"Sometimes I hear banging sounds in there. He's throwing things. Breaking them."

❖ ❖ ❖

Each parent takes turns tapping their knuckles against the door, his wife gingerly and Mr. Dorton, too. On day three he converts to a fist.

"Talk to me!" he screams. "Just talk to me."

From the room, nothing but silence.

One must not walk away from a child, Mr. Dorton reminds himself. Wisdom passed down by none other than the Young Savior.

That night, Mr. Dorton drags a folding chair into the hallway. Perhaps his troubled boy will gain comfort from a caring presence just outside the door. A few hours in, Mr. Dorton hears a bright crash inside the room. A shattered high school trophy, most likely. He calls to Daniel, asks him what he needs. *Go away,* his son tells him.

All through the night, Mr. Dorton talks to his son. He shares stories of his own life, fluttering tales of his boyhood right on through to last week's staff meeting. He offers up new stories, stories he has never told anyone. The crude buzzing of a large insect, the distant hammering of the prison expansion, all float sadly in the pale air. His son does not make a sound.

By sunrise, Mr. Dorton has yet to move. He calls in sick from work for the first time in a decade. "Talk to me," he pleads with the door. "Please just talk to me." A haze descends over his vision, his lids are heavy, he can stay awake no longer. And then, finally, he hears the gentle rub of an opening door and feels the presence of his son. Daniel is standing over him.

"You want to know what I saw?" Daniel says.

Mr. Dorton, stiff from a night on the folding chair, nods. He does not stand. He does not think he can.

"Week one," Daniel says. "Here's what happened to me. Four a.m. Commander wakes us up. Not the whole company, just a group of six. Irv's there, too, that's my only friend. First Lieutenant marches us out to a landing strip; it's still dark out. There's a helicopter, two fucked-up looking animals painted on the doors, some insignia, I don't know what. We get in, and right away I see that this thing is loaded down: rocket pods, thirty-millimeter cannons, guided missile subsystems. Outside, it's dark, but it's still hot out, we're already sweating. Irv gives me some piece of jungle fruit from his pocket. The fruit is red and prickly and tastes like old soap when I bite into it. Irv sees me and starts laughing, tries to tell me to peel it. Rotor blades are up and I can't hear him, so I bite it again. Irv laughs some more, mimes the motion. I peel the fruit. It's sour, and it stings my tongue. Up in the air First Lieutenant opens his pocket, pulls out some pills, starts handing them out. *What's this?* I think, but I can't ask, because it's too loud but also because First Lieutenant is a total asshole. I look at Irv. He shrugs, pops it down his throat. Wind is blowing, light is starting to come up. Down below, I can see green hillsides, huge trees. Get 'em out, First Lieutenant says. Irv heads to the gunner's well. I'm just supposed to use my standard weapon. Whatever pill First Lieutenant gave me, I can feel it now. My shoulders are strong, my chest is huge. I can feel that pill making me purple inside, little drips of dark juice flowing into my blood. Each drop has a different flavor, and they all taste good. My whole body is one big beating heart. My point of vision turns narrow, like my two eyes are just one big telescope. There. First Lieutenant points. We're hovering over a series of low buildings, some type of factory, a refinery, I don't know. Pipes, pumps, turbines, filters. Smokestacks pour out this bright green smoke, just a never-ending stream. The smoke rises, and we sense it on our skin, sticking to our bodies, even from way up. Below, there are small ponds everywhere, man-made, all square and lined up in rows. We're low enough that I can see outlines of people. The ponds, the green smoke, they stink, but somehow the pill makes me not mind, lets me see the smell as a series of shifting colors. Night is pretty much over, it's light, but the whole world is blue. Blue people, blue buildings, blue ponds, purple blood, green smoke. Get 'em, First Lieutenant says.

I wish I could see Irv, but he's strapped in behind the pintle mount. My rifle is as light as a pencil, my eyes are quick. We mow those little humans down, pop them over in the cold blue light. Whatever those ponds are, lots of people are around them, protecting them maybe, like human shields. Foreigns do that. My new purple blood rushes through me, loves all of this, wants more. I keep shooting. The little people fall right into the ponds. The more Foreigns we off, the more green smoke pours out of those smokestacks. Inside, I'm on fire, it's hot, it's wet, it's raining and blooming and steaming all at once. My aim is perfect. One by one by one I pop the little guys off. What's that? says First Lieutenant into his radio. He nods. We power up, return to altitude. Good job, boys, First Lieutenant says. Irv slips out from his position and moves back over to me. He's smiling, so I smile back. His blood has turned purple, too, I can see it. Take another, First Lieutenant says, digging in his pocket. We're just getting started. That was my first hour of war."

23.

A shake of leaves, a distant howl from some catlike creature. Plenty of sounds, but no one to talk to. By Joe's second morning in the cabin, the lack of conversation had become a physical pain, a dull ache that stretched from the insides of his ankles right up to his thighs. The longing surprised him. In the city, an accidental brush from a stranger would make him bristle. But now, days into the solitude, he felt desperate to find someone to talk to. Outside, he heard a strange rustling. Against all that he knew, he still hoped for Benny.

He rushed over to the door and pulled it open. Immediately he felt a quick burst of wind and found himself greeted by a small metal eye, unwinking. The barrel of a rifle. A rapid series of twists and turns twirled through his head. Had the Registry tracked him down? But First Tuesday was tomorrow; he wasn't even officially delinquent. No, this woman aiming a weapon between his eyes could not represent the Homeland.

"And you are?" The woman was calm, her breath steady.

Joe could see that her finger was outside the trigger guard. She hadn't yet decided whether or not to shoot.

"I'm a friend," he stammered. "My friend Benny, he said—"

"Benny? I don't know any Benny." Her right hand pulled back on some sort of lever, the high-pitched noise of a mechanical system locking into place. Slowly her index finger moved until it rested lightly on the trigger.

"Wait, wait, wait! Sorry. Benny is my friend. His uncle, that's who owns this place."

"Mort."

"Right, Mort. Benny is Mort's cousin—sorry, nephew. And Benny is supposed to meet me here. Mort said we could stay." Had Mort said they could stay? Joe had no idea.

"Well, why didn't you say so?" The woman lowered the rifle. A few more relieving clicks and slips from the gun that Joe hoped were the sounds of disarmament. "I live on the other side of the lake. I watch the place for Mort when he's not around."

Joe wanted to invite her in, to talk to her, to open up about his problems, but to invite her in would be to expose the shattered window and scattered glass, and he did not want to make his story any more complex than it had to be. And yet, he could not let her go.

"Can I walk you back to your cabin?" he asked.

"I think I know the way, thanks."

"Well, I could use some company."

"Young man, I've got a lot on my plate. I've already wasted half my day coming over here to check on this place."

Joe wondered how she could have wasted half her day before he had even had breakfast.

"I can't even walk you back to your cabin?"

"And for what? I don't like to explain myself to people. I don't want to do any explaining."

"Same here. I hate explaining, too." Anything to make her stay.

"Truth be told, I can guess why a young man like yourself might be here, and I don't much care for it."

"No, no," he protested. "I'm not a runner." And it was true. He wasn't. Not yet, at least.

"I apologize for implying otherwise," the woman said. "Still, I've got to be getting back. Hope I didn't cause any offense. It's just, the papers write about these young boys not wanting to do their part when the time comes—"

"An apple," Joe said. "I'll give you an apple if you let me walk you home." He apologized in advance for bartering away the apple meant for him and Benny, their celebration apple for once the future was clear. The last apple on the dying tree.

A balmy lust spread over her face. "Now you're talking. It's not a far walk, no more than twenty minutes. But once we get there, you're going to have to leave me alone. I've got things to do, you hear?"

"You've got yourself a deal."

24.

Trance is not the right word, neither is daze, spell, or dream. Words, after all, line the books whose pages Alan turns every day, in the jungle, in the library, in the dim glow of his bunk before lights out. Words, he knows, don't mean what he wants them to, but instead have lives of their own, undulating charges of electricity traversing the world on self-directed terms. Now Alan pushes up against the window of the headmaster's office. *No word*, he decides, *can ever explain what I'm doing. Or why I'm doing it.* But what exactly he is doing is still forming like the clouds of a dream. *Make it wild.*

The creak of the window is loud, but the skittering songs from the dance are louder. With two palms flat on the wooden floor, half his body is already inside the forbidden office, the mission now under way. A long pause, the magnet pull of his intentions sliding the rest of his body through the window cleanly, no crash of ankles against glass.

No one he knows has ever been in the headmaster's office. In respect of this fact, Alan stands up and looks around. After four years at the School, this office has become mythical, a roped and gated legend that produces a nervous condition in any student threatened with a visit. Even the most troubled miscreants are whipped and yanked elsewhere. In one corner of the room, he spies a large stack of newspapers. Flipping through them, he spots titles not carried by the school library. "Charcoal Attacks Still a Mystery," screams a bolded headline. "Largest Induction Center in Homeland to Expand," shouts another, followed by the subhead: "Western City North Reaches Capacity." A few blinks, and Alan's eyes move to yet another paper: "Coyotes Gain Ground in Parliament."

In the center of the room he sees a large wooden desk, just as they have all been told. Around school, tales of the headmaster's desk have long been constructed on principles of fear and mystery. "That will do well on my desk," the headmaster is known to say as he takes the Y-shaped wood some boy has spent months sanding and smoothing into the perfect slingshot. The desk, too, has a reputation of holding not only contraband but also new plans, platforms, and pillars, rumors of untried policies or dreamed-up futuristic punishments. No student has ever seen this desk; they only know that it can churn out directives that harm or help them, depending on its mood. You are weak, the students are told; the desk is powerful.

Artlessly, crudely, joyfully, Alan spits on the desk. What next? The voice of the Majority Group lady, rising from the wavering world behind his eyes, softly singing in his ear: *Make it wild.*

He pulls on the first of four drawers. Top drawer: locked. Middle drawer: a heavy-looking stapler, some old rubber stamps, a pile of pay stubs, a carved pipe with a crusted rim. Third drawer: a bag of bright green apples. Never before has Alan seen so much fresh fruit at once. Their skin is clear: no brown spots, the surface free of oozing mush marks. He takes one and puts it in his bag, then takes another. After a moment's pause, he lifts the entire netted sack out of the drawer and places it in his bag. The rusty receptors of his brain shoot to life, reminding him of their long-forgotten taste. *But no,* he reminds himself. *Don't eat the apple, Alan.*

On the back corner of the desk is a thick, bulging envelope with the word VOUCHERS printed on the front. The free tickets for the bus ride home for graduating students to offer their final good-byes before shipping out. Reaching into the envelope, Alan grabs two of them. For a moment, the idea comes to him that he will find the Registry assignments and destroy them. But he knows that this small act will lead to nothing. He can destroy any letters the Registry might have sent, but without hesitation, they will simply send new ones.

Next to the vouchers, steady and unflinching, sits a small, square box of matches. Alan pauses, stares up for a moment at the coffered ceiling, his eyes racing in circles around the perimeter beams, his ears listening to the rumbling sounds of the dance as they vibrate the office walls. Ricky X-P, were he ever put in this position, deep behind enemy lines, would have a perfect plan. But Ricky X-P, Alan reminds himself, is just the transmutation of some writer's thoughts into words. He doesn't need made-up stories anymore; he has a real person to look up to.

Thank you, Woody, Alan thinks. For he now has a plan. Now he knows. Words from the pamphlets run to and fro in his mind, tagging the wall of his skull before skittering back to the other side. *Quotas.* The disproportionate numbers of Homeland Indigenous combat deaths. The health of his people, he reminds himself, is holy. And as Woody Gilbert had said, one must do whatever is necessary to keep it that way. He will burn the whole place down.

Still, the thin sticks in front of him are incapable of lighting anything more substantial than a small cigar. These matches are not matches at all. They are possibility, for it is these weak matches that jump his mind to an image of the bright orange zippered pouch his father gave him so long ago, the small kit with the sturdy survival matches, their phosphoric orange heads just waiting to be struck. As the Young Savior said: *Strike the proper chord, and you shall make history.* Now those matches, he could work with.

❖ ❖ ❖

"Now!" he yells to Gad, pulling his elbow hard. "You need to come with me."

"What?"

Gad can't hear him; the music is too loud, the stomp of dancing students too strong. Alan's timing is off as well. Gad is taking a break, greedily sipping the sticky red juice the nuns and priests provide only at the final ship-out dance. Each boy has made sure to have at least three cups. Will they get red sticky juice in between fighting Foreigns in the jungle? All of them know they will not.

"I'm not kidding!" Alan shakes him with both hands.

"Why would I leave?"

"Just trust me."

Gad leans in close. "Why are you wearing a backpack?"

"If you don't come with me, there's going to be trouble." Is he begging or ordering? Alan does not know himself.

Before Gad can respond, the music stops. A bony nun finger points to the woven wire that covers the gymnasium windows. Alan turns, too, ready to see the light sparkings of the timber-frame storage shed, but when he looks, he sees there is no structure at all. The entire shed has completely vanished, and a roar of spreading flames has circled two dormitories and the dining hall, and is now extending its rage quickly, zigzagging toward them.

"Run!" yells a tall boy from his Homeland History class.

Nobody moves.

"RUN!" yells a nun.

Everybody moves.

Gad drops his cup. A small pond of sticky red liquid rolls over the smooth wooden floor.

Grabbing Gad's hand, Alan pulls him away from the crowds, away from the school, away from the fire, and down the path of low grasses that leads toward the closest town, which leads to the small bus station, which leads to larger bus stations that in turn connect with the most distant corners of the Homeland. Students scramble, nuns scream, priests bellow, and Alan and Gad slip through the barbed wire and into the night.

As they run, Alan turns back to Gad to make sure he's following. And even through all the sharp cries of fear, he is sure he can make out the sounds of one he has forgotten: Hazel the guinea pig, locked in her cage, tiny teeth chomping on the scalding metal bars while the fire consumes her.

❖ ❖ ❖

The two of them are breathing hard. In a few minutes, there will be an emergency roll call. In a few minutes, everyone will know they are gone.

The moon is large and gives off a crinkled, hazy light. Behind them, a dark pillar of smoke. Gad has stopped running, so Alan does, too. Finally, a moment to talk.

"Wait, *what?*" Gad says.

"She came to me, the lady in the pamphlets."

"And she told you to set fire to the whole school?"

"Well, no. She told me to do something big. *Wild*, actually. I thought of the fire myself. But I didn't think it would spread that far."

"And while you were lighting the fire—"

"That's when it came to me! What it's all been leading up to. This is what the pamphlets have been telling us."

A hungry bark in the distance. Would the younger priests bring their nattering sniff-dogs to track them down? Alan crinkles his face at Gad, hoping he'll realize that there is no time to spare.

"And what have the pamphlets been telling us?"

"To get the hell out of here. So here we are, right? We escape, right before they snap us up and send us off. And we go right at them, just like the pamphlets said. We go to their biggest induction center, and we burn it to the ground."

Two more barks, closer now.

"And where is that?"

"Gad," he says, trying to sound as confident as possible. "We've got to keep moving. We've got to get to the bus station in town."

Gad does not move. "If we go," he says, "we'd be—"

Alan nods slowly. "Dodgers." Down the long country road, he sees two sets of headlights, coming fast. "Gad," he says. "You should come with me."

Gad does not move. "Come where?" he says.

The headlights are getting closer.

"We haven't even gotten our assignments yet. I might get rejected. Or placed in Intelligence or something."

"Everybody is infantry."

"You don't know that."

The bright yellow lights will be on them in seconds.

"If you don't come with me," Alan says, "I'll tell them you lit the fire, too."

The lights of the car are upon them. Before Gad can respond, Alan pulls him into the long narrow trench by the side of the road and rapidly begins covering them with the small, prickly brush at hand. "Gad," he whispers. "You know what's next, right?" But he's not sure Gad can hear him, his voice lost beneath the sweeping wind, and so Alan whispers it again, though mostly to himself. "Western City North," he says.

❖ ❖ ❖

A few hours of unclean sleep in the swallowing bushes across the street from the bus station until first light. They are fugitives now; all movement is weighted. After breakfast, solemn nuns and priests will have handed out Registry letters telling each boy what he already knows.

"You know I was just kidding," Alan tells him first thing in the morning. "Heat of the moment and all that."

Gad nods.

With his new status as a fugitive, Alan finds that he feels lighter. Each new step he takes is gleeful with secrets. "Once we do this, Woody Gilbert, he'll find us," Alan tells him. "You have to do an action before you join HIM. Or find the baldheads and get cleared by them. That's how they know you're not a Reggie."

"Whatever," Gad says.

But Gad always wakes up cranky. Shoulders low and eyes puffed, the two of them walk into the station and up to the ticket window, pilfered vouchers in hand. "I'd like to exchange this," Alan tells the woman at the ticket window. "We need to go to Western City North."

She frowns through the waved layers of glass. Below the window separating them, a steel drawer pops open. The ticket lady motions for Alan to place his voucher in it, and when he does, she slams the door shut, nearly catching his fingers.

A flat look passes over the ticket lady's face. "This is a voucher from the school down the road. The kids use these to go home for a week, to say good-bye to their families before they ship out."

"Right," Alan says. He wills himself calm. News of the fire has not yet reached the ticket lady. "That's us. We got early permission. I'd like to exchange this voucher for a ticket to Western City North." On the edge of his vision, he sees people lining up behind them. The ticket lady is taking too long. They must get on a bus before word of the fire spreads to the town.

The ticket lady frowns again and holds the voucher up to the light as though she's trying to see into a sealed letter. Her eyebrows draw close, hovering beneath her wrinkled forehead. *We're doomed,* Alan thinks.

The ticket lady holds up a slender finger, then turns around, pulls out a book of timetables, flips through it, and takes out another book from the shelf behind her. "Much as I'd like to accommodate a boy in his last week before shipping out, you'll still have to make up the difference," she says.

"What?" Alan says. It is hard to hear through the thick glass, so he leans into the perforated grille carved into the window.

"Prices are by distance," she says, not speaking any louder or closer to the opening. "This voucher you have, well, you're talking about a few hundred distance-units total. The trip you want? That's a whole other type of ticket. More distance-units. Much farther. Distance equals Currencies."

"How much?" Alan asks.

The woman frowns again and quotes them an astonishingly high number. "Not including," she says, a gleeful shudder passing through her, "the repaving surcharge."

"The what?"

"We've got to fix these roads somehow. Plus a security fee."

"Security fee?"

"What with all the attacks on buses, we have to manually check every bag."

People in line are shuffling and starting to grumble. Alan and Gad step aside.

The floor of the bus depot is dirty; neither of them want to sit in the muck, so Alan takes off his pack and they lean against the wall. His pack is light; there was little time to grab the essentials. Inside is an extra pair of socks, the zippered pouch of matches, the stolen sack of apples, all of the HIM pamphlets, and his folding steel-bladed hunting knife. Not wanting to be caught with illegal literature, he stuffs the HIM pamphlets down his pants.

"A question for you," Gad says. Alan recognizes that Gad won't quite look at him. "How far have you thought this plan through?"

"Well," Alan begins to answer.

"Because we could still go back," Gad says. "Deny the fire had anything to do with us, get our assignments, and everything goes back to normal."

"Are you crazy? Normal is over." Alan leans forward. "Now how the hell are we going to get on this bus?" Alan hopes that his tone is strong, charismatic even, but beneath his clothes his knees shake and his fingers wiggle. At any moment some smirking priest could show up, his long black robe now cleaned and victorious, wrap a thick hand around their wrists, and drag them away. Just as Gad is about respond, a Majority Group man approaches them. The man's tongue drags at the corner of his mouth, and sweat gathers at the bridge of his nose and pools in the basins of his ears. A mercenary, dispatched by the school to capture them?

Alan stands up straight to take the Majority Grouper's artificial height away.

"I couldn't help but overhear that you guys are in a fix," the man says. An amazing amount of perspiration drips from his forehead to the floor. Though he's never been anywhere else, Alan knows that the sun spins faster, whiter, hotter, in this part of the Homeland. In some ways, the suffering man in front of him is a treat. Alan had never heard any of those complaints personally; he'd only read about them in books. Now, in front of him, as promised: a man who clearly cannot take the heat.

"Yeah, you could call it a fix," says Gad. Alan pops an elbow into Gad's ribs.

"You have anything worth trading?" the man says, wiping his forehead.

"Not really," Gad says. "You see, there was this fire at our school and—"

Alan elbows him again, this time harder. Clearly, Alan thinks, Gad is less suspicious of strange Majority Groupers walking up and offering helpful information than he is.

And then it comes to him. "Apples!" Alan nearly shouts. "We have fresh apples."

Several heads of waiting passengers turn their way.

"Well there you go!" The gap between the man's two front teeth is wide enough that he can surely get a unique and deep whistle out of them. "If they truly are fresh, just name your price."

After a few brief negotiations, they make the trade.

"Enjoy Western City North, my friends." His smile is like a dog's— big and droopy. "That place is wild."

❖ ❖ ❖

It's been twenty-two hours since the bus left Southwest Sector. Shouldn't take this long, a lady with twins and a toddler turns to tell them. All these damn stops, she mutters.

In the seat next to him, Gad seizes large clumps of his own hair while tapping his foot against the floor.

"Get it together," Alan hisses. "You already look guilty of something."

A chain of drunken Homeland sailors in khaki uniforms files onto the bus in Village 82. They sing songs Alan doesn't know, and the babies on the bus cry even harder.

"You!" A drunken sailor points at Alan. "Soon you'll know these songs."

"Maybe," another sailor slurs. "But maybe not. Some of these kids still slip through."

"Not him." Talking about Alan as if he isn't there. "Look at him. Homeland Indigenous. They all serve, every last one of them."

❖ ❖ ❖

In Western Town R, Alan and Gad exit the bus to wait for their transfer, the final leg of the journey before Western City North. People buzz around, angry; the lounge of the small depot is packed, the articulated movement of a stumble ten people away sends waves through the rest of the crowd moments later. The air is heavy, and Alan finds it harder to breathe than he'd like. Gad still has questions for him, sure, but they succumb, momentarily at least, to the need for elbow room. Too many people in one small space. Alan grabs the arm of a thin woman next to him and asks her to explain the unfolding crowds surrounding them.

"Are you single?" she asks.

She must be twice his age, older than his mother. "I ship out tomorrow," he says. He counts on the fact that she is looking for more than one night's companionship. By her frown, he can see he is right.

Almost three feet of snow over Mountain Range J29, she sighs. Everything is backed up. No buses in, and no buses out.

A smile slides across Alan's face. By now the School has surely sent forth some hired lackey who likes to treat kids with a strong hand and is willing to track them down for just a few Currencies and the fun of beating on some Homeland Indigenous kids. And though that someone is coming, the two of them have a head start. The snow in some distant place has given them time.

"What about you?" the old woman says to Gad. "You got yourself a lady?"

❖ ❖ ❖

The snack bar has oranges, but they're six times the cost of a small loaf of bread. Gad and Alan spend the last of their Currencies and split the bread in two. Hours pass. A weary voice comes over the loudspeaker: *There are no buses in the depot,* the voice says. *Please do not approach the window; the buses will come when the roads open.* A pause, followed by one last beleaguered crackle: *We have no idea when the roads will open.*

The crowd buzzes, one step away from a stampede. Misery and anger are packed in tight, a mental unity so strong that Alan thinks they all might rush the ticket window, light a fire, rip some chairs from their bolts, no planning necessary. *We all hate each other,* Alan realizes, *but we all want to leave this place.* At this point, a power outage would be catastrophic, unbearable; they need their light. More people want to sit than there are seats. A young man with a nasty cut on his face has a portable radio. At first, the only sounds it throws out are tinny squeals and muffled buzzes. Finally he adjusts the dial, and a voice comes through. The man whose radio it is smiles and starts to speak, but people tell him to shut up and crank the volume. A blizzard in some distant place finally moves the way it should, and people start to cheer. Moments later, a faraway summit is deemed passable, and the crowd erupts again. But in the depot, no announcements are made; the loudspeaker remains silent. A few people approach the window anyway. There are no buses anywhere. The only information they return with is that no one else should approach the window.

Gad goes to wait in line for the bathroom, tells Alan he'll be back.

"Hey!"

Alan looks up and sees a man around his age with close-cropped military hair. The man is tall, and the upper half of his face is blotched and sticky looking.

"Hey, yourself," says Alan, hoping he has struck the right tone of casual. The man's eyes look wet and desperate.

"You need ID?"

Alan says nothing. People around them jostle and elbow for more space.

"ID. Papers, man." He is whispering.

"I don't know," Alan says, whispering back. *If I do need ID,* Alan thinks, *I should be the kind of person who knows I need it.*

"Either way, seventy Currencies and I'll get you good papers in an hour. You got time. No one here is going anywhere."

"I don't have seventy Currencies."

"Sixty."

"I don't have that, either."

"C'mon, kid. Fifty-five. That's my lowest. What are you, Homeland Indigenous?"

"I have eleven Currencies. And yes."

"Eleven Currencies? That's all you got? Well, it will be a good thing when the Registry gets you. At least you'll get some clean clothes and a hot meal." He shakes his head, a small smile on his lips. "Homeland Indigenous, eh? Why not become something else with one of my papers. Minority Group C, maybe. There are no quotas for Cs."

"What are you, crazy? I can't pass for C."

"Not my problem," the man shrugs.

"How do you know about the quotas?"

"You ever seen a Homeland Indigenous who is eligible *not* serve? I don't know anything about any quotas, I've just been paying attention." The man shrugs again. "So look, let's talk Currencies. I'm open to negotiations, bartering, that sort of thing. You gotten your greetings yet?"

"My greetings?" Alan pauses. And then, in between the silence, a new voice rushes in and hooks his arm, this new voice answering the question that is meant for him.

"Nope. Haven't gotten those greetings yet, right, honey?"

Artlessly, he looks at the woman who has grabbed him, who is pulling him away from the man with the papers. He opens his mouth to ask who she is.

"Just shut up for a second, will you?" she hisses. Her eyes are wide and knowing, and he estimates that—in a good way—these knowing eyes occupy far more real estate on her face than that of the average woman. She pulls him into an unoccupied corner of the station. "That guy is setting you up. He's a Reggie for sure."

"A Reggie?"

"Undercover agent for the Registry. You've never heard that term? Where are you *from*?"

"How do you know he's undercover?"

"How *don't* you know? Walk slowly. Just follow me, okay?"

Alan's eyes again trace the outline of her face. She's not full-on Majority Group. No, she's a halfie, he thinks, almost positive. There were a few untouchable girls like this at school, alpha women who struck blows in every passing boy's heart, some Homeland Indigenous grandparent who entered the bloodline long ago only to rise in certain members of their Majority Group descendants, but with enough subtlety to register only the softest projection of difference.

Gripping his arm, she angles the two of them back into the waiting crowds of the bus station, slipping them away from the Reggie. Alan can see that she is somewhere around his age. After treating himself to a brief stare, he can also see that she is very, very beautiful.

Her name is Terry, she tells him, her family owned the smallest mansion on an Eastern Sector block of very large ones, and yes, her grandfather was Homeland Indigenous, Group T, or maybe P, she can't quite remember right now. She has dropped out of a three-digit university and left the hollow-hearted people she came from to find, she tells him, the real.

"The what?" he asks, just to make sure he has heard her correctly.

They sit on a somehow unoccupied corner bench of the still crowded depot. However long that line for the bathroom Gad is in, Alan finds himself wishing it longer.

He likes, he decides, the bones of her face, the curve of her cheeks, the slope of her forehead. An idea presses itself forward. "You know," Alan tells her, drawing directly from the pages of *Tiny Rock*, "I can teach you the ways of my people." Though his ethics and morals threaten suicide as these words leave his mouth, the rest of his body—the part that wants to fuck her in some wayward stall of this crowded bus station—cheers these empty words on. He leans back to gauge her reaction and finds himself gazing at her beautiful hands and feet.

Terry bursts into laughter. "Seriously? I may not know what the real is, but I know that you don't believe what you just said any more than I do." She has the confidence, Alan sees, of someone who has sat across from any number of slavering men.

He nods shamefully and admits the source of his inspiration. Terry launches into a lecture, learned, apparently, at that three-digit university, about how the author of *Tiny Rock* took a false name, sold his book as a meditation on some slice of Indigenous life, and cemented his way into libraries and classrooms throughout the country. Plus, she says, the author is a huge proponent of expanding the war, just one final surge, and if sixteen-year-olds are what it takes—

"So he's not Homeland Indigenous?" Alan asks.

"Once we thought he was," Terry says, "and now we know he's not."

"Oh."

"Does that matter to you?" she asks.

Alan shakes his head. "I just thought it was a pretty shitty book."

She opens her mouth wide and laughs again, a small seed revealing itself between her two front teeth. Her neck is a smooth maze of soft lines. Even the smallest bones within him are terrified. She is that beautiful.

As the conversation floats on—a perfect admixture of jokes, insights, damages sustained, influences, and the beliefs that shape them—Alan realizes that this is the longest conversation he has ever had with a woman. Gone for now are thoughts of some mercenary sent to chase him, his lack of Currencies, the unknown location of his next night's sleep, his doubts about his ability to find the baldheads and pass their test so he can be introduced to Woody Gilbert. Those distant worries are not a stunning woman with a small seed in her teeth, sitting next to him.

Around him, people begin to cheer. *The Expressway has been reopened,* the loudspeaker rumbles. *Please approach the window if you need to make new travel arrangements.*

"I have to ask," she says, "or to warn you, really."

A convoy of buses pulls into the station.

"Are you going? Has the Registry gotten to you?"

Now boarding.

"Sorry, that's my bus. Now answer my question."

He wonders whether this might be some sort of test, so he says nothing.

She shows a joyful blaze of teeth, her cheeks rising into her eyes. "Good," she says. "Never reveal your status to anyone." She places a hand on his shoulder. "The quotas, the one hundred percent conscription rate for Homeland Indigenous that everyone talks about? They're reading the wrong papers. It's not real."

"How do you know?"

"You still have a chance—"

Now boarding.

"I have a plan," Alan hears himself say. "Hiding isn't something I want to do. In fact"—he can feel the fire within himself now—"I want to make *them* hide from *me.*"

She mumbles something about male ego that he doesn't quite catch.

"Have you ever been to Western City North?" he asks. "Do you know about the baldheads?"

She snorts and tells him that she has just come from there, that she has seen plenty of baldheads around town and that all they do is play some strange psychological game. "They can't get you out of war," she tells him. "You need to prioritize. So keep this in mind: the quotas are a trick. They just want you to think it's inevitable. Those are dirty papers that report on that, government funded." She reaches out to touch him, her soft fingers landing on his wrist. "But don't get caught up in anything stupid. You're a person, you're not a group, understand? The only change that violence brings is to create a more violent world."

He understands that she is warning him against HIM, against the ideas put forth by the pamphlets he has hidden in his now swelling pants. But what does she know? Of course she'd say the baldheads just play games; curing addicts was their cover. Sure, she is beautiful, but her beauty hasn't led her to the information on the crushed paper folded into small squares and now resting just below his backbone. She thinks that the baldheads are just some cult of wackos. Which means that she doesn't understand that for real freedom, you need to sink below. Not that her inability to comprehend makes her any less attractive. He would like to kiss her stomach, behind her ears, the back of her neck. He decides to give it a try.

"You must be kidding," she says.

Now boarding. Now boarding.

"Fine," he tells her. "Your loss."

With a tight smile, she reminds him to always keep his Registry status to himself. If someone does ask, make sure to—

Last call for boarding. Final call.

"Whatever," he says, standing up. "I can take care of myself."

With the buses once again running, the crowds around him have thinned. Still, the bathroom line must have been insane. Navigating his way through the remaining crowd, he is already weaving together for Gad the story of how he has kissed a girl. He knows that if another person believes the new facts now forming on the edge of his mouth, they will in some way become true.

He arrives at the bathroom. There is no line; every stall is empty. The depot buzzes with people, but Gad is not among them.

Alan leans against a small piece of wall. Back at the School, he had watched over Gad's shoulder as he filled out the Registry form: *Name and Address of Person Who Will Always Know Your Address.* Gad had printed Alan's name, and Alan had done the same. Alan looks around for Gad. But Gad isn't anywhere.

25.

Bitter, flashing cold, the cruel Interior City atmosphere. Lance could feel it before he debused, felt the polar air slice his lips as he and the passengers of the Broken Bus floated down the aisle, groggy from so many hours in motion. A hopping, one-footed man gripped his arm for balance. Eyes drawn to the man's waist, Lance saw a small protruding pouch that lifted his shirt and gave Lance a clear view of a torn and ruptured stomach.

"Bomb metal," the man said. "Passed through my spleen on the left and my liver on the right. Left my intestines alone at least."

Too many hours on this bus with the men whose weaponized bodies had doubled as targets for the Foreigns. Men just like his brothers, save for the beat of their hearts and the flow of their blood.

He led the one-footed vet to a chair in the main terminal of the depot, whereupon the two of them, along with everyone else, were plunged into darkness. No surprise; Lance had arrived in a blackout.

Through the second-story windows, small stars shone bright above the powerless city, and the thought came to Lance that the small nips in the sky added up to some celestial set of directions, complete with a smiling Lorrie at the endpoint. He zipped up his coat, pushed outside, and looked upward, ready to follow. The bitter air cracking his skin reminded him that although he was far from his hometown of dead brothers, he was now much closer than he preferred to be. But those old versions of who he had been didn't matter now. Finding Lorrie wasn't just a task. It was an obligation.

And yet, where was his courage? Too much fire, he thought, and not enough light. To be so close to her, to be so ready, was nearly unbearable. He needed to calm down, to dull the waving rushes of oncoming delight. He needed a cup of coffee.

Nothing was familiar. As he walked the strange, blacked-out city, a roaring wind followed him around every corner, hurling itself against his face in cold slaps. Soon a hum and a whirr brought the lights back to life. Finally he could see. And on the corner of the newly lit block, there, shining through the bitter night, were the lights of a coffee shop.

Lance pushed open the doors and immediately felt at home, then confused, then at home again, though still confused. The owners had clearly studied the coffee shops of Western City North and done their best to replicate the experience here in Interior City. But then something even stranger: there, in the back corner, on an old couch near the entrance to the restroom, reading a book, sipping tea, and biting her fingernails, was Lorrie.

❖　❖　❖

Her cavernous apartment was fouled and filthy, very un-Lorrie-like. Once Lance had seen the coffee shop girl up close—her Lorrie-like features almost immediately transfigured into some defective substitute—he had nearly turned away, ready to move on. But at the moment of his gloomy recognition that his luck was not what he thought it was, the strange face in front of him had broken into a sad sizzle of a smile. Sure, this woman wasn't Lorrie. But so what? To regain the love and affection of the real Lorrie would take some work. For now, this shadow Lorrie was as close as he could bear.

Back at her place, the unspoken agreement became clear: this woman—had she even said her name?—loved a man who had no more life in him, and Lance, well, Lance knew what his problems were and hadn't felt the need to share them. The two of them recognized the various types of starvation in their hearts, and now, in her grim and cluttered space, they were ready to punish each other for not being who they wanted the other to be. Thank goodness for the many windows of her apartment, Lance thought, because the lights, as usual, were out again. He reached out to hold her, to feel the differences between themselves. Small waist, his hands told him. Large lips.

They stood in her hallway.

"Chase me."

"What?" he said.

"You heard me."

And she began to run.

He chased her from living room to bedroom, her clothes falling from her body. He could see this was a game she had played with her dead solider, and he found that being someone else—a someone who was chasing a long-legged, naked stranger—was an effective salve for keeping the world away. Forget the war. Forget the old fuck running the country who was unable to die. Yes, he thought. Yes yes yes. And then he caught her.

She was not ready, not wet enough, and he knew as he pushed into her that she would feel pain. Not that such dryness felt good for him, either, but at least he was in control. Her upper lip quivered, and her discomfort only made him want to push harder, deeper. And so he did.

"That's it?" she said when he had finished.

Lance nodded and turned over on his back. At some point the lights had come on, and in the terrible moment when he finally looked at her, he could see how little her bulged-out cheeks and rounded nose resembled Lorrie at all. She sat next to him, propped up on one elbow, ready to listen. This posture, at least, Lance appreciated, because he found himself ready.

"You know why I'm here?" he told her. "I'm not from around here."

"Listen, I was thinking, maybe you could—"

"I just got off a bus, from Western City North."

"Great. So listen, I didn't quite get to—"

"Three days I was on that bus. That's a long time. Awhile back I took this same drive, under other circumstances—really different circumstances, you could say—but things were way different this time around. Last trip, I wasn't looking for anything, and this trip I am."

"Aren't we all." She ran her fingers over Lance's chest. "So I've got a little proposal."

Lance frowned. "I'm trying to tell you a story here."

"About who?"

"About me." He paused. "My story."

She laughed. "How about you skip story time and we move on to something a little more grown up?"

"This trip, this one I just took to come here, there was so much garbage. Four ovens, I counted, tossed in ditches on the side of the road, and that was just when I was awake. I mean, I left some stuff behind, too. Well, I tried to donate my art. Anyway, I took this run-down bus full of mangled vets and . . ." His own story was jumbled, leaping from his mouth without strand or pattern to hold it in place. He tried again. "What I mean is, I first drove across the Homeland with this woman who was, who is, really important to me. The three of us, her friend Terry was there, too. And we went. I mean, we found . . ."

What kind of story, Lance thought, was he trying to tell? He couldn't even properly string a bunch of verbs together.

The woman reached under the sheets and began to stroke him, tugging just a little too hard in desperation to bring him back to life.

"Hey, how many anti-Registry centers are here?" Lance asked suddenly.

"Here where?" Still stroking.

"Here-here. Interior City."

"What, you scared to go?" She laughed. "Real original." She continued her clawlike stroke. "How about I save the welcome-to-Interior-City tour for later?" she said, her voice dropping down to a soft whisper. "How about you do something for me. I'll tell you what I like. What I want is for you to take my—"

"How many?" Lance interrupted, pulling away. He heard his voice grow slower, louder. "How many centers are there in Interior City?"

She lowered her eyebrows for a moment, but then seemed to think better of it and continued. "You'll have to spank it out of me."

At that moment, Lance sprang up, pushed the woman onto her back, and sat with his legs spread across her torso, flattening her breasts and pressing her into the mattress. Out came his hand, and his four fingers pressed on one side of her throat, his thumb on the other.

"How about you just answer my question?"

He could feel the rapid bumps of her heart pressing against the underside of his thigh, the swooshing of the blood in her neck.

"What are you doing?" she yelped. He squeezed harder, long fingers around tight neck. "Why?" she gasped.

"How many?" he roared.

Water flooded her sclera and drowned her small pupils until two small tears dripped across her cheeks.

Harder still.

"I just want to know how many anti-Registry centers are in this city! Is that too much to ask?" More force, a tighter grip. Beneath his fingers he could feel the air struggling to pass.

She wheezed and stared at him from beneath his hand, silent and still, until she finally gasped out the answer. "One. Just one. Two if you count those Fareon freaks."

She offered up an address, and he let go, her throat begging for air on the bed. Enough with this hollow apartment. He was ready to head toward the real version of this woman, leaving behind this sorry imitation who he hoped would cease to exist the moment his feet touched the outside pavement.

"You're no good," the woman said to him, her voice raw, the sheets pulled up to her neck as he slid on his pants. "You know that, right?"

"Yeah," he said. "I do."

26.

Enough with the shit work. All those weeks of wooing Jane, her ally in reform, and one day Jane was plucked away. Over a breakfast of burnt toast and hard butter, Lorrie considered her tactics. She filed for the Center, she collated for the Center, she took notes on the Center's meetings, subdividing and cross-referencing to ensure as many access points as possible. But she was not allowed to counsel. She could not sit behind the desk across from the quivering men with a gnawing at their windpipes—men so paralyzed by fear they could not even speak—and help them decide what to do. Jane's disappearance didn't scare her, but it did slow her down. Now she would have to go straight to the source. "Put me on the front lines," Lorrie told Eric. "Let me get out there."

The two of them sat in the back room, chairs swiveled across from one another, the power failed, the naked light of the window allowing their shadows to meet. It was morning, just after another one of Eric's inspirationals, the same room in which Lorrie had repaired a sentence and Susan had splattered a radio.

Eric's inspirationals had taken a new turn since the disappearance of his mother. The talks were less practical now, less focused on the progress of the Coyotes or the ineffectiveness of the prime minister's latest troop surge. Now Eric tended to speak more broadly about the nature of mischief and disobedience, or instead focused on the historical, such as the Homeland's slaughter of its Indigenous. But as for actual counseling, the advice the Center gave remained exactly the same. When and if his mother did come back, Lorrie could see that Eric wanted her to return to a world exactly like the one she had left behind. But Lorrie could not wait any longer. For the war, she knew, did not wait for anyone.

Eric's deep curls were matted down, wilted plants that needed watering. "We seek," he began, "to save the lives of our brethren—"

"We're not in the morning circle," Lorrie said, her good ear angled toward his graceful mouth. She rose from her chair and walked toward him. "Just say what you want to say to me. Can you do that, please?"

As Eric nodded, Lorrie saw that she could talk to men like this now. After she had sex with the peeled-skin artist, word had gotten around the Facility. Dozens of disgusting men had wanted to fuck her. They thought that because she had been available for one of them, she should somehow be available for all. Daily shame-reduction exercises had offered the gleaming realization that saying no did not leave her responsible for their feelings. Lorrie wondered if Eric could recognize that same thing in himself that she had finally learned, but doubted it. Some people can't see themselves in anybody.

"Do you know the issues, Lorrie? You need to know them inside out in order to counsel." He stood up. Men, Lorrie knew, don't like it when a woman towered over them. "Do you read the papers?"

"Of course I know the issues. And what actual news has there ever been in the papers?" Lorrie read at least ten newspapers a day, but knew he would like this response.

"Fine, let's do this. Question one: Should we support the Coyotes?"

"What good has come from any of our legislators?" Lorrie said, clearing her throat. "By participating, we become accomplices."

Eric smiled in just the way she knew he would. "Exactly. Okay, where should we stand on Fareon?" A much more difficult question. Around the Center, Fareon was generally dismissed as some sort of collective pathological response to an extremely stressful situation. Certainly no one in Lorrie's circles ever took the accusations seriously. Eric, of course, knew this, and the simple nature of his question made her suspicious.

"Nothing?" smiled Eric. They were faced off like boxers.

"Shut up for a second and let me think." Crouched deep inside: the knowledge that Lance would be horrified and proud of her strength.

"So you don't have a ready answer on the curious aging of our leaders? On the prime minister's chief of staff fathering a child at eighty-four? On any of the Fareon rumors?" He untangled his crossed arms, allowing them to dangle by his sides, and Lorrie saw a faint hint of triumph in his actions.

The question was a ball, burning hot and furious in her hands. As Eric knew quite well, save for the tin bones of the prime minister and his fellow aging ministers, no one had any tangible proof of anything. None of these supposed octogenarian offspring had ever been photographed. Certainly, it was possible that the prime minister and his fellow cabinet members simply took good care of themselves, consuming some perfect amount of fiber and nutrients. After all, if anyone had access to fresh fruit and vegetables, it was these men. But the pictures: the ninety-something secretary of the interior out for a jog, the eighty-two-year-old national security advisor and his beaming thirty-one-year-old wife smiling for the cameras after a night at the theater.

She needed time, just a few more seconds to think. The prime minister, of course, always justified everything with the need for punishment. First Aggression, he had said, hurt our people, but did not kill our spirit. Even now, he often gave thundering speeches on how there could be no closure without justice, and no justice without the annihilation of the Foreigns, who had committed the ultimate in cruelty.

Such a message, Lorrie knew, resonated deeply with huge swaths of the Homeland. Broad zones of Eastern Sector were still uninhabitable, even all these years later. Relocated Homeland citizens didn't just forget where they had come from.

"Fareon, Lorrie," Eric said again.

She knew that Eric wanted her to drown, that he saw his missing mother every time he looked at her. "Well," she began slowly, "with Fareon. I mean, the thing is—" Lorrie stuttered, began a new sentence, stopped, and tried to start again. "You see, it's just . . ."

A slow conversion ensued, and Eric's handsome features began their ugly turn toward loftiness. Never the learner; always the learned.

"How about a clear answer, Lorrie," he said, sitting back down.

"I don't know, Eric. The Fareon question is a complicated one. There's no proof, and when you tell the Fareon freaks that, they point to it as evidence. Some of them are just crazy. But really, I have no idea."

Eric smiled. "So you don't know. Good, Lorrie. That's what I was looking for. That's what this job is about, knowing when you don't know. And for the most part, I'm with you. Those people *are* crazy. But every now and then, you have to wonder. I mean, so many of the prime minister's people, all hearty and hale right into their nineties? You know I don't go in for that Young Savior stuff, but there's that one quote of His I've never been able to let go of: 'All truths are double or doubled, or they all have a front and a back.'"

So the self-righteous little shit didn't have an answer for everything. She felt a brief sadness at the loss of her image of him as a total prick. "So you'll let me counsel?"

"I'll admit to not having given this much thought. A woman counselor. I'll think about it, I'll talk to Jane and Tom, and I'll open up a dialogue."

Both of them paused.

"I mean Tom," Eric said. "Just Tom."

"Thank you, Eric." Lorrie stood. "About your mother. I just wanted to say—"

"Look," he said, standing up, "Susan's gone, and the new girl isn't here today. And we're way behind on our filing." With a wave of his hand, she was dismissed.

As she filed, she cursed herself for letting Eric once again dominate the conversation. Why had she answered all of his questions when the questions he asked were not the ones that needed answering? Where was the data about the effectiveness of the Center's tactics, the continuing education for counselors in order to keep up with the latest shifts in Registry policy? Forget Fareon. Men wanted to know the best way not to die. That was it. Anything else was spinning in circles.

The Center, Lorrie saw, was a frozen field. And Lorrie was sure she knew how to thaw it. With the Homeland more than two decades into the sacking and bundling of boys toward their final acts, the Center was short on volunteers—solely, of course, because the only volunteers allowed to do anything substantial were men. And almost all of them were new, as the ones with experience had been dragged away.

She needed fresh air. Outside the building, the men in line covered their faces with bandanas, not willing to risk being seen. An older woman drove by in a taxi, screaming at the masked men for their cowardice. A few minutes later, a concrete mixer passed. Slowing down, the driver rolled down her window and shouted at the covered faces that had her husband been alive, he would kill them himself. After that, Lorrie decided the fresh air outside the Center wasn't worth it. She took a ten-minute walk and then came back.

Upon her return, she saw Eric talking to Doug, the two of them laughing so hard that Eric felt moved to take his large fist and thump Doug's back so as to help him breathe normally once again. Both men became silent as she approached, though she could see Doug suppressing a giggle. Lorrie threw her purse on the round table in front of them.

"Once the filing is done," Eric said, "I have a few leaflets I'd like you to hand out."

"What about my request to counsel?"

"It's under consideration."

"Under consideration by whom?"

Doug giggled. "Tell her about her special visitor."

"What are you talking about?" Lorrie asked.

"He means some guy was looking for you," said Eric.

"Who?"

The two of them shrugged, helplessly.

"Tall?"

Blank faces.

"Clean-cut? A wildhair?"

"I didn't really take notes."

As usual, Doug broke into a fit of halted little snickers at anything that came from Eric's mouth. "Actually," Doug said, catching his breath, "I did write down the time he came in." He handed her a piece of paper.

As Lorrie bent to grab it, she thought she saw Eric glance down her blouse. Quickly she pressed her hand against her chest. The note had nothing but a time of day written on it, nothing to make the situation any clearer. "Come on, guys, I'm serious. Was someone actually asking for me?"

"Yes, Lorrie," said Doug. "Someone was actually asking about you."

"Was he, you know, how did he look?"

"A little tired," said Eric.

"No. I mean, was he, you know, particularly handsome?"

Another flood of giggles.

"I wouldn't know," said Eric.

"I'd rather bone Eric, given the choice," said Doug.

Eric punched him in the shoulder. Doug attempted a headlock, but Lorrie's voice disrupted their scuffle.

"And you didn't think about asking his name, or paying enough attention to tell me one little thing about the guy?" She passed her glare over both of them.

"C'mon, Lorrie." Eric, the voice of reason. "You know how busy it gets in here. What do you want me to say? I see hundreds of faces a day. Some guy asked me, then Doug, if we knew you, what days you came in, that kind of thing. Said he was an old friend of yours from Western City North. Man, that's a wild city, you know?"

I do, thought Lorrie.

"Crazy eyes," Eric said, "I remember that much. Super shiny and bright, but creepy, too."

Lorrie felt her legs begin to crumble into cold grey ash. "Did he say he was coming back?"

"I don't—"

"Of course he's coming back!" said Doug. "If you were looking for someone and you couldn't find them, wouldn't you keep coming back until you did?"

Eric snorted, somehow finding the whole situation humorous.

"You're nervous about some friend of yours politely asking to see you," Doug said, "and you want Eric to let you counsel?"

At this comment, Eric's interior world seemed to spill outward, and he was unable to suppress a hearty laugh.

"How dare you," Lorrie said to him.

Immediately, Eric's face exploded into a human spider web, all crossed lines emerging from a central point. "Who the fuck are you?" he yelled. "You can't talk to me like that."

The anger on his face was all too familiar. Shame and talk groups and a general sense of how people should be all coalesced in Lorrie's mind, a screaming reminder that the nature of a man with this much hate wasn't a state of affairs she needed to accommodate, no matter where his mother was.

"All I'm asking for," Lorrie said, "is the chance to be taken seriously."

But in Eric's head, the elephants were still roaring. He stood up and screamed, "Men don't want to sit across from you and take orders on how to protect themselves. What's it going to take to get that through your head?"

Lorrie leaned forward, palms flattened against Eric's desk, and spoke slowly. Let the asshole look wherever he wanted. "*Fuck*," she said, curling and stretching her tongue around the sound, "*you*."

She stood up, grabbed her purse, and walked toward the exit, pushing the glass doors open. On her way out, she slammed them behind her with a firework bang.

Only after she had walked a few steps did she realize Lance could be out there, waiting. The concealed men, their faces wrapped with scarves and bandanas, were now lined up under awnings, studying their reflections in the specular windows. Lorrie studied the rows of slitted eyes. None of these men wanted to be pointed. Thankfully, none of them seemed to be Lance, either.

The head coverings, the fear, all of it made sense. These were men, she knew, who had been told by their fathers to act like soldiers ever since they had first skinned their knees or been popped in the jaw by a ground ball that took an unexpected bounce. *That's right, killer,* their fathers had told them. *Shake it off.* To a man, all of their fathers had served, though mostly in peacetime. To a man, all of them wanted to act in a way that was different. To a man, none of them knew how. *The advice of our fathers,* Lorrie thought, angling her shoulders through the clump of men blocking her path to the sidewalk, *is burying us alive.*

On the walk home, she saw Lance at least twice, dissolved into dark corners, leaned against empty storefronts, eyes calling out to her. Each time she got close, he managed to convert himself into a strange, unassuming man as soon as she passed. This was not a way to live. Her privilege to wander had been ripped away the moment she knew Lance was in town. The streets were different now, and she could head no place other than home.

A strong rush of wind swept the small tears from resting in the corners of her eyes to the ground below. Her cheeks were hot, and she tripped over a rise in the cement where a sidewalk slab had been upended, mutilated by an extensive system of twisted roots. It all seemed so random. Once inside the Center, no matter who counseled them, it would be someone who could not recount the absolute truth: twenty-two years into the war and the Center no longer had any real ideas on how to save them.

With each step, her darting cat eyes swiveled the streets for anyone the least bit Lance-like. The air felt empty, and the wind blew dark and heavy against her skin. Good people died, and Lance lived. Of course Lorrie knew that was how the world worked: the wrong hearts were always beating.

I already gave up my body to that man, she thought. That would be all. Her new life was hers. No one else's.

Down the street, a woman walked toward her, both hands waving wildly. The woman's upturned palms juddered closer, shuddering with intensity. Quick glints of light broke through open holes in the clouds and caught the rings on the woman's fingers, the tinsel of her hands painting streaks across the avenue. Who was she? A fellow reformed crazy from the Facility Lorrie now failed to recognize? The arms continued the two-handed wave, moving closer.

Lorrie considered whether or not to cross the street. There was no one behind her, no one else the woman could possibly be gesturing to. As the wild-palmed woman closed more distance, the velocity of her finger wiggles increased with each step. The shadows lifted from her face, and Lorrie saw that it was her old antigrammarian acquaintance, the radio-shattering Susan.

How much time had gone by since Lorrie had last thought about her? Susan had stopped coming to the Center, and in that absence Lorrie could see she had lived dozens of lives. She had no makeup on. Gone was her short, fanciful dress; now she wore brown corduroy jeans, work boots, and a light blouse with long sleeves that fell over her wrists. Oversized aviator sunglasses with a hint of yellow covered most of her face. Next to Susan, Lorrie felt gigantically small. *She must think I'm so uptight,* Lorrie thought. How much, she wondered, did Susan hate her?

"So glad to see you!" Susan squealed.

Or maybe not.

Hugging one another on the sidewalk, they exchanged where-have-you-beens and what-are-you-doings.

"You're still at the Center, right?"

Lorrie nodded, though after today, it was quite clear she wasn't. Neither brought up dangling modifiers or predicate nominatives, and both avoided all talk of the smashed radio. While Susan asked about mutual friends—a few volunteers had already been shipped over and quickly shipped back, some alive, others barely—it came to Lorrie that the two of them hadn't known each other at all. From Susan's perspective, she was as an overly corrective envelope stuffer, a filer. Susan knew nothing of her bugs, her angry ex-boyfriend with the wild temper—possibly watching from around the corner or up some tall tree this very moment—the Facility, all the things that everyone else seemed to think added up to who she was.

And it went both ways, Lorrie knew. All her Susan thoughts were formed by the unfortunate day she had chosen to wear a revealing skirt and her strong aversion to the rules governing syntax. Their lives had danced around each other, but never really touched.

"Eric still running things?" Susan asked. They were stopped under a large tree.

Lorrie wanted to mention Eric's hateful outburst, but found that she could not. "Yes," Lorrie said.

"And his wolf of a mother?" Susan smiled. "Is she still there?"

"Jane?"

"Yeah, Jane." Susan snorted as the name left her lips.

"You didn't hear about Jane? We were walking in the park, and two agents just came and took her."

"What's she charged with?"

"That's the thing. No one can find her. She's just vanished."

Susan shrugged. "I don't know what they would want *her* for."

The tough new Susan in front of her made Lorrie shy, but what Jane had done to Susan besides embarrass her for that short skirt awhile back, Lorrie couldn't imagine. This new Susan didn't seem like she would hold such a fragile grudge.

What she wanted, Lorrie realized, were Susan's secrets, an explanation of the way her posture made it seem as though she might grab a flowerpot and smash it over someone's head. In a flash, Lorrie saw how timid she had been, how she had let her ideas leak out in tiny, polite drips and drops rather than speaking her mind with the loud and bold voice in her head. But could Susan see that, too? Susan had gutted whatever house she had been living in, that much was clear.

Talking to Susan on the street, Lorrie felt far too exposed. "How about we grab a cup of coffee?" she suggested. At the entrance to the coffee shop, Lorrie paused and looked in. There wasn't an inch of free space along the walls. The owners—probably three-digit university boys whose daddies helped get them Respected Doctor notes for asthma and pigeon toes—had clearly studied the coffee shops of Western City North and done their best to replicate the experience here in Interior City. And it was working; the café was packed with women and vets. This was, she thought, just the kind of place Lance used to piss away his days in. Still, Lance didn't know his way around Interior City. Wherever he was, there was little chance he would be here.

Feet still street-side, Lorrie's mind traveled back to the slightest hesitation she had felt before entering a photo studio/bookstore to chat with a nice-looking rural boy while Terry fixed the car; the doorway of her Western City North apartment that smelled of old cigarettes and new foods; the entrance to each and every closet in which she had pushed up against the peeled-skin artist; every threshold she had crossed before her started-over life in Interior City back when bright-eyed bugs still distorted her life and decayed her veins. She had exited all of it: the up-country entryway of the Facility, the double-glass doors of the Center that failed to stop men from going to war. Most of all, she had left Lance, whose boiling-water temper was more unstable than an industrial reactant. From her place on the sidewalk, the odor of the sugar maples rolled through her nostrils and mixed with the roasted beans of the café. Immediately Lorrie knew that the swirling aroma was the air of her started-over life. She was not with a man in Western City North who beat her. She was not in a Young Savior–obsessed crazy-person clinic near the border of Allied Country N. Those doors were gone. Now she was outside a coffee shop with a woman in strong clothes who had almost smashed her toenails with a radio and had no idea about any of her other doorways.

"You all right?" said Susan.

"Perfect," Lorrie said. "Just perfect."

They walked inside and twisted themselves through the makeshift aisles and narrow spaces toward the back of the café. One man sobbed softly in the far corner, another held his oversized mug in front of his face, ashamed to be seen. One of his ears was scabbed and tattered, the other seemed to have been blasted off completely.

"How about over there?" Lorrie pointed to a battered couch on the other side of the room with deep depressions in each of its cushions.

"What? Oh, no. Not that. Just a friendly little reminder, Lorrie: never sit on the couches here, even if they just zapped them." She paused. "They're filled with bugs."

Lorrie shuddered.

Susan seemed to pick up on her discomfort. "How about my place instead?" she asked. "This coffee shop looks like they're scheduled for a blackout anyway."

Susan's smile was greedy, and Lorrie could see that she, too, was ready to flee the empty human lives that were all over the café. Again she looked at Susan's impressive new swagger. If Lorrie could plug the right ideas in, she decided, then Susan was the right one to deliver them.

"Just come," Susan said.

"There is a lot of stuff that needs to be done at the Center," said Lorrie.

Susan raised an eyebrow.

For a moment Lorrie had forgotten the loud music of her departure. No, she would not be going back to the Center. Doug, the worst counselor ever, could continue shooting Substance in the bathroom before returning to his desk to scribble divergent loops while men across from him cried. Though the Center might be slowed down by the lack of a woman to file their intelligible notes, their problems were much more severe than that.

❖ ❖ ❖

Susan lived on the tenth floor of a condemned building. Interior City simply had yet to bulldoze the place, she explained, and so Susan and a few hardy neighbors on floors two, three, and five stuck it out, occupying the large, airy rooms with the knowledge that on any day a crew of old men and newly trained women in hard hats might bang a warning on their doors that today was the day the building was to be reduced to rubble. In the lobby, they walked past the elevator bank and straight to the stairs. Even if the elevators had been working, in this time of constant blackouts neither of them was foolish enough to ride one.

Once in the apartment, Susan pulled out a fifth of rum from beneath a cushion, and the two of them sat on her couch and took short slugs right from the bottle. Looking around the apartment, Lorrie saw no newspapers or magazines. In Lorrie's circle, such a lack of media was unheard of. To be informed, to be up to date with as many publications as possible, was to show you cared about stopping the war. "No newspapers?" asked Lorrie. She was curious; she couldn't help it.

Susan looked at her with a stretched smile that almost bordered on pity. "The way to understand the war," Susan said, "isn't to read about it in the papers. All that so-called news is just noise. And the more noise there is, the harder it is to hear what's really going on." Susan leaned toward her. "Now have some more." The rum was sour and burnt her insides.

The echo of Susan tugging at her tiny skirt in the circle of the Center, of Susan bragging about her excellent filing skills, of Susan being anything other than the woman in corduroys taking deep swigs from the bottle in front of them, those old Susans were gone. This Susan had been exposed, dazzled, and Lorrie knew that she would have to soak herself in whatever world Susan was living in until it coated all of her, right down to the last column of her spine.

"Can I ask you a question?" Lorrie heard herself say. "Why did you stop coming to the Center?" She took another gulp from the bottle of rum in front of them.

"Why? Because their tactics were stale. I wanted to really do something."

"Jane used to talk about that."

Susan snorted. "Forget about Jane, Lorrie. Don't you see she's dust? None of them can counsel us. They've got nothing. Especially not some old broad like Jane."

"So what, she's old? What have you got against Jane? She had a lot of influence around that place. I was working her, getting her to get Eric to let women counsel? She was into it, too. But she's probably suffering right now in some secret prison."

"Sure, that sucks for Jane the individual. But don't forget what Jane was all about. 'War is not a healthy thing for children.' Mother's Day cards to Homeland officials. 'Girls Say Yes to Boys Who Say No.'" Her voice had a low, mocking tone. "She was just being nice to you. She would have never been in favor of women counselors."

She passed Lorrie the rum. Lorrie turned the bottle upside down and opened her mouth wide. Nothing came out. Susan had finished it. "Jane thinks—thought—we should be more sympathetic to the Coyotes. They hate the war, too."

Susan ignored this. "You got a kid?"

"No."

"Me neither. But it's like we shouldn't say anything unless we're talking about how it affects our babies. Jane's whole authority came from motherhood. She would go on and on about 'mothers this, mothers that.'" Her hands performed wild gestures she seemed to associate with mothers. Susan lowered her voice. "I don't give a fuck about babies, Lorrie. I care about stopping this war."

Lorrie's eyes cut downward.

"And if you want to stop this war, you'll quit talking about Coyotes, at least until they can triple, no, quintuple their membership. What are they now, like, five percent of parliament? This war is about to turn twenty-three years old! I don't know what Jane's agenda was, but I know it's irrelevant. I mean, don't get me started on that 'girls say yes' shit." Susan stood up and went to the kitchen.

"But she doesn't mean—"

"Really, Lorrie? Do we have to talk about what we do and don't get to do at the Center?" Susan pulled another bottle from a cabinet, twisted the cap, and handed it to Lorrie.

"True."

"Exactly. Now let me hit you with something real. No more typing Eric's bullshit notes. I'm on a new grind, a hustle that actually stops the Registry."

Lorrie tilted the bottle up and pursed her lips around the opening. The river of rum pricked at the walls of her throat as she gulped it down.

Susan went on. She knew, she said, a way that could help the men ensnared.

"Gay?" Lorrie guessed.

"Oh, gay is out. They're giving them full rights and then snapping them up the moment they peek their heads out. Besides, the gay angle is pretty unethical, if you ask me. That whole ruse the Center runs about pretending to hate gays so they'll think you're gay?"

"What about it?"

"It validates the hate! So wrong. But again, what I'm into is way beyond any of that."

"Fake papers at a three-digit university? Respected Doctors notes?"

"Don't joke. Those have been gone for months now." She wiggled her fingers, a signal for Lorrie to pass the rum. "Even the kids with mommies and daddies who shit Currencies can't snag those notes anymore. I'm telling you, this is different. Can you get out of town for a few days?"

Lorrie thought about her started-over life once again. In high school she had taken a few classes in Foreign before the ban kicked in, and she knew the language had a word for the concept. She had looked for that started-over word, asked around, even queried a librarian at the neighborhood branch with the smooth stone walls and the well-kept window trim. She had never found the word, but the way Susan smiled at her, she knew she was living inside one, even if old shadows were still about.

"So are you in?"

"Is it dangerous?"

Susan gave a sad shake of her head. "Let's do something that matters. We can't let another year go by. Let's do something real, Lorrie." She held the bottle toward Lorrie with an outstretched hand.

"But is it dangerous?"

"Of course it is."

27.

Tuesday morning in the cabin. No one to talk to, no one anywhere. Benny did this to you, he told himself. Pumped his body full of Substance, got caught, and left you up here to rot. Outside the cabin were jagged trees, a massive boulder field, the harsh quiet of total emptiness. No sounds but those of his own deep breaths. In the silence, Joe could see clearly that no one should have to pursue their own ruin unless they chose to. But running on your own was no kind of life. Induction was at six p.m. To show up was an either/or proposition. Either you surrendered your freedom at sundown or you didn't. One could not report late; today is Tuesday, he thought. This is the night.

First Tuesdays are the worst days.

28.

Leaving the truck, the unchecked darkness in front of him, Benny counted steps. Knowing he was far from the city, after every hundredth step he started the count again, the numbers edging out all pain, thirst, and desire. Large tasks, he knew, were less daunting when chopped into small, manageable pieces. Getting back to the city was a large task.

As he walked, he asked himself why he was going back to Western City North at all. Most of his friends had been snapped up, a few had disappeared, and others had simply lost it, wandering around the city like starving dogs. And yet, the city called to him, from its small neighborhoods of low-slung buildings to its massive steel skyscrapers, their sharp tips pointing toward the stars. New waves of people would replace those he was missing, other like-minded souls who managed to give the Registry the slip. Each day could still be an adventure. His ankles became weak, every new step igniting a small wildfire. Just a hundred more.

Sometime after first light, Benny reached the city. He could sense his own stink from the way people flung their eyes elsewhere as he passed. He found a bench and sat, caught in a dark turn between fear and exhaustion. Now, drawn out by the rise of the sun, people emerged from their houses, on their way to work, to school, to some life Benny couldn't conceive of.

The slatted wood bench was painted dark green, though most of the paint had peeled. To finally sit was to experience, if only for a moment, a perfect world. No past, no future. But as he sat, he stuck his hands into the huge pockets of his coat, and the world to come invaded. No Currencies, not a one.

"You're all pinned-up, aren't you?" A girl slid onto the other end of his bench. She was young, maybe a few years younger than him. Her face was long and slender, topped with wide, ranging eyebrows; he had noticed those right away. Bushed and crow-colored, they hung over her sockets in a way that shielded her eyes. "You've got it bad, I can tell. You're knotted up, big time."

"Fuck off," Benny told her. He didn't need this right now. He was bone-tired, and besides, women in Western City North were always coming at him. Part of him couldn't blame her: undamaged men stood out like exotic animals surrounded by drooping cats and limping dogs. But when had he last slept? Again he felt around in the big canvas pockets of his coat, unable to shake the dim memory that there had been a few Currencies in there earlier. Glossed and slippery paper touched his fingers, and he pulled out a bus ticket. Benny studied the destination to see what he could make of it.

"Going somewhere?" the girl asked. "Me, I'm trying to get out of town. Maybe make it down to Western City South."

She hadn't taken the hint, he noticed, but a woman not taking the hint wasn't surprising. Most of them, once school was over, barely got a chance to speak to a man their own age in possession of two arms, two legs, and a small serving of sanity. This one next to him didn't seem willing to let the opportunity slip away.

"I don't feel like talking," he told her. With these women who were not used to male conversation, directness was essential. The bus ticket in Benny's hand was yellow and crumpled; it would have looked fine under museum glass. A closer look showed it had expired. He couldn't quite make out the numbers.

"What's the big deal? I'm just being friendly."

Benny shrugged. What the fuck was this ticket? The sky was grey, blanketed by one gigantic cloud. Benny looked down at the paper in his hand. *Destination: Rural Sector M.* His uncle's cabin.

Joe.

Out of survival mode and momentarily safe from the Registry, arteries fully sober, only now could Benny recognize what he had done to his friend. He knew he had convinced Joe to head to the cabin and was somewhat sure he had passed off the key. Joe would be fine without him; Joe could be all right on his own, as long as he had the key. Desperately, he again plunged hand into pocket.

"Lose something?" the girl asked. She was turned sideways and hugging her knees.

The pads of Benny's fingers touched cold metal. "Fuck!" Wrapping his hand around the key ring, he ripped it from his pocket and threw it as far as he could. It landed in the grass with a soft plop.

"No one can stop me from leaving," the girl said. "I'm getting out of here. Western City North." She shook her head. "It's completely wild, right? Too wild."

"Sure, sure," Benny mumbled. If she had an agenda, he couldn't focus on it.

Responsibilities pierced him. Events from his dealer's house, the squalid truck, the Blue Unicorn Café, all of them were now connected and destroying what little harmony he had. Who he was, what he had or hadn't done; it all came back to him. Joe had gone to the cabin to think about induction.

Joe alone was not a good thing. Like no one else in his life, Benny felt a responsibility toward his somber friend. It wasn't just the fact that Joe secretly loved him—Benny had known about that for as long as he could remember. Instead, the responsibility came from a different place. Joe was as soft as a soap bubble. He took jokes too personally, he couldn't dance, his frail body unable to perform any of the required graceful motions, but most of all, those childhood religion classes had seeped into him in some deep and haunting way. No, Joe was not like any of his other friends. Joe needed him. And he had let him go.

The keys sat on the damp grass in front of him.

And still there was more. *My greetings from the Registry*, Benny thought, *my order to report*. He was sure he was up on the same day as Joe—hadn't that been what they'd talked about in the Unicorn?—but he needed confirmation. The Substances were fucking with his head—that much he could tell. But Joe was up at the cabin—that was right. Only he couldn't be inside it. And how cold was it up there at this time of year? Cold as fuck. Had he been somewhere close to Joe last night, stuck in the back of a truck? Hard to say. All Benny knew was that his greetings had called for him and that Joe was alone and waiting. Had his greetings been for yesterday? Today? The particulars escaped him. If the induction date was yesterday, he'd missed it. But then again, missing it was okay, if missing it was what he wanted to do. But that meant he was again a criminal, a dodger. It was all too much. A pretty moth or an ugly butterfly settled on the wood of the bench between Benny and the woman.

"What day is it?" he shouted at her. His voice sounded like rubble.

"Monday," she told him.

So his greetings were tomorrow. The first Tuesday of the month, he knew, that arrogant, fatal day for a huge chunk of men. *First Tuesdays*, the phrase went, *are the worst days*.

"What's that book?" the woman said. "I could use some reading for my travels."

"What book?" She had no way to understand his problems. Her tomorrow could be anything. Benny actually had to be somewhere, and so did his oldest friend in the world, who was stuck outside a cold cabin with no keys.

"That little book in your pocket." The girl was still talking, nodding her head toward his coat.

Benny looked at his other pocket, the pocket that hadn't held the bus ticket and the keys and the reminders of his orders to report. With his hands tied behind his back in the truck, all the information in his pocket had been moot, unreachable. Now, the coat continued to cough up little bits of paper that helped him recall the various people and institutions he had let down.

"You're a real dazed kind of guy, aren't you?"

The pleasant thought came to Benny that maybe his coat had a bad-news pocket as well as a good-news counterpart, a left-hand path and a right-hand one. And the woman was right—from the top of the good-news pocket poked the pages of a tiny book, smaller even than the pocket scripture carried by Offshooters attempting to convince passersby that the terror they all bore was just another plan of the Young Savior's.

Benny looked at the engraved title pressed on the bonded leather. *One Thousand and One Ways to Beat the Registry.*

Incredible. Someone in the dealer's house must have slipped it in his pocket. To think, there could have been anything in there: a few Currencies, one of those little scissors to cut fingernails, some last bits of Substance. But there was a book, the best of all books, the only book he had ever needed. Benny looked at the girl. She was here, he saw, for him, set down in his midst to point out the small soft book in his humongous pocket.

"That sure is a lot of ways to win," she said. The sun bent around the girl like a spotlight.

"You," Benny said, sliding toward her. Paint chips from the slats of the bench crinkled under him. She was glowing. "You're an—"

"Just trying to make my way up north." Benny could have sworn she'd said she was going south a minute ago. The whites of her eyes were fresh and laundered; the dazzling sunlight poured over her.

She was in flames, and Benny told her so. "You're glowing," he said. "On fire." She smiled because the flames could not consume her; she was meant to do what she had just done: bring the dawn and exile the doom. He pulled her close and wrapped his arms around her. She was hot all over, and her chest rose up and down, sweet and panting.

"What do you think you're doing?" She did a wiggle dance and pushed herself from his grasp. Just as quickly, the light was off her and so was the fire. "You think because there's no men left," she said, leaping off the bench, "you can put your dirty hands on me whenever you feel like it? I'm out of here." She sailed across the park, a small little spot. "And by the way," she stopped and turned, yelling over her shoulder, "you smell like death!"

Benny shrugged. It didn't matter if she was going north or south, or what he really smelled like; the girl had done what she needed to do.

His hands flipped the book like a fan, and his eyes jumped up and down the cascading pages. Surely Joe would tire of waiting for him at the cabin, would surrender to what he thought was his fate and head back to the induction center. Only what Joe didn't know was that Benny would be there, bathed in bright light, ready to intercept him with whatever was inside these pages. There were one thousand and one ways to beat the Registry, but Benny needed the number that was right for him. He looked down, into the book.

25. Stretch yourself on a rack till you're so tall they won't take you.

26. Marry your mother.

27. Marry your father.

28. Blow up a bridge.

29. Marry your sister.

30. Wear pants made of pudding.

31. Grow nine toes in the middle of your forehead.

32. Make the world go away.

He stared at the pages and tried to rearrange the letters into opportunities that meant something, actual, real ideas that were usable. Maybe there was still more Substance left in his system than he had thought. Maybe numbers twenty-five through thirty-two were jokes. He flipped toward the end.

896. Solder your eyelids shut.

897. Round up your friends and get them to crucify you.

898. Develop a language that you speak only from your anus.

899. Tell the Registry that you'll leap into your own grave laughing.

900. Grow old fast.

A dark horror started at the base of his back and coiled a wicked path up his spine. Like a dog digging for a buried bone, he rubbed the words on the page with his thumb and forefinger, wishing hard that these sentences were the painful trick of the final drops of Substance in his body. But the words didn't rearrange themselves, didn't change at all. The cells of his nerves were sick, and the book made them sicker. Leaning forward, Benny pressed his body in half and vomited on the grass in front of him. Out poured a thin, yellow bile.

A bunch of jokes, he thought. His sentence was carved in the form of a thousand and one stupid jokes. He wiped his mouth with his sleeve and swallowed.

So the angelic eyebrowed girl had been entirely mortal. Of course she was. When had the Young Savior ever done anything but make a mess for him?

Another spasm in his stomach, and he knew his body had more to empty. Fingers loosening, he dropped the book to the ground, a direct hit into the yellow pool by his feet. A small splash on the legs of his pants, and the edges of the paper began to darken, soaking up his juices. Another go, and Benny heaved a final load of yellow onto the cover. The book was fully soaked. Huddling knees to chest, Benny curled into a ball, his chin tucked in, an attempt at darkness. A book of jokes. His hot breath was as old and flavored as a dying man's. He pressed his eyes shut. Not to sleep, but instead to stop, if only for a moment, the rest of the world from coming in.

One thousand and one ways to beat the draft, and he had vomited on all of them.

29.

I have left Gad, Alan thinks, *or he has left me. Either way, we are separated.*

One final bus ride away from Western City North, he feels that his life until now has been a series of extended naps. Upon arriving in that city, he will surely be forever awoken. So tomorrow, he can weep for his missing friend. Or maybe find a new one. But right now, he has a ticket to Western City North. Ten minutes till departure.

Through the stained window of the depot, Alan sees an unmarked bus pull into the parking lot. One by one, young men, their heads newly shaven, step down to the concrete. All of them exit with a thicket of nervousness. They are, Alan realizes, being bused off to war. A few circle up in a vacant space near the bus and begin a game of keep-it-up with an old ball. Others pull out cigarettes. Enjoy it while you can, Alan thinks.

Without Gad, there's no one to inform him of the genius of his plan. No matter. Alan steps outside. As he exits the station, the heavy hiss of idled motors whizzes through his ears. The panel doors of the Registry bus are open; he can see the driver resting up before the next shift. The air is warm and smoky. With a nearly invisible gesture, Alan reaches into his bag and wraps his fingers around the smooth steel handle of his hunting knife. Just a quick check to make sure.

"How long till your bus leaves?" he asks the group of soon-to-be soldiers.

"Half hour," comes the response.

Wherever HIM is, whenever Alan links up with the group, he will need some sort of lurid souvenir. Now is his chance. Thanking the soldiers, Alan slinks away, turning the corner and walking to the other side of the bus where he cannot be seen.

I don't know how tires work, he thinks. *I haven't learned the proper angle, the most effective way to stab.* Would there be a loud pop, a rush of air? But as Woody Gilbert wrote in the pamphlets: action must divest itself of awareness in order for true skill to occur. Removing the hunting knife from his bag, Alan slides the blade from the sheath and, in one smooth motion, plunges it into the sidewall. The rubber is tougher than he expected. Pushing down, he grinds the serrations of the blade against the tire. Finally he hears the small hiss of air. *Funny,* he thinks, *I thought it would come so much quicker.*

On the other side of the bus, he hears the yelps of the future soldiers and their game of keep-it-up. Alongside the deflated tire is another one, parallel, just waiting to experience the same impersonal pain. Looking over his shoulder, Alan sees no one. Lifting his arm high in the air, he feels the crude and shapeless joy of destruction as the point of the blade enters the rubber. Each stab is natural, a reflex. When he finds HIM, when the baldheads make the introduction, he will find people who understand. He will show them this slice of Registry rubber. And they will show him—

He does not know what they will show him. And that is exactly the point.

Alan checks his watch. His ticket will expire if he does not get on the next bus to Western City North. He gets on the bus.

❖ ❖ ❖

Safely in his seat, Alan allows himself a moment to feel. Whatever was awakened within him by lighting the fire only became more enlivened by slashing the tires of the Registry bus. If only there had been someone to admire his work! But Gad was weak, too convinced by a sense that the Registry was inevitable—that must have been it. Without a model for another way of life, he had simply jumped back to his old one. So sad. That path of his would lead nowhere. A jolt in the road as the bus runs through a pothole, and the thought strikes him: Will Gad allow him a path of his own?

There are a thousand ways in which he is not safe. All of the other passengers on the bus are women. But women might be Reggies just as often as men. He considers the blunt possibility that Gad might have told people, alerted some team of agents in a windowless room that Alan will be arriving in Western City North as a Registry-runner with an intent toward arson, and that all of these innocent-looking women are just waiting for the right moment to spring up from a reclined seat and wrap their hands around his throat.

The roads are now open. Policemen, Registry agents, whoever they send after rogue Homeland Indigenous who burn their schools down and run toward a second taste, anybody could be coming for him. But not because of Gad. How can he think that? Gad, he decides, would not betray him. And even if he did, so what? He had not been caught for the fire, had not been spotted as he let the air out of the tires of the Registry bus. In the pale light of the rising sun, it comes to Alan that he might actually be good at something.

Unclear on when he last slept, Alan's tiredness forces a protective clarity he has never known. His dried-out eyeballs make high-pitched clinks every time he blinks. *I'm not sorry for anything I've done,* he thinks, *only that my best friend might have told someone I've done it.*

"Last stop," the driver announces. "Downtown. Western City North."

Alan reaches into his bag, pushing aside his beloved hunting knife, gliding over his one pair of socks, before finally coming to rest on the zippered pouch from his father. The industrial matches are still there. With grace and tenderness he slides his fingers over them. It's time to burn down the induction center.

❖ ❖ ❖

Downtown Western City North: people everywhere. Older men in suits rushing to get to wherever they have to go, women with high-heeled shoes clicking across the street. Even the air seems different—Alan can feel the salt and smell the water. No agents or policemen greet him; either Gad has not snitched or the authorities are unable to find him. Both scenarios are entirely possible.

The ocean wraps around this place—he's seen the map—but now he truly understands what it means to be a peninsular city. Wet air slurs around Alan's face. His stride is a breaststroke that breaks apart the little wet particles floating all around him. The buildings are taller than any he has ever seen.

How to begin, where to start? Briefly, he wishes he had made a pitch for Terry to join him. She had said she knew the city. But would she have supported his cause? Like Gad, she was not full-on Homeland Indigenous. And like Gad, she is not here with him.

He comforts himself with future accolades. Once he has committed his magnificent act, he will find the baldheads and get an introduction to HIM. Perhaps he will even be fast-tracked to a leadership position. Obviously he will have to strike during nighttime; that is a given. And of course he'll have to find the place first, watch the security comings and goings. Surely there will be other necessary reconnaissance, from determining the induction center's primary materials (the best burns can never be one size fits all) to more basic concerns such as escape routes and getaway plans. A young woman standing on the sidewalk hands him a free newspaper. First Tuesday, the paper tells him, is this evening, the biggest induction day of the month. Alan wonders whether he can fast-track his plan.

Still, there are other, more pressing needs. First food, then sleep. He has not eaten since sharing a loaf of bread with Gad the night before.

Peeking through the tall buildings, he sees the ocean. Finally he has reached the edge. No more civilization until some alien country thousands of distance-units away. A strange shoulder collides into him.

"Watch where you're going!" the shoulder yells. It's true; he can't look at the expanse of water and the people in front of him at the same time.

Yellow sodium lamps are lit up even though it's daytime. It could be that Western City North is immune from blackouts, he thinks, and that in this magical city the lights stay on every hour of the day. Trolleys and buses roll down the street, shiny black antennas sticking up from their backsides, crackling and dragging on overhead wires. Does a grid of wires web the entire city? And what about the blackouts? Do these wires somehow circumvent the lack of electricity in the Homeland? But no matter, an instinct of food propels him forward, directs each turn he makes. The overhead wires follow him everywhere he goes. Maybe he judged Gad too harshly; they had somehow just gotten separated, and amid the chaos they will run into each other on the streets of Western City North and embrace like old friends.

Down the street, a police officer with a wide gap between her two front teeth smiles and heads toward him. *I am her prey,* Alan thinks. This officer has spotted him, exiled and alone in her exotic world, and she is laughing with the knowledge that her brutal coworkers will soon hop from behind corners to cuff and detain him. For kids soaked in evil, for uppity Homeland Indigenous who burn down the precious facilities we provide for them, the cop's face says. At any moment, she will signal the others. But she doesn't, instead passing Alan with a bouncing-ball step. *Calm down,* Alan tells himself. *Relax.*

At the end of the block is a gleaming bronze statue, a glowing beacon that pulls Alan in, mothlike, toward its shining metal plates. The statue is a mess, a tangle of metal men pulling hard on a humongous punch press, each sinewy man wrestling with the lever. Even working together it seems doubtful they could operate the thing, and Alan wonders why this strange city wants to memorialize their failure. Even so, it's a beautiful statue, larger and shinier than any he has seen before. A man in a ragged vest sits on the plinth of the statue, directly below the bronzed action. He has one arm, small bruises around his eyes, and has surrounded himself with large piles of newspapers.

"I am much unappreciated," he tells Alan. The man smiles, and Alan can see he only has a handful of teeth.

"Sorry," Alan says, meaning it. "Do you know where I can get something to eat?"

He does, but first, he says, allow me a quick story. From under the punch press statue, the man explains that he has waited his entire life for the Young Savior to take notice of him and help him out. But the Young Savior, it seems, is distracted, preoccupied, tied up in handling His other affairs. Food? he says. Of course he can tell Alan where to get food, he snorts. That's not the point. It's bigger than food. A request, the man says. He sees that Alan is young, and could he please wait his turn for the Young Savior's help, as he himself has been waiting, he explains, a long, long time, a situation in which it is only fair that he should get to go first. Not to eat—Alan doesn't have to wait for that, the man is quick to say—but for the bigger stuff, the true favors from on high. "The things I saw in the jungle," the man says before trailing off. "If you have any manners at all, you won't cut me in line."

"But where's that food?" Alan asks again. The man points him toward a church.

The church is clearly an offshoot, its congregants and clergy not adherents of Homeland Religion proper, but whatever denomination it is, Alan doesn't pay attention and heads straight toward the line of pensive-looking men awaiting their peanut butter and white bread sandwiches. Most of the men are vets, but a few of them are healthy. Snatches of their conversation float through. "My last day of freedom," one says. *First Tuesdays are the worst days.*

Alan considers asking any of these men whether the quotas are real, a second opinion on whether all Homeland Indigenous men really do have to serve, but save for a couple of Minority Group Cs, this hungry knot of men around him are all Majority Group. Though they might have an answer, Alan knows that to most Majority Groupers, the problems of Homeland Indigenous are nearly invisible.

Instead, he asks a morose man with a severe gash between his eyebrows where he might find a safe place to take a nap and whether he knows who the baldheads are. The man tells him about a park a few blocks away with plenty of benches and minimal harassment. "Don't know what you want with those baldheads," the man says. "They just play games. They're not going to help you."

Alan thanks the man and moves on. It's been too long since he's slept, and his feet drag against the pavement. It seems impossible that happiness has ever bothered to come his way, so he tries to remind himself that he has lived a life in which good things have come to him and that he is on a journey, a quest to do something important. Even so, his lack of sleep colors everything.

Each sight his eyes fall on is sick: the dirty toddler running naked while his scarred and hobbled father tosses wood chips at a pigeon—sick. A bald man in a wheelchair with a thick mustache and matchstick legs mumbling to himself, insanity on wheels. Sick. At least he can see the park now. It's true: there are plenty of benches. As the sun lowers into the clouds, a deep, coppery light covers the world around him. Spotting an empty bench, Alan puts his bag under his head and uses it as a pillow. His bent eyes push themselves closed. Within moments, he is asleep. Soon Gad comes to him, calm and forgiving, and they develop a true plan, a direction.

"Hey," a voice says. *(Name and Address of Person Who Will Always Know Your Address.)* We could find each other, Alan thinks. I could explain. "Hey," repeats the voice.

Gad has found him.

But the voice isn't Gad's. Alan looks up and squints into the morning sun. However long he has slept, it doesn't seem to have been enough. A man is speaking, telling him that where he's sleeping isn't a good place to sleep.

"A young guy like you? Alone on a First Tuesday?" the man says. "Might as well just go report for duty."

The man has gold crowns in his mouth that wink when he talks. He is also missing one arm. On closer inspection, the man's furry voice sounds nothing like Gad. Is the sound of his closest friend already fading?

"But I don't have a good place to sleep," Alan says. He blinks the sun out of his eyes.

"Well, I can get you a meal."

The man, Alan sees, is bald.

"A kid who doesn't have a good place to sleep could probably use a meal," the bald man says. "But first, you have to play a game."

"A game?" Alan says. A shuddering joy comes over him. Though he knows his path is a long one, it seems that he has stumbled upon the trailhead. Perhaps the rubber slice of Registry bus could serve as the sincerity of his intentions. Maybe he doesn't have to burn down the induction center tonight after all.

"Come take a ride," the baldhead says. It is as though the man is reading a script from his pamphlets. Everything is how it should be. "Get ready for the most important game of your life."

Let the journey begin.

30.

Benny woke up shivering, the cold sun drilling holes in his eyelids. He had slept, it seemed, from the afternoon of one day to the morning of the next. A thin film of dew had wrapped itself around him while he slept. Hours on the bench had made him stiff, though the thought of making his way toward the induction center offered up a much worse feeling. *First Tuesdays are the worst days.* At least he had till sundown.

Sitting up, he could see that his bench was not the only one in the park that had been slept on. Other men around him slowly groaned to life, pushing off the wet morning as best they could.

As his stomach spun, Benny thought of Joe. How had he spent his nights up there in the mountains? Hopefully Joe had been smart enough to somehow break into the cabin. *One Thousand and One Ways to Beat the Registry* was still on the grass, dried and caked with bile, pages stuck and mashed together. If his throat could have handled it, Benny would have coughed up some more, just to punish that book filled with words all pointed in the wrong direction.

There was, Benny thought, nothing to intercept Joe with if he showed up at the induction center, nothing to save either of them. A one-armed man with a shaved head and a pair of horn-rimmed glasses moved into Benny's line of sight. People in this city just couldn't leave each other alone.

"I don't need it," Benny said.

"What don't you need?"

"Whatever your angle is."

"Fair enough. We don't need you, either." The man sidestepped the vomit-caked book and sat down on the bench.

Benny turned to look at him. "Does whatever you have that doesn't need me have a meal somewhere in it?"

"Yup."

"Okay."

"But if you want the meal, you're going to have to play a game." The gold crowns flashed again. The man seemed to be enjoying himself.

"What kind of game?"

"The most important game of your life."

"Look, I just want something to eat, okay? I'll listen to whatever you say, but I have to be somewhere important by sundown."

"First Tuesday, eh? That's nothing compared to the Joust. First day of the rest of your life, brother."

"That's the game? The Joust?"

"You got it."

"Meal first?"

"On my word." He placed his hand to his chest.

The man led Benny to the edge of the park, where a large van idled on the street. Inside were two other men with shaved heads—one of them definitely Registry age, a situation that immediately tensed Benny up—alongside a bald woman and three other guys with hair who seemed to have also been sleeping in the park. The youngest— even younger than me, Benny thought—looked to be worse off than any of them. Bags under his eyes and a nervous look on his face, this kid was Minority Group L, Benny thought, or maybe even Homeland Indigenous, but definitely tired, hungry, and new to the city. As the van pulled out into the street, the kid's eyes, though hemmed-in and hungry, clamored to take in as much of the city as his weakened state would allow.

"Now right there"—Benny pointed to the kid, eager to act as tour guide—"that's the island just off the coast where—"

"Wow," the driver said, turning around to interrupt. "You guys smell like corpses."

Who the hell was this bald-kid driver to talk to him like that? And on a First Tuesday? Benny would have swung an axe right through his neck if the situation had allowed for it. That his last day of freedom should have to be spent cadging free food from strangers was a hollow truth that the driver's smug words seemed to magnify. What about good-byes to friends, to parents? But again, he still had till sundown. If he could just get a good meal, his mind might clear a bit and he'd be able to think. "Now where was I?" Benny cleared his throat and pointed out a few more landmarks to the possibly Indigenous kid. No one brought up the fact that it was First Tuesday, but everyone was well aware that a good chunk of the populace was due to report. Even those who had never interacted with the Registry knew how the last day of freedom worked. Show up by six p.m. or else.

Through the window, Benny looked at the pedestrians—women mostly—their faces cracked with grief as they went about their day. First Tuesdays made it even worse, he knew, even if their men were long gone. All it took was the pain of another to be reminded of their own misery.

A few more turns and Benny saw the van was headed into the northern part of the city. They drove uphill, past high fences shielding the large homes of the sort of folks who wouldn't think twice about calling the Point Line on some wildhair wandering their streets. Not like the rusty quadrants surrounding the induction center. Today the place would be packed, and for a brief moment he worried about finding Joe once he got there. A quick meal from these baldheads and then he would duck over to look for him. The timing shouldn't be hard; if he knew his oldest friend, Joe would have made the decision not to run and would wait for him outside the center, even if it meant walking in just as the blaze of the sun lowered below the horizon. They would find each other, and Benny would tell Joe he was sorry for demanding he follow and then leading him straight to nowhere. Not that an apology would do either of them any good in the jungle.

Benny turned to the possibly Indigenous kid next to him. "So what are you here for?"

The kid frowned. "A meal, just like you."

"No, I mean, why were you sleeping in the park?"

"Why were *you* sleeping in the park?"

Fine, so the kid didn't want to talk. Probably had to be at the Registry by six himself. The van drove on. The driver wavered the knob of the radio, pausing for a moment on a tearful ballad. Just as the song reached its highest, most impassioned state, the driver shifted the station. Even though Benny still hated the guy for calling him smelly, he couldn't blame him for the switch. Sometimes turning off a piece of yourself was the only way to get through the day.

Now, a news station: *At a press conference on the steps of the highest lawmaking assembly in the Homeland,* an announcer intoned, *four more legislators announced that they would now caucus with the Coyo—*

Again the driver twisted the knob.

"Hey!" said Benny. "I wanted to hear that."

"Like four more make a difference," the driver said.

The other baldheads laughed, as did a few of the park dwellers. All of them but the possibly Indigenous kid.

31.

These baldheads are strange, Alan thinks. But whoever they are, the bald-heads are also, he knows, outside the main lines of communication, downwind from the visible. And below it all is where he needs to be. The van speeds onward, past manicured bushes and verdant lawns, the houses themselves mysteriously hidden.

Wherever HIM is, Alan knows that from now on, he, too, will need to occupy the hidden spaces of the Homeland. Just like Woody Gilbert did. You had to if you were going to unslave young Indigenous from the Homeland and wage war on its way of thinking. How lucky he feels that he has been exposed to the truth at all.

Perhaps all it takes is to get behind the curtain. Perhaps every-thing he needs is backstage. On the radio, commentators rattle on about First Tuesday, the war turning twenty-three, the prime minister's recent absence from the airwaves. A whole bunch of surface stuff that he doesn't need to pay attention to. Someone makes a joke he doesn't hear, and the entire van breaks into mindless laughter. These baldheads are the stagehands, hinging open the trapdoors on the surface and leading him to all that is hidden below. Alan feels a tap on his shoulder. The talkative stinky guy from the park asks him another annoying question.

32.

"Out," said the driver. The van had pulled into the driveway of a massive house. In the front yard, baldheads darted in quick bursts all around them, eyes angled downward. "Follow me," said the man with gold crowns.

Outside, two or three of the baldheads were focused on watering the large and healthy plant life in the front garden. Other baldheads scurried about with urgent postures, hustling around frantically and making wild, jerkwater motions with their hands. Inside, the mansion was immaculate. Dark woods, bright rugs, all bejeweled and gleaming.

The place around Benny seemed charged with a latent rapture that might erupt at any moment. Why these young men should be so happy on a First Tuesday—chances were, some of them had to be up today as well—he didn't plan on sticking around to find out. Once the promised food came, he would try to slip away before they started their weird little game.

The baldhead led all the park-dwellers from the van into a large room with a platter of stale sandwiches set out on a lengthy table decorated with ferns and a bowl of grapes. The park-dwellers attacked the spread. Of course the grapes were waxed; real grapes would have cost a fortune. Even so, Benny had to touch them. He didn't care that the sandwiches were stale. They were stacked high, and he ate five of them before he nearly popped a wax grape in his mouth for dessert; it had been so long since he'd had a real one. Benny watched the possibly Indigenous kid stuff two sandwiches into his mouth without chewing. Each bite was fabulous, joyful to the point of hallucination. An incredibly tall baldhead appeared and pointed to the possibly Indigenous kid.

"You asked for me?"

The tall man and the possibly Indigenous kid disappeared down a stairwell.

Once Benny was done eating, another baldhead walked him to the bathroom and handed him a thick red towel. Fine, first a shower, and then he would make his way out of here. On the way to the bathroom, he passed a group of men with full heads of hair. A good chunk of these visitors to baldhead house seemed war age, and all were well dressed. Blue suits, red ties. He studied them for subtle signs that they, too, were up for First Tuesday this evening, but nothing on these men's faces indicated anything but excitement. They were dressed up and ready to play. But play what?

❖　❖　❖

After his shower, a waiting baldhead directed him to a large main room with a group of folding chairs arranged around a central circle in the rug. For the first time in recent memory, Benny's body felt fresh, light, even, and he sucked in the unfamiliar smells that had materialized on his skin. The other park-dwellers had scrubbed up, too, seemingly in other bathrooms planted in distant corners of this massive home, all of them except the Indigenous kid, who he didn't see anywhere. Benny felt a stab of jealousy that the Indigenous kid had probably done exactly what he had wanted to: eaten their food and run. Through the window, the high sun suggested it was midafternoon. Plenty of time until sundown. Maybe he would just check out this game for a minute.

His thoughts were interrupted by the touch of yet another Registry-aged baldhead. "That way," the man said. "The Joust is over there."

The grand room held a mixture of baldheads, young men in suits, and freshly scrubbed park people. The very tall baldhead motioned for them to sit in the folded chairs arranged in a circle.

"Listen up, losers," the tall man boomed. "We've brought you here to play a game." The men on either side of him looked like children. "Only it's not just a game," the tall man continued. "Of course, it *is* a game, but if we thought it was *just* a game, we wouldn't go around finding you crumbs to come play it with us."

A few of the park-dwellers, Benny included, moved their eyes toward each other.

The tall man noticed the glances. "You don't like the word *crumbs*? How about Substance Q-heads? What am I saying, I saw some of you get dropped off this morning. If you were just on Substance Q, that would be the least of your problems."

How long would this bullshit take? He'd had the meal, Benny thought, the luscious warm-water shower, and the puffy towel. Now it was time to head to the induction center, find Joe, say sorry, and break the news that the both of them were beyond saving. Maybe he should just stand up and walk out.

"So what are we going to do?" the tall man went on, his eyes gliding across each person in the circle. "Well, what are we not going to do? We are going to not hold back. This is a Joust, understand? Engaged combat. A Joust isn't some cocktail party chatter. It's an attack. You can yell anything, anything that comes into your head."

"What are the rules?" asked a park-dweller.

"Rules?" The tall man smiled broadly and raised an eyebrow. "Three rules. Don't Joust drunk or high on any Substance, not even Q. No physical threats. And no holding back."

Well *that* sounded interesting. Benny listened as the tall man explained the theory of the Joust: "We attack the lies in your lives, the hypocrisy. We take your poisonous attitudes and cure them. We expose and free your secret fears and guilt," he said, "thereby reducing the tendency for you to pour your distress into some Substance. No line of thought is out of place. Lies are in the service of truth. None of you are clean. Confess, assholes. Dump your shit, or we *will* extract it. Like it or not, we are your only alternative to total failure."

The guy was clearly an overconfident prick, but Benny couldn't help but like him. Most of what the tall man had said felt silly or slight, but Benny could see how much the guy was enjoying himself. He liked that; he hadn't been around such a magnitude of happiness in a long time.

"And now," the tall man yelled, "let's Joust!"

Benny shrugged and stared up at the ceiling beams, all angled to the center of the room like spokes on a wheel. So this was it: a nice shower, a sandwich or two, and some crazy game, followed by a trip across town and a loss of freedom. Why the hell not?

❖ ❖ ❖

Two hours of listening to people vent their rage was more than enough. With their voices now scalded from yelling, the group seemed angrier than before they had started. None of these people seemed to be able to accept the unfairness of life. Before the game had begun, they had all seemed resigned to their unfortunate circumstances. Now they were incensed.

"You think prime ministers would want to go to war if they Jousted?" the tall man said. "You think if those Coyote weenies in parliament knew how to Joust that they'd still be crouching at podiums, whining and begging 'oh pretty please stop the war'? The Joust can change the world, folks. Six days a week, right here for members. The more you Joust, the better you feel. Monthly dues only ten Currencies. You can pay on your way out."

Ridiculous. The baldheads, Benny saw, were just another group that regulated your life in return for the empty promise of happiness.

"Bring your friends," the tall man told them.

And yet these people lived here. Men, young men, ones who had not shipped off to war. The game was bullshit, but still, these baldheads were on to something. He needed to get back to Joe and bring him here. Somehow these people would hide them. Somehow yelling and screaming at others could be their substitute for war.

Benny walked over to the tall man, who was standing alone by the table looking at the waxed grapes longingly. "I want to Joust some more," he said. "I don't quite get it. But I like it."

"So you want to have another go-round?" The tall man handed Benny a cup of coffee and motioned for him to follow. For a moment Benny paused. There were no clocks anywhere in this place, but if they had started the game at noon and played for three hours, he didn't have much time to chat before he needed to leave. He had no idea how long it might take to get from this far-off neighborhood to the induction center, but it was best not to play it too close.

"You coming or what?" the tall man said.

33.

Alan and the tall man, alone in a windowless room. Three chairs, a small table with a newspaper, and a vase of purple flowers atop a small box. Does the tall man know anyone from HIM? Alan asks.

"Of course I do," the man tells him. "We're all down here together."

Though they are in a basement, "down here" seems metaphorical. Alan does not press the point. So the man has interacted with some rank-and-file HIM members. But how about Woody Gilbert? Has he met the mastermind himself?

"Saw him last week," the tall man says.

"I need to meet him," Alan says. "I need to talk to him."

"Need is the fuel of life, no?"

"What?"

"You need to meet Woody Gilbert, and I need someone to help me with something."

"Tell me," Alan says, "about that something."

"Wait here," says the tall man. "I've got a Joust to run."

"A Joust?"

"It's just a distraction that we use for cover. I'll be back in a bit. Read the paper. Make yourself comfortable."

34.

The tall man had to have known it was First Tuesday, had surely heard Benny say today was his day. So whatever he wanted to tell him, Benny thought, at least he understood Benny's situation. The two of them headed down a staircase and into a long, narrow basement hallway, baldheads darting out of one doorway only to pop into another. Large blue sacks of charcoal rested on the floor, lining the length of the passageway. The overhead lights were dull; the plaster had been painted a somber shade of grey. Gone were the upstairs odors of hard work and joyful cleanliness. Down below was sticky and dark.

Farther, deeper, they headed down the hall.

"What's the deal with all the charcoal?" Benny asked the tall man's back.

The tall man kept walking and didn't turn around. Instead, he simply raised an index finger over his head. No stopping. The two of them wound through the corridors beneath the massive house. Every few steps, the tall man ducked below a naked lightbulb, cradling his coffee gently.

How long was this going to take? The entire Homeland understood the six p.m. deadline. If he owed Joe anything, it was to be there when they took him away. Unless.

Finally the tall man came to a stop. "In here," he gestured.

So the possibly Indigenous kid from the park hadn't left after all. He was sitting in a metal folding chair reading a newspaper. The walls were bare. No windows. Three chairs in all, and a small standing table. On the table, a rectangular wooden box, on top of which rested a small vase of bell-shaped flowers, the blues and purples a shock of color in the otherwise bland room. As Benny entered, the possibly Indigenous kid didn't even look up. On the front page of the kid's newspaper, the headline: *Another Terrorist Bomb Fails to Detonate.*

The tall man took his seat. Finally Benny could look at him. When standing, the guy's face was so high up it was hard to make out his features. Small swirls of possibility thrummed through Benny's head. To be able to crap and clean himself in those sparkling bathrooms on a daily basis, what wouldn't he trade for that? He would move Joe in here, too, save them both from the Registry. And along the way, if he happened to find himself some baldhead lady to keep him warm at night, no big deal, right? Besides, even if these guys were on some crazy kick in which the only way to live was shaving his head and yelling lies around a circle, Benny had to admit that right now was the longest time he'd gone without wanting some Substance as far as he could remember. "I just want to express my interest in—"

"Shut up," said the tall man. The possibly Indigenous kid smiled into his newspaper.

Benny shut his eyes lightly before opening them again. The bags of charcoal in the hallway, the smirking expression of the tall man, the long silence of the Indigenous kid. Something was very wrong.

"In case you didn't catch names in the van," the tall man said, "this is Alan." He gestured to the kid.

The name didn't sound very Indigenous, but then again, Benny had never met a Homeland Indigenous person before. "Great to meet you," Benny said. He could sense he was in some sort of danger, but he couldn't place it. "But I should be going." He stood up from his chair.

"Nope," said the tall man, placing a heavy hand on his shoulder. "We're not done yet."

Benny sat back down.

"You asked," the tall man said slowly, "why we really do this."

Benny hadn't asked, but now didn't seem like the time to object.

"Do you ever watch television?"

A strange question. No one watched television. All the shows were either old men playing twenty years younger, barely believable women in drag, unretired athletes tackling each other gently, or, of course, the news. "Nope," Benny said. "Do you?"

The tall man smiled and grabbed his mug of coffee from the table beside him. "Of course not. Just like you, or your parents, probably, I used to watch, back in the war's early years. Back then it was different. The Homeland sold the war as some noble adventure. At that time, watching the news or reading the papers might get you an honest moment about our progress."

"And now?"

"Well, now, just like everybody, I've come to recognize that there aren't any new facts available. And still, once a week some new newspaper pops up and starts publishing. But it's all the same: we're still fighting. Sometimes we're winning, sometimes we're not."

"So instead you get Substance-smashers to yell at each other and charge a fee for participating?"

Reaching toward the small bouquet of purple flowers on the table, the tall man rubbed a flared petal between his fat thumb and slender index finger. "Nah, kid, you're missing the point. I got clean, dropped all the Substances, and when I did, I saw a little clearer, you know? I came to see some real fundamental things."

"Oh yeah?" Until now, Benny had been sure that he had long since given up on any hope for real meaning, but now, with a tall man rubbing purple petals and dangling the possibility that Benny could somehow be the master of his own life yet again, he saw how badly he wanted some sort of answer. How *was* he supposed to live amid all this shit around him? "What do you do?" he asked, more passionately than he meant to. His voice was soft. "And why do you do it?"

"That's right," the tall man said. "You're finally asking the right questions." He leaned in and lowered his voice. "Now you want to know *why* we do what we do? Why we take Substance-smashers and have them yell at each other?"

Enough with the buildup, Benny thought. *Just skip to telling me whatever the fuck it is that you do.*

"You know when I finally started to see what crap the news was?" the tall man said.

Benny stifled a sigh. The tall man took up as many words as he did inches. "When?"

"When I started making it."

Okay, Benny thought. He would bite. "What kind of news do you guys make?"

"Unfortunately, not the kind we want to. We've had some troubles, you see. Equipment-wise." He cocked his head toward Alan.

Benny looked at Alan, whose expression was still obscured behind the newspaper. He returned his eyes to the tall man. The tall man nodded. Again Benny looked at Alan, whose eyes still refused to meet his. Finally he looked once more at the headline. *Terrorist Bomb Fails to Detonate.*

"That's right," the man said. "That's what we do."

"You guys are bombing the Homeland?"

"Easy there. First off, read the headline. We're *not* bombing the Homeland."

"So you're trying to bomb the Homeland?"

"Not the Homeland. The Registry. We're certainly not the only ones. Three weeks ago, that attack on an induction center in Western City South? I have it on good authority that it was done by some Fareon folks."

"And you guys aren't the Fareon folks."

"Hah." The guy gave a fake smile. "Didn't I just explain it? As far as anyone is concerned, we're an experimental outfit using unusual methods to heal Substance-smashers."

"But what about the Fareon people?"

"Don't believe in that piece of fiction for a second. Ridiculous. The prime minister doesn't need some mythical drug to keep his blood flowing."

A hurried look he had taken at an old newspaper headline on the way to some party popped into Benny's head. "And those attacks on the Strategic National Stockpile? That's the Fareon people, too?"

"Nope. Those are Foreigns hiding in the Homeland trying to make it look like they're Fareon folks. Real-deal Ideology Fivers."

"But you're trying to kill people. Even if you haven't done it right."

"Slow down, kid. That's not what's happening here."

Benny's mind flashed to the hallway, the large blue sacks piled high against the walls. Hadn't there been some attack somewhere involving charcoal? If only he had read the papers. "So the charcoal—"

"He's finally getting warm," the tall man said to Alan.

"You filled all these Registry trucks with charcoal. In a bunch of places. I heard about that. You didn't hurt anyone, you just confused everybody. Why charcoal?"

"Well, truth be told, we've had some technical problems. According to our research, you mill down charcoal, add some everyday root killer, blenderize with a little sulfur, introduce a solvent or two, and you've got your hands on some pretty powerful explosive. Or you're supposed to."

"So you *do* want to kill Homeland citizens, but you just need to perfect your methods?"

The tall man laughed. "You make it sound so simple. But what you just saw upstairs, that's important, that's part of what we're trying to do, too." The tall man smiled, showed his landing-strip teeth. "We're rewriting the words to the song, Benny. A little street theater—I don't know if you heard about our little fashion show with stolen Homeland uniforms, but that was us—toss in some fake bombs that are never meant to go off, and, into that mix, some real bombs that *are* meant to go off. Keep people curious, keep things playful, right until they're not. Phases, understand?"

"All this so you can stop the war?"

"Oh, we don't want to stop the war. You think the prime minister would listen to us?"

"So you support the Coyotes?"

The man snorted. "Kid, you're not getting it. The Coyotes, the prime minister. They're the same thing. Just different systems of control."

"The Coyotes didn't start the war."

"No, but this sick culture did. We don't want to stop the war. This civilization, it's too sick to be saved. We need to start over, and we know how to do it. First, you mock the culture. Then you flummox it. And finally, right when things are at their most confusing, when it's spinning around and dizzy, you kill it. New culture, new world."

Benny could see from the tall man's face he was very serious.

"So why am I telling you any of this? First off, just like Alan here, you're going to help us."

"Help you what?"

"Second," the man continued, "your help is not being requested here."

Benny didn't understand. Apparently the tall man could sense his confusion.

"What I mean," the tall man said, "is that your assistance in this project is required. You have no choice but to help us."

Benny was starting to resent the tall man's vague mixture of arrogance and assumption. He turned to Alan. "You want to help these crazy mother-rapers kill people?"

"You don't know me," Alan said. "You don't know what we've been through."

"Who the hell is *we*?"

"Don't talk to him, listen to me," the tall man said. He was leaning forward now, his face close to Benny's. "This is phase three. Right now. We've got the entrance to the induction center fully rigged. First Tuesday, everybody is going to be there. We have figured out this charcoal shit, and the games are over. When the place opens at six tonight, we're going to explode it on the first person who walks through that door. We can't get too near without raising suspicion, so we're going to need someone to signal us, a kid who looks like he's got his greetings. That's you. As soon as the sun sets, it's going down."

"And what if I don't—"

The tall man reached for the purple flowers, lifted up the vase, and opened the small wooden box upon which it rested. A small flash of light reflected off the object, and Benny saw that it was a small gun. The tall man removed it from the box, wrapped a hand around the grip, and pressed the muzzle into Benny's earhole. *First Tuesdays are the worst days.*

35.

"You want to help these crazy mother-rapers kill people?"

The words hover in Alan's ears, a screaming rage coursing through him. That Benny had labeled him some unthinking murderer showed that the guy not only had no sense of the immorality of the Registry, but also of Alan's larger purpose. Once again, Alan is in a van, the tinted windows smoothing all colors into elephant grey.

The only reason he is in this van is to meet Woody Gilbert, and the only way he can meet Woody Gilbert is to fulfill the agenda of the baldheads. The tall man had laughed at his piece of Registry bus rubber. If this stunt is the only way to get introduced, so be it. Woody Gilbert *is* change, Alan knows. Woody Gilbert will purify him. Once the tall man presents him to HIM's mysterious leader, Alan will shackle himself to the man, nibble at his mind, inhale each small puff of wisdom. Together they will make the world free.

But what do any of these Majority Groupers know about freedom? With Woody Gilbert, he will be fighting for more than the small indignity of sitting out the war. In the row behind him, Benny and his privilege occupy the middle seat, a terrified expression smeared across his face. Look, Alan wants to tell him. If you escape the Registry, that's it. You're just a Majority Grouper living his life. But whoever heard of a Homeland Indigenous escaping anything? Whether the words belong to the Young Savior or Woody Gilbert, Alan cannot remember. Either way they apply: *A people cannot be free until they are able to determine their destiny.*

Just as he is about to explain this to Benny, the tall man turns to him. In the tall man's massive grip is a small device, all black save for a red button in the middle and the slim silver of a protruding antenna. "You keep your finger ready," he says to Alan. Only a truly weak man, Alan thinks, could develop a plan that involved death and not see it through. No matter. All he needs from this baldhead is an introduction. Push a button? So be it.

The whole ride over, Alan practices his first words to Woody Gilbert. *Sir, I greatly admire your work.* Too formal. *Mr. Gilbert, I am Alan, Group F.* No, too pandering, too eager to play the Homeland Indigenous card. Through the window, Alan watches the trees shake in the wind, the light slowly fading. Turning around, he can see the small pistol one of the baldheads has pressed against Benny's ribs. The tall man drives, quietly explaining to Benny that the baldheads have rigged the doorframe of the main entrance along with a flower box in the first-floor window, ready to blast the first inductee of the day. But even if the bombs work—and the baldheads have yet to explode one successfully, Alan knows—the blast will do small damage at best, maybe knock off a limb of whatever unfortunate mother-raper happens to be first in line. Nothing too major, just another page seven article in a few dozen newspapers. Earlier, when Alan had been alone with the tall man, the modest scale and size of the attack had been made clear. But now in the car the baldheads are claiming the whole place might blow. Alan can see from the drop of Benny's lip that he is scared, that impalpable sirens are screaming in his ears, that he feels both furious and helpless at the situation he has fallen into. Probably, Alan decides, the baldheads can see this fear too, and are trying to capitalize on it by inflating the bomb's magnitude. Oh well.

A massive pothole jolts the van. Finally they arrive at the induction center. A baldhead sends Benny out to a bench and tells him to stay seated until he gets the signal.

"One more thing," the tall man calls to Benny. He whispers in Benny's ear as he hops down to the street.

"Anything else I should know?" Alan asks.

"Just keep your finger on that button," the tall man tells him.

36.

A tiny border town at the northernmost edge of the Homeland. Nothing had happened yet, Lorrie thought, but anything could. The plan was fuzzy to her, the only fathomable parts being the ludicrous amounts of someone else's Currencies they carried and the fragile fear that at any point—one incomplete step or sloppy signal—and she would be reborn into a new life of uniforms and cages.

What on good roads might have been a half-day journey had stretched into an all-day drive. Now, Susan roughed the air of the small motel room with one cigarette after another. Outside, grey-blue clouds covered up the warmth of the sun while specks of frost dotted the dirty window that looked out over an old swimming pool. The entire town consisted of two gas stations, one bank, a barber shop, three churches, a diner, and, at the end of the street, a large, windowless box of naked concrete over which two banners were draped, one announcing the grand opening of the new police station, the other, a Homeland classic encouraging people to use the Point Line. Plus their motel. Lorrie and Susan occupied a corner room. The solemn open spaces, the endless discolored farmland, suites of undisturbed lakes—all the stillness unnerved her. In the city, life was everywhere, and there were multiple opportunities for moments of connection. The great gulps of vast land-scape left her feeling lonely. At least she had Susan.

Susan twisted her hair with a finger. Lorrie stared out the window at the curved swimming pool, its lines forming the perfect shape of a kidney bean. No two moments, she thought, were ever alike. A small electric pump attached to a hose slowly sucked the water from the pool and flooded a nearby strip of grass. The seconds crawled forward, and the cursive neon sign of the motel gave off short flicks and long buzzes, sounds that passed easily through the thin windowpane. The room stank, but she was happy to be there, and even happier that Lance had no idea where she was. Let him search. Let him keep looking till the end of time.

If the plan worked and they didn't get caught—though there was every reason to expect they would—Lorrie knew she would be on that brilliant path toward actually making a difference. But there were so many ways it could go wrong. "Let's go over the plan again," she said to Susan.

Susan sighed. "It's simple. This kid, he snuck out of the Homeland and into Allied Country N. But he can't find work because he snuck in."

Sneaked, Lorrie thought. "Got it," she said instead.

"And Country N, nice as they can be, won't give work papers to people who enter illegally. They only want stand-up immigrants with lots of money and a job."

"So we smuggle him out of N—"

"And back into the Homeland," Susan interrupted. "That part shouldn't be too hard. And then, once he's in the Homeland, we help him get back to N legally. That's where all this cash comes in. Plus, I lined up some fake employment papers."

A puff of air landed on Lorrie's cheek as Susan waved the envelope stuffed full of Currencies. Who knew where all that money had come from?

"And even with the Currencies and the fake promise of a job, they still might not let him in?"

"Right, it's called getting landed. And then, if they don't land him, we've got a problem, because the Homeland will be right there, waiting to snap him up."

"Do we think we have a good chance?"

For a long while, Susan was silent. "They'll give us more directions over the phone," she said. "We should get a call soon."

What were the penalties for smugglers, for collaborators? Lorrie didn't know, didn't want to ask. They sat beside one another on the outer edges of the old queen-sized bed. Neither dared scoot off the ledge due to a concave impression in the very center, an effect that gave the mattress the look of having been impacted by a small but determined asteroid.

The two of them watched the phone. For a long time now, Lorrie saw, she had been waiting for whatever she was now waiting for.

Susan leaned forward and flicked the ash of her cigarette into the tray. Opening her purse, Lorrie searched her eyes around its insides, just to have something to do. A slight stink wandered around the room, possibly emanating from Lorrie, possibly from the mildewed curtains and the heavy rug. Fear and excitement always made her sweat. The phone rang.

"Tall," repeated Susan, taking two short puffs of smoke into her lungs. "Okay, okay, right. Mustache. Check." She hung up the phone.

A question charged through Lorrie's brain. *Don't ask,* she told herself. *Do not.*

"What?" said Susan.

She asked. "Could it be a setup? Could he be a Reggie?"

Susan made it clear that yes, Reggies were everywhere, even in other countries. "Anyone," she said slowly, "could always be a Reggie."

Ducking into Susan's car, they headed toward the border. Deep holes in the road were marked by ad hoc signals, usually a piece of bright fabric tied to a stick. As they drove, roadside signs updated their progress. "Country N Border: 1 Distance-Unit Ahead." Susan flicked her ash through the window and drove on. "Country N Border: ½ Distance-Unit Ahead."

"Do you think all this is worth it, just to save one guy?" she asked Susan.

"You know, for the most part, I don't go in for that Young Savior stuff," Susan said. "And not to be cheesy, but you know that one quote? 'By making a difference in one life on an individual level, we begin to change and repair the world.' I actually buy that."

Lorrie considered the sentiment, doing her best to ignore the source. A warm, yellow feeling rippled throughout her body and she found that without a doubt, she bought it, too.

Ahead, all lanes converged on bullet-resistant booths with sliding doors where drivers presented their documents to agents of the Homeland. Large armored trucks were parked on both sides of the road. Spirals of rusted barbed wire curled around every possible illicit exit, followed by a trench and an impossibly tall electrified fence. To pass through a booth was the only way out.

Susan pulled in the middle lane, away from the border store selling rare items untaxed by the Homeland. Perhaps Allied Country N was a land of bright pumpkins and juicy grapes, Lorrie thought. A begging, one-legged man tapped their window with his elbow stump. Lorrie handed him a few Currencies and forced herself to concentrate on the task at hand.

A Homeland border agent motioned for their papers. After scanning the car inside and out for hidden men, he waved them through. Ahead, another agent, this one adorned with the mitered pocket flaps and purple epaulets of Country N, looked at their papers, rescanned for hidden men, and, upon finding none, welcomed the two of them to his country.

Save for a family trip when she was seven, it was Lorrie's first time in Country N. From the passenger seat, it was clear to Lorrie that this was a nation that possessed far greater agricultural prowess than the Homeland. Rows of what seemed to be alfalfa stuck out from the dirt, followed by fields of plums and peaches and other varietals of stone fruit of which Lorrie could no longer recall the taste. Deer grazed on blooming flowers by the side of the road. Perhaps such success was because Allied Country N, she thought, was allied with the Homeland in name only, a country that had not yet shipped off all the men who knew when to water and when to pick.

As instructed, they stopped at the first bar in the second small town, a low-slung brick building with a domed awning over the entrance and two neon beer signs in the window, exactly as the caller had described. So far, so good. Lorrie's and Susan's eyes fell on a young man with a semblance of a mustache, alone at the bar, a small club soda in front of him. He was slumped forward in a manner that forced his upper back into a sharp, painful-looking curve.

For a moment, the two of them stood in the entryway and watched, amazed there really was a man with a mustache who needed saving. Even more amazing were the other men around the tables, their eyes blooming, hair clean, all of them seemingly unaware of their fortune as they laughed and drank and thumped one another on the back.

Focus, Lorrie thought. The young man's pointed cheeks were specked with sparse stubble, his mustache—if he could be said to have one at all—was slight. Deep lines crossed his face. He couldn't have been more than twenty. His clothes were simple except for a large and garish belt buckle that had been soldered into an unrecognizable shape. He was, Lorrie saw, only a kid.

Lorrie exchanged looks with Susan. Setup? Clandestine Registry agent illegally operating in another country, waiting to bust them as soon as they returned to Homeland soil? "Well," Susan said. "There's only one way to find out."

The kid began an extended coughing fit, as though little kernels of rusted popcorn were bursting right there in his chest. Lorrie smiled; even the Registry couldn't fake that.

"You're really here," the kid said.

"That's right," said Susan.

The kid shook his head. "It's just, I can't believe it. I thought it was all over for me."

"No promises," said Lorrie. "But the chances are good." She ignored Susan's frown. "Tell me," Lorrie said to the kid, "about Allied Country N."

Allied Country N, it seemed, was filled up and overflowing with his kind, the generous social services stretched thin by a daily influx of Homeland deserters whose numbers no one had a realistic estimate of. "No one will hire us," the kid said. "Not without the right papers. Runners are always last on the lists. When I first heard about you guys, I thought it was just a fairy tale."

Even so, the kid went on, "you wouldn't believe the food up here. Strawberries so juicy they"—Another series of coughs, his inflamed lungs working overtime to push the phlegm out of his airways. "Of course, I was eating them out of garbage cans."

The kid shuffled off to the bathroom, and Lorrie took a look around the bar. Loud music with the volume adjusted to soft levels drifted from hidden speakers. The bar itself was angled like a bent elbow. Susan and Lorrie sat on two stools right in the crook.

"He seems hungry," Lorrie said to Susan.

"He *is* hungry."

The kid came back from the bathroom, and soon they were back at the border, headed toward the Homeland. A creeping reminder came to Lorrie that if they didn't do this right, it wasn't just the kid who was going to suffer. The Country N border guard waved them right past, no inspection necessary. The Homeland guard did not.

"Citizens?" the Homeland guard asked.

All three nodded. As they had been told would happen, the guard gave the kid a hard stare but didn't check his papers. What dodger who had made it out would ever sneak back in? In the backseat the kid tried to suppress the terrible coughs and hacks that came from deep in his chest. Lorrie wished she had something in her purse to give him. "My parents won't talk to me," the kid told them. "In our last conversation, my father told me he wished I had been shot in the jungle instead of killing him slowly the way I am now."

On a billboard, a massive portrait of the prime minister welcomed them to the Homeland.

"Ready?" said Susan.

"Ready," said Lorrie and the kid. It didn't matter which one of them Susan had been talking to; they were in this together. With a flip of the turn signal, Susan cut the wheel and crossed the painted lines, turning back in the direction they had just come from.

"What now?" said the kid. Lorrie smiled at him and almost laughed. The kid knew even less than she did.

As Susan killed the engine, Lorrie and the kid stepped out of the car.

"No," said Susan. "The fewer people the better."

"Sorry," said Lorrie. "But I came all this way. I'm going to see this through."

Susan shrugged, and the three of them headed to the closest guard booth. "Asylum!" yelled Susan. "This man is applying to be landed in N. Leave us be!"

Where they had expected a fight, they were instead received with shrugs and apathy.

"Thataway," one helpful Homeland guard grinned, gesturing toward Allied Country N immigration. "You think this ever works?"

"Hope you've got the Currencies!" called another.

"We'll be waiting," yelled a third. The rest of them laughed.

The Allied Country N officials seemed to be getting ready to close for the night even though it was barely late afternoon. No one was behind the service counter.

"Excuse me?" Susan leaned over and threw her voice into the empty row of desks.

"Yes?" A head poked out from a door.

"You have the papers?" Lorrie whispered. The kid nodded. "Currencies too?" He nodded again. Lorrie heard Susan speak the much-practiced lines. "This young man wishes to apply for landed immigrant status in Allied Country N."

The agent sighed and bent over to dig up some forms. "Don't bother," the agent said, "unless you have all three thousand right now, on your person, plus a letter of employment."

The kid began counting out the Currencies one by one.

Lorrie and Susan went out to the car and waited. If the kid was refused, he at least deserved a witness as the Homeland took him away.

Five hours later, the kid emerged with the first smile they had seen. He coughed out a million thank-yous. Lorrie offered him a handshake, but the kid shook his head slowly and reached out, wrapping her in a sloppy hug. "You saved me," he said. His voice was soft. "I won't ever forget you."

Susan cut over to the expressway and headed south, back toward Interior City. As the darkness descended, they rushed through rows of white and red pines, spruces, and aspens. These were the same kinds of trees Lorrie had seen on the way to the Facility, the same trees she had seen on the ride up to the border, just in different places now.

"Well, that's the end of that," said Susan. "I'm glad it's over."

Over? Lorrie laughed. Even on the outskirts of everything, she still knew they hadn't achieved any sort of ending.

It was too cold to open the window, but Lorrie did it anyway, just a crack.

"Hey!" said Susan.

But Lorrie didn't care. She stuck her fingers through the slit and into the ice-cold night as they hurtled down the expressway to Interior City, back toward her life that was more started-over and begun-again than ever before.

"You okay?" Susan asked.

Lorrie was so touched that someone thought to ask that she almost broke down. A single tear fell from her face, and she told Susan that yes, she was pretty sure she was all right.

"What's next?" Susan asked.

"What are you asking me for?" Lorrie almost shouted. But as they drove on, past empty fields and large billboards for the Point Line, Lorrie realized that she did know what was next after all. "Pull over at the next rest stop," Lorrie said. "I have to make a phone call."

Lorrie stepped from the car into the night. Her fingers shook as she dialed. Numbers she knew so well but had never dialed before.

"Hello?" said the voice on the other end. "Point Line."

Lorrie's voice waddled, catching in her throat.

"Name of person you would like to report, please."

The wind stopped, the grasses around her stood straight and tall, and watching the stillness, Lorrie knew there were periods in her life that would always be with her.

"Name of person, please."

The wind blew harder, the voice asked for a name yet again, and Lorrie cleared her throat, ready to speak the name.

"Who did you call?" Susan asked her when she returned to the car.

But Lorrie only smiled and clicked on the radio. The two of them were partners now, that much was clear. But even the closest confidantes must sometimes be steered away from the truth.

Back on the expressway, a break in the music, an interruption. From some other world, the prime minister's vibrating vocal folds billowed and fell as he imparted the news: our enemies have struck again. His voice sounded hoarse, pinched even. Terrorists have attacked a military base outside Interior City. Emboldened, the prime minister warned, by our own waffling, encouraged by our own legislators. Ideology Five is the most dangerous system of thought ever known to humanity. At first, the prime minister said, I thought the Coyotes were an awfully bad joke. Now I see how dangerous they truly are.

Lorrie switched over to music.

37.

Someone, Lance knew, had pointed him. Had to have been. There had been too many agents, too much of a firestorm for a regular capture.

Now there were five of them—all dodgers—in a temporary holding cell meant for two. To stay out of each other's way they spent the hours in silence. On the third day, a guard told Lance he would be sent to a Homeland penitentiary any day now.

"When?" asked Lance.

"Soon," she said. "There's no room for you yet."

But there was not enough room in the holding cell, either. Two more were added that night.

A few of his fellow cellmates had visitors, some of whom brought in newspapers from the outside world. With the overworked guards too busy to review the titles, even the smallest, most antiwar publications circulated freely. In his head, he authored his own profile: a crap job in a bookstore that was always empty, painting stuffed birds with cracked eyes, followed by a relocation to Western City North that soon gave way to bugs and tears. And now, of course, all signs pointed to betrayal. Pointed by the woman he loved, he was sure of it. But there was no room for this type of story; in the underground newspapers, men who resisted were nothing but heroes. Even if these men were able to rot away nobly behind bars, no newspaper made it clear that all their prison time meant was that the Registry would find someone else to take their place and die. There was always someone else.

"Come out here," a guard said to him. A self-satisfied grin spread across her face.

"Why?"

The other men in his cell muttered nervously.

She didn't answer, but unlocked the cell door, sliding it open hard. "You're happy about this shit, aren't you?" the guard said.

"Happy about what?" asked Lance.

"Shut up, you Fiver."

Lance was not an Ideology Fiver. Whatever depravities or virtues were in that system of thought, he had no idea.

"That's what you are, right?" the guard said. Small pearls of sweat dripped from her puffed face.

How could Lorrie have pointed him?

"I don't like Fivers," said the guard. She held Lance's forearm in a tight grip.

Lance knew this type. She had probably lost two husbands and a boyfriend.

"Don't like them at all," the guard repeated.

Was it truly Lorrie who had done it? Impossible. Maybe he hadn't been pointed, just caught. What did it matter? "Well, yes," Lance said. "I'm a Fiver then."

A seething, incandescent rage spread over the guard's face. She called out, and two more guards appeared at the entrance to his cell, all three of them gripping their clubs tightly. "Say it again," the first guard said.

Lance said it again.

The guard kicked him in the scrotum. As he bent over, she knocked him over the head with her club. Lance curled into a ball as she continued to beat him. He could see that he had so far lived his life entirely off-key, his mind full of misapprehensions, dazzled by all the wrong things. The rare and unmistakable odor of his own blood wafted through his nose. More voices, more guards arriving to join in the beating. A practiced boot connected to his floating ribs. The pain was strong and vivid. Lorrie had put him here, and there was no way to take anything back. Even her ghost refused to visit.

That night, as his sore body rested on the thin jail mattress, he found himself desperate to talk to someone, to share his misery. His cellmates, terrified that association with Lance might lead to a beating of their own, turned their backs.

Some hours later, Lance was strip-searched, poked, and inspected, given the clothes he had shown up in, and led outside.

"Am I getting a new uniform?" he asked.

"You kidding?" responded a tall guard with fiery eyes. "We're all out of uniforms. You wear what you came in with."

Outside, there was no sun, only a series of thick, layered clouds. Lance, he was told, was off to a Homeland penitentiary, Prison Complex J.

❖ ❖ ❖

Two elderly guards floated Lance toward the bus, one at his elbow, the other gripping the crook of his armpit. The only male guards he'd seen since his arrival. Though it was the middle of the day, the sky looked dull and ragged, and the round sun sputtered pale, barely visible through the thick cover of clouds. With each step, his body ached.

They shoved him onto a bus with what he was sure was extra force. Behind this bus was another bus packed with prisoners, and behind that bus, two or three more. Though he was dressed in his own clothes, they had taken his shoes, replacing them with canvas slippers a half size too tight. Leg irons poked the balls of his ankles. A chain was wrapped around his belly with one cuff on each side, forcing his hands to his waist. He could not have clasped them together if he wanted to.

The prison bus hurtled down the highway. Small seats, one man per row. The aisles were narrow and the rows close together, and like the rest of the men, Lance found his knees pushed into the slatted metal seat back in front of him. None of the men looked at each other. Three guards sat in front, protected in a special cage of their own. Though he could not make out their conversation, the laughter of the two women and the old man echoed throughout the bus. An extra bar ran across the windows, but by slumping his shoulders, Lance found that he could still see the outside world. Mountain slopes appeared, mostly loose rocks and gravel. Soon the rocks gave way to bushes with long, flowering stalks, their dense leaves whipped around by the wind. Lance thought it might be nice to have that same feeling through his hair.

The bus drove on. After a while, the view was all spotted scrub and patchy yellow mountainside. Each new pothole shook the men like a rattle of dried-out seeds. Lance closed his eyes and did his best to summon Lorrie, the Western City North Lorrie, the Lorrie who was not brainwashed by her parents or the Center or some new big-dicked boyfriend or whoever it was who had encouraged her to do the pointing. *Come back,* he whispered. But Ghost Lorrie would not appear.

After a brief nap, he popped his eyes open and saw what he thought was a migrating bald eagle crossing over the pale, dry mountains. Cheek against the glass, he did his best to follow its flight. He had found that though his arms and legs were constrained, he could rotate from side to side as well as lean forward and backward without much obstruction.

"I think that's a bald eagle," Lance said, half-twisting to address the man seated behind him.

"I don't know you," the man said. From his constrained angle, Lance could only see half the man's face, enough to tell that he was older, past Registry age, with a fat middle section and a shaved face. A short scar about half the length of his lower lip ran horizontal across his chin, a raised slice that someone had done a poor job of sewing up and as a result was now even fatter and more visible than it had to be.

"I know," Lance said. "But I'm pointing out a bald eagle to you."

"I don't give a fuck about some little bird. They said I knocked off a bar in the middle of the day. Who would be dumb enough to do that? I didn't do that."

"I believe you." Lance ducked and dodged around his chains as best he could, hoping he could still track the flight path of the eagle. The bird was gone.

"I don't think that was an eagle you saw."

"I thought you didn't see it." Lance turned back around as much as the chains allowed.

"You've never done time, have you?" the man said.

Lance made a sharp twist with his body, cutting the belly chain into his hip, and took a closer look at the man behind him. He was surprised at the agility the chain allowed, though the cold metal driving hard into his already sore oblique was not a pleasant sensation. Perhaps the guards had left his bindings too loose. Lance saw that the man behind him had gulched diagonal lines across his forehead, lines that established hard times and worry.

"You've been here before?"

The man was disgusted. "Of course I've been here. What do you think, I'm some kind of fresh meat? I've been here plenty. I'm not like you; I served right after First Aggression. But then I got caught up in some drama. Either way, no one comes here just the once. No one."

"Come here," Lance said. The chain cut into him harder. "You lean in close."

"What's that?" the man said, but he leaned in toward Lance anyway.

The coarse laughter of the guards up front echoed down the aisle.

From his twisted position Lance saw how close the man was to him. In one deft movement he lunged over his right shoulder, caught the lobe of the man's ear, and pulled it into his mouth. He was twisted too much, the belly chain protested, chafing and pulling against him much too tightly, rubbing his skin raw. Lance didn't care.

"Listen to me," Lance said. The man's lobe was salty and smooth. He spoke in low, deliberate tones, moving his tongue over the flesh of the man's ear, every word a slur: "You can pull back, you can move back right now," Lance hummed into the man's ear. Every part of his abdomen was in pain, cut off from blood and air by the belly chain. "But I've got your goddamned earlobe between my teeth, you hear me? And I will rip it off. Because I am here just the once, one time only, understand?" Lance's words sloshed around the lobe. "Just the once."

The other prisoners looked at them, then quickly looked away. Lance guessed that this hands-off approach would set the tone for the next years of his life.

"Let go of my ear, you crazy mother-raper," the man said. "Please don't rip my ear off."

Lobe still between his teeth, Lance twisted his body even more, the tautness of the chain around his waist nearly unbearable, a warmth crawling to the surface of his skin. He gasped. The sides of their foreheads touched and Lance could feel the sweat exiting from under the man's skin and onto his own.

"Help me, Young Savior," Lance heard the man whimper.

Lance circled his tongue around the man's lobe once more and leaned back, releasing the ear from his mouth and loosening the grip of the chain around his waist. A drop of saliva fell from the man's ear to his lap. Both of them were breathing heavily.

"I'm just here now, you got me?"

The man gave off a series of sad, short pants. His face was damp and flushed. Lance turned around and stared at the panoramic stretch of mountains on either side of the road.

"Oh, man, you just bought your ticket," the man told the back of Lance's head. "You know I'm going to kill you, right? Not right now. But I'll really kill you."

From the outer reaches of his vision, Lance saw a second eagle—which he knew may very well have been the first eagle now farther inland—fly overhead before it disappeared for good beyond the mountains.

The bus slowed to a stop, and Lance slid down into his seat to get a better view. "Prison Complex J," painted in large black letters on a high wall. They passed through a heavily armed iron gate, tire spikes clanging down as the wheels of the bus pressed them into the concrete. Lance saw houses, little homes with front yards strewn with children's toys, all of it passing by as the man behind him pushed out a fiery stream of threats. From his window, he glimpsed a fenced-in piece of lawn packed with tents, several of them with men lying just outside the entrance flaps. "That doesn't look too bad," he heard one prisoner say.

"Stupid mother-raper," said another. "That's not the prison. That's the detox zone. Substance-smashers. Those boys are just here to sober up a bit before shipping out."

The bus continued to roll through the complex, and soon the tents and houses faded, replaced by a series of long and flat cement boxes with gun towers on every corner. Razor wire was twice coiled around the fence tops. The thought came to Lance that for the first time in his life, the rifles in those gun towers weren't for his own protection, but instead were there to keep him away from others, to save and spare Homeland citizens from having to glimpse the face of a man who wouldn't fight.

Finally the bus stopped. "Do not stand!" A new guard stepped onto the bus to yell at them. "Remain in your seats." Like all of the women officers, her hair was pinned closely to her head.

"Dead," the salty-eared man behind him whispered. "You're already dead."

"On my count," the guard screamed, "the first row will begin deboarding."

The sensation of tiny little bugs crept over Lance, small creatures running round and round the tubes that led to his heart, biting his insides all along the way.

"Move it, inmate!" he heard the officer yell.

The little bugs fell away. Who was he kidding? It was just a sensation. He would never understand what had been inside of Lorrie, he thought, although as the guard pulled him up by his armpit, he realized he would have plenty of time to try.

❖ ❖ ❖

Lance knew his fists were out of practice and that as a new resident of Prison Complex J, he had arrived at a period in his life in which the ability to fast-track his rusty skills into usefulness was surely in his best interest. No sooner had he prepared for his first fight with the man whose earlobe he had tasted than he saw that man pop a guard in the face—a punch that sent an immediate geyser of blood into the air and was later said to have broken the guard's nose in two places. Dragged by his ankles to some interior chamber of the prison, Lance never saw again the man whose earlobe he had tasted.

Though the man with the salty earlobe was gone, there were all too many men entirely. Lance's thoughts were dirty and rotten. Brushes and paints were not allowed, but charcoal pencils and paper were made available to him, and so he drew. Lance drew pictures of women with huge breasts and blurry faces, he drew pointed breasts, meager breasts, breasts that were round and full, breasts with puffy stretch marks on their sides, textured breasts, breasts shaped like teardrops, athletic breasts, swooping, sagging, and tubular breasts, nice breasts, mean breasts, apathetic breasts, and before long, his fellow inmates took notice. Lance began to barter, primarily with an Eastern Sector breast aficionado two cells over who brewed a briny hooch from pilfered yeast rolls sneaked from the dining hall in balled-up napkins.

One day he brought the bootlegger his latest work.

"No good," the bootlegger said, shaking his head. They were in the yard, their one allotted cell-free hour in the sunlight.

"Why?" Lance asked.

"Sicker," the bootlegger said. "Draw me something sicker."

Lance returned to his cell and began to draw. He realized that it was not just the bootlegger who wanted a new level of vulgarity in his work. Without paints, he could not embark on his grand project, and so his project was forced to change. From his pen emerged women, bodies, really, women crouched on their elbows, asses in the air, and other women, legs stretched so far back their toes tickled their earlobes. He felt no need to add faces.

The small cell was crowded with men, all of whom agreed that Lance should have the worst bunk, his feet nearly pressed against the cool metal of the seatless toilet. Each time someone went to the bathroom, Lance was forced to hug his knees.

Though he was not invited to participate, the men in his cell talked. Some recent attack on the Homeland was the worst ever, a higher body count than the last ten attacks combined. Word around the prison was that after an initial volley of speeches blaming the Coyotes, the prime minister was laying unusually low. Health problems, people said. But then again, people had been wishing health problems on the prime minister ever since he turned eighty. The man was ninety-six years old.

❖ ❖ ❖

On day three, the library cart came around, pushed by a casually dressed young woman with uneven eyes—a volunteer, most likely—who treated the resisters with an extra dose of guilt and admiration.

"Don't you want something to help you pass the time?" she asked Lance with a nervous smile. "We've got tons of books. No newspapers, though." Lance shook his head. What, he asked himself, would he want to read for?

The woman smiled and pushed her cart toward the next cell of men.

Before the bugs, Lance remembered Lorrie reading one of her Foreign books to him, looking up at him and quoting out loud: *As soon as you trust yourself, you will know how to live.* Here in his cell the words finally seemed right. He didn't trust anybody, not the guards who couldn't help but slam him against the solid steel bars to clear a bad mood, not the longtime convicts who looked at him with disgust because their service in the timid early years of the war was still fresh for them, and certainly not himself. He had given Lorrie bugs, small creatures that had turned into something else and driven her crazy. When confronted with her eroding mind and body, he had responded with fists. That was what mattered; the rest of his life was just a distraction.

The next day, the woman with the library cart came around again. "You got any Foreigns?" Lance asked.

❖ ❖ ❖

"New assignment," the guard told him in the morning. "Facilities."

"Is that kitchen duty?"

"Nope," she said. "The warden put you with a suit. A big shot. Arranges the furniture, chooses the lamps, I don't know."

Escorted by the guard, Lance passed three checkpoints. Watchwomen from the towers kept their rifles by their sides, glaring down from above. He was frisked twice. The administrative area of Prison Complex J was new to him. In the hallway were large portraits of the elderly prime minister looking young and the Young Savior looking even younger.

"Kid," the guard said. "Meet your new boss."

The man was circular: little stick legs poked out from a round chest. Large bags swallowed most of his eyes, and the buttons on his shirt strained against the strength of his stomach. On his desk was a bowl of fresh strawberries, their long, wedged shape so distant that Lance could not recall the experience of ever having eaten one.

"Good to meet you," he said. "And glad to have you." He put his hand out for Lance to shake.

As if I have a choice, Lance thought. The hand hung in the air.

"I'm Mr. Dorton, son. What should I call you? Help yourself to a strawberry."

38.

Benny Dorton knew his role. The tall man had explained the function he was expected to serve in a violent and threatening manner on the ride over to the induction center: Sit on that bench. Wait until six; the sun will set, and they'll open the doors. When the first recruit is about to step over the threshold, flash the signal. "Oh, and one more thing," the tall man had whispered. "Do anything different and we shoot the Indigenous kid right between the eyes."

Could these baldheads really have rigged the whole place to blow? Wasn't the induction center smothered in security? Still, the intentions of the baldheads did have their own mangled logic. If visibility was what they wanted, now was certainly the time to strike. On a First Tuesday, everyone would be at the center: print, television, and radio report-ers, sobbing mothers, bitter protestors, and, of course, the inductees themselves.

Now Benny sat on a bench across the street from the induction center, the spectacle unfolding before him. He had expected more from the actual building that wanted to take him. It was an unassuming twelve-story box, tiny compared to the compound he had conceived of as having a city block all to itself. The air grew cooler as the sun settled lower in the sky, the colors around him increasing in volume along with the number of protestors. Half the city, it seemed, had gathered in front of the building.

Benny was having trouble keeping his knees from visibly shaking. Why not find the first official-looking person he could and shout a warning? But the tall man had made it clear: "You can't see us," he had whispered, "but we can see you." So Benny stayed put on the bench. Though the baldheads could keep him sitting, they could not control his eyes. And so, in the slowly dying light, he scanned the crowd for Joe.

Overhead, the streetlights flickered on, brightening the faces of the arriving inductees. Were all these men destined to die? Was he one of them? It was 5:50. Ten minutes to go.

A group of protestors to his left began to organize.

"Circle up!" said one.

They walked counterclockwise, chanting and high-stepping at each other's backs. A young woman in tight jeans and a denim shirt approached what seemed to be the leader. "I've got a class in a half hour," she said, shoulders shrugging. "It's a lab. I can't miss it." The protestors in front and behind her moved forward and back to close the gap; in a moment, Benny would have never known she had been there at all.

His eyes swept the crowd for Joe. What kind of decision could he have made without him?

"Hey, brother. A moment of your time?" The man speaking had feminine lashes, long and straight and the color of coal. A bright blue book was tucked below his armpit.

"Go away!" Benny hissed. He did not want the baldheads in the van, wherever it was, to think he was snitching. The man's simple approach could mean the Indigenous kid's brain might now be splattered across the fabric of the van.

The curly-haired man had a joyful weariness to him. "I just wanted to let you know that whether you are going in there or you aren't, it doesn't matter. The Young Savior loves you either way."

"Just leave," Benny said, pleading. "Just get out of—"

Before he could finish, a series of yellow lights clicked on, bathing the crowd in a heavy shine. Immediately the male protestors began to scatter. Just before six, and the news cameras had arrived. None of the eligible protestors wanted their faces filmed for fear of being seen and reported to the Point Line. The curly-haired stranger shrugged at Benny's lost soul and headed into the crowd. As the remaining group of protestors—all of them women—took up another chant, a new sound cut through the clamor. Benny could hear it clearly: a voice, not just any voice, but a specific voice that possessed a particular sonic quality and could only mean one thing. From deep within, he screamed with pleasure. He knew the sound of that voice; he had known it all his life.

39.

In the kitchen, Mr. Dorton hears the dragging sounds of his wife's tears. He goes to her, caresses the back of her neck. His wife takes a deep, muscular breath, but is unable to stop crying. "He just needs some time is all," Mr. Dorton tells her. He takes a large gulp of coffee. "He's strong."

Mr. Dorton kneads his wife's shoulders and thinks of the boy who works for him at the prison. A handsome kid, nice eyes, somewhere around Benny's or Daniel's age. Clearly a dodger, though the boy addresses him respectfully and sees his assigned tasks through in a quiet and capable manner. A thoughtful boy. Mr. Dorton has seen him reading during breaks, more than he can say for most of the prisoners. Still, the boy had shirked, run away from courage, not toward it. Who could ever understand that? A rusty sob escapes from deep within his wife. He realizes she is still crying. "He'll come out soon," he assures her. "Daniel is strong, I told you. He just needs some time." But his words are not working. Soft and swollen tears continue to fall from her face.

"Benny," she sobs. "Where can Benny be?"

A rage pours through him. A ceramic mug shatters against the wall, thrown, he sees, by his mottled right hand, which is now popping with thin, swollen veins. Brown streaks of coffee slide down the wall. "Our

Homeland-decorated son has locked himself upstairs and all you care about is our dodger?" screams Mr. Dorton. "Daniel saw some truly messed-up things in that damn jungle, but no, your thoughts are with our youngest—a boy who, pardon me, doesn't give two shits about helping out the country that gave him everything. No, by all means, keep your thoughts on the son of ours who won't even call his parents to let them know he's alive, doesn't even bother to find out whether his brother made it back from the jungle. I'm the one who has to walk everywhere in town, to go to work with the stain of a dodger on my back. Me! That's the boy you care about?"

He screams more, cursing the Young Savior, dousing his name in gasoline, stomping it in mud. He understands that the screams are upsetting his wife, but he finds that he cannot stop, that he is falling in love with his anger at the unfairness of it all, and so he lets the rage course through him, curling his fingers until his thumb rests tightly between his middle and ring fingers, a clenched fist, he realizes, the perfect shape and posture for striking. He chooses the wall closest to him. For a brief, peaceful moment, he is released from the knowledge that his family is falling apart.

The impact to the plaster is minimal, but moments later, the pain makes its entrance: sharp, stabbing streaks flitting from fist to elbow, a hurt that Mr. Dorton does his best to ignore. A thin river of blood flows over his knuckles.

Sally Dorton runs upstairs and slams their bedroom door. Another room, Mr. Dorton thinks, that he can no longer enter.

His oldest son has disappeared into his childhood room. His youngest son has vanished into the murk of Western City North, a place probably only a smidgen friendlier to a faithful Homeland citizen like himself, Mr. Dorton thinks, than the jungles in which Homeland boys were being picked off one at a time like ring-necked pheasants. The country he loves is not doing well.

That morning's papers had told him all he needed to know: the metabolic machinery of the Coyotes is at full throttle. Each day their numbers grow as some new cowardly legislator announces he or she has joined up with the other spineless lawmakers. And the man who the Young Savior—fearing citizens of the nation have put their trust in, who allowed decades of war to pass like a dream, the man whose moon-bright vision is the only one that can extract them from the quagmire, the man who designed the plans, has missed yet another of his weekly radio addresses.

Daniel is upstairs and empty. Benjamin is nowhere. The gripping quiet of his own house is choking him. Darting up the stairs, Mr. Dorton bangs on his oldest son's door, his fingers swelling rapidly. He has not spoken to Daniel since his son's violent show of emotion the other night.

"I need to talk to you!" he cries. "You didn't do anything wrong."

From the other side of the door, silence. The wind whirls outside, vibrating the glass of the windows. As Mr. Dorton turns to walk away, he hears the gentle skid of paper being slid over the threshold and under the sweep. His knees gripe, his back whines, but he cannot go slowly. With the speed of a much younger man, he bends down to see what his son has slipped under the door. Immediately he recognizes the pamphlet. It is the same one the mangled vet gave to him on his last visit to Daniel in the hospital. *Fareon*, the pamphlet screams. *The Real Reason for War.*

40.

Whenever someone says he'll gladly point you in the right direction, you know that person is full of shit. How was Joe supposed to know where the induction center was? He had never been to that part of town. But clearly the noseless vet he'd asked for directions had sent him off in the wrong direction. Only after two buses and a long, uphill climb did he finally arrive at the induction center. Now he saw he hadn't even done that right. His shabby route had plunked him down on the wrong side of the building.

The lack of a rear entrance didn't surprise him. Joe had seen photographs of First Tuesdays in the newspapers before. If the long line of men were to stream toward whatever open door the induction center flung open, what sort of image would that be? No, the men needed to be arranged, one behind the other. When the Homeland projected order, people felt like there must be a plan. All must pass through the front. But for Joe, there was no version of his life in which he walked through that door alone.

His eyes shifted toward a bright flash of sun shining on an open steel grating. Could it be so easy? The words of the Young Savior came to him: *Everything with wings is beyond the reach of law.* And with that, Joe started up the fire escape.

41.

On Mr. Dorton's desk, the bowl of strawberries was always full, and he was never stingy with them. From this, Lance took that Mr. Dorton must have been a wealthy man and a very good father. Though he must have known why Lance was there, probably could have cleared up definitively whether he had been pointed or not, their daily exchange of words never included anything but questions from the older man regarding the former life of the younger one. Had he ever been to Western City North? Of course, Lance told him. That's where I lived. Western City North was wild.

"Did you cook food or eat out?"

"Both."

Did he own a television, did he ever go see any of the retiree leagues play? Mr. Dorton wanted details. This guy, Lance thought, is trying to piece together a life that's based on mine but doesn't belong to me.

"You know," Mr. Dorton said, his voice lowering, "I have a son in Western City North."

"Oh yeah? It's a big city. What part does your son live in?"

Mr. Dorton gave an exact address.

A rainbow of shock shimmered inside Lance. That a father would know his son's exact address from memory. But even more, that such an address would also be the very space where he and Lorrie had lived and breathed together.

"Are you okay?" Mr. Dorton asked.

Lance had begun an extended coughing fit. Four units. He could narrow down all the residents immediately. Which one had been a Dorton? His internal census began on the bottom floor, striking out the asthmatic widow. Moving across the hall in his mind's eye, he came to the door of Tim and Rebecca, or just Tim once Rebecca had left him on her Indigenous quest. An upward gush of fear entered him. Had he held a knife to the throat of Mr. Dorton's son? Impossible. Tim had talked about his father before, said he was one of the few casualties in those first years of war. Lance studied Mr. Dorton some more and let his internal surveyor climb those familiar stairs. Mr. Dorton clearly wasn't an immigrant from Neutral Country P, so that ruled out the many war-aged cousins who had often crashed in the apartment across the hall from his own. Only one apartment left: the empty place, the place that had belonged to the runners.

He could see the faces of two men, one of whom he had bumped into on the stairs with a duffel bag, the guy clearly headed out on the first step in a long series of Registry dodging, and the other one, a quieter guy with an indistinct face who tended to follow the loud one around. The guy he had caught on his way out—the loud one—Lance had seen him before, staring at Lorrie as though she might be his next catch. The quieter one he had seen around as well, but that one had always kept his head down, barely able to compose audible hellos and good-byes. But what were their names?

"Benny," Mr. Dorton said in a whisper. "That's my youngest."

No shit. Mr. Prison Administrator Big Shot had a runner kid. The guy was no different from anyone else.

Excited for any news, Mr. Dorton pressed him for questions about where Benny might have gone. Still unclear whether Benny was the loud, lusty one or the silent follower, Lance offered as much as he could, which was very little. Soon Dorton's questions reverted back to general queries regarding life in the building. Did Lance read the papers? Did the other young people his age in Western City North? The media up there was very biased, did he know that? They probably under-reported the body count of that recent attack outside Interior City. Damn Ideology Fiver journalists.

"Doesn't matter," Lance said. "I don't read the papers anyway. Who can keep up?"

More questions. Did they regularly tune in to the prime minister's weekly address, had they heard of the Coyotes, this thing called Fareon? The questions continued, though, really, each one was the same: What had happened, Dorton seemed to be asking, for the world to come to this?

42.

Just what I don't need, Craig Camwell thought. Twice in one week he had run into Dorton at the front security gates on the way home from work. And on today of all days. Surely even Dorton looked at him with disgust; at least his Daniel had valor medals and other honorifics, the most decorated soldier in the entire sector. Now, he noted Dorton's grin, the whole smile cataloging every accolade the Homeland had heaped on his eldest. More than ever, Craig Camwell wished his coffee table contained a scrapbook of clipped articles denoting the bravery of some phantom son of his own, anything to cancel out Joe's cowardice. But his coffee table was empty. Joe was all he had.

The morning had started off well. The papers were reporting that the prime minister had recovered his health and planned on giving his first radio address in weeks. With a huge chunk of boys reporting for duty on First Tuesday, Craig Camwell had no doubt that these young inductees could benefit from the prime minister's charismatic words as they were shaved and suited up. Perhaps his wayward son Joe would finally get some sense and be one of them. Plus, today the war turned twenty-three. Yes, even with Joe missing, Craig Camwell had been cheered by the news that the prime minister would return for this evening's radio address. Sure, the prime minister was quite old, but wisdom, after all, is a gradually accumulating resource. Besides, the ever faithful had always known: any prophet among them would be marked with signs of wonder.

At 5:50 p.m., with the sun slowly disappearing behind the horizon, Craig Camwell headed out to the parking lot, eager to drive to church and listen to the speech with his fellow congregants. But there, in front of him, was Dorton.

They started off with small talk, soon establishing that both of them, per some whim of the warden, had been assigned convicts to assist them with menial tasks. Word around the complex was that Dorton had gotten a dodger, but of course the topic of runners went unmentioned. And yet, it could not be ignored completely. Not too long ago, the warden had turned away a shipment of Registry-running Substance-smashers caught in the net of Operation Lowlife. Both men agreed that their boss was a soft man. What harm could there be in packing the overcrowded boys in the detox zone a bit tighter?

"How's Daniel?" Camwell asked. Questions about Dorton's wayward son, Benny, were awkward, but his colleague's war hero son was fair game. For sure, Craig Camwell thought, he was ready to gloat; any of the dealerships or real estate agencies in town would snap that kid up the moment he walked in the door asking for a job. Who wouldn't want a Homeland war hero on the payroll? Why the hell did Dorton keep him cooped up in the house?

"Ah, yes. Daniel," Dorton said. His voice sounded sunken, far away. Craig Camwell noticed that Dorton's eyes seemed brackish and misty.

The two men stood, paused in front of the second security gate, colleagues shuffling around them, eager to head home. Neither mentioned that today was First Tuesday, that the rapidly fading light around them meant that the deadline to report was near. Both knew that the other's son was up for induction. Neither had any idea what his boy might do.

Dorton tried to speak, but nothing came. It was, Craig Camwell thought, quite out of the ordinary.

"If you find him—" Dorton began.

Craig Camwell waited.

"If he doesn't go in this evening. If you hear from Joe—"

Dorton seemed to be having trouble swallowing. After a moment, Craig Camwell bounced an open palm against his shoulder. "You all right, Dorton?"

The sunlight had all but vanished. If the Young Savior had any sway at all, Craig Camwell thought, their two boys would be approaching the front door of the induction center at this very moment. A voice came over the mounted weatherproof speakers. *This is an emergency announcement.* Both men turned upward toward the sound. *Please return to work and gather in the chapel immediately.* A gust of wind burst forth, and the leaves of the trees began to shiver and shake.

"Now that's unusual. What do you think that's—"

"Snap his fingers off, Camwell," Mr. Dorton said. "Shoot him in the foot if you have to. Don't let your boy go over there. Don't let the Registry get him." Even his ears drooped downward. "Just don't let him go."

43.

From the roof of the induction center, Joe can see it all. To his left, a thick bank of fog has rolled over the eastern half of the city. To the right, the soft light is slipping away with the sinking sun. It must be close to six. From below, the sounds of protestors, of lined-up men, their weight shifting from one ankle to the next, of tearful good-byes, sobbing mothers and brothers and sisters and wives. Two birds circle overhead, two birds of a kind he has never seen before, though he doesn't know bird names anyway. From out of nowhere more join in and begin to circle with them. They are perfect, these birds, cleaved together with no leader, not questioning for a moment that the loose and sloppy circles they make in the air are exactly what needs to be done.

Below, the faint click of camera lights. Like startled bugs, the men scurry away. Immediately the chants of the protestors take a distinctly feminine turn. After a moment, the sounds from below melt away, and Joe hears his parents begin to sing. They would be in church now, as they were on all First Tuesdays, listening to the prime minister's speech before breaking into their favorite hymn, voices bouncing off the great window above the balcony in which the Young Savior commands that every last one of their flock preach the gospel to all those with ears to hear.

Above him, the birds circle lower and tighter. Joe can hear the sweet, tuneful voices of his parents. He knows that the words to these hymns are in his mother's and father's hearts, that their eyes will not look to the lyrics even once. *I shall wing my flight to worlds unknown,* they sing.

Worlds unknown are the only kind that have any appeal. Joe watches the birds. The thought comes to him that if he leaps into the air, they will accept him as one of their own. *I can be them,* he sees. *I can leap, and I will enter their world, and we will join together to make a clean thing from an unclean one.*

Leaning over the cold aluminum handrail, he looks at the crowd below. Six o'clock must be minutes away. "Where are you?" he shouts down to Benny. "Why aren't you here?"

Benny doesn't answer.

Maybe I won't fall, he thinks. *Maybe I'll enter with the birds into their loose circles over the rocks and thistles and streams and be received and complete. Even just a moment of being them will save me. They'll brush their wings against me.*

One foot over the rail, then the other. The birds circle. There is one step between Joe and those worlds unknown.

"Benny!" Joe screams again. The shifting crowds below drown out his cry. But what does it matter? Benny is not among the skittering heads down there. No, he is probably wilting away in some rotten cell or perhaps is already on a plane to the jungle. Even so, Joe wants Benny to tell him that his plan is okay. With Benny gone, Joe decides to ask Him, but he knows that he cannot think the universe, that he knows nothing about the Young Savior except what He is not. Ridiculous, Joe thinks, because he can see that He is not anything. That is how it has to be, he decides: His silence is His speech, and His words and His silence are the exact same thing, and maybe His answer is already up there circling. Maybe silence is the only help the Young Savior can give.

The thoughts come: *I don't belong to the Homeland, I don't belong to the Registry, and Benny, who belongs here, with me, is nowhere.* A key change to the hymn in his head, his parents' voices rising along with the rest of the congregation. The birds circle tight. Joe edges his toes forward until they rest on nothing but air. Just a bit farther. Young Savior, help me.

❖ ❖ ❖

There are no more rules, Benny thinks. Minutes till six and the tone of the crowd shifts into one of frantic and feverish good-byes. But still, he cannot have imagined it; he had heard that voice. But there are too many sounds and too limited a view from the wooden bench. "It can't be true!" he hears a protestor say. If Benny leaves the bench, the Indigenous kid gets shot between the eyes. If he stays in place, the whole crowd might get blown to bits. But what about standing? Had the baldheads prohibited standing on the bench? If he stands, he might spot Joe and shout to him, tell him to come to the bench. Before, the crowd was just a crowd, a bouquet of strangers who could not be saved. Now Joe is hidden in that crowd, and this knowledge changes all that he must do. Benny rises to his feet and climbs atop the bench. The tops of the heads before him are a complex geography, sobbing, chattering, moving, small bits pushed around by a large storm. He even hears the unmistakable sounds of laughter. Laughter? Why are these people in the crowd so nuts? There are too many strangers among him; the dim light of the few working streetlights is not enough.

A distant church bell begins to chime. At the same time, the first man in line starts his approach to the front door. In seconds, the van will be expecting a signal. Another chime, the first recruit nearly at the door. Again the sounds of laughter from the crowd. Benny leaps from the bench, apologizing to the Indigenous kid whose time on this earth he has cut short. Joe is somewhere in this crowd, he must be, and he cannot let Joe down. He pushes his way through the knots of people. "It is true, it is!" he hears as he twists through the crowd. "All the stations are saying it! All of them!" Benny grabs shoulders indiscriminately, whipping them around in the hope that one of them will be Joe. Joe, who has been here all along. Waiting for him. The clock strikes six.

❖ ❖ ❖

Inside the van, the heat rises. On the radio, an announcer is talking. Both the tall man and the Indigenous kid see the shadow they know to be Benny rush from his bench, and both understand his leap to mean that there are now only moments until he makes them, seconds until he taps the shoulder of a uniformed police officer or one of the obvious undercovers circling the crowd to point out the unmarked van full of baldheads and an Indigenous kid with a detonator in his hand. Only, Benny is not running away from the site where the blast will be. Benny, they see, is running toward it. *Time of death*, the voice on the radio says. *Not yet available.*

"Turn that down," says Alan.

"What the hell is he doing?" screams the tall man.

"Hold on," says a baldhead. "Turn that up."

"Stay ready," says the tall man to Alan.

All watch as Benny makes his way through the grip of chaos, separating the rapturous crowd. Each moment expands; the seconds are swollen and full as Benny races toward the front doors of the induction center.

"What is wrong with these people?" asks the tall man. Even from inside the van, all can sense the collective shock clattering through the crowd in front of them. Nostrils widening, eyes blinking in an effort to adjust themselves.

After so many years in power, the radio says.

"All these people are crying," says a baldhead.

"Of course they're crying," says the tall man.

"No," says the baldhead. "This First Tuesday is not like the last one."

"Should I push it?" says Alan.

"They're not crying, they're laughing," says another baldhead.

On the twenty-third anniversary of the conflict he championed, the announcer continues.

A third chime from the nearby church bell. From the van, all eyes squint through the dusk as Benny grabs someone, sees his face, and moves on, rotating another man by the shoulders, the two of them directly below the first-floor flower box stuffed with explosive charcoal.

He was ninety-six years old, says the radio.

"Did you hear that?" says a baldhead.

"Quiet," says another. "We need to focus."

"Now," says the tall man to Alan. "Push it now."

❖ ❖ ❖

In the low candlelight of her apartment, Lorrie holds the letter in her hand. *I have heard about what you've been up to*, she reads. *I have heard about what you are doing*. Her lips are pressed tightly together. *We've had our differences, but the Reggies will have me any day now and I need your help*. Lorrie's cold breath dissolves onto the paper. Eric's handwriting is unchanged, but behind his words, for the first time, there is a flicker of humanity. Of someone who needs the aid of another.

Because it is First Tuesday, Lorrie knows the Center will be open late. Ten minutes before six, she pushes through the double-glass doors of the Center, her stride strong and free. Back through another old doorway. Almost all the faces she sees are new, unfamiliar. Eric appears from behind some dark corner and asks her to follow. His posture is uneasy, and he moves in slow, halting steps, a man who knows what he wants to say but is unsure of how to say it. In the same back room where she had labored away typing his notes, Lorrie wonders how she has allowed herself to come back to this place. She makes a silent promise that she will not let her old surroundings degrade her new self.

"It's the twenty-third anniversary," Eric tells her.

She understands why he mentions this, that to confer meaning on such a number is both real and meaningful in one sense, though completely unreal and meaningless in another. Also, he says, his mother is back, released from some unmarked prison, though Jane has returned a poorly assembled version of the woman she once was. Lorrie begins to ask for details, but Eric stops her. "I don't have much time," he says. "I'm supposed to be at the induction center in ten minutes."

"Well, go ahead, then," Lorrie tells him.

He does not apologize, makes no expressions of regret or sorrow for his past arrogance. His words are clipped and quick, and Lorrie must lean forward with her good ear to take it all in. A rosy shine of evening sun falls onto his face just as Lorrie begins to understand. Eric's time is done, over with. The Center is stagnant; almost all his volunteers are reporting this evening. As for Eric himself, the Registry has knocked on his door for the final time. He begins to wax on about the superhuman splendor of the human spirit, but sees Lorrie's expression and catches himself. "Pardon me," he says. His shoulders slump, and his little eyes shoot around the room. She knows he cannot say it, so in her mind, she finishes his sentence for him. *I've become too used to having people listen to whatever I have to say.*

"What is it," she asks, "that you are saying?"

"My time is done," he says again. "What I've tried to do for this place, it hasn't worked."

"And you finally want me," she asks him, "to come in here and help?"

Finally Eric looks into her eyes. His forehead is damp, his voice is pitched several octaves above his normal speaking tone. "Come in here and help the Center?" A small, bitter laugh escapes from his throat. "The Center doesn't need you, Lorrie. The Center is done. I need you. I need you to save me."

Lorrie stands to leave. No one, no matter who they are, jumps ahead in the queue.

"Put in a good word for me?" Eric calls over her shoulder. "Please. Just see what you can do."

In the car, she switches on the radio and hears the somber announcement. Year after year, and finally it is here: the news too large for any one reaction. She pulls over to gather herself, the wheels of the car perched unevenly on the crumbling concrete beneath a large and ancient tree, somehow unscathed by the passage of time. For despite what she has just heard, she is sure that there will still be men who need saving. At the base of the tree a swath of small ferns envelops the trunk in a sweet embrace. Lorrie lifts her chin upward, the back of her skull settling in between her shoulder blades. She would like to see how tall this tree is, but from her point below, there is no top, only the endless stretch of long branches and brittle leaves. How high the tree goes, how far up its branches stretch, she cannot imagine.

❖ ❖ ❖

After his meal, another walk for Lance back to his cell, past the politicals, the bootleggers, and the Substance-smashers. Back in his cell, he starts to pick up his Foreign book, but soon puts it down to stare out of the thin bars of his window, where he can see bushes and trees and even a backyard with a small, empty sandbox. The sun begins to set, dinner will soon be served. A guard walks by and slides his mail for the day through the slot. For a moment, he is sure he recognizes Lorrie's neat and stiff handwriting, but before he can inspect the letter, the guard interrupts.

"Did you hear?" asks the guard.

"Hear what?" Lance says.

"The prime minister," the guard tells him. "He's dead. Right now on the steps of parliament, those coward Coyotes are giving speeches. Seems there's more of them than we thought. And that's not all. Just as his death was announced there was an attack up in Western City North, a bomb right in front of the induction center. The prime minister dead. Hard to believe, no? May the Young Savior forgive him for all his sins."

Through the window, Lance can see the deep red shine of distant craggy mountains, a tall and heavy tree just beyond the perimeter fence swaying in the hot wind, and a fully grown eagle circling over the bare, dusty courtyard. The tents of the men in the detox zone are empty, ready for new arrivals. Though the colors of rock, bird, and tree overwhelm him, even amid such overwhelming beauty, there are times we should not be so happy.

ACKNOWLEDGMENTS

A special thanks to Larry Sirott, the kindest, bravest person I have ever known.

I thank Charles Baxter, whose fiction and thoughts on its creation are my own kind of scripture. Further thanks to Wendy Lichtman, the first person to tell me I needed to write every day.

The majority of this book was written in public libraries in Minneapolis, Berkeley, and San Francisco; I extend my utmost appreciation to these three library systems.

I am enormously appreciative of Noah Ballard's guidance and insight. Carmen Johnson's deep understanding of my project and her remarkable talent for spotting the unnecessary improved this book immeasurably.

I'm indebted to Michael David Lukas for his perceptive readings of early versions of this work. Special shout out to Benjamin Rombro and my fellow Freakersons.

The love and support of Harriet Charney and Irisa Charney-Sirott have been invaluable.

Thanks to Lo, my earnest companion on a million walks around the city. You've expanded my heart in new directions.

Finally, I am grateful for Leah, my dream come true.

ABOUT THE AUTHOR

Photo © 2015 Jameson Costello

Jonah C. Sirott, a graduate of the University of Minnesota's MFA program, grew up in Berkeley, California. He lives in San Francisco.